In the latest in the #1 *New York Times* bestselling series, homicide detective Eve Dallas sifts through the wreckage of the past to find a killer . . .

The body was left in a dumpster like trash; the victim a woman of no fixed address who offered paper flowers in return for spare change—and informed the cops of any infractions she witnessed on the street. But the notebook where she kept track of litterers and other offenders is nowhere to be found.

Then Lieutenant Dallas is summoned away to a nearby building site to view more remains—decades old and wearing gold jewelry—unearthed by construction. Now she must enter the world of New York real estate and a web of secrets to find justice for two women whose lives were so casually discarded . . .

Titles by J. D. Robb

Naked in Death

Glory in Death

Immortal in Death

Rapture in Death

Ceremony in Death

Vengeance in Death

Holiday in Death

Conspiracy in Death

Loyalty in Death

Witness in Death

Judgment in Death

Betrayal in Death

Seduction in Death

Reunion in Death

Purity in Death

Portrait in Death

Imitation in Death

Divided in Death

Visions in Death

Survivor in Death

Origin in Death

Memory in Death

Born in Death

Innocent in Death

Creation in Death

Strangers in Death

Salvation in Death

Promises in Death

Kindred in Death

Fantasy in Death

Indulgence in Death

Treachery in Death

New York to Dallas

Celebrity in Death

Delusion in Death

Calculated in Death

Thankless in Death

Concealed in Death

Festive in Death

Obsession in Death

Devoted in Death

Brotherhood in Death

Apprentice in Death

Echoes in Death

Secrets in Death

Dark in Death

Leverage in Death

Connections in Death

Vendetta in Death

Golden in Death

Shadows in Death

Faithless in Death

Forgotten in Death

ANTHOLOGIES

Silent Night
(with Susan Plunkett, Dee Holmes, and Claire Cross)

Out of This World
(with Laurell K. Hamilton, Susan Krinard, and Maggie Shayne)

Remember When
(with Nora Roberts)

Bump in the Night
(with Mary Blayney, Ruth Ryan Langan, and Mary Kay McComas)

Dead of Night
(with Mary Blayney, Ruth Ryan Langan, and Mary Kay McComas)

Three in Death

Suite 606
(with Mary Blayney, Ruth Ryan Langan, and Mary Kay McComas)

In Death

The Lost
(with Patricia Gaffney, Ruth Ryan Langan, and Mary Kay McComas)

The Other Side
(with Mary Blayney, Patricia Gaffney, Ruth Ryan Langan, and Mary Kay McComas)

Time of Death

The Unquiet
(with Mary Blayney, Patricia Gaffney, Ruth Ryan Langan, and Mary Kay McComas)

Mirror, Mirror
(with Mary Blayney, Elaine Fox, Mary Kay McComas, and R. C. Ryan)

Down the Rabbit Hole
(with Mary Blayney, Elaine Fox, Mary Kay McComas, and R. C. Ryan)

FORGOTTEN
IN
DEATH

J. D. Robb

St. Martin's Paperbacks

Published in the United States by St. Martin's Paperbacks, an imprint of St. Martin's Publishing Group

FORGOTTEN IN DEATH

For information, address St. Martin's Publishing Group, 120 Broadway, New York, NY 10271.

Library of Congress Catalog Card Classification Number: 2021016217

www.stmartins.com

ISBN: 978-1-250-77414-9

Our books may be purchased in bulk for promotional, educational, or business use. Please contact your local bookseller or the Macmillan Corporate and Premium Sales Department at 1-800-221-7945, ext. 5442, or by email at MacmillanSpecialMarkets@macmillan.com.

Printed in the United States of America

St. Martin's Press hardcover edition / September 2021
St. Martin's Paperbacks edition / January 2022

10   9   8   7   6   5   4   3   2   1

She lived unknown, and few could know
When Lucy ceased to be;
But she is in her grave, and, oh,
The difference to me!
—William Wordsworth

I do perceive here a divided duty.
—William Shakespeare

1

For a homicide cop, murder often started the day. For the mixed-race female sloppily wrapped in a tarp and stuffed in a construction site dumpster, it had surely ended hers.

Lieutenant Eve Dallas ducked under the crime scene tape and strode across the demolition rubble. She'd already been on her way downtown to Cop Central when the call came through, detouring her to one of the construction sites in Hudson Yards.

The day had a soft feel to it, a breezy warmth as May of 2061 made way for June and the heat that would surely follow. Construction types stood around in their hard hats and steel-toed boots, gulping coffee, shooting the shit, and goggling at the dumpster where a couple of uniforms stood by.

Civilians, Eve knew, couldn't resist goggling at the dead.

She could hear the hard, staccato, machine-gun echo of an airjack at another site. The whole sector, she knew, was full of them.

The dumpster sat on the north side of the seventy-story spear of a building, on the edge where a trio of lesser towers huddled. The trio, post–Urban Wars toss-them-up-and-cross-your-fingers construction, showcased the dinge and wear of the years, the shrugged shoulders of neglect.

She noted broken windows, the pitted, graffiti-laced walls, crumbling facades, old beams now bent and twisted, and the big, muscular machines, the strangely delicate sway of the towering cranes, and the mountain range of lesser tools lined up to deal with them.

To her eye, it resembled the aftermath of a war zone, but the only casualty she could see lay wrapped in a dumpster like so much debris.

Whatever the plans, the schedule, the budget might be, it all stopped now.

The civilians could goggle at the dead, but she stood for them.

She carried her field kit to the cops at the dumpster, tapped her badge. "Who's first on scene?"

"That would be us, Lieutenant. Officers Urly and Getz."

"Run it for me," she said as she took a can of Seal-It from her kit.

Urly, a tall Black woman in her early forties, took the lead.

"Getz and I responded to the call at oh-seven-thirty-five. We confirmed the DB in the dumpster here, and secured the scene. The nine-one-one caller, a Manuel Best, stated he found the body shortly after he reported to work at seven-thirty."

"Maybe the blood trail gave him a clue."

Urly's lips twitched—the closest she got to a smile. "Yes, sir. Best stated he thought someone had dumped a dead or wounded animal in there."

"He's pretty shaken up, Lieutenant." Getz, white, husky, thirties, chin-pointed to the left. "Just a kid, college boy, summer job. Just started this week."

"Hell of a way to enter the workforce. I'll want to speak with him when I'm done with the body."

She stepped up, avoiding the drops of dried blood, and, a tall woman herself, peered into the dumpster.

She could see the side of the victim's head through the plastic sheeting. Scraggly hair, the color of dust, spilled over it. Blood matted the hair, smeared the sheeting.

Her hand fell out when the killer tossed her in, Eve thought. Rush job, bash, dump, run.

"Severe blunt force trauma to the right side of the victim's head is visible, as is a blood trail starting approximately four feet from the dumpster on the far side of the security fencing. Blood on the front of the dumpster, on the plastic sheeting used to cover the victim. Likely used to carry the victim to the dump site."

When she had the interior of the dumpster, the position of the body fully on record, she hissed out a breath.

She sealed up, passed her field kit to Getz.

And boosted herself into the dumpster.

Construction crap—not garbage, so lucky day. But construction crap could include nails, glass, toothy metal, and all kinds of sharps.

"She can't be more than five-two," Eve judged as she found a corner of the sheet, drew it up, and exposed more of the head wound. "Blood, bone shards, gray matter. Hand me my kit. Looks to me like . . ."

She took the kit, pulled out microgoggles. With them, she leaned in. "Yeah, murder weapon's going to be a crowbar. I can see where the two-pronged hook went in, the flat handle indented."

Gently, Eve turned the head. "Two strikes, right temple, upper back of the head. One probably did it."

"Oh hell. Lieutenant, I know her. Getz?"

He rose up a little, leaned in. "Yeah, shit. Sidewalk sleeper, sir. She roamed around this area, did some unlicensed begging."

"We looked the other way there," Urly added. "She was harmless. She'd make little flowers or paper animals out of litter, pass them out to anyone who gave her some change, you know?"

"Got a name?"

"No, sir. She used the Chelsea Shelter mostly in the winter or bad weather. Or flopped in one of the condemned buildings here like a lot of them. She didn't hustle or hassle, but she kept a little book, and wrote people up for rule violations."

"What kind of violations?" Eve asked as she got out her Identi-pad.

"Jaywalking, littering—she was fierce about littering—shoplifting, trespassing, not picking up your dog's poop." Urly shrugged. "She'd write down a kind of description of the violator, the violation, the time and place. She'd hunt up a cop and read off the page. Ask us to make a copy."

"Mostly, we would, and we'd thank her, give her a couple bucks," Getz added. "We all called her CC—for Concerned Citizen."

"Spotty on the ID data, lot of blank spots. But she comes up as Alva Quirk, mixed race, age forty-six. No fixed address. No current employment. No family listed on her ID. We'll do a run there."

"Alva," Urly repeated. "Lieutenant, if it turns out she doesn't have family, the cops in the Tenth would take care of having her cremated. She was kind of a mascot."

"I'll make sure you're notified. TOD, zero-one-twenty. COD, blunt and sharp head trauma. ME to confirm."

Eve heard the clomping, recognized pink cowgirl boots. "Peabody," she said without looking up. "Just in time. Everybody, seal up, and let's get her out. I can get her up," Eve said before Getz could climb in with her. "I can get her up and pass her to you."

It was a process, and not a pleasant one, but Eve slid her arms along and under the plastic, got a grip.

Even deadweight, the victim couldn't have been more than a hundred pounds.

Urly reached over, took some of that weight, then Getz and Peabody helped lift the legs.

They laid her, the sheet still wrapped around her lower body, on the ground in front of the dumpster.

Eve crouched down to check the multiple pockets of Alva's faded gray baggies. "No book, no nothing."

"She usually had a backpack, but she kept the book and a pencil in her pocket."

"Not there now." She looked back at the dumpster, thought: Fuck.

She looked up at her partner. It still took her an extra instant to adjust to the red tips and streaks in Peabody's dark, now flippy hair. In fact, Eve thought she registered a few more of both streaks and flips.

"Peabody, Officer Getz is going to take you to the wit who found her. Get his statement. There has to be some security around this site—get copies of any discs or hunt up any security guards. And make sure whoever's in charge knows this site is shut down until I say otherwise."

"I got it."

"Let's open up the rest of this plastic."

When she and Urly unwrapped the lower body, Eve saw the stub of a pencil in the ragged cuff of the baggies.

"Pencil stub, caught in the cuff of her pants," she said for the record as she took out an evidence bag. "Dropped it when she got bashed and it got caught in there. Someone didn't want to be in her book. I'm not going to find the book or her backpack in that dumpster. Gotta look, but the killer took all that. Missed the pencil, but this was a rush job."

She sat back on her heels a moment, because she could see it. "Murder weapon may be in there, but smarter, if they were going to leave it, to wrap it up with her. We're going to find the kill site. Cleaned up some of the blood, but it was dark—even with the security lights, you wouldn't get it all. And he was sloppy, didn't wrap her nice and tight, so she started coming out of the sheeting, dripped some blood.

"Maybe she was flopping here for the night. They've got the buildings locked up, fenced off while they're doing what they do, but it's familiar here, so she comes here for the night. Nice night, who wants to be ass to elbow in a shelter on a nice night? Hears something, sees something. Can't have that, gotta write that down for my police friends."

"Oh crap, Lieutenant, that sounds right."

"Illegals deal, rape, mugging—it's not going to be littering or dog shit. He could take the book, but what's to stop her from telling somebody? Only one way to fix that. Where did he get the crowbar? Because that's what it's going to be."

As she spoke, she ran her hands over the victim, checked for other wounds, offensive, defensive. "Just the two strikes to the head. Back of the head when she'd turned away, right temple on her way down, to make sure. Take the book, the backpack, check her pockets and take whatever she has. Get the sheeting—has to know where to find it—wrap her up, carry her over to the dumpster, drop her in."

"Why not just leave her where she fell?"

"Somebody might come by, find her. You've got to get away, ditch that pack, destroy that book, and clean up. You got blood on you, you got spatter. Nobody's going to find her for hours. Likely a couple hours more than the wit did because of the sloppy."

"She said to me once, she had to take care of New York because New York took care of her."

"That's just what we're going to do, Officer. We're going to take care of her."

Rising, Eve called for the sweepers and for the morgue.

"Stay with the body," she told Urly, then boosted herself back into the dumpster.

Urly gave her that hint of a smile again. "Those are really nice boots."

"Well, they were. Describe the book."

By the time Eve swung out, empty-handed, Peabody was waiting for her.

"The wit just started working for Singer Family Developers, and on this job," Peabody began. "His uncle's one of the crew, got him in for the summer. He saw the blood, thought there was an animal in the dumpster, maybe just hurt, so he took a look. Saw the body and, in his words, 'went freaked.'"

"Did he touch anything?"

"He says no. Too freaked. But he called it in, then tagged his uncle."

Peabody shifted on her pink boots, careful to keep them away from the dried blood.

"The wit was one of the first on the job this morning—trying to make good—and his uncle was just pulling up. Uncle took a look, too, and they waited for Urly and Getz. While they waited, the uncle—Marvin Shellering—contacted the foreman, who contacted Singer. That's Bolton Kincade Singer, who took over from James Bolton Singer, his father, about seven years ago. Singer is cooperating. I've got security discs, but am told they don't cover this area—just the buildings. Nothing back here that needs security according to Paulie Geraldi, the foreman."

Peabody glanced down at Eve's now scarred and filthy boots. "You know, the sweepers would've done that search."

"Yeah, and they're going to do another. I had to see if the killer tossed any of her stuff in there with her. Or the murder weapon. Any human security on-site?"

"Not at this point. They have the fencing, the cams, and

right now it's a lot of demo. When they start bringing in new materials, they'll add to security."

"A job this size has more than one boss."

"Right now, it's demo, and that's Geraldi."

"All right." Eve pulled a wipe from her kit to clean her hands. "We're going to fan out, find the kill site. The trail leads that way before it stops—or before she started to drip. I'm leaning toward somewhere along the other side of the security fence line, but out of the lights."

She started along the trail of blood. "We need to run Singer, the foreman, and anyone else who has access inside the fence after hours. We start there and—"

She broke off when a woman—eighteen, maybe twenty—called her name as she ran over the rubble.

T-shirt, Eve noted, jeans, boots, candy-pink hair spilling out of a fielder's cap.

Eve concluded one of the crew, and wondered if someone had found the kill site for her.

"Lieutenant Dallas." Her breath whooshed out; sweat streamed down a pretty face nearly as pink as her hair.

"That's right."

"I recognized you, and you, Detective. You have to come. You have to come right away."

"Where and why?"

She pointed. "A body. There's a body."

Eve gestured behind her. "That body?"

"No, no, no. Manny—um, Manuel Best—told me about the woman, and I'm sorry, but that's how I knew you were right here. And I told Mackie I'd run, I'd run right here and get you."

"You're saying you found another body?"

"I didn't, not exactly. Mackie did. Or some of one, and he said work stopped and call the cops, and I said how you were here, and he said go get you. You have to come."

"Officers! Stay with the victim until the morgue arrives. Secure the scene until the sweepers get here. Where?" she asked the woman.

"We're about a block up."

"Part of this construction site?"

"No, no, it's not part of this. This is Singer Family Developers. We're on Hudson Yards Village, residential and office buildings, a shopping arcade, and a green space."

To save time, Eve left her vehicle; taking a block on foot would be quicker.

"Let's have a name."

"Oh, sorry. I'm Darlie Allen."

"And how do you know my witness?"

"Your . . . oh, you mean Manny. Some of us go for a beer—or a cold otherwise—when we knock off. We just hung out a couple of times since we started. He just started with Singer. And we're, you know, going to go out this weekend. He tagged me about that poor woman. He was really upset. And somebody told him you were in charge, and then when we found the body, I came to find you."

"How'd you find the body?"

"We already demoed the main part of the old building. It was a restaurant. We were jacking up the floor, the old concrete platform. The boss says it's substandard—hell, a good chunk of it had already decayed—so we're taking it all. I was watching because I want to learn how to use the jack, and this big piece broke off, and I could see how they were right about it being a crap job in the first place all that time ago, because there was a lot of hollow, and that's not safe. There's a cellar below—and that's already had some cave-in. And it was in there."

"A body under the concrete? We're talking remains then. Bones?"

"Yeah, but they came from a body. It's not like an animal.

I didn't look real close after, because it was sort of awful. But I saw how it was mostly dirt and rotten supports and broken beams under the platform, and the body—remains—that was in a kind of hollow place."

They came to a set of iron steps manned by a security droid. It nodded at Darlie.

"You're cleared, Ms. Allen, Lieutenant Dallas, Detective Peabody."

"It's up on the platform over the old tracks. We're revitalizing what they started before the Urbans, then that got all screwed, so they threw up all this substandard after just to get them up, you know."

"Yeah."

Boots rang on metal.

"It's going to be done right this time. Mackie says we're building an urban jewel, and we're building it to last."

She didn't see a jewel. She saw construction chaos, with a section roped off, and farther north the beginnings of a skeleton that, she assumed, would be one of the residential buildings.

"Who's in charge?"

"Mackie. I'll get him."

"Yeah, do that. But who owns it? Who's in charge of the project?"

"Um. You are."

Eve looked into Darlie's big, puzzled green eyes. And said, "Crap."

Darlie raced off to where a number of people stood around the roped-off area.

"I can tag Roarke," Peabody offered. "He's going to want to know."

"Yeah." Her husband, the owner of almost everything in the universe, would want to know. "We'll see what we've got first. Crap," she said again, and started over as a Black guy who looked like he could curl a couple of the airjacks without breaking a sweat peeled away from the rope and came toward them.

She judged him at about forty, ridiculously handsome, and built like a god in his work jeans, safety vest, and hard hat.

"Jim Mackie, just Mackie's good. I'm the job boss. I had them rope off the section where we found it. Her, I guess."

"Her?"

"Yeah, I'm thinking her because it's them. Sorry. It looks to me like maybe she was a woman. A pregnant woman when it happened, because there's what looks like baby or infant or fetus remains with her. Sorry."

He took off the hat, swiped his arm over his forehead. "That got me shook some. The little, um, skeleton."

"Okay. How about you move your people away from there, and my partner and I will take a look."

"You got it. If you need to go down to her? I gotta fix you into a safety harness. The old stairs collapsed even before we took down the building. I don't trust the supports, and the street-level building below is just as bad—condemned for good reason. This was a shit-ass job. Sorry, sorry. I'm upset."

"Shit-ass jobs upset me, too."

That got a smile. "Heard you were okay. Figured you'd be because the big boss, he's okay. No shit-ass jobs when you do a job for Roarke. You do quality, or you get the boot."

"She's the same," Peabody told him, and earned another smile.

Then he turned around. "Get on away from there, move back. Anybody on Building One, get on back to work."

The way people scrambled told Eve that Mackie did that quality work, and knew how to run a crew. She stepped to the rope.

She didn't know much about building, about concrete and beams and rebar, but even she could see a lot in this section was some sort of filler, more like dirt than stone. And curled in it, about eight feet down, between two crumbling walls, the remains of one adult, one fetus.

Too small to be called a child, she thought, and also curled, likely as it had been inside the womb at the time of death.

"Do you know when this was built—poured—whatever it's called?"

"I do. Not the exact day, but the year: 2024. If the really half-assed records are accurate, late summer, early fall of that year. I expect if there's a better record of it, Roarke can tell you the day, and the hour."

Yes, he would, though he wouldn't have owned it in the late summer of 2024. He wouldn't have been born quite yet, she thought.

But he'd know who had owned it. He'd know the owner; he'd know who developed it. Whatever he didn't know, he'd find out.

"I'll take that harness, Mackie. Peabody, contact DeWinter, get her here."

They'd need the forensic anthropologist, but in the meantime, Eve needed a closer look. Whoever they'd been, they, as much as Alva Quirk, were hers now.

"I'll tag Roarke."

While Mackie sent for a harness, she pulled out her 'link.

Caro, Roarke's admin, answered. "Good morning, Lieutenant."

"Caro, sorry. You need to get him."

Always efficient, Caro merely nodded. "One moment."

As the screen switched to holding blue, Eve considered she'd have gotten exactly the same response in exactly the same tone from Caro whether Roarke sat alone at his desk enjoying a cup of coffee or ran a meeting involving the purchase of Greenland.

She didn't think Roarke could actually buy Greenland, but if he could, if he was planning on it, Caro's response would have been the polite: One moment.

Eve glanced over as Mackie held up a safety harness. "Give me another sec."

She took another couple steps away as Roarke's face filled the screen.

He didn't smile. Not annoyance, she knew, but concern. Those wild blue eyes held steady on hers. Making sure she was in one piece, Eve thought.

"Sorry," she began. "I hope you weren't buying Greenland."

"Not at the moment." Ireland shimmered like morning mists in his voice. "Something's wrong."

"I caught one on my way in, but that one's not the issue. It's the one I caught about a block away from the first. That one's on, or maybe it's under, your Hudson Yards Village project."

"Which part?"

"Ah . . ." She looked back at Mackie. "Which part is this of the project?"

"Right here's the Sky Garden phase."

"Sky Garden. Some restaurant you took down, in the cellar of that. They jacked out the concrete over the old rails, and we've got remains, human remains. Two. What appears to be a female and a fetus. I'm calling DeWinter in to examine and confirm."

"A pregnant woman buried under the platform there?"

"The way it looks from where I'm standing. I can only confirm two human remains, which I further speculate, given the platform was built and poured, according to your job boss, nearly forty years ago, have been there a few decades. Again, DeWinter will take that end of things."

"Bloody hell." He raked a hand through that gorgeous

mane of black hair. "I'll be on my way to you within ten minutes."

"Okay. I'm going to have to shut down your project until—"

"Yes, yes, we'll deal with that. I'll be there," he said, and cut her off.

"That'll be fun," she muttered. She looked over at Peabody, who nodded, wound a finger in the air. More fun, Eve thought, with the fashionable Dr. DeWinter coming up.

She stepped back to Mackie, looked at the harness, looked down in the hole. "All right then, let's get me suited up so I can make sure this isn't some sick prank."

Hope lit all over his face. "Oh, hey, like maybe it's fake?"

"I'll know in a minute."

It wasn't, but she had to make that determination even if it meant hanging by a damn cable over a bunch of broken concrete, rebar spikes, rocks, and Christ knew.

"It'll hold ten times your weight," he told her as she put her arms through the straps. "It's got good padding, so it's not going to dig into you, and that adds protection."

He adjusted the straps, checked the safety buckles, the D rings.

"You ever use one of these?" she asked him.

"Yep. I'm not ten times your weight, but I bet I more than double it, and no problemo."

"Good to know."

"DeWinter's on her way." Like Eve, Peabody looked down in the hole. "Do you want me to go down with you?"

"No point. I'm going to get it on record, confirm we've got human remains, and see what I see. I need my field kit."

"We're going to hook it on this ring right here," Mackie told her. "Keep your hands free." He handed her a pair of work gloves. "And protect them. You ever do any rappel-ling?"

"Not if I can help it." When he laughed, she shrugged. "Yeah, I know the drill. Check in at the other site, Peabody. Start lining up interviews. We need a full run on the victim."

"You're set," Mackie told her. "We'll take it slow. Lot of rubble down there, and where she is, between the walls? That wasn't poured, so it's not going to be real stable."

"Yeah, I see it. Peabody, DeWinter needs to bring recovery equipment."

"She knows."

Of course she knew, Eve thought, and admitted she was stalling.

"Okay." She ducked under the rope, took another careful look so she could mentally map her route down. Then turned her back to it as she pulled on the gloves.

She gripped the belay rope, took up the slack, leaned into it, and started the descent.

Obstacles, she thought, checking left and right behind her as she went down, feet perpendicular to the wall, keeping her pace slow but steady. She adjusted right, left to avoid rubble and rebar and busted beams.

Six feet down, she called up, "I'm moving a couple feet to the left. I can get closer. She's right below those beams, between two walls. Say, how stable do you figure those beams are?"

"They held up so far. We got you, Lieutenant. You're not going anywhere."

While she didn't want to end up somehow breaking through the ground and splatting on the rubble, she'd actually worried more about the remains.

She eased down on a broken beam, gave it a little testing bounce. "Feels solid enough."

Kneeling, she pulled off the work gloves, then resealed her hands. And took a close look at her second and third victims of the morning.

2

Not a prank, Eve thought as she took out a flashlight.

"Human remains, one female. I can confirm that without DeWinter. DeWinter to establish approximate age, race, height, weight. Second remains, a fetus or very small infant. No more than a foot and a half in length."

She played her light over the adult skull. "Some damage, cracks in the adult female skull, and a broken left arm—possibly from the fall. It looks like the left shoulder—if she hit the way we found her, she hit on the left side. There's something . . .

"Gold ring, wedding band? Third finger, left hand. Still on there."

She took tweezers out of her field kit, used them to slide the ring off the curled finger bone. "No engraving. Plain yellow gold ring."

She bagged it.

"I see splintering, second and third ribs, left side."

She leaned closer. "Heart shots. Those are going to be from bullets. Plenty of guns around thirty-five to forty years ago if that's when she went in. We need to locate the slugs when we bring up the remains. I see something."

She shifted her light, then used the tweezers again. "Earring." She used a brush to carefully clean it off. "Post style, yellow gold circle with a silver or maybe white gold triangle inside. I can't look for the second if it's a pair or I'd disturb the remains. Recovery team needs to locate. Got a gold necklace, too, still attached, so I'm leaving it in place. Gold chain maybe ten inches long holding a what do you call it—swans, a pair of swans twined together at the neck to form a heart.

"Got an old watch, gold watch." Girlie, Eve thought. Expensive. "One shoe. Ladies shoe, probably leather because it hasn't fully decomposed. No sign of a 'link or ID. Recovery team should do a thorough search. Maybe a mugging, maybe, but wouldn't you want the jewelry? Is she going to refuse when she's pregnant or has a baby with her? I don't think so. Shoot her after you have the valuables, okay, but before? No point."

Eve shifted, and focused on the second remains.

So small, she thought as pity rose up. Hell, her cat was bigger.

"Probability on second remains is fetus given the positioning with female. That's not a damn coincidence. Indeterminate gender. I'm not sure I could tell even if it wasn't curled up. The top of the skull . . ." She remembered Mavis talking about Bella's soft spot. How the skull didn't knit hard for weeks after birth.

"Soft spot," she murmured. "No visible injuries."

Because it died in there, died inside its mother before it took its first breath.

Some sort of exterior wall, she noted. Concrete blocks. And brick, a brick wall on the other side of the hollow. About three feet in from the exterior wall.

Walled you in, didn't they? Fuckers.

"Dallas? You good?"

"Yeah." She held up a hand to verify to Peabody, and

slowly, carefully eased off the beam to balance on some rubble.

Something shifted; she held her breath.

When the world didn't fall in around her, she played her light closer to the remains.

"I've got slugs here. Bullets. I see two bullets. I can't safely retrieve them without disturbing the remains or, you know, burying us in here."

"You should come up," Peabody called out, and the nerves in her voice sounded clearly. "You've got enough on record."

"Probable COD on unidentified female, two gunshot wounds to the chest. Probable COD on second remains . . . it comes to the same, doesn't it? Dr. DeWinter and ME to confirm."

She secured the evidence bags, put on the gloves.

"Bring me up."

When she came up again, she unhooked her field kit, passed it to Peabody. "We need sweepers who can get down there once the remains are removed. Call it in, set it up."

She pulled off the gloves as Mackie unclipped her.

"I gotta shut you down, Mackie."

"The whole project? Building One—the one we got going up? It's a half block away from this projected green space."

"The projected green space is a crime scene." But she considered. "Is there any way to secure this area off, to access that building from another location?"

"Yeah, yeah, we already access it from two other locations. And I can have a security fence up in three hours, tops, to cordon off this whole area. This elevated space here, it's going to be all park, see? Open to the public and all, and over there, we'll have some private green space for the towers. Mixed residential and commercial. More commercial down on street level."

"Why are you jacking up just this one area?"

"We tested all the platforms, and this one here, this section came up hollowed out in spots. Well, you saw that yourself up close. We've updated and reenforced wherever we need to for the new designs. A lot of what got started in the way back ended up bombed out or torn up during the Urbans. And when construction started up again, a lot of it was rushed or subpar."

Eve tugged at her own memory. "There used to be shops and restaurants up here. Over The West Side, right?"

"Yeah, yeah, but it was crap construction, and they never got the people glides to work right. Plus, they never finished it, so it ended up overgrown, falling down until the boss bought it a couple years ago."

"A couple years ago."

"He's got ideas. Well, you'd know, right? Took some time to get the design the way he wanted—it's a big project."

"I can see that. Bigger than the one Singer's developing."

"Oh yeah, more than double that. So it takes awhile to get the design, get it all engineered and approved and permitted, and . . ."

She saw his eyes widen. "Is that one of yours? She looks too fancy to be a cop."

Eve turned and thought he had a point. Garnet DeWinter looked too fancy to be a cop. Then again, she wasn't one.

"Forensic anthropologist. Bone doctor," Eve added as Mackie continued to watch DeWinter approach.

In heels, for Christ's sake, Eve thought. Scarlet stilts to match the body-hugging red dress. A statuesque woman, she carried an enormous bag. She'd changed her hair, Eve noted. Not the style so much, as she had it in her most usual sleek roll at the nape of her neck. But she'd gone sort of copper colored, which Eve had to admit looked good with her mocha-colored skin.

Peabody tapped her hair, tapped at DeWinter. "Love it."

DeWinter flashed a smile. "Me, too. And yours." Then she looked at Eve, smile fading. "Dallas."

"DeWinter. This is Mackie, he's job boss."

DeWinter offered a hand, and not a smile so much as a very female sizing up. "Mr. Mackie."

"Aw, just Mackie's good."

"Mackie. I've got a recovery team coming in," she said to Eve. "But I'd like to see the remains in situ."

"Are you planning on going down there wearing that?"

"If I feel I need to examine the remains in place, I have the proper gear with me. Down there?"

With Eve, she moved to the rope. "This was part of the old elevated train platform?"

"Yes, ma'am."

"And the plan was when this concrete was put in to convert it to residential and commercial space?"

"Yes, ma'am."

She smiled at Mackie again. "You needed to demolish this platform?"

"Yes, ma'am. The material—we tested it—wasn't top grade. It shouldn't have been used for this purpose, and we detected some hollow spots, suspected some of the supports might not've been up to code—at least not up to today's codes. So we started jacking it out, and we found them."

"We had a DB at another site, a block south," Eve told her. "We responded here."

"Busy morning."

"Mackie tells me this would've been done in 2024."

"That's helpful. I'll be able to confirm if they've been here for that amount of time. A female and a fetus. I'll go down and examine them."

"I've been down." Eve considered the trip down and back, and while she and DeWinter weren't the best of pals, she'd spare her that. "And have it on record. It's hard to see from here, and at this angle, but there are two holes in the female. Left side, second and third ribs. I could see the two slugs. Couldn't get to them, but I have them on record."

"You're sure the damage was from gunshots?"

"As sure as I can be from a visual. She fell on her left side, most likely. Broken left arm, dislocated left shoulder. Some damage to the skull, but it doesn't read blunt force trauma. Probably from the fall. Bang, bang, and in she goes."

"We'll see."

"I took what looks like a wedding ring off the third finger of her left hand. No visible injuries on the second remains."

"The mother's heart stops, blood flow stops, oxygen stops. The fetus wouldn't survive. I can and will give you cause of death, year of death, the ages of the victims, and so on. I'll extract DNA if possible, and if she was in the system, you'll have her name. Otherwise, we'll generate a sketch and a holo."

"You can do that?" Mackie asked. "Figure out what she looked like?"

"We can." DeWinter's lashes swept up, swept down. "I have a brilliant reconstruction artist in my department."

"How long will it take?"

Flirty girl banished, DeWinter glanced back at Eve. "Until it's done. Once it is, finding the who did this and why is up to you."

"You do yours, I'll do mine." She spotted Roarke, turned, and walked to him. "Before you were born," she said.

"Understood." He looked over at DeWinter. "And still, the second time for the three of us, isn't it? Let's hope it doesn't become a habit."

"I know you want to see, but first, who'd you buy this property from?"

"Actually, there were two sellers, since I wanted all of it and part had been sold off about thirty years back, maybe more, then again about a dozen years ago, before I had enough to finance it myself. The far west section I bought from Nolan and Sons, which had overestimated their scope, you could say, particularly since they overpaid for the air rights, and this section I wrangled from Singer Family Developers two years ago."

"Singer. Is that right?"

"It is. Would I have it right your first call was to their project?"

"You would. I can't see a connection between the bashing of a homeless woman early this morning and the murder of a pregnant woman nearly four decades ago. But you never know, do you?"

"You will." He kissed her forehead before she could stop him.

"On duty."

"Aren't we both?" Then he walked over to the rope.

"Hell of a thing, boss."

"It is, yes. Garnet. Christ, what people will do. Did she fall, do you think?"

"Dallas found what she believes is damage from bullet wounds, upper left ribs, and the spent bullets."

"What people will do," he repeated. "Well then, Mackie, the NYPSD is about to shut us down for a bit."

"The lieutenant here said we could put up a security fence and close off this area. We can keep Building One on schedule."

"See to that then, won't you? And see that the steps up to this area are locked down. I'll see the cops have codes for entry if needed."

"I'll get it going. If you need anything, Lieutenant, Detective, ma'am, just send somebody for Mackie."

As Mackie jogged off, Roarke turned to Eve. "Is there anything you need from me?"

"A lot of information, and any data or plans you have or can access from when this building went up. I'm going to have a talk with Singer."

"It's Bolton Singer now," Roarke told her. "Fourth generation. He and I made the deal on the property."

"I need their records. They would've had a Mackie back then, maybe still have him or her. I need to know who worked or had access to this area when she went in. It's not impossible somebody didn't bust up the concrete more recently, then cover it up again."

"I suppose it's not. There would have been several buildings along here being built about the time she died."

"So somebody decides to kill her, has access to the building over the pad, jacks it up, dumps her, does a quick cover-up. Possible."

And a lot of work, Eve thought.

"More likely they dumped her in before, then covered her up. Either way, I need what building was over that section, and who had access."

"I'll have all that for you by this evening."

"Good. Get me how long she's been there, DeWinter. That's a factor into finding who put her there."

"It'll take longer than this evening, but you'll have it. Here's my recovery crew."

"And the sweepers. Earring, bullets," she reminded DeWinter. "And she's still wearing a necklace and a watch. I need those and anything else your team or the sweepers find."

She looked at her wrist unit. "Peabody and I have to get back to the first scene."

"Do you want what they find sent to you at Central or straight to the lab?"

"Lab. We'll get by there at some point today, or tomorrow."

"I'll be here for a while yet," Roarke told her.

"I'll be in touch."

With Peabody, Eve clanged down the metal steps.

"It's a stretch," Peabody commented, "to connect a murder from potentially thirty-seven years ago here with the murder of a sidewalk sleeper last night a block and a half south."

"The Singer organization owns and is developing the first scene, owned and did develop the second scene at the probable time of the unidentified victim's murder. But, yeah, still a stretch. And they have a partner. I did some looking when you were examining the remains. Singer partners with Bardov Construction for areas within what they're now calling the River View development."

"Bardov?" That was a name she knew. "Did you get any specifics?"

"Not yet, but I can dig."

"Yeah, do that, and we'll look at the partner, seeing as that company's owned by a Russian gangster."

"Really?"

"Feels like kind of sloppy for the mob," Eve considered, "but then again, it was effective. She could have been part of the company, worked for any of those companies—if they had access to that site, that building under construction. There's a reason you cover up, hide, basically bury a body. They walled her in there, Peabody."

"I saw the interior brick wall. No other reason for it. Mackie said the same thing."

"You don't just want her dead, you want her to vanish—want to cut off any connection between you. Otherwise? You'd dump her in the river, hell, toss her in a dumpster."

"She had a wedding ring?"

"Right type of ring, right finger for it, so high probability. And, yeah, if we ID her, we look at the spouse first."

"Gotta do it. The baby . . . The way the remains looked, it had to be close to full term, Dallas, or a newborn."

"That's DeWinter's area." But she'd thought the same.

"Post-Urbans—again, high probability—and this area settled down and into rehab, renewal, rebuilding. It's unlikely somebody got shot a couple of times on an active construction site in broad daylight. So what was she doing there after hours, after dark?"

"That's our area."

"Yeah, it is. We pin down when that particular building went up, then when the wine cellar section went in. Following probability—unless and until DeWinter tells us otherwise—we search for records of missing persons reports with that time frame. Pregnant female, which again, with DeWinter, we can narrow down to an age span, a race, and we'll eventually get an image reconstruction.

"Until we do," Eve continued as they climbed up to the initial crime scene, "we gather as many names as possible. Who had access, who among those had a pregnant spouse, sister, daughter, ex, mother, and so on. Who, among those, can we confirm is alive, or was alive beyond our time frame."

"That's all going to take time."

"Yeah, well, I don't think she's in a hurry."

She moved over the debris and back to the platform. "Now, Alva Quirk. She came from somewhere, had connections to someone at some time."

Eve spotted the head sweeper still in her white protective gear and headed that way. "And we go back to access. Who had reason to be up here last night? CSI Yee."

"Lieutenant Dallas, Detective Peabody."

"Any prints or trace on the dumpster or the sheet?"

"No." Yee, an Asian woman who barely hit five-two, shook her head. "Workers tossing things in the dumpster are going to be wearing work gloves, and whoever wrapped the body sealed up or wiped down. We got what might be a shoe or boot print on the plastic, but it's going to be too smeared to give us anything. Blood, hair, fiber on the inside of the plastic, but at on-site exam, it looks like the victim's. We'll turn it over to Harvo."

If there was a speck of hair or fiber not the victim's, Eve knew Harvo would find it.

"Any good news?"

"We found the kill site."

"Thought you would. Toward the southwest, near the security fence."

Yee smiled, nodded. "You must be a trained investigator."

"That's what they tell me."

"Me, too." Yee turned to lead the way. "Blood trail starts here, due to crappy wrapping job. So the plastic loosened enough for her to drip out after he/she/they carted her along the fence line, through the gate, and into the dumpster. It's just over twelve feet."

Near the southwest corner of the security fence, beyond its gate, its cams, Eve studied where Alva Quirk died.

Blood soaked into the ground, spattered over the fence, through it to where a sweeper took samples of the spatter on the side of a large backhoe.

"Some overgrowth on this side," Eve observed. "She'd be out of the lights, the cams, be able to snuggle in pretty good. Is this area cleared?"

"On this side, yeah."

Eve moved over to the fence, crouched down, scanned. "Good view from here. She could see the city, and she'd see anybody who, say, walked in or out of the gate. Can't see the access from the street from here, but if anybody walked to or toward the gate, she saw them. Unlikely the killer arrived armed with a roll of plastic sheeting or a crowbar. I bet they'd find both in that equipment shed over there.

"Peabody."

"I'll go find out."

"I assumed you'd already looked. I'm sending sweepers in there next."

Eve shook her head at Yee. "We got called to another murder just south. Another construction site."

"I heard something about it. What gives?"

"Human remains closed off in a portion of what was supposed to be a wine cellar of a post-Urban-built restaurant. DeWinter's on it."

Interest bloomed on Yee's face. "Do you want me and my team to take that one? We're about finished here, and can send a runner to take what we've got to the lab."

Save time, potentially, and she knew Yee's work was top-notch and thorough. "Yeah, tag your dispatch and clear it. You're going to need to rappel down about ten feet from where they broke through the top of the basement—cellar. Ask for Mackie."

"Got it. Give me a second."

Yee turned away as Peabody came back through the gate.

"Storage shed, tools, small equipment. Organized," Peabody added. "I saw rolls of plastic sheeting. Crowbars, sledgehammers, wedges, shovels, picks, nail cartridges, cutters."

"Yee will get some of her people to process it. The victim sees you, or hears you—or both. You're doing something you shouldn't be, saying something you shouldn't say. Quirk gets out her book. Has to write down the infraction or crime, describe the perpetrator or perpetrators. Let's have EDD check out the security on the gate, see if it's been compromised. If not, they had a way in, they had access. They see her or she makes her presence known. 'Sorry, but I have to report this.'"

She circled the kill spot.

"What do you do? Maybe you try to intimidate, charm, threaten, maybe you offer her a bribe. Maybe, but it comes down to she's a witness to something you can't afford a witness to. So you've got to know you can get a weapon and the sheeting in the shed there. You've got to have a way through the gate."

Closing her eyes, Eve ran it through in her head.

"Got to be two of them. At least two. One has to keep her engaged, keep her right here, keep her talking while the other goes for the weapon. She wasn't a big woman, why not just beat her down or strangle her? Takes time maybe. But a couple bashes is pretty quick. Cut some plastic off the roll, wrap her up—but you gotta get gone, so you rush it. Dump her in. Maybe it buys you a day or so. Crew tosses shit in. Why would they look in there? Another day or so before she starts to smell, right? Or maybe before that, they haul the dumpster off to the recycling center."

Eve gauged the ground again. "You can't see the blood unless you look straight over here from the gate. You don't see it from the work area inside the fence until you move the heavy equipment. You take her backpack, whatever she had—especially that book. Do you take time to clean the murder weapon and replace it? Smarter if you take it with you, shove it into the backpack, get rid of all that somewhere else. We're not talking big smarts here, but maybe smart enough for that."

"We'll check any tools for blood traces," Yee told her. "I'm going to leave a couple of my team here to finish, and the rest will start on the second site."

"Appreciate it. You'll be able to tell which roll they cut from. They hadn't started any work this morning, so it would be the freshest."

"Yeah, we can, and when we do, we'll take the roll for full analysis."

"Over to you then, Yee. Peabody, let's go have a conversation with the job boss."

"Good hunting, Dallas," Yee called out.

"Same to you."

"Geraldi, Paulie," Peabody began. "Officer Urly tagged me and said with the shutdown order, he was going to Singer HQ to talk to his boss."

"Two for one. We'll have a conversation with Bolton Singer, too."

"His office is walkable. Just a couple blocks east, another couple north."

"You looking for loose pants again?"

"That could be a side benefit. It's just a really nice morning."

Eve couldn't, and wouldn't, deny the appeal of New York in the spring.

"Maybe so, but we need the car. After the conversations—unless they lead to immediate arrests or further conversations—we'll go by the morgue, see what we've got on Quirk. Then we're at Central, doing a full run on the vic—again, she came from somewhere. Her ID has gaps, so we need to fill them."

She reached the stairs, started down with Peabody clanging along with her.

"And digging back into the missing persons on our other vic. We need more background on the partners, on the sales of the second site. We don't have time for strolling."

"When you put it that way."

When they reached Eve's DLE, Peabody slid in. "Can I get a diet fizzy? It got warm up there."

"Go."

"Coffee?"

Eve started to say yes before she pulled out because coffee was always a yes. "Tube of Pepsi."

While Peabody programmed the drinks from the in-dash AutoChef, Eve ordered a run on Geraldi.

Geraldi, Paul Tomas, age sixty-two, her computer began. **Caucasian, male. Married Theresa Angela Basset, age sixty, June 2032. Three offspring, Paul, male, age twenty-eight; Carla, female, age twenty-six; Anthony, male, age twenty-five. Employed by Singer Developers 2023 to present. Demolition expert, supervisory position.**

Eve listened to the employment record, the financial data, education data, the criminal—small change in Geraldi's early twenties.

"He'd've been with the company in 2024," she commented. "Puts him on that list if those dates line up. Let's see about the big boss. Computer, run Bolton Kincade Singer of New York City."

Acknowledged. Working. Singer, Bolton Kincade, age fifty-nine. Caucasian, male. Married Lilith Anne Conroy, age fifty-five, December 2033. Three offspring, Harmony, female, age twenty-seven; Layla, female, age twenty-four; Kincade, male, age twenty-two. President and CEO of Singer Family Developers, based in New York City. Employed by Singer Family Developers 2026 to present.

"Pause," Eve ordered. "Where was subject employed and/or residing prior to 2026?"

Subject attended Irving Allen Conservatory from 2020 to 2024 as full-time student. He resided in Savannah, Georgia, from August 2020 to February 2026.

To save time, Eve zipped into a loading zone a half block from Singer HQ. "Degrees and employment during that period."

**Subject earned degrees, with honors, in music com-
position, instrumental arts, and vocal arts. He was
self-employed as a musician/performer during this
period.**

"Hold the rest. An odd education for the head of an urban development company."

"My guess would be he had other plans for his future. Singer wanted to be a singer."

Eve nodded, then realized she hadn't cracked the tube of Pepsi. She let it sit where it was as she flipped up the On Duty light. "That's my take. Guess he changed his mind, or his finances ran thin."

"He gave it a decent shot," Peabody said as they got out of the car. "Either way, it lowers the likelihood he was here when our unidentified woman was murdered."

"Or he was here on a college break, hoping to butter up his wealthy parents so they'd fork over more dough. They gave him his shot. A year or so after college to make it or break it. You don't make it, it's time to face the real world, earn your keep."

"I looked up the conservatory. They don't take just anybody. You have to take written tests, and audition, then they have a panel that votes on your admission. It's pricey, and it's exclusive."

"And it would've been away from the hot spots still flaring up during the Urbans. You could pull some strings to get your one and only son in, I bet."

"Cops are cynics, because I can see that." Peabody paused outside the entrance of the Singer Building to take stock.

"It's impressive," Peabody decided, "and it's got that old-timey New York and dignified look to it. But it's not as big or impressive as Roarke's Midtown HQ."

"What is?"

Eve swung in, crossed the marble-tiled and, yes, old-timey New York and dignified lobby to the security desk.

She held up her badge. "Paulie Geraldi and Bolton Singer."

"Are either expecting you, Lieutenant?"

"I don't think they'll be surprised."

"One moment." Security turned away to consult with someone on his earbud.

While she waited, Eve scanned the lobby. Activity coming off or going on elevators. No shops or cafés, but a large screen displaying various Singer projects—completed, projected, under construction.

"Mr. Geraldi is in Mr. Singer's office at this time. You're cleared to go up. Elevator bank A, fiftieth floor. Someone will meet you. Please sign in."

Eve scrawled her signature with her finger on the pad, then moved to the A bank of elevators.

"That was easy," Peabody commented.

"Let's see how easy the rest is."

Eve waited for a trio of suits to hustle off an elevator, then stepped inside. "Bolton Singer, floor fifty."

Enjoy your visit to the Singer Building, the computer told her. **Singer Family Developers is dedicated to building a vital and vibrant New York.**

"A couple people might disagree." Eve slid her hands in her pockets as the elevator headed up.

3

The elevator doors opened on fifty to a spacious reception area that continued the dignified theme in tones of navy and cream and dark, glossy wood. Two people manned stations at opposite ends of the tall counter backed by the floor-to-ceiling company logo.

Eve heard the one on the right chirp cheerfully to a caller on her station 'link, "Good morning! Singer Family Developers! How can I assist you?"

The woman who waited to greet them didn't look as if she'd chirp, cheerfully or otherwise.

She wore her ink-black hair in a kind of skullcap with the ends honed into keen spikes. While her lips curved in polite greeting, her eyes—a tawny gold that made Eve think of various unpleasant reptiles—stayed as keen as those spiked ends.

Her dress, blue as cobalt, skimmed down to the knees of a tough, athletic body and showed off well-cut arms.

"Lieutenant Dallas." She offered a ringless hand and a very firm grip. "Detective. I'm Zelda Diller, administrative assistant to Mr. Singer. He and Mr. Geraldi are meeting in Mr. Singer's office. I'll escort you back."

"Okay."

She started back and through a wide doorway to the left of the counter. Open doors on either side showed outer offices where admins or secretaries or both worked busily at stations with closed inner doors where Eve assumed the execs did what execs did.

"Due to the unfortunate circumstances"—Zelda flicked a glance at Eve—"I've cleared thirty minutes of Mr. Singer's schedule for you. I assume that will be sufficient."

"We'll find out, won't we?"

As expected, the big boss's offices boasted double doors.

Dignity continued its reign with a sand-colored carpet, dark wood, chocolate leather visitors' chairs, and the central desk, where a man in a navy pin-striped suit worked his comp.

Through the open door on the left, Eve saw a man in shirtsleeves pacing as he held a conversation on his 'link. The firmly closed door on the right had the admin's name on a brass plaque.

Zelda moved straight to the double doors behind the central desk.

She knocked briskly before opening one side.

"Lieutenant Dallas and Detective Peabody, sir."

"Yes, thank you, Zelda. Please, show them right in."

Bolton crossed the wide space from desk to door in his sharp gray suit as a second man in work clothes rose from a chair.

"Lieutenant, Detective. Bolton Singer and our project supervisor Paul Geraldi. A difficult day for all. Zelda, could we get some coffee, please?"

"I'll arrange it."

She stepped out, closed the door behind her.

And, Eve would've made book, started the thirty-minute timer.

"Please sit." He gestured not to the chairs facing his desk, but to the two-seater sofa in that chocolate-brown leather, then waved Geraldi to one of the forest-green chairs facing it. Bolton took the other rather than the power position behind his desk.

Eve figured an office told you something about the person who worked in it. The vibe, her oldest friend, Mavis, would've called it.

This one struck her as friendly—the comfortable seating, the thriving plant in a cheerful pot at the corner of his window wall. Involved, as she spotted several framed wall photos of Bolton Singer in hard hats at job sites as well as more formal ones of him at ceremonial first shovels or ribbon cuttings.

Busy, most likely. She couldn't see his comp screen, and the wall screen pulsed on holding blue, but she'd spotted a legal pad and some handwritten notes on his blotter.

"Paulie's been filling me in," Bolton began, "as best he can. My first questions are do you know what happened, and what can we do to help?"

"We're at the very beginning of our investigation. We appreciate your cooperation thus far, and continuing that cooperation aids our investigation."

"You can count on it." He paused when the knock came again. This time Navy Pin-Stripe came in, wheeling a coffee service.

"Thanks, Terry. I'll confess I read Nadine Furst's first book, and have already started her second, so it's black coffee for Lieutenant Dallas, coffee regular for Detective Peabody."

He had a strong face, clean-shaven, that just missed handsome. Direct, pale blue eyes took it over the line into appealing, as did the dark honey hair curling over his ears and collar.

He wore a thick, ridged, white-gold wedding ring, a slick

and sleek black-banded wrist unit, and a single stud in his left ear.

Beside him, Paul Geraldi looked tanned and burly with his barrel chest in a black T-shirt, his scarred work boots, his small, scruffy beard and gray-streaked brown hair clipped militarily short.

Bolton waited until Terry slipped back out of the room.

"Is there anything you can tell us about the woman who died? If there's anything we can do for her family?"

"Our information to this point is she lived on the streets."

He nodded, looked down at his coffee. "There'll be expenses regarding her burial or cremation. If there's no family, I would take care of that."

"She was known to the cops at the Tenth Precinct, and if we can't locate next of kin, they'll make arrangements for her."

"You know who she is?" Geraldi spoke up, then glanced over. "Sorry, Bolt."

"No, don't be."

"I didn't really get a look at her. I'd just gotten on the site when the kid found her. I figured we weren't supposed to touch anything before the cops got there."

"You were right. We've identified the victim as Alva Quirk."

"Don't know the name." Geraldi looked back at his boss again. "Don't know it."

"Peabody."

Peabody brought up the ID image—one a few years out of date—turned her PPC so both men could see it.

Bolton started to shake his head, but Geraldi leaned closer.

"Ah, shit. Sorry. Damn it. I knew her. I mean to say I didn't know her so much as I saw her a few times, talked to her a couple times."

"Where?"

"On the site. She came up a couple times—some do even though we've got the old steps blocked off. They get around it. And we have crew coming up and going down, so it ain't hard. Nothing up on that side of the fence right now, so it's not a big problem, but I move 'em along when I can. She was . . . she gave me a flower."

"A flower," Bolton repeated.

"Folded paper flower. Like that origami stuff. Out of part of one of those damn flyers they try handing out on the street nobody wants. She said I was lucky to work in a place with such a nice view, and how it was good we were building places for people to live. She kept coming back, and I had to keep telling her it was private property. She'd just smile and give me a flower or a bird or whatnot."

He scrubbed a hand over his face. "Got so I liked seeing her now and then. She'd camp some days down on the sidewalk by the steps. She wasn't hurting anybody. She told me how she was sorry she had to report one of my crew to the police."

"Why?" Bolton demanded immediately. "Did someone harass her?"

"Nah. She'd been up at the fence, saw one of the crew tossing stuff in the dumpster there. He missed with something, left it on the ground. She said littering was against the rules, showed me how she'd written it all out in her book."

"She showed you her book?"

Geraldi nodded at Eve. "Yeah, she had this book—sort of like those diaries little kids like to write in. A paper one. She showed me where she'd written it down. What the guy looked like, what he was wearing, the time of day, the litter. She said how we had to keep our city clean, and I said it wouldn't happen again."

"When was this?"

"Oh, man, this was back . . . last month. Three, four weeks

easy. It gave me the idea to ask her how about she write down people who came up the steps who didn't work for us. Figured it would keep her from coming up. I guess it didn't."

"When's the last time you saw her?"

Geraldi scrubbed a hand over his beard. "Gotta be a couple, three days ago. I worked out a kind of deal with her, see? I'd stop by down below after work every Friday, and she could give me her report, you know? I'd give her a few bucks for the weekend. I made a kind of game out of it, because I didn't want her coming up all the time, maybe taking a spill, or getting through the gate and picking through one of the dumpsters. We got broken glass, nails, sharp shit—stuff goes in there. We're doing a lot of demo. I didn't want her getting hurt. She wasn't hurting anybody.

"Goddamn it, Bolt, I'm sorry."

"It's not on you, Paulie." Bolton reached over, gripped Geraldi's arm briefly. "It's not on you, and I'm sorry, too."

"Who has off-hours access to that dumpster area, and the secured area, the building, all of it?"

"I would," Bolton began. "Paulie, of course, our head architect and engineer, head electrician, lead plumber." He stopped himself, held up a hand. "I'll give you a list of names and job titles."

"That would be helpful. We'll need to speak to all of them."

"I'll have Zelda set that up. Wouldn't it be more likely it was someone who got through the stairs on that side of the fence? Just some . . . opportunist?"

"More likely doesn't apply at the moment. Can you tell us where you were last night, Mr. Geraldi, between midnight and two A.M.?"

Geraldi blew out a breath. "Takes me back," he murmured. "I had a couple little brushes back in my misspent youth." He tried a half smile. "Nothing like this. I can tell you I was

home, from five-thirty or so—grabbed a beer—a couple—
with some of the crew before I went home. Two beers because
my in-laws are visiting from Scottsdale."

He rolled his eyes toward Bolton, who let out a sudden
laugh. "You'll get through it, Paulie. Stay strong."

"Been married going on thirty years," he told Eve and
Peabody, "raised up three good kids. Got two sweet-faced
grandkids so far. I make a good living, got a good, responsible job and respect on it. But I'm never going to be good
enough for their girl. They don't say it right out loud so much
anymore. But they think it, and always will."

He huffed out another breath. "Anyway, I was home, had
dinner with my wife, the in-laws, my youngest boy, who
came by with his new girlfriend. Medical student, pretty
thing, speaks French like a native. And believe me, she'll
never be good enough for their grandbaby. Anyway," he said
again. "I was home from five-thirty, hit the sack about ten
because my day starts early."

"Okay. Mr. Singer?"

"My wife and I had dinner with friends, and I'd say we
got home about the time Paulie hit the sack. My day doesn't
start so early. I checked on some work—habit—we watched
the first part of *Knight at Night*, then settled in. Or my wife
did. Our youngest is home from college. When he—or any
of them—are away, I sleep like a rock. But when they're
home, I can't drop off all the way until I hear them come in.
Which he did at twelve-forty-eight—because I looked at the
clock."

"Thank you. If you could ask your admin to generate those
lists?"

"Yes, of course."

"My partner can go with you while it's set up. If we could
have a space to conduct interviews with anyone in the building at this time, that would also help."

"Absolutely." He rose. "This shouldn't take long, and I'll have you set up in the small conference room on this floor. Detective?"

When Peabody went out with him, Eve turned back to Geraldi. "You've worked for the Singers for a long time."

"Longer than I've been married. Longer than Bolton, come to that. Turned me around as I was heading in the wrong direction. Nothing big, but not doing anything with my life. I got a job with Singer, and it helped turn me around."

"You'd have worked for them when some of the buildings you're taking down first went up."

"Yeah, just a laborer back then. I had a lot to learn. Learned pretty quick I like demo. I thought it was so I could just bust things up, but I learned more. How to take something down, when, when to save and salvage. What's safe, what's not. What you can repurpose or donate. You don't just tear something down and throw it away."

His eyebrows drew hard together as he stared down at his hands. "That's what someone did to her. They just threw her away.

"It's not right. It's not right."

"No, it's not. Have you had any trouble on the job site? Pilfering, sabotage? Anything?"

"Nothing like that. We had some trouble when we started with sidewalk sleepers and squatters trying to get back in those buildings—the old ones. That's why we added security fences around the buildings in addition. They weren't safe, Lieutenant. I swear to you, they weren't safe, and if we weren't taking them down, they'd sure as hell start falling on somebody's head in another five, six years."

He leaned forward again. "They weren't built to last, see? It's not on the Singers, it's the system. Or what was. You're too young to know, but people were desperate for a place to live back then. So many buildings down or bombed out, torn up. It was get something up fast, get people off the streets. Or get people coming back into the city again. Get things going again."

"I know. A lot of the projects in Hudson Yards—just like elsewhere—ended up with that sort of construction. The Singer Family sold off a larger chunk of it."

"Couldn't do it all, not efficiently, not timely, and you know, you've only got so many resources, right? As I recall, the old man—that's Bolt's father—had partners, and when Bolt was coming up in the business, he wanted to focus in more. His old man had already sold most of the second site, I think, by then anyhow. That's awhile back."

"Did you work on both construction sites back then? Right after the Urbans?"

"They bounced me around plenty." Nostalgia put a wistful smile on his face. "Like I said, I was green labor. Young, strong back, so I'm hauling trash, mixing cement, carting materials. Crap stuff, like I said. I didn't know better then."

He looked up as Bolton came back in.

"The detective's getting things set up with Zelda. It won't be long."

"I appreciate that. If I could have a few more minutes of your time, Mr. Singer. We're done here, Mr. Geraldi."

"Go home, Paulie. We'll shift over to the Houston site tomorrow, get a jump on it. I'll meet you there at seven-thirty. How's that?"

"Can do." He rose. "I'd sure like you to let me know when you find the person who did that to her. Alva, you said. It's a nice name, and it suits her. I'd like to know when you get them."

"All right."

Bolton sat down again as Geraldi left. "He's taking it hard. It's that personal connection. It makes it even harder. He's a good man."

"He's worked for you a long time."

"He's a fixture. Loyal, reliable. He takes pride in his work. Whatever his in-laws think, his wife couldn't have done better. Now, what more can I do to help?"

"Your company developed a second project in Hudson Yards at the same time as the one you're currently rebuilding."

"Yes, Hudson South-West, I think they called it at the time. Then the Urban Wars put a stop to that. I don't know a great deal, as I wasn't interested in the business, and then was away at college. I do know the buildings went up fast and cheap once the dust cleared."

"Your father sold off a portion of Hudson South-West."

"Yes, years ago. He wanted to build the tower. The Singer Tower. He wanted that signature, you could say, before he retired. He'd hoped to develop the entire project, but he had some health scares. When I took over, I decided there were other areas that took priority. And I wanted that project, where my father had built his signature, to be worthy. It takes time and resources, so I sold the rest of South-West."

"What was Hudson South-West is also being developed now."

Bolton smiled. "I'm aware, Lieutenant. And certain that it will also be worthy. Roarke builds to last, and with the integrity of the city in mind. It's exactly why I approached him about buying the property."

"My partner and I answered a call to that site this morning."

"I'm sorry?" He looked blank for a moment. "But you're . . . You're Homicide. Dear God, not another murder."

"This one, if it proves to be murder, happened a long time ago. The crew found human remains in what had been part of a wine cellar—walled off, perhaps deliberately, to conceal those remains."

"Jesus." His fingers shot through his hair. "How long ago? Do you know who he was?"

"We have to determine that, and will. That, too, will take time. If we date it to when the building itself was being constructed, it would be roughly thirty-seven years."

"Thirty-seven years." More nostalgia, Eve noted, and wistful with it. "I was in college—or just out—and living in Savannah. I didn't want any part of the business back then."

"Why?"

"I wanted to be a rock star." He offered that half smile now. "The troubadour for my generation, like Dylan, like Springsteen." Now he laughed. "More or less. I wanted to write music, to perform. I wanted everything that wasn't my father at that point in my life."

"You left New York to study for it."

"Yeah. I guess you checked. It was about as far away from urban development as it gets. But I know—and I was young and critical—that buildings there, as in other areas, went up hard and fast and cheap. I know some who worked on them weren't . . . there weren't many Paul Geraldis, if you understand me. One of the agreements my father and I made when I said I'd come into the business was the return to our tradition of quality builds. I was very full of myself, even though I'd failed miserably as a performer."

When he shook his head, Eve caught more than self-deprecation in his eyes. She caught just a hint of sadness.

"What was I . . . twenty-four, I guess? My mother appealed to me. Just give it two years. They'd given me four years of college to study my dream. Give the family business two years. So I did, and discovered I could make a difference."

He waved that away. "Sorry, this just took me back. Do you know if this was some sort of accident? A job accident?"

"We don't believe so, but will pursue all avenues."

"I suppose it's not the first time or the last. I hear stories about animal remains, and have heard about human ones as well. The building in Hell's Kitchen you and Roarke transformed into a school. All those poor girls. Was this like that?"

"Something like. Is your father well now?"

"He is. He's needed a few replacement parts, as he puts it. And doesn't appear to take after my grandmother, who's hale and hearty at a hundred and five. His own father, my grandfather, died fairly young. Not as easy to replace parts in his day."

"I may need to speak with him about that development project. He may remember something that would aid in our investigation and identification. Yours is, as you said, a family business," Eve continued. "Would your mother have been involved in the project, or is she involved in your current development?"

"My mother? No, she's never been part of the building or planning. She has excellent taste, a fine eye, so she has, over the years, made suggestions for colors, fabrics, fixtures, furnishings if that applies. But Mom's not one to put on a hard hat and tour a site.

"My grandmother, now," he said before Eve could thank him and stand up. "She was an equal partner with my grandfather, and basically took over when he died. And believe me, she'll still give her opinion, solicited or not, on a project, on details big and minute."

He smiled when he said it. "She's a true matriarch, and shows little sign of slowing down."

"I look forward to speaking with her. I appreciate your time and cooperation, Mr. Singer."

He rose as she did. "I personally, and as head of this company, will help in any way we can."

He walked her to the door, stepped out with her.

"Terry, show Lieutenant Dallas to the small conference room, would you?"

"Yes, sir."

"Let me know if there's anything else I can do. And I'd appreciate notification as soon as we're cleared back on-site."

"You'll be the first."

The small conference room wasn't that small, Eve discovered.

It held a table that would easily fit eight on either side, a massive wall screen, a refreshment station, and a trio of mini data and communication units.

The stone-faced Zelda, on the point of leaving, paused to aim those weird eyes at Terry.

"You're to coordinate, contact the names as Detective Peabody or Lieutenant Dallas submits them, and have them come here immediately."

"Yes, ma'am."

"Detective Peabody has your 'link code and will contact you. After this initial contact, you can continue to work from your desk."

"Yes, ma'am."

When she walked out, Eve studied the room. "Give us just a minute, Terry. And don't *ma'am* either one of us."

He opened his mouth, closed it, nodded, stepped outside the door.

"She's creepy," Peabody said immediately. "She talks like an authoritarian droid and she has eyes like a snake."

"Yes!" Eve jabbed her finger into Peabody's shoulder. "She has snake eyes. How many have we got?"

"We've got twenty-six who'd have access codes, but only five are in the building today."

"Why? Where are the rest of them?"

"Working on other sites or in outside meetings. Three of those took the early shuttle this morning to a plant near Dayton, Ohio, to check out some man-made stone under consideration."

"Okay, we'll start with what we've got, then round up the others." She checked the time. "I'm going to tag Jenkinson, see what's what, let him know to handle things until I get there. You can send for the first of the six."

"Five."

Eve just gave Peabody a sad look. "Really? You think Snake Woman doesn't have the access codes to one of her boss's pet projects?"

"Well, now I do. The first is Danika Isler, head architect."

"We start there. Do a quick run on her while I tag Jenkinson."

They went through the architect, and Eve eliminated her from the older murder, as she'd have been four at the time, then put her bottom of the list on Alva's because she had a solid alibi up to thirty minutes before TOD, as she and her husband had attended his sister's birthday party in the Bronx, shared a cab on departure just after midnight with two other partygoers, and had arrived home to dismiss the babysitter at around twelve-thirty.

She eliminated the engineer, Bryce Babbott. He'd been sixteen at the estimated year of her unknown victim's death—more than old enough to kill. But he'd lived in Sydney, Australia, until 2049, so unlikely.

"He still has the accent." Peabody lifted and wiggled her shoulders after Eve dismissed him. "Sexy."

"People with sexy accents murder people all the time. He's got two dings for assault—bar fights, but he's not averse to violent behavior. And his alibi for the time in question is that he was home asleep with his current cohab, with his ten-year-old son asleep in the next room. He stays on. We'll take a closer look at him. Who's up?"

"Snake Woman."

"Good. This'll be fun."

"I think she's going to be really pissed."

"That's part of the fun."

Pissed hit the mark.

Zelda marched in, lips tight, jaw set.

"Is there something Terry couldn't handle for you? He's at your disposal."

"Does Terry have access to the Hudson Yards project?"

"Of course not."

"Then we don't need him for this. Have a seat."

"I'm very busy. Accommodating your inquiry has interfered with today's schedule."

"Well, that's too bad. Somebody interfered with the rest of Alva Quirk's life. Have a seat. Or we'll arrange for you to take one in an interview room at Central."

"What for?"

"Let me give you a heads-up. Lying to a police officer during an official investigation can land you in all sorts of . . . difficulties. So you're going to want to be careful when you answer my first question because my partner and I are very good at what we do. It'll be a snap for us to determine if you lie, and if you lie, difficulties. A lot of them."

Eve looked straight into those reptilian eyes. "Do you have access codes to Singer's Hudson Yards project?"

The way Zelda looked at her, Eve half expected to watch the woman's tongue—forked, of course—lash out from between her lips.

"As his admin for the past seven years, I manage Mr. Singer's codes, passwords, swipes—which are routinely changed every two weeks for security purposes."

"That's a yes. Have a seat, and start off by explaining why you didn't put your name on the list of those who had access."

"Because it didn't apply."

Eve could tell the woman wanted to remain standing in a show of defiance and personal power, but she finally sat.

"I manage his security codes, seeing that they rotate, that he has them. I don't *use* them unless he specifically requests that I do."

"Has he ever specifically requested that you access the gates at the project in question?"

"No, he has not, and I have not."

"When's the last time you were at that location?"

"I accompanied Mr. Singer to that particular site in March."

Zelda turned her wrist, tapped at her wrist unit. "March fourteenth, from nine to nine-forty-five A.M. While I do occasionally accompany Mr. Singer to sites if he has need of me, it's more usual for me to work out of this building or from my own home."

"You haven't been at that location since March fourteenth?"

"I have not. Now, is that all?"

Eve glanced over at Peabody, spoke pleasantly. "Hey, Peabody, do you think that's all?"

"No, sir, I don't. We're just going to have to interfere with today's schedule a little bit longer." Peabody held out her PPC, and the ID shot of Alva Quirk.

"Do you know this woman?"

"No." Something changed in her eyes. "No," she repeated.

"Difficulties," Eve said. "Lots of them."

"I don't know her. But . . ." Shifting, she looked closer at the photo. "I saw her. I think . . . She gave me an origami flower."

"When and where?"

"On that day, on March fourteenth. Bolton—Mr. Singer— wanted to see that the security around the buildings to be demoed went up properly. He'd delayed that until as close as he could to warmer weather. The buildings weren't safe, but there were squatters, and he worried they'd have nowhere to go over the winter. He's a good man. He delayed locking that area down as long as he could."

"She was at the site. You and Mr. Singer saw her, spoke to her?"

"No, she was down on the sidewalk. I don't think he saw her. It was cold, and had started to sleet. He insisted I go down, wait in the car while he finished up. He gave me some busywork to do to override my objections. I saw her when I went back down, and yes, used his access code to unlock the security gate we had in place until the area, the unstable buildings were fully secured."

"You spoke to her."

"She was by the gate, and she said we were locking people out, and some people lived up there. I started to just go by her, but she got in front of me. She had this book and a pencil. She said she would have to report me for locking people out because some of them had nowhere else to go."

Back ruler straight, Zelda folded her hands.

"Frankly, I didn't want Mr. Singer to come down and have to deal with her. He already felt considerable guilt about displacing the squatters. I just told her the buildings weren't safe, they were dangerous, and my boss needed to fix them, to make them safe so no one got hurt. He'd feel responsible if someone got hurt. And, again frankly, if that didn't work, I intended to call the police and have her moved along."

"Did it work?"

"She smiled at me, as I recall, and said that was different. That was being a good citizen. She gave me the paper flower, thanked me, and walked away. She's the one who was killed?"

"Yes."

"I never saw her again. I haven't been back to the site since then."

"What did her book look like?"

"I don't really recall."

"Like a diary? A kid's diary—the paper kind?"

"No." Zelda narrowed her eyes, frowned. "No, not like that. It was more . . . ah, like an autograph book. Like books celebrity watchers carry around to get signatures. Like that, I think."

"Okay. Can you give us your whereabouts from midnight to two A.M. this morning?"

"God, this is absurd. It's intrusive."

"It's routine. Somebody killed her and tossed her in a dumpster like she was garbage. You can deal with some intrusion."

"I had a date," Zelda snapped. "I'm divorced, which if you're even marginally efficient you'd know by this time. I've been divorced for three years, I have no children. I had a date with a man I've seen twice before. We went to dinner, to a club to hear some music. And . . . we're unencumbered adults."

"What time did he leave your place, or you his?"

The faintest, the very faintest of a flush rose up on Zelda's cheeks. "He left just after seven this morning."

"Okay, we'll need the details. Where you had dinner, what club, his name."

Zelda stared straight ahead as she reeled off the data.

"Just to wrap this up, we are marginally efficient, so we know you've worked for this company for thirty years."

"I came on as an entry-level secretarial assistant right out of business school in 2031."

"How did you work up to your current position with the top boss?"

She aimed a withering look at Eve. "I'm good at what I

do, and received regular promotions. I was assistant to Ms. Elinor Singer's admin for four years before she formally retired, then I served as Mr. J. B. Singer's admin's assistant for five years before Mr. Bolton Singer, who was at that time vice president, operations, asked me to serve as his admin. I remained in that position when Mr. Bolton Singer took over as CEO."

"Did you work on anything related to the Hudson South-West project?"

Her brow furrowed again. "Yes. The Singers divested themselves of much of that property before I joined the firm, or certainly shortly thereafter. And in my position at that time, I wouldn't have had any part in the larger projects. But I did assist Mr. Singer—Mr. Bolton Singer—with the sale of the remainder of that property to Roarke Industries two years ago."

"Okay. Thanks for your time."

She didn't march out, but she did sort of sail. Eve had to give her credit for it.

"We'll verify her alibi, but that's going to check out. I wonder where Alva kept all her old books."

"Backpack?"

"Depends on how many she had, doesn't it? Something to ponder. Have Terry send in the next."

4

Once she'd finished with the available interviewees, Eve considered those remaining on the list.

"See how many of the others we can get to come into Central, and juggle them in."

She got into her car for the drive to the morgue.

"We can split those up, and hit any remaining at home or on a job site." She tapped her fingers on the wheel as she braked at a light. A river of pedestrians flooded across the intersection.

New Yorkers doing the fast-clip dodge and weave; tourists doing the neck-craning goggle shuffle.

Everybody had somewhere to go, she thought. Where had Alva gone? A couple of shelters, maybe Sidewalk City, her little nest in Hudson Yards.

But like everybody had somewhere to go, everybody started somewhere else.

Where had Alva started?

While Peabody worked her 'link setting up more interviews, Eve used her in-dash.

"Search all state records for any and all data on Alva Quirk, female, Caucasian, age forty-six, New York City ID on record in 2048 through 2052, no fixed address, no employment listed."

Acknowledged. Working . . .

It continued to work as she threaded through traffic, parked again. She transferred the search to her PPC.

"I've got the electrician, the IT team—three have access," Peabody told her. "I couldn't tag the head plumber, but I got the foreman on the job site he's working now, and she said she'd have him contact me once he's freed up. That's as far as I got."

Eve considered as they started down the white tunnel. "Find a place, stay on this. I'll take Morris and the victim."

"Works for me."

Eve kept walking, her bootsteps echoing. The lemon-scented chemicals, the air filtration, never quite defeated the underlying scent of death. She wondered why she found visits to the morgue less fraught than stops at hospitals and health centers.

She pushed through the double doors of Chief Medical Examiner Morris's autopsy suite to find him wrist-deep in Alva Quirk's open chest cavity. On his music system, a throaty female voice sang about long, sweet goodbyes.

"I'm a bit delayed on your victim," he told her.

"It's no problem. I appreciate you getting to her this fast. Do you want me to step out? Or come back?"

"No need. Why don't you get yourself a cold drink?"

It reminded her she'd yet to crack the tube of Pepsi from her car, so she went to his friggie, got a fresh one.

As she cracked it, he continued to work.

He wore a suit under his protective cape. She supposed the color was lavender or orchid or whatever they decided to call that palest of pale shades of purple. His shirt bumped that hue up a few more shades, and the precisely knotted tie took it back down again.

He'd braided his midnight-black hair into three sections, then braided those into one, using both shades in the cording. She supposed, like his musical talents, he considered the various ways he styled his hair a creative outlet.

"Do you know how long she was on the streets?" Morris asked her.

"Not yet. Working on that, but at a guess, at least ten or twelve years."

He glanced up, his eyes dark behind his safety goggles. "She was in remarkably good health considering that length of time. I'd say the fact I've found no signs of illegals or alcohol abuse factors into that. She's a bit underweight, marginally malnourished, but I'd say she made use of free dental clinics and screenings. She never gave birth to a child."

He looked back down at Alva. "She took care of herself as best she could. She has a kind face."

"She passed out paper flowers and animals—made them out of litter. Folded up from flyers and other litter."

"Origami?"

"Yeah, I guess. And she kept record books on people she spotted breaking the law—the rules. Jaywalkers, litterers, street thieves, and so on."

"A concerned citizen."

"That's what the beat cops called her. I'm thinking that's what got her skull caved in."

"Two strikes, and I agree with your on-site. A crowbar."

He switched to microgoggles, gestured for Eve to take a pair from his counter. "You see the indentations from the prongs, how the killer struck downward, then pried out and up. She wouldn't have felt the second blow. She fell forward, bruising her knees as you see, her body rolling slightly before the second strike to the temple. No defensive wounds, no sexual assault.

"But."

Eve frowned. "But?"

"A dozen years or so on the street, you said."

"She's got official data—bare minimum—on record from '48 to '52. A lot of sidewalk sleepers don't update their IDs. It only gets updated if they get pulled in for something, or the shelter they use gets around to it."

"Yes, we see that here often. Take a look at the screen." After ordering it on, he moved to his sink to wash the blood from his sealed hands. "I did the full body scan. You see the damage to the skull, of course."

"Hard to miss."

Eve drank some Pepsi as she studied the internal scan.

"It looks like she had a nose job. Or busted it at some point."

"Yes." Morris reached into his friggie, chose a tube of ginger ale.

"Cheekbone, too. Right cheekbone, a fracture there, not recent."

She understood the "but" now and moved a bit closer.

"Got a pair of fake teeth, lower left." Eyes narrowed, Eve jabbed with her right, hooked with her left. "Broke her right shoulder, right forearm, wrist—both wrists—two fingers right hand, three left. Looks like those fingers were broken more than once over the years. Some of those ribs were cracked. None of it recent, none of those injuries happened in the last weeks or months. Those are old injuries."

She looked back at Morris. "Could've been a bad accident. Vehicular wreck, serious fall, but. Did they happen at the same time?"

"In my opinion the ribs were broken and healed before the injuries to the arm and shoulder. The fingers—and the right index, the left ring finger were broken at least twice, at different times—both before and after the arm and shoulder. Even with your keen eye, you'll be forgiven, as you're not a medical, for missing the slight displacement of the right eye socket."

"Magnify it, will you?"

When he had, she nodded. "Okay, yeah, I see it."

"I estimate the orbital and cheekbone injuries, and the second break on the right index finger, occurred after the others."

"Somebody tuned her up regularly," Eve murmured.

"That would be my initial conclusion."

"How old are they?"

"My analysis, and comp-generated probability, puts them at fifteen to twenty years. But I'd like to send the scans—and if necessary the victim—to Garnet for an expert confirmation."

"Yeah, let's do that. She's already working on one of mine."

"Another?"

"I'll get to that in a minute. I need to . . ." She circled the body, studied it, studied the screen.

"You're not going to be off, or not far off on your estimate. You're too good for that. So that's going to put her in her mid-twenties to early thirties. Not a child, so unlikely parental abuse. More likely a relationship. A spouse or lover."

She held up a finger as her PPC signaled.

"No results, no data on record in the state outside '48 to '52," she told Morris. "Recalibrate search to nationwide and run."

She pocketed her PPC. "Maybe she went rabbit. One too many tune-ups, she goes rabbit. At some point, she wipes her data, or has it wiped so whoever uses her for a punching bag can't find her. But then she puts it back up, or creates a new identity, for these four years. And it takes some skill to fully wipe out official data. Or money to hire the skill. Takes that to create fresh.

"I need an e-man with the skills."

"I suspect you know where to find one."

"Yeah. It'll take time to run the national, then if that comes up zip, a global. I'll get Feeney and his team on it. I'll hit on Roarke for it."

She looked back down at Alva. "It's not going to apply to her murder. I'm not stretching coincidence that she ends up bashed by whoever smacked her around a couple decades ago."

"But you need to know. She deserved the knowing."

"I do. She does. Let DeWinter know this takes priority over the other. For now. Her killer's still out there. For all I know the one or ones who killed my other victims are as dead as they are."

"Victims?"

"Female and apparently a fetus or newborn, remains potentially close to forty years old."

Once she filled him in, Morris took a long pull of ginger ale. "You've had a busy day."

"And it ain't half done. Thanks for the quick work on her. I'm going to find who put her in your house, and as a bonus round, I'm going to track down who beat the crap out of her twenty years ago."

"I trust you will."

When Eve left, Morris walked back to Alva. "We'll all look out for you now."

Eve signaled Peabody to meet her at the car, and considered her options. Rather than tag her former partner and captain of the Electronic Detectives Division, she'd prefer to run it by him face-to-face.

She wanted to set up her board and book—or boards and

books, she amended, as she'd been running two cases and three victims.

Still, the remains were in DeWinter's hands now. Until she got something from the bone doc, she had little to do or explore.

When she spotted Peabody, Eve got behind the wheel. Peabody picked up the pace, then slid in.

"I've got everybody but the head plumber, an electrical engineer, two hardscapers, and the security chief. One of the hardscapers is on his honeymoon in Belize, has been for four days. I left a message for the other, who happens to be the groom's sister. The others are on other job sites."

"Good start. I need to talk to Feeney, so if we have any come in before that's done, you take them. Keep it routine, just crossing the t's. We need to evaluate everyone with access."

"You need to talk to Feeney about any potential break in the security at the crime scene?"

"Yeah, that. If there was a breach, what for? Theft, sabotage? Access, it could still be either of those. But it's most likely someone who knew the site, somebody who worked on the site, knew where to get the crowbar, the plastic. But I need to talk to him about the victim. I got stiffed on a regional run on her. National's still in progress. And what Morris found tells me we need an e-man on it."

She filled in Peabody, finishing up as she pulled into the garage at Central.

"It sounds like a hard life," Peabody said as they crossed to the elevators. "And she gave people paper flowers and animals."

"And kept her law-and-order book. I wonder what Mira has to say about those habits. Meanwhile, DeWinter will put Alva at the front of the line."

When the elevator doors opened, the stench rolled out

ahead of the occupant. Eve recognized the undercover Illegals detective despite the stringy hair, the scruffy stubble, and the filthy trench over equally filthy baggies.

"Jesus, Fruicki, did you bathe in piss?"

"Pretty much." He grinned, showing blackened teeth. "Got a meet with a Zeus dealer. Somebody's added an extra zing to the street sales. He's my in. Do I look crazy enough for a fix?"

"You smell bad enough."

"Yeah, but that gets me a private ride down."

He shambled off, leaving the fetid odor lingering in the air. Eve eyed the elevator.

"No," she said, turned on her heel, and aimed for the stairs.

"He really looked like a jonesing junkie," Peabody commented as they clanged up.

"He smelled like a corpse covered in cat piss."

She went up two levels, hung a left, and took an elevator from another bank.

It might have been packed with cops, but it smelled normal.

"I'm heading straight up to EDD. Get what you can going, and I'll check in. If you don't need me to take an interview, I'll set up the boards and books. Just keep me in the loop."

"Can and will."

At the first opportunity, Eve slithered out of the elevator to take the glides to EDD. More noise, as voices echoed, but more air to breathe and fewer bodies pushed together.

Then she made the turn into the carnival that was EDD.

Colors clashed and smashed. Patterns streamed and soared. Bold, bright, bewildering. Neon baggies, skin pants, overalls in tones only known to nature in solar systems far away. Zigzags, spirals, lightning bolts, and starbursts.

E-geeks sat in cubes, at desks—always bouncing—or

danced along from one point of the big bullpen to the other to the strange music playing in their heads.

She spotted Ian McNab, Peabody's main dish, at his station, skinny hips ticktocking as he stood, tapping fingers on a screen, rainbow airboots shuffling, his head bopping so his long blond tail of hair swung with the movement.

Beyond the usual circus, she got the impression of speed and focus. So something was up.

She headed for the relative sanity of Feeney's office.

He, too, stood, one old brown shoe tapping as he worked a screen. His silver-threaded ginger hair exploded—like a cloud of shock—around his basset hound of a face. His eyes, all cop, focused on the screen.

Unlike those in the bullpen, he wore a suit—the color of dung that had baked a few hours in the hard sun. The knot of his brown tie had gone crooked at the collar of his industrial-beige shirt.

She smelled cop coffee and sugar.

He grunted, stepped back a half step. And spotted her.

"Don't have anything yet. I sent a couple of boys out as soon as I could spare them."

"Okay. You're working a hot one."

He held up three fingers. "We're nearly there with the first—got nearly thirty hours on it, and we've broken through. Second just came in last night. And the third, the big, hit this morning."

He held up a finger, this time as a signal to wait, and stepped over to his AutoChef. "Want coffee?"

She accepted she'd been spoiled, but good coffee, Roarke's blend, waited in her office. So she could wait, too.

"I'm good."

"Spitzer Museum took a hit. It's a small, exclusive joint, Upper East. Privately funded, heavily secured—got all the bells and whistles. And somebody melted right on through, looks like about midnight. Only took one. A painting by that French guy, that Monet guy. Water lilies. Curator said it was insured for a hundred and twenty million. Get that? For a picture of flowers."

Feeney shook his head, slurped some coffee. "Anyway, I couldn't send top tier on your case. We're booking it here to find out how the living fuck they got through enough security it should've slammed shut on a housefly buzzing in."

He slurped more coffee, gave her a long eyeballing over it.

"Jesus, Feeney, you know he wouldn't—"

"Shit, Dallas, I'm not saying that. I'm thinking about maybe tagging him up, seeing if he's got time and room to consult on it."

"That's up to you and Roarke."

"I'm thinking about it. It's a challenge, this here. Pretty slick, pretty fucking smart. I can't say I'm not enjoying it, but Roarke could maybe add to it."

"Was it one of his security systems?"

"No, and that might be their mistake. Who knows? They had it privately designed. It's good, and I'm saying it's goddamn good. Somebody knew his shit to get through it."

"Like maybe one of the designers."

Feeney smiled, full teeth. "Looking there, but we're on the tech. Once we get through the one that's breaking, make a little more headway on the second, I can spare McNab or Callendar for you, for short sprints. You know the kid's spending his off time working with Roarke on a personalized security system for the house Mavis and Leonardo bought."

"Yeah, I knew that. And Peabody's burying me, when she catches me off guard, in tile samples and paint color and Christ knows for their end of the place." Then she shrugged. "It's going to be good for all of them. Anyway, there's no real rush on my e's, not yet. I've got other avenues to work."

"Give me an overview. I need to clear my brain cells for a few."

So saying, he picked up a wonky bowl—his wife's creation—from his desk and offered Eve the candied almonds inside.

Unlike his coffee, his almonds were top-notch. She popped one into her mouth as she started her rundown.

"Looks like we're both looking at inside jobs. You likely have two a few decades apart."

"Yeah, and the Singer business has hooks in both."

And that bugged her. Bugged the crap out of her.

"The guy in charge now, he doesn't give me the buzz, but some hide that really well. He's pretty well covered on the older murder—away at college—and since he owns the place, it's hard to work out why he'd bash somebody for seeing him there. But you've gotta look."

"You've already got the expert consultant, civilian, on the construction angle. Still . . ." Feeney looked back at his screen. "I might give him a tag."

She looked at the screen, and couldn't decipher the figures and symbols. But Roarke could. "He'll have more fun with you. I've got to get going."

She popped another almond on her way out. "Good hunting."

"Back at you," he said, and refocused on the screen.

As she made her way to Homicide, her PPC signaled.

No results, she read on her national search. She tagged Roarke. Feeney could do the same, she thought—and, yeah, Roarke would enjoy the challenge, but she needed an e-man now.

"Lieutenant."

"Yeah, that's me. Listen, I know you're tied up with the Hudson Yards site, but there's nothing much I can do on that one until DeWinter's done her thing. And I had to put my first vic ahead on that. Morris found some old injuries—it looks like regular physical abuse—and I need her to confirm a time line."

"All right."

"Meanwhile I need some e-work, and Feeney's slammed. He's probably going to tag you on the hottest of the three they're working."

"The Monet."

"You know about it?"

He smiled at her. "Not directly. *Water Lilies*, 1916. A brilliant work, and worth well over a hundred million. Double that to a private collector. Wouldn't it be fun to consider how it was done, and who wanted that particular painting?"

He would have once, she thought.

And nobody would have caught him.

"I figured, and what I need's not so much fun. My vic doesn't show up on a national search. She popped up as Alva Quirk for a space of time, but nothing before. No records. So she had them wiped. I figure she got tired of being tuned up, took off, did what she could to go into the wind. I need to find her."

"A thorough washing of official records takes considerable skill or money. Or both."

"You could determine if it's that thorough."

"I could, yes. I've still some scheduling to untangle, and if I understand you, we'll be shut down for several days or more, but for Building One."

"I have to prioritize."

"Understood. Send me what you have on your victim. I'll see what I can do when I can do it. Ah, and Feeney's tagging me now."

"Me, first."

He smiled again. "Darling Eve, you're always first. Now, I do wonder what the NYPSD did without me."

"I look at it this way. We're saving the world from some-body who can steal a dead French guy's flower painting. See you later."

She clicked off, and turned into Homicide.

The only carnival in her bullpen lived in Jenkinson's tie. To her eye, it looked like a sunset on Pluto, after the sun went nova.

She wondered it didn't burn through his shirt.

Deliberately she walked down into her office, retrieved the sunshades she put in a drawer. She slid them on and walked back to the bullpen.

When he saw her, Jenkinson smirked.

"Status."

"Healthy, not close to wealthy, but pretty fucking wise. Baxter and Trueheart caught a floater—East River. Carmichael and Santiago are in Interview with a suspect on the knifing on Avenue B they caught last night."

He jerked a thumb over his shoulder to where his partner barked into his 'link. "Reineke's running down a lead on the case we caught day before yesterday. We're moving on it. Peabody's in Interview with one of yours."

She scanned the case board as he spoke, nodded. "I'm in my office."

"You got a twofer this morning. If we wrap this up, we can give you a hand if you need it."

"I'll let you know."

In her office, she tossed the sunshades back in the drawer and hit the coffee. She gave herself a moment, just one moment, to stand at her skinny window, fueling up, looking out at the city she'd sworn to protect and serve.

A lot of Alvas out there, she thought. She could have been one of them. Her beatings had started young, ended when she'd been eight and killed the man who'd beat her, raped her, terrified her.

Maybe Alva had killed her abuser. Maybe she'd killed, then run, then tried to vanish.

A hard life, Peabody had said. And a damn hard end to it.

Eve turned away from the window. She set up both sides of her office board. Front for Alva Quirk, back for her unidentified victims.

She sat, started a book for Alva, another for the Jane Doe.

She continued on the book when she heard Peabody's bootsteps.

"Status?"

"I interviewed the security chief. He's clear, Dallas. I was kind of hoping he'd be the link, but he was—and I verified—in Connecticut at his parents' seventy-fifth anniversary party. There's video of a lot of it. He and his husband took a limo to and from because they wanted to be able to drink and stay late. I have the limo company, talked to the driver. He dropped them at home on Third Avenue at zero-two-twenty-two. There's security on their building, and they didn't go out again until they both left at zero-eight-sixteen this morning."

"Okay."

"I want to add he's upset. He'd like clearance to check on the security, find the breach. I told him we were on that. He'd seen Alva around. Not on-site, but on the street."

"We'll clear him when we've cleared the scene. He may spot something, since he's worked it. Feeney's got people on it now. Do you need me on the next?"

"I've got it. It's the IT guy, and he's coming in now."

"If you get a buzz, pull me in."

"I will. I like you're letting me handle this part."

Eve glanced up. "You know what you're doing."

"And I like handling it. I'll go write this one up, take the next."

Eve nodded. Alone, she got more coffee. She put her feet on her desk, studied her board.

Old injuries, a hard life. A believer in rules. Who broke what rule, Alva? Where's your book?

Where's your place? Other books, others breaking rules.

Inside job, she thought again. And a sloppy one. A goddamn unnecessary one. Panic or meanness?

Or both?

More than one killer, almost certainly. No drag marks. Bash her, wrap her up, carry her, dump her.

"I'll find them, Alva," she murmured. "Then I'm going to go back and find who broke you."

Since Peabody had the interviews in hand for the moment, Eve dug into the Singer family. The connection between the two murders on her board ran through them.

The company had its beginnings in the mid-twentieth century, when the current CEO's great-grandfather, James Singer, leveraged a loan—from his father-in-law—to purchase his first rental property: a three-story, sixteen-unit walk-up on the Lower West Side.

James Singer and his son, Robert James Singer, expanded, developed, and built. On his father's death—heart attack—R. J. Singer and his wife, Elinor Bolton Singer, took over the business.

And on R.J.'s death—lung cancer—Elinor Singer ran the company, until she retired and turned the reins over to her son, James Bolton Singer.

Eve brushed through the history, as the founders had been long dead and buried before the Hudson Yards projects. But it gave her a sense. By the time J. B. Singer took over, his family had a solid and expanding business in place.

Under Elinor Singer's lead, and with her son as CFO, they bought the Hudson Yards properties—their biggest acquisition, biggest project not only to that date, she noted, but their biggest development still.

Since construction also began on their watch—with an interruption for the Urban Wars—she took a closer look, beginning with Elinor Bolton Singer.

The daughter of Henry Bolton and Gladys McCain Bolton, she'd grown up wealthy—Park Avenue mansion, and another country home in the Hudson Valley. One brother—and digging there, Eve concluded he'd been groomed for political office before his death in a plane crash. One sister—who'd developed a drug and alcohol habit and died of an overdose at twenty.

Elinor attended Radcliffe, studied business management and finance. Which hadn't helped save her family business, which floundered after her mother's suicide.

Eve made a note to dig into more details later when she could pull the unknown victim's murder into her focus.

Less than a year after her mother's death, Elinor married R. J. Singer and gave birth to J. Bolton Singer, their only child, the following year.

The Bolton financial business went under in the eighties, and Eve made more notes to look into—or hopefully have Roarke translate—what she saw were multiple legal issues.

Upon her father's death following a series of strokes, Elinor sold everything but the Hudson Valley estate. Though it looked to Eve like she'd juggled some of the acreage into Singer for development.

Eve breezed through the society stuff—galas, politics, benefits, fashion—taking away the impression of a woman who'd enjoyed her position, her lifestyle, and knew how to use both.

A widow at sixty, she stepped into the big chair, increased holdings, profits. Maybe a figurehead, Eve thought, maybe not, until she retired.

Interesting.

She lived in her longtime family estate, kept an apartment in the city, maintained a flat in Paris.

Though fully retired for about twenty years, Eve noted she was still listed on the company letterhead as consultant.

J. Bolton Singer was not.

"Did you step aside, J.B., or get tossed?" Eve wondered.

She started to shift to his background when she heard Peabody coming down the hall.

"I think you're going to want in on this interview. I'm getting a buzz—not from her, Chloe Enster, hard- and landscape—but what she's telling me."

Eve programmed her search, rose.

"What's the buzz?" Eve demanded as they walked to Interview.

"It may apply to Singer's partners in the project. Enster says she and her brother saw a couple of people they think are questionable characters on the site."

"I'm always interested in questionable characters."

5

Eve opened the door to Interview. She studied the petite
woman in work pants, a scruffy T-shirt, and beat-up boots.
She wore her midnight-blue hair in a short braid and studied
Eve in turn out of emerald-green eyes that reflected nerves.

Petite she might have been, but she had strong swimmer's
shoulders and diamond-cut arms.

Strong enough, Eve thought, to have bashed in a skull with
a crowbar.

"Chloe, this is my partner, Lieutenant Dallas."

"Yeah, I got that."

"We appreciate you coming in, Ms. Enster," Eve began.
"I'm sure Detective Peabody explained this is routine."

"Easy for you to say." She took a glug from her water bottle. "I know there's somebody dead, and there's a finite number of people who had access to the Singer site. Me and my
brother are two of them."

She blew out a breath. "Deke's covered, my brother's covered because he wasn't even in New York last night. But I
was, and I got nothing. I busted up with my boyfriend a couple days ago—to be known forever as the Cheating Bastard—
and I was home, alone, sulking. I didn't talk to anybody. I
didn't want to talk to anybody, especially my friend Lorna,

who'd I-told-you-so me to freaking death. Or my mother, because the same."

"All right. Did you know Alva Quirk?"

"That's the woman who's dead, Detective Peabody said. I didn't know her name. But when I saw the picture there"— she gestured to Peabody's folder—"I recognized her. Deke and I saw her up at the site a few times. Early, before the crew. Before they broke ground the first time. Deke told her she wasn't supposed to be up there, how it wasn't really safe. But she said something like it was safe under the stars and gave him like this little origami dog."

Chloe drank again, sighed. "We spotted her little nest when we were doing the early site work, but we let it go. She wasn't hurting anything. I guess if we'd made her leave, kept her out, she'd still be breathing."

"That's not on you unless you killed her."

"I've never hurt anybody in my life. A lie," she said immediately. "I lie. I kicked the Cheating Bastard in the balls when I found out. And once, I punched a drunk who grabbed my ass in a bar. But that's it."

"Both of those sound justified."

Chloe managed a smile. "Felt good, too."

"Detective Peabody told me you saw someone else on the site."

"Yeah." Now she rubbed the back of her neck. "We've done other jobs for Singer, and we did one for Bardov—that's one of the partners on this. Deke and I, we've only been in business four and a half years. We're still building a rep. We keep the overhead down, do the design and prep work ourselves. We've got a tight crew, and pay fair, and we don't cut corners. Quality work for a fair price, that's how you build your rep and your business."

"Okay," Eve said when Chloe paused.

"Okay, well. We did two other, smaller jobs for Singer, and

we worked our asses off to get this one. We'd work for them anytime. They pay on time, listen if there's an issue. But we wouldn't do another job for Bardov."

"Because?"

"In construction—like in anything, I guess—some cut those corners. Or know which palms to grease. We did good work for Bardov, but we saw some of that. So unless we're squeezed, we won't bid on their projects.

"This job? It could make us. We didn't know about the partners until we bid, but we wouldn't have backed out any-way. The way we heard it, Bardov's sort of silent partners, and consultants. Singer's in charge of the build. It takes a lot of scratch for a build like this. Most are going to need part-ners, for the scratch."

"All right."

Chloe shifted. "Okay, so we're up there doing some sur-vey work, and we see a couple of Bardov guys doing a walk-around. This is a few weeks ago, and we saw them by the buildings northwest of the tower. Demo's going on, right, and me and Deke just came back on-site to check some measure-ments for our design. And the one guy—Tovinski—he's an engineer. We don't get why he's there because we know the engineers on the job, and that's really how we copped to Bar-dov being more in it than we thought. We dealt with this guy on the job we did for Bardov. He's a corner cutter for sure."

"In what way?"

"He knocks down the quality of the supplies and materi-als. Right on the edge of it, you know? You're doing a qual-ity job, and you bid fair, then he's pulling down the quality to save more money. We argued it—'cause the cost was in the damn bid, right?—but he went over us. Didn't show on the invoice, get it? But we know what we're working with."

"You're saying this Tovinski padded invoices."

"I'm saying Deke and I know what we're working with,

and on the Bardov job we did, what we were working with wasn't what was on the order sheet. It was cheaper grade, down the line."

"Okay."

"And we saw him with a couple of inspectors. Maybe we didn't see him grease the palms, but we sure didn't have any trouble passing any site inspections. And we should have."

Now she shrugged. "It happens, right? The way it is sometimes, but it's not how me and my brother work. And we saw a couple of the Bardov guys on the Singer job—I don't know the names except Tovinski—get into it with a couple of the other subs. Not punch-outs, but it looked close."

"And you think Bardov's company cuts and greases?"

"Well, Lorna—the landscaper and the I-told-you-so pal—said that's what she heard on the job. How they had ties to the Russian mob."

After blowing out a long breath, Chloe took a hit from her water bottle again.

"I don't know from that, but she said she heard it. It could be bullshit. It could all be bullshit, but that nice lady's dead, and somebody did it."

"Do the Bardov people have access—codes and swipes?"

"I don't know. They shouldn't, not at this point in the project anyway, but we're just subcontractors. Just cogs in the wheel, right?"

"Have you heard anything about substandard materials on this job?"

"Not a peep on that. And not on the other two jobs we worked for Singer. But we haven't started our work yet, other than prep, design, ordering. And I only saw Tovinski on-site those two times. We're not on-site much right now, so maybe he's there more."

"Got a first name on Tovinski?"

"No, sorry. We just called him Ivan. He's got the accent and everything."

"Have you worked with Bryce Babbott?"

"Quality," Chloe said instantly. "And . . ." She lifted those strong shoulders, gave them a wiggle. "Frosty supreme. And with Angelica Roost, solid, in my opinion. And Mr. Singer—he takes an interest, knows his ass from his elbow. Not J. B. Singer. We haven't met the old man. We saw the grandmother—she came on-site on both our other jobs a couple of times. Got eyes like a hawk. A little bit scary, if I'm honest, but she gave the work a nod, so we got the second job. Now this one."

"Okay. This is good information. When's your brother due back?"

"A week from Monday. Well, Sunday night, but Monday morning at work."

"We'd like to talk to him. Just see if he remembers anything more than you have."

"Sure. I'll make sure he tags you. I guess you don't know how long we'll be shut down."

"Not yet, no."

"I know you've got to do what you've got to do for the lady who got killed. It's just we put almost all our eggs in this Hudson Yards basket. Biggest job we ever bid on. It's dumping some stress right now."

"As soon as we clear it, we'll let Mr. Singer know. Thanks for coming in."

"I'm all done? You said it wouldn't be too bad," she said to Peabody. "It wasn't." She rose. "Um, you bring murderers and like that in this room?"

"It's a room for interviewing, both suspects and witnesses."

"I can kind of feel them. The bad ones. I'm like half-assed a sensitive. I mostly block it because it creeps me out. But I can sorta feel them."

She shuddered once. "I sure wouldn't want your job."

When Peabody led Chloe out, Eve sat a moment, considering.

Corner cutting, palm greasing. Why not some high-dollar pilfering? She couldn't see how anyone had legitimate business on the site in the middle of the damn night. And being there led to murder.

Tovinski looked like a very good place to start.

She rose when Peabody stepped back in. "Good call bringing me in. It gave me a better sense of her. I'd say a sharp eye and maybe tossing in the half-assed sensitive gives her a solid take on what's going on."

"My father worked construction as a teenager—before he met my mother and started the farm."

"Pre–Free-Ager?"

"I guess he was a half-assed Free-Ager before Mom, but he was always a full-on sensitive. Anyway, he says that some jobs, most jobs, ran clean, and with people having pride in the work. But some, you had that corner cutting, the palm greasing, material walking off the job. And greed ran the show."

"Sounds about right."

"The Bardov company. Do you think they still have ties with the Russian mob?"

"Jesus, Peabody. Yuri Bardov *is* the Russian mob. He's Bardov Construction."

"I've got to catch up."

So did she, Eve thought, because she'd never tangled with Bardov or his crew.

"You hear he's mostly retired. Has to be hitting toward ninety. But maybe he's still got fingers in the pie. Alva sees a midnight bribe going on, or witnesses material walking away, something of the sort, alerts whoever's doing it—because that was her pattern—starts writing in her book and, panicked or pissed off or both, they kill her, dump her."

"And take her book."

"And take her book," Eve agreed. "Write up the interview. I'm going to look into this Tovinski, and take a harder look at Bardov. Didn't have the feel of a mob hit," she said half to herself. "Too damn sloppy."

"I bet Roarke knows the company."

"Yeah, I'm counting on it."

She didn't want to tag him on it right then. She figured he was either catching up on his own work, dealing with the shutdown of his site, or having a little fun helping Feeney in Geek World.

She went back to her office, hit the AC for more coffee, and found Tovinski by using his last name and his employer, the city.

Not Ivan. Alexei.

She studied his ID shot as she generated a hard copy for her board. A hard face, she mused. Sharp and lean, as if any excess had been meticulously whittled away. White-blond hair cut close to the scalp, pale skin, pale blue eyes.

The nephew of Marta Bardova—Yuri Bardov's wife— Tovinski immigrated to the United States in 2023 at the age of fifteen. Now just shy of his fifty-third birthday, he held the title of chief structural engineer for Bardov.

One marriage in 2048—Nadia Bardova, daughter of his uncle-in-law's cousin. Two offspring: son, Mikael, age twelve; daughter, Una, age eight.

Numerous identifying marks in the form of tattoos. Prints and DNA on record.

Juvenile record sealed in Kiev—which meant he had some early bumps.

Adult bumps included three assault charges—and six months inside for the third one—at the age of twenty-four.

Carrying a blade over the legal limit, two counts, ages

eighteen and twenty-two. Fines, community service for the second charge. No time served.

Questioned and released over the beating death of a shop-keeper. Questioned and released over the drowning—in a toilet bowl—of a city inspector.

No wits, no physical evidence, suspect alibied.

Nothing since.

Because you got better at it, Eve thought.

If she had to conjure the face of a professional enforcer, it would look like Alexei Tovinski's.

"I'm going to enjoy chatting with you, Alexei. And soon."

She rose to add him to the board, then found herself circling around to the other side.

She studied the remains, and the area—essentially a pit—walled off from the rest. Deliberately, she was certain. It occurred to her that if the dates on the plans and construction of that building, of the so-called wine cellar were accurate, Tovinski would have been in New York.

Still a teenager, but old enough. She still needed DeWinter to verify the time of death on the Jane Doe, but speculating, if the victim had gone in at the right time, if Bardov had any part in the plans . . .

She generated a second copy of Tovinski's ID, studied it again.

"Oh yeah, you were born to kill."

She pinned him up on the second side.

And when she looked over, Roarke stood in her doorway. The man moved like a ghost.

"Didn't expect to see you."

"I've been in EDD for a bit. Some progress there, but then Feeney had already made inroads. I've just added some . . . alternative perspective."

"From a thief's point of view."

He only smiled. "It's all fascinating, and gave me a very nice distraction. Feeney's had to shift to something else for now, and it occurred to me it's very unlikely my cop has eaten anything since breakfast.

"So." He moved to the AutoChef.

"I'm right in the middle of—"

"Mmm-hmm. As I am myself. But let's have a bite. Pasta salad sounds good enough."

He programmed two portions, then glanced at her board. "And who is this hard-bitten individual you've put on my murder?"

"My murder," she corrected. "Alexei Tovinski. You don't know him."

"Not his face, no, but the name sounds familiar. How are you linking him to the murder?"

"On that side, pure speculation. He's a relation and employee of Yuri Bardov—Bardov Construction."

"Ah yes, Bardov. What you'd call a shady sort of character."

"Would I?"

"You would, yes." He took out the bowls, handed her one. "A great many of the flops and tenements thrown up post-Urbans are Bardov Construction. He very likely bought the properties, or won the bids by intimidation, bribery, or other means. Just as he'd done prior and during the Urbans. I've purchased a few from him over the last decade or so. He tends to divest when the buildings are on the edge of falling down—or condemned. As he has considerable—you could say influence—in some areas of city government, many that should be condemned aren't. Until after the sale."

"Do you know if he ever had a part in your property in Hudson Yards?"

"Not overtly, not that I've seen. I'll look closer. But he often, so it's said, keeps any interest quiet and off record. Make a loan, you see, but off the books. Pull in a tidy profit—or call in an enforcer to persuade the borrower to cough up the vig—or perhaps renegotiate at a higher rate, or take a share of the property itself as payment. His ties to the Russian Mafia are well-known. He likes it that way. It makes him more formidable."

"Why would Singer partner with him?"

"Ah well, cash flow's always a sticky point, and Bardov has deep pockets."

Money always rang a murder bell. "Hold on. Does Singer have cash flow issues? You'd know," she said before he could answer. "You bought the property from Singer, so you know, because if they were in a squeeze, you could use that to squeeze them down on the terms."

He ate some pasta, took his time. "And if they have cash flow issues, as you put it, you'd chalk that up on the motive end of the scoreboard. What I can tell you is Singer's cash flow, their bottom line, and their profit margins have steadied up in the last few years."

"Because?"

"Better management, top down. A more careful eye on cost overruns, on waste. And the sale of non-profitable properties such as the one I bought two years ago."

She frowned up at the crime scene pictures on her board. "If it wasn't profitable, why did you buy it?"

"For one, I was able to buy the whole of it, the plot that had been sold, and sold again, and the section Singer held on to. And that increased the development and profit potential. Bolton Singer, wisely in my opinion, calculated they were already deeply invested in their River View development, would stretch their resources too thin if they attempted to finance yet another major job—particularly when the bulk of the site belonged to someone else."

"Okay, so sell that, use that take to plow into the other project."

"Exactly."

"But they're still partnering with Bardov on the River View project."

"I expect the ties there have been in place for some time, and may be difficult to untangle. In any case, Bardov's well established in New York, and parts of New Jersey. He has his own suppliers, at least for some essential materials."

"How about substandard materials?"

"I can attest he used them post-Urbans, but then so did many. The push was to get people under a roof, to bring the city back. It was much the same in Dublin when I was a boy, and everywhere, I'd say, the wars hit hard.

"Eat."

"Right." She scooped up some pasta, and realized she needed it when it hit her empty stomach. "I have a wit who saw this Tovinski on the Singer site a couple of times, and says the word is Bardov was supposed to be silent partners, and Singer was using their own engineers. That's what Tovinski's supposed to be. She also saw a couple of Bardov's people getting into it—verbally—with some of the subcontractors. She said Tovinski pads invoices—or cuts the quality of materials ordered."

Like Eve, Roarke studied the board, and wondered as he often did what she saw that he didn't.

"An easy way to pocket a bit—or more—on a job. I don't know this particular man, but I can say in the last decade or so, Bardov's divesting some of his . . . we'll call them sidelines."

"Such as?"

"Weapons, ID theft. He had more global interests in such things well back. Back when I was very young. The old man had dealings with them."

More bells rang. A cacophony of bells. "Patrick Roarke had connections to Bardov?"

"Back in the day," Roarke repeated. "He'd have been very low-level, so I doubt Bardov even knew his name. And nothing I can see would thread through to all of this."

"But they had connections?"

"My word was *dealings*, which is entirely different." He reached over, trailed a fingertip down the dent in her chin. "The old man was always looking for an angle, and Bardov's interests at that time were more global. As I said, long ago, and I was very young. It wasn't the building trade, as even the shoddy sort requires real work, and the old man was more interested in breaking legs and thieving."

That calmed the bells.

"You've never met him? Yuri Bardov?"

"I haven't, no. My sense would be Bardov Construction was, for the most part, a front for those sidelines. And in the last fifteen or so years, it's less a front and more an actual business. Remodeling and the suburbs are more the target these days. It's a smallish company as compared to Singer's."

"Or yours."

"Or mine."

She looked back at the board. "But they have an interest in this particular urban development. Makes me wonder why."

"I've no doubt you'll find out."

"What do you know about J. Bolton Singer? I haven't run him yet."

"Not a great deal, though I've met his wife a few times. Her Open Hearts Foundation does good work."

"'Not a great deal' means you know some."

He sighed a little. "Relentless, you are. All right then, if the historical gossip is valid, he stood as more of a figure-head and his mother ran things after his father's death, and continued well into his tenure as well."

"I wondered about that. So his mother still ran the show?"

Roarke shrugged. "From what I know, or heard, that suited

J.B. quite well. His father, I'm told, was canny and clever and knew the business from the digging of footers and up. His own father had him work as a laborer, so he learned how to build."

"And generation three?"

"J. B. Singer, so it's said, was born into wealth and privilege and liked it very well. Squandered quite a bit of what he had, and was bailed out by his parents more than once when a deal went south. Preferred the, well, you know, the swanning about, and the talking of big deals—and making poor ones, or running them into the ground. So his mother kept the reins while indulging him."

"Indulging him into cash flow problems, and partnerships with Russian gangsters?"

Roarke lifted his shoulders. "This is, as I said, talk and gossip. I've never met the man."

"It's interesting talk and gossip. If you keep making poor deals, swanning, running things into the ground, money starts to be an issue, right?"

"One would think."

"And one might have to bring in a shady partner or two to keep things going."

"Very possibly."

"Enter Bardov."

"Deep pockets there."

"Filled with ill-gotten gains."

Still eating, she walked around her board. The yesterday, the today.

"Mother and son would have been in charge of Singer, most likely, when the old murder went down. Cash flow issues, Urban War delays. An outside loan, a silent partner, might've seemed just the thing. I'd like to see those records."

"At that point in time, there might not be any but what I've dug up already, and what there are doesn't—officially—include such partnerships."

"I'd like to see them anyway."

"I'll see what I can do, but I'll warn you going as far back as you're thinking, they're likely spotty at best."

It pulled at her, fascinated her. But . . .

"Don't worry about it now. I've got to focus on the front of the board—and if any connections to the back turn up, I'll use them."

"Such as Tovinski."

She studied the eyes in the photo. A killer's eyes. "Exactly as."

"I'll dig into Alva Quirk's ID wash as soon as I can settle in to work on it. I can tell you, from the quick look I managed, a wash is what it was. She either knew what she was about or had some help with it, as it's very clean."

Eve turned away from the board and back to him. "You'll find the rest, no matter how well she washed it."

"I will, given time and some focus. Well then, since we've had our working lunch, I'll leave you to it." But he stepped back again, to look at the back of Eve's board. "She might have family who never knew what happened to her, or the child inside her."

"I know it. I have to zero in on Alva Quirk, but I won't forget her."

"And I know that." He stepped over, rested his hands on her shoulders, his brow on hers. "Part of me thinks she's been waiting for us."

"That's the Irish talking."

"It may be, but I feel it nonetheless. Waiting for me to buy that property, waiting for you to be all but on the spot when they found her. What do you say about coincidences, Lieutenant?"

"They're bollocks."

"There you have it." He touched his lips to hers. "So she waited for us. And can wait a bit longer knowing we'll take care of her now."

He flicked a fingertip down the shallow dent in her chin again. "Let me know when you're heading for home, and I'll catch a ride with you."

"I will, but I may be out in the field."

"If you are, I'll find my own way home. And to you."

He would, she thought. They always found their way back.

And maybe, Irish woo-woo or not, he had a point. The woman who'd lived and died so long before had found her way to them.

She sat down, began to write up everything he'd told her before she did her own searches and runs to verify what she could.

Because talk and gossip or not, it all clicked right into what made sense.

6

Eve ran J. Bolton Singer, and to her mind verified at least some of Roarke's talk and gossip. He'd graduated from the Wharton School at the University of Pennsylvania, got his degree—but his official data listed nothing outstanding there.

The society pages she threaded through her search gave her a picture of a rich man's son who liked to travel, to party, to sail, to golf.

Lots of different lovelies on his arm, she noted, in his youth. Then a big, fancy splash of a society wedding to a Marvinia Kincade—one of the three daughters and heirs of the Kincade fortune. Candy makers, founders of Sweet Treats.

Damn good candy, she thought, and reminded herself to check her office stash to make sure it remained hidden from the nefarious Candy Thief.

One and only marriage, which produced one child, Bolton Kincade Singer.

She shifted to a quick look at the wife—summa cum laude at William & Mary, worked briefly for her family business in PR. Stepped out upon the birth of her son. Founder of Open Hearts, a nonprofit centering on children and families in need.

And apparently put in the money, time, and energy.

Eve noted her son currently served on the advisory board.

She found no criminal on J. Bolton Singer, but did find reports in business news articles of failed enterprises, and interviews with him touting major deals that either never came about or went under.

The Hudson Yards project—which had at the time included the property Roarke now owned—was one of them.

She dug there, sifting through the business jargon to find the gold. Big loans, big plans, high stakes. The tower was his shining star.

Then the Urbans turned the city into a war zone. Construction stopped or slowed to a crawl. But she'd bet the interest on those loans continued to pile up.

He still talked a good game, she noted when she skimmed interviews. Singer's rock-solid foundations, their vision for the future, blah blah.

She found a snippet about Elinor B. Singer selling thirty-three acres in the Hudson Valley as the Urbans ran down. The buyer? Eve sat back, shot the board a satisfied look.

"Bardov. It goes back at least that far then, the connection."

Had to be a major infusion of cash. Then another when she sold the Park Avenue mansion to Yuri Bardov.

Since coincidences were bollocks, she didn't see a coincidence when Singer started up construction in Hudson Yards again.

New bold plans. Quick, efficient, affordable housing, restaurants, and shops. An urban rebirth.

Substandard, the job boss—and Roarke—had concurred. Built fast and cheap and never to last.

Then sold the part of the South-West project—still not fully completed—less than ten years later.

Took the money and ran, she concluded.

But kept the section of that property where a body lay walled in a cellar.

She pushed up, paced.

Risky to sell if you knew about a murder, about a body decomposing behind a brick wall. Why take a chance on that?

But then, more recently, they had. If they had any part in the murder, why risk it now?

Something to chew on once she got DeWinter's conclusions.

Singer kept the other property, had the grand tower— flanked it with lesser builds, some apartments, some offices, some shops. But that left a good portion undeveloped.

Ran out of money again? Lost interest? Other projects took priority?

She paced to the window and back, thinking, speculating, and paused when she heard Peabody's boots clomp.

"You're J. Bolton Singer," Eve began when Peabody came to the door. "Rich kid. Stupidly rich kid with family money on both sides."

"Okay."

"You're being groomed to take over the family business— the Singer business. You like to play, you like to party, you like pretty girls."

"Sounds normal."

"You get into a fancy college—big deal college. Probably had some help there as in family grants. Greasing palms maybe. But you played and partied around the globe on your breaks, and got the degree.

"Nothing I found shows he learned the business from the ground up like his father. And most of what I found indicates he was a fuckup. Losing money on bad deals, buildings that went unfinished or cost more than they were worth. But the parents bail you out. Besides, you marry a rich girl—one with smarts, one who, at least on the surface, has a social conscience, and you produce a son. Yay, another Singer, the next generation."

"That would be the current one."

"Right, but when the current one's still a kid, the Urbans happen. They happen after you secured great big fat loans for your massive projects in Hudson Yards. And your signature tower you want to loom over the city."

Peabody tried a bright smile. "Can somebody as rich and important as me get a cup of coffee?"

Eve jerked a thumb toward her AutoChef.

"Now you've got a wife, a kid, a business, and people are blowing up buildings, occupying them, camping in the street, and your business can't function at capacity—or close to it—and you've got those great big fat outstanding loans."

Knowing her partner, Peabody handed Eve a mug of black coffee and took her own. "Interest piling up. Hard to collect rents from a burned-out building, or from a tenant who's armed, or from squatters with ball bats and pipes."

"Cash flow dries up," Eve agreed. "They had a fancy place on Park Avenue, and a thirty-six-room mansion in the Hudson Valley and a whole lot of acreage. J. Bolton's mother, Elinor—who actually ran the show—sold off more than half that acreage. To Yuri Bardov."

"Well." Over her coffee, Peabody studied the board. "That gets an aha."

"He built some summer cottages—and another big mansion for himself. He still owns them. Singer has a property management department. They handle rentals on the cottages. She also sold Park Avenue—Yuri Bardov."

"More aha. We've got a long-term connection."

"We do. With a company with reputed ties to the Russian mob—and Tovinski's rumored to be an enforcer."

"Bad company."

"Meanwhile the new generation has no interest—so he told us—in running the company. He wants to rock it. He focuses on music in college—stays out of New York and the business to give this a try. Doesn't appear—from what I've found—to be the party animal his father was."

"He was good, too. I was curious," Peabody added. "I dug up a couple short vids of him performing. Really strong voice—made for ballads. Solid talent on the guitar and piano—he played one in each of the vids I watched."

Shrugging, Peabody eased a hip down on Eve's desk. "It's a hard road, though, especially if you're trying to live on what you make at it at the start, and you don't have pro management and some support."

"He got tired of living on the edge," Eve concluded, "came home, invested himself in the business. And, according to at least one of his contractors, isn't stupid about it. So how much does he know about people like Tovinski?"

"Looks like we need to have another conversation."

"Sure as hell does. Check and see if he's still in his office."

Peabody took out her 'link as Eve turned back to the board.

"First generation starts it up," Eve murmured. "Second digs in and expands it, grows it. Third generation fucks it up. What does the next in line do?"

"When do you expect him to be out of the meeting?"

At Peabody's words, Eve turned back. "Is that Diller?"

When Peabody nodded, Eve took the 'link. "Lieutenant Dallas. You should be able to answer a couple of questions that came up."

The eyes came across no less reptilian over a 'link screen. "I'll be happy to help if I can, of course."

"Do any of Bardov's people have access to the Hudson Yards site?"

"Bardov Construction is an investment partner, and representatives from same had input on the design and scope.

They are not part of the actual build and would have no off-hour access."

"Okay, who brought them into the deal?"

"I . . . I couldn't tell you. I wasn't privy to the negotiations."

"Do you know an Alexei Tovinski?"

"I don't believe so."

"You make and keep Mr. Singer's appointments, field his calls, correct?"

"I do."

"And that name doesn't ring a bell? It's not a common one."

"I don't recognize the name."

"Okay. You said Mr. Singer's in a meeting?"

"He is. I'm not going to interrupt unless it's of vital importance."

"Not yet." He had to go home sometime, Eve thought, and home might be a better place to pin him down. "Thanks for the information."

"Mr. Singer's orders are to cooperate as much as possible. He spoke to me about hoping you find the poor woman's family so he could speak with them personally. He feels a responsibility."

"Me, too. We'll be in touch."

Eve clicked off, handed the 'link back to Peabody. "I think I'll take a pass at him at home later. Out of the power center. We're going to set up interviews with his father, his grandmother. Let's find out how much they had to do with bringing in the partners."

"They may be able to tell us more about the second site," Peabody put in. "It's most likely they were in charge then."

"Most likely isn't definitely. We need DeWinter to nail down the TOD, as close as she can. Right now she should be working on Alva Quirk, analyzing how long ago she got the shit kicked out of her."

Eve shoved a hand through her hair. "Roarke's going to

work on finding out when she washed her ID—he said that's what it was. He needs some time on that."

"I had a ten-second conversation with McNab about an hour ago. He said Roarke was up there helping them out."

"Yeah, he'll look into Alva tonight. And it won't hurt to have him with me when I drop by Singer's home. They aren't pals or anything, but murders, even decades apart, make a connection."

"Maybe you can take him with you and track down the plumber. I'm still waiting for him and one other to get back to me so I can set up interviews. The other's the second IT—the one installing the building systems. But her place is like a block from my apartment, so I was going to try her there after shift."

"You take her, I'll take the plumber, and we'll wrap up that part of it. I need a name and address."

"I'll send you both."

"I've got a couple more things I need to do here, then I'm going up to see how much longer Roarke figures he'll be. If it's awhile I'll take the plumber and come back for him. And I'll tell McNab you're in the field if they're still wrapped up in it."

"Works." After draining the coffee, Peabody set the mug aside. "I'll give both these people another push. I've gotten the unavailable on both all damn day, but it's got to be close to knock-off time for them. Or after it."

"Let me know. I can still take one of them at home, then hit Singer."

Eve sat again, and decided to start with the oldest living generation. She used the 'link number she had on Elinor Bolton Singer.

A woman of about forty with brown poreless skin and sea-green eyes came on-screen. "Mrs. Bolton Singer's residence."

"This is Lieutenant Dallas with the New York City Police and Security Department. I'd like to speak with Mrs. Singer regarding an investigation."

"Yes, Lieutenant. Mrs. Bolton Singer has spoken with her son and grandson and has been apprised of the situation. Unfortunately, she's resting and can't be disturbed at the moment."

At a hundred and five, Eve decided the woman was entitled to a nap. "I'd like to make arrangements to speak with Mrs. Singer, at her convenience. My partner and I can come to her."

"Of course. I'll check with Mrs. Bolton Singer's assistant on her schedule and availability. If I can have a contact number, I'll let you know as soon as possible."

Eve relayed the number. "And your name?"

"I'm Sheridon Fitzwalter, Mrs. Bolton Singer's head housekeeper."

"Given her age, is there anything I should know about your employer's health before the interview?"

"Mrs. Bolton Singer is quite well, thank you. She is very mindful of maintaining a healthy mind, body, and spirit. I believe if she tires, she won't hesitate to inform you."

"Okay then. I'll wait to hear from you."

Maiden and married name, every time, Eve thought. Very formal, very fussy. Curious, she did a quick run on the assistant.

Mixed race, unmarried, age forty-three, with the Hudson Valley mansion as her official address. She also had a certification as a nurse practitioner. Five years under her current employment.

Live-ins knew things, heard things, intuited things.

She might want a separate conversation with Sheridon Fitzwalter.

She tried J. Bolton Singer next—same address, different

contact number—and got a recording stating he was currently unavailable. She left her name, number, and the request he contact her as soon as possible.

She sat back and considered.

The three generations had talked. Normal, she decided, for family, especially with the business interest. It also gave them an opportunity to coordinate stories, details.

She'd judge that when she talked to all of them.

She got up, gathered what she needed. She walked out to the bullpen as McNab pranced in.

Like a ringmaster, he brought the EDD circus with him. His baggies, the color of lemons infused with plutonium, glowed. The shirt over his skinny torso exploded with polka dots.

He pumped a fist in the air. "Score!"

Jenkinson shot out a finger. "And you rag on my ties, boss."

Eve could only shake her head.

"Where's Roarke?"

"Just putting some finishing touches on Feeney's deal. Mine is . . ." He spread his hands, turned his thumbs up while he executed a strange little dance in his rainbow airboots.

Eve felt her eyes shake in their sockets.

"Stop. I beg you."

"The cap said you can have me as needed since me and my team have scored."

"I'll let you know. Take him out of here," she told Peabody. "Hit the IT interview, write it up at home. We're going to take on Elinor Bolton Singer tomorrow, and J. B. Singer if I can get through. Read my notes on both of them. And we'll track down Tovinski, bring him here—in our house—for interview. With his background, he's used to being in the box. Yuri Bardov's on tomorrow's list, and a swing by the lab to give DeWinter a push. I'll send you the timing when I work it out."

"I'm all in." Peabody gathered her things. "McNab can speak IT to the IT." She smiled at him. "We can pick up a couple of brews, take them to the house, and see today's progress. We need to settle on tiles, and the cabinet doors, and—"

"Take Insane House Project with you," Eve ordered. "Get gone."

"We're out."

At least, Eve noted, they waited until they hit the doorway to link hands and swing arms.

"It's one crazy house," Baxter said from his desk. "Trueheart and I dropped by the other day. A crazy, big-ass house. I liked it."

"It's nice they're moving into the attachment with Mavis and Leonardo." The fresh-faced Trueheart kept writing up a report while he spoke. "With the kid and another coming, it's good they'll have cops right there, and friends."

"Yeah, it's a good deal all around. What's your status?" she asked Baxter.

"Funny you should ask. I was about to come to you to approve a little OT for me and my boy. We've got a hot angle, and we want to have ourselves a stakeout tonight."

"On the floater? Who, what, why?"

Once he ran it through, she signed off, and started out herself.

She'd just reached for her 'link to tag Roarke when she saw him stepping off the elevator.

"Did you score?"

"I had an entertaining couple of hours." He took her hand before she could evade, and drew her into the elevator with a load of change-of-shift cops. "And you?"

"I've got two stops to make, so if you want to hitch a ride, you're making them, too."

"I don't suppose one of them is at a fine dining establishment and includes a good bottle of red."

"No. The first's an elusive plumber—head guy on Singer's site. And the next is a follow-up with Singer—Bolton Singer. I want to drop in on him at home, see what shakes."

Not nearly enough cops got off at the next stop; far too many got on. It was, to Eve, like being hedged into a can with an overload of sardines carrying badges and weapons.

"Well then, I'm with you, Lieutenant. We could make three stops and go by to see how things are progressing at Mavis's."

It surprised her to realize part of her actually wanted to.

"Too much work to do, and not enough brain left for more construction." She did an inner scan to see if she felt any guilt over that, found just the slightest twinge. "How is it going? You'd know."

"Both kitchens and all the loos are gutted, several walls are down, and a landscape crew has started clearing out the overgrowth and so on. There's considerable fretting over choices—finishes, appliances, colors, fixtures—but time yet for firm decisions. McNab and I, and Feeney's in it now, are designing the security system, the communication systems, and the rest of the IT. More entertainment for me."

"I bet."

"I will say Mavis and Leonardo are both very decisive about what they want and need in their work areas. McNab and Peabody are coming to terms with what they want and need in theirs. It's the rest of the space that seems to fluster them."

"Did you call in Redheaded Big Tits to work with them?"

Roarke gave her the slow side-eye. "I assume you mean our very qualified and creative interior designer. And she's consulting, yes."

"She does good work," Eve said, and all but exploded out of the elevator on her garage level.

She waited until she was behind the wheel. "Did you ID the thief?"

"I believe Feeney's, as we speak, giving the investigators all they need."

"How'd he get in?"

"She was already in. In fact, both were at different times. Two women, identical twin sisters. And very, very clever."

"Really? Let's hear it—what I'd understand, I don't need all the tech and geek stuff."

"A shame, as it's nearly brilliant."

He settled in as Eve drove.

"Two sisters, using one official ID. They'd wiped the second—and quite well—so when Irina Hobbs was vetted and hired by the museum as a curator several months ago, no twin—Iona—existed on record. Irina had all the qualifications, the résumé, and recommendations. A very, very attractive young woman as well, with an encyclopedic knowledge of art. Apparently both of them had that knowledge."

"Do you know them? Had you heard of them in your . . . circles?"

"Not a whiff, no, which tells me this was their first major job. They likely pulled off a few others, smaller, less impactful, for practice. In any case it's clear they both knew their way around security systems—which was not in their official records. But even if they had no more than rudimentary skills, they could have pulled this one."

"Why?"

"Irina Hobbs left the museum—it's clear on the logs and the security feed—at eighteen-oh-five on the night the Monet went missing. She met several friends for drinks and dinner. Her apartment building's security shows her entering at just before midnight, and not exiting again until zero-eight-sixteen the next morning. In a rush, obviously upset, as she'd just gotten the notification about the Monet. She rushed to the museum, and has cooperated in the investigation fully."

"Easy to be two places at once if there's two of you."

"Exactly so. One of the twins entered the museum an hour before closing. Disguised—wig, face putty, body padding. Well done again. Very well done. She didn't leave. The investigators missed that initially, as there was a slight glitch in the feed at closing."

"Which you found they generated?"

"They did indeed. Just a couple of blips as patrons left or were escorted out. By then, she would have been hidden, out of the disguise. They would both have known the building, its crannies, inside out."

"Plenty of time to study the place, from the inside. Taking turns."

"Yes, indeed. And no doubt had studied every angle of it beforehand as well. Very good work," he said in a tone that had her casting her eyes upward.

"And so," he continued, "one leaves as usual, along with colleagues. The security is set for night duty, locks engaged. But the sister's inside, and from her location shuts down the system—the whole lot. It must have taken them considerable time to craft the device or devices that so cleanly cut through."

"You admire that," she muttered.

"Skill is skill, after all, Lieutenant. And in four minutes, thirty-three seconds, the system rebooted. She'd already taken the painting, rolled the canvas into her bag, and walked out. Rebooted the system from a safe distance, and very likely went directly to the client."

"Client." This time Eve's breath hissed out. "That's a name for it."

"It's unlikely they took the Monet to hang it in their own parlor, now, isn't it? So client works well enough."

"Have they picked the twins up?"

"That's where more clever comes into it. Irina Hobbs put in for her two-weeks vacation months ago. Beginning two days after the heist. Not enough time for the long arm of the law to work it all out, and just enough for her to be cleared, as she was."

"They're in the wind." She gave him a hard look. "You're glad they got away with it."

"It's difficult for such as me not to admire their ingenuity, taste, and teamwork. And they're but twenty-four. Young for all this, and long gone by now."

"So's a painting worth millions of millions."

"I think not, as the client wasn't half so clever as they. He took a vid of it hanging in his private room in his country home upstate. We ran a search for it, as sometimes people are just that stupid and vain. I imagine the investigators are knocking on—or more likely knocking down—his door right now."

"Good, and maybe he'll lead them to the twins."

Roarke just patted her hand. "You can dream, darling."

She hit vertical, did an airborne one-eighty, and dropped into a barely adequate parking spot.

Roarke didn't blink.

Eve shifted. "They'll do it again."

"Possibly. Probably," he conceded. "Though they'll have more than enough to live on, quite handsomely, for a very long time. Still, with that talent . . . they'll come to miss the rush of it."

"Like you."

"I get my rush in different ways these days." He leaned over, kissed her.

Since she couldn't argue with that, she got out of the car.

"Plumber's half a block down. Carmine Delgato," she continued as he joined her on the sidewalk. "Age fifty-eight, employed by Singer for twenty-two years, moved up to head guy eight years ago. Married, twenty-six years, Angelina Delgato. Three offspring, twenty-five, twenty-three, twenty."

She paused in front of a white-brick townhome with a three-step stoop, flowers in pots, a solid security system.

"Unclogging sinks pays," she observed.

"It's a bit more than that, but it does, yes."

"When he stayed unavailable all day, I looked a little deeper. He likes to gamble, and he doesn't hit often. He likes the horses, but they don't seem to like him. Oldest kid's in law school—that costs. Middle one's in grad school, looking for an MBA—that costs. Youngest is in college."

"So some financial squeezes. The spouse?"

"Manages an upscale home decor place. She's got twenty in—and it looked to me like she opened her own account about five years ago. She's got herself a nice nest egg."

"I assume you'll be taking a hard look here."

"Hard enough. He has access, he gambles, he's got a lot of bills to pay. So you order more than you need, or fake an invoice, and the order's for cheaper material and you pocket the change. Or you just slip some material or equipment off-site when no one's there."

She shrugged. "Or he's just a hardworking guy who likes to bet on the horses."

She walked up to the door, pushed the buzzer. Glanced at Roarke. "We can have some fine-ish dining and a good bottle of red when we get home."

"That we can."

"And you could, after that, try to find Alva Quirk."

"I can—and I did take a couple more steps there after lunch. I haven't yet . . ."

He trailed off as the door opened.

The woman who answered wore a trim black suit. Her hair, the color of cranberries, swept back in wings from a face dominated by lips the same color as the hair.

As her feet were bare, Eve judged she'd just gotten home from work—suit, full makeup—and kicked shoes off feet she'd likely been on most of the day.

"Mrs. Delgato." Eve held up her badge. "Lieutenant Dallas, NYPSD, and my consultant. Is your husband at home?"

Angelina Delgato slapped one hand on her hip. "What's that son of a bitch done?"

"Ah—"

"Cops coming to my door now, and after I put in eight hours on my feet? Doesn't surprise me one damn bit."

"I'd like to speak to him, ma'am, that's all."

"Bull hockey! Cops at my door! Well, he's not here, is he? And he won't be here because I kicked his stupid, lying ass out eight months ago. Nine. Almost nine."

"You're separated?"

"Damn right we are, because I've had enough. Twenty-six years, and he promises no more gambling. But does he stop? Hell to the hell no, he doesn't stop."

She was winding up, Eve saw, and would keep right on winding.

"We could've lost the house where I'm standing right here!" Angelina rapped a fist on the doorjamb. "But he doesn't stop. Lost most of our middle boy's college fund, so we had to take out a loan, but he doesn't stop."

"I'm sorry to disturb you, Mrs. Delgato, but the separation wasn't listed on his data, and this address was."

"I see he hasn't changed it. You have to pay a fee to change it, so why should I pay more to cover his stupid ass? Man's got a good job, he's got a skill, but he can't keep away from the horses. I'm done."

"Could you tell us where to find him?"

"Took himself off to some flop." She rattled off an address, included a room number, which told Eve she kept such things in the memory banks.

"And if you don't find him there, try the track or Delancy's Bar and Grill, they have offtrack betting and he can't stay the hell away. And you tell him he can stop tagging me up and making his lousy promises and whining about coming home. I'm done."

"Could I ask if you know if he ever sharked out a loan?"

She snorted. But the glitter in her eyes didn't come from anger. It was grief.

"He'll claim he hasn't, but I know damn well. More than once he's come home with a black eye or worse, and claimed he got hurt on the job. More than once I've heard him whispering and pleading on his 'link when he thinks I don't hear. I said you need help, Carmine, and he'd say he was going to meetings. Bull hockey!"

Eve took out her PPC, brought up Tovinski's photo. "Do you recognize this man?"

Angelina frowned at it. "Maybe. Not sure. But I recognize the type. The type who gave Carmine the black eyes and bruised ribs, and one time broke his fingers so he couldn't work for a week. Trash. I recognize trash, and I'm not having it in my house anymore. I'm done."

"Yes, ma'am. Thank you for your time."

"You tell him I'm done!" she called out as Eve and Roarke walked away. Then slammed the door.

"I have a feeling Carmine Delgato just popped up several rungs on your list."

"Damn right."

Roarke wrapped an arm around Eve's waist as they walked back to the car. "She still loves him."

"Come on."

"She's too angry not to still love him. I saw a broken heart in her eyes."

Eve sighed. "Yeah. So did I."

7

New York, Eve knew, merged different worlds into one big, crowded, diverse city. Traveling a few handfuls of blocks, Carmine Delgato had moved from a tidy neighborhood of upper-middle-class townhomes, apartments, and the shops and restaurants they patronized, to a dingy corner of flops, dives, low-rent street LCs, and the downtrodden who patronized them.

He'd chosen a squat post-Urban box squeezed between the dirt-fogged display window of a pawn shop boasting a sign reading $ 4 U, and a dive bar called The Hard Stuff.

The four-story box had plenty of graffiti and no security.

When she walked inside—no need to buzz in or use her master—it surprised her to find the closet-size lobby looked and smelled clean. The tiny counter held a sign:

RING BELL FOR ASSISTANCE.
WE'LL BE RIGHT BACK!

Eve eyed the single elevator, swiveled to the stairs.

No litter or graffiti in the stairwell, and again that sense of clean.

"Somebody scrubbed the place down recently."

"It's more than that," Roarke commented. "I expect it's next to impossible to keep the exterior tag free, but someone maintains the inside. No soundproofing to speak of, as we can plainly hear."

"Yeah, why is there always a baby screaming like somebody's jabbing a needle in its eye?"

"I couldn't say, though someone else appears to be enjoying themselves."

Over the baby's wailing and someone's choice of trash rock, the sound of sex thumps and grunts came through, enthusiastically.

"A long way from flowers on the stoop."

She pushed through the door on the second floor, spotted the skinny, pint-size Black guy hammering a fist on 2B.

"I know you're in there, Carmine. Open the effing door."

He paused when he spotted Eve and Roarke, and dropped his fist. "Help you?"

Eve held up her badge. "Are you a friend of Carmine Delgato's?"

"Not exactly. I'm the building super. My partners and me own the place. Is there a problem?"

"I need to speak with Mr. Delgato."

"Yeah, well, get in line." His shoulders hunched the second the words spurted out of his mouth. "Sorry, don't mean to be a jerk. He hasn't paid the rent in four effing weeks, and I gave the GD SOB plenty of chances on it. I told him how this was his last one, and he's dodging me."

"Are you sure he's in there?"

"Pretty doggone sure. I had to turn one of the rooms and I saw him coming in when I looked out the window. We keep the rooms clean, see, between the thirty minutes and hourly rents. Wasn't more than a half hour ago. Look, I gotta kick him out. I'm sorry to do it, but it's been four effing weeks."

The little guy, Eve thought, had an expressive face that managed to look aggrieved and apologetic at the same time.

"You're within your rights to enter the premises."

"Yeah." He blew out a breath that had his lips vibrating. "I was gonna. Makes me feel like a jerk, but I was gonna."

Eve switched on her recorder. "Can I have your name?"

"I'm Dell, Jamal Dell. I'm the in-building super. My brother and my two cousins, we rotate when we can, but I'm the in-building. We own the building. I know it doesn't look like much, but—"

"It's very well maintained," Roarke told him.

"Thanks." Jamal brightened right up. "We work at it. We pull in enough, we're gonna add some security and sound-proofing, but we can't do that if SOBs like Carmine try stiffing us."

"Mr. Dell, we have official business with Mr. Delgato. If you enter the premises, do we have your permission to do so as well?"

"Jeez, I'm sorry if he's in any cop trouble. He's got a sad story—which is why I let him sob-story me into four weeks. Yeah, you can come in."

He pulled a passkey out of his pocket. "Doggone it, Carmine. I'm coming in and you're going out."

He unlocked the door, shoved it open. After one step inside, he froze.

"Holy cow! Oh my gosh!"

Eve had already rushed past him to grab the legs of Carmine Delgato and shove his limp body upward. It hung from the rope around his neck tied to a hook in the ceiling.

"Call nine-one-one," she shouted at Dell. "Call for an ambulance. Now. Now!"

"Oh my effing goodness."

Roarke righted the chair on its side under the body, then, pulling out a folding knife, sawed at the rope. To help with the weight, he wrapped an arm around Delgato as he cut through.

"He's still warm." Roarke let the knife fall and used both hands to help lower Delgato to the floor.

Eve yanked at the rope to loosen it, felt for a pulse.

"I've got a pulse. Just barely, but he's not breathing."

She straddled him, started CPR.

"They're coming! The ambulance. Holy cow, holy cow."

"Go down, lead them up. Tell them I'm doing CPR."

Roarke crouched beside her as Dell raced out. "I can take over."

"I've got it, I've got it. Goddamn it. He's swinging up there while we're standing outside the door." She pumped, pumped, pumped, pushed her breath into him, pumped.

"There's drywall bits on the floor from putting that hook in. Fresh. Fuck, fuck, come on, you asshole. Come back. But where's the tool? Need a tool to get it into the what-do-you-call-it."

"Joist."

"That. Just into that ceiling? It wouldn't hold him. Wouldn't hold the weight. Could've put it away, but why? Place is a pigsty."

She heard the sirens. "I need my field kit."

"I'll get it." But he waited, stayed beside her as she fought to bring Carmine Delgato back to life.

He rose when the MTs rushed in.

Eve swung off Delgato, gave them room as they got to work.

"No pulse."

"He had one when we got him down. Faint, but he had one."

They shocked him, once, twice. Eve watched the line on the portable lay flat.

They shot adrenaline into his heart, but the line stayed flat.

She pushed to her feet when Roarke came back with her kit. And shook her head before the MT called it.

"He's gone."

"I'll take it from here." She held up her badge.

"Yeah, I recognized you, Lieutenant." The female half of the MT team glanced up at her. "I've mopped you up before. Nothing we could do for this one. Likely he was gone when you cut him down."

"Appreciate the effort."

"We all do what we can."

While they packed up, she walked over to Roarke. "I won't waste my breath saying you don't have to wait while I deal with this, so I'll use it to tell you to seal up."

She took a can of Seal-It out of her kit, coated her hands, her boots, then passed it to him.

"You can play Peabody, collect some of the drywall bits."

When the MTs moved out, she went back to the body to formalize the ID.

"Victim is Delgato, Carmine, currently of this address. TOD, seventeen-forty-three. He died when I was doing CPR."

"The MT was right. He was, essentially, gone when we got to him."

"Yeah. COD, asphyxiation, strangulation by hanging. No visible defensive wounds, no visible trauma other than severe bruising around the neck."

She put on microgoggles, leaned close. "Bruising is consistent with the rope used to . . ."

Leaned closer. "There's . . . it looks like a slight, possible anomaly in the neck area. A lot of bruising, swelling, but . . . it looks like . . . potentially a faint circle. Pressure syringe. It's from a fucking pressure syringe. ME to examine and verify."

She sat back on her heels, tagged Morris as she scanned the room.

"Dallas? How's your evening going?"

"I'm looking down at a dead guy."

"So, as usual then."

"Ha. I need you on him, Morris, and right away. I'm sorry to ask, and it would read as a self-termination by hanging, but . . . Wait, let me magnify this area and show you."

Once she had, Morris studied the magnified area. "Yes, I see what you mean. I'd want to take a look—in the flesh—to confirm. But from the visual, it appears to be the mark left by a pressure syringe. It's very nearly blurred out in the bruising, which would have been a smart and efficient way to mask it. Send him to me. I'll head back now."

"Sorry to screw up your evening."

"The dead are demanding creatures, as we both know. I'll verify, and run tests to see what, if anything, was injected. Do you have a TOD?"

"About ten minutes ago."

"Ah, well, that'll make my job easier. I'll send a team out now myself. I want him fast. Before any substance—and some can quickly—dissipates from his system."

"Thanks."

She pocketed her 'link again, looked at Roarke.

"Open window over there, fire escape outside. Hook recently added to the ceiling. We're going to look for the drill or other tool that installed it, but we're not going to find it because whoever came through that window took it back with him. Like he brought the hook, the rope, the syringe full of whatever he jabbed into Delgato so he could just string him up.

"His neck's not broken. That doesn't automatically mean homicide, because it doesn't always snap when somebody puts on a noose and steps off the chair."

"And when it doesn't," Roarke said, "you choke to death. Slowly."

"Yeah. Not an easy way. No broken neck, it's one more added to the hook, to the mark, to the fact Delgato makes an excellent fall guy."

"Dead men tell no tales."

"You got that." She stepped away from the body to walk to the window. "We'll get some uniforms to do the canvass, but we're not likely to get a cooperating witness around here. Could luck out, but for a solid ID—a long shot."

She studied the windowsill, angled her head, then put on her goggles again.

"What did you say about the building?"

"It's well maintained."

"Yeah, and these jimmy marks look real fresh. They're faint, careful, but they've scratched the paint a little. And . . . son of a bitch! Son of a bitch. I need tweezers and a small evidence container. The lidded vials, not a bag. I've got a couple bits of fabric. Not so smart as you think, you murdering bastard fuck. Jimmied open the shitty window lock—didn't take much, but you scratched the paint. And when you climbed in, the scratches caught at your pants. Didn't even feel it, just a couple threads."

She drew them out, put them in the container. Still wearing the goggles, she studied them. "But I've got Harvo, the fucking Queen of Hair and Fiber."

She labeled it, initialed it.

"He was waiting for him, that's how he did it. Knows Delgato's routine, so he times it. He was probably leaving by the window about the time we were coming in the damn building. Dell saw Delgato coming in about a half hour before he started banging on the door. Killer grabs Delgato when he comes in, jabs him. No defensive wounds so he's either able to control him or the stuff he put in him takes him out. He's already installed the hook—maybe somebody heard that, we'll check."

She looked up, climbed up, examined the hook. "That's going to hit zero, most likely. It couldn't have taken more than a few seconds to drill through."

She hopped down. "Now he's got time to get the rope ready. No drag marks I can see, so he hauls Delgato up, gets the noose around his neck. He's the one on the chair, not the vic. Stand on the chair, haul on the rope—got some muscle—loop it around the hook, tie it off, good and strong. Step off while he's dangling, knock the chair down, and then leave the way you came. Sealed up—we're not going to find prints, and I'm betting the rope came off a job site, one Delgato worked. I'm betting that."

She glanced toward the door when she heard footsteps. "That's going to be the morgue team. Morris is quick. Go ahead and let them in. I'm calling for sweepers, then we'll do a quick search."

They didn't find any tool for installing the hook. Roarke did locate a fake soup can with a roll of cash. Enough—maybe—to pay a couple weeks' rent. She didn't find his 'link, and that told her she would've found some kind of communication on it to/from his killer.

"No 'link, no appointment book, job schedule, no PPC or tablet."

"You believe, and I'd agree, they went out the window with his killer."

"Yeah. Why risk it? You had to communicate some way or other. And he could have your name listed somewhere."

Roarke looked around again, considered the small, sad life ended there. "And you believe Delgato was responsible for Alva Quirk."

"He was responsible, he was part of it, or he knew who was. Ducked Peabody all day, and damn well told whoever put that noose around his neck the cops wanted to talk to him."

As Roarke did, she scanned the lost-man mess of the single-room flop. "Sweepers won't be much longer, then I'll turn the scene over to them—and they can get the evidence we already collected into the lab tonight. Still . . ."

She looked at Roarke. "That fine dining and bottle of red has to wait."

"I may not be a trained investigator, but I deduced that."

"Sorry. I need to talk to Dell, then I have to go notify the victim's wife. She's still next of kin. And a drop by Bolton Singer's is still on the plate. I can pull Peabody in for all that."

"Why? I'm here, and you don't need either of us for those tasks in any case."

"Partners sometimes hear or see something you don't, or think of a fresh angle."

"Then I'll do my best to be a good partner."

"You already are."

When the sweepers arrived, she and Roarke went down to the lobby. Dell paced the tiny space, literally wringing his hands, while another man, not quite as skinny and clearly a blood relation, sat behind the counter.

"Officer!"

"Lieutenant," Eve corrected.

"Sorry. So sorry. I'm so twisted around. I don't know what to do. We decided we should close to new bookings until . . . We have some week-to-week and month-to-month tenants, but we closed down for now for the rest."

"You don't need to do that, Mr. Dell."

"Told ya," said the man behind the counter.

"My brother, Koby, we're partners—with our cousins. I called Koby. I hope that's okay."

"It's fine. We'll need to seal off 2B. It's a crime scene. We'll clear it as soon as possible. I have a couple officers coming in to canvass—to check and see if anyone saw anything."

"I don't know how I can go in there again. Carmine eff-ing killed himself. I had to get the rent, but I wouldn't have pushed at him so hard if I'd known he'd—"

"Mr. Dell—Jamal—this isn't your fault."

"Told him that, too. Jamal takes everything to heart. He's a GD softie."

"Okay, I'm going to ask. What's with the language cen-soring? I'm a cop. I've heard it all. I've said it all."

Koby snickered. "Bone-deep habit. Our mama, she won't allow hard language. We said something off when we were kids, we got all heck to pay. No screen time, or no ice cream if that was coming. We got older and slipped? A dollar for every word. You're working and saving your money, you learn. Besides, no telling if she'd hear us where we stand now, even though she lives clear across town."

"Mama's got her ways," Jamal agreed. "I was dogging him on the rent, I can't forget that. I can't forget how I walked right in there and saw him that way. How he got so down he hung himself."

"We haven't determined if he self-terminated."

"But—"

"We're investigating."

"You think it was murder!" Now Koby got up. "That's what you do. Murder."

"She doesn't kill people. She's a police officer!"

"Jamal, you dumb-A. She's the one from the vid, the one who solves murders and stuff. From that vid, *The Icove Agenda*."

"The one with the clones and the murders and that scary business? I didn't watch it," Jamal told Eve. "I watch stuff like that, I don't sleep right."

"No problem."

"He's in it, too." Koby grinned at Roarke. "The rich dude. I saw it twice. It's a solid vid. You guys kick butt. So maybe somebody killed him and made it look like he did it himself?"

"We're investigating," Eve said again. She took out her PPC. "Have you seen this man around? Have you seen him with Mr. Delgato?"

Jamal shook his head. "I can't say I have. But I'm not on the desk twenty-four/seven. We rotate, but even then. We got repairs and such, and we try to get to that right away. And you gotta turn the quick rooms. That's why we have the bell. It'll ping on the 'link of whoever's on the shift. It's mostly me, but not twenty-four/seven."

"He looks mean," Koby added as he studied Tovinski. "A mean white dude, but I don't think I've seen him around."

"I'd like to check with your cousins. You said you rotate."

"Sure. Meesha and Leelo. I can tag them now. Meesha, she's a nurse and works nights right now. Leelo, he's an accountant. He keeps the books."

"Let's do that. And can you tell me when the hook in the ceiling of 2B was installed."

"We never put that in there. I didn't see it. Was there . . . I guess there was. I didn't see, but we never did that to any of the rooms. Carmine must've."

"Or the killer did," Koby said. Darkly.

"Knock that off sideways," his brother ordered. "I won't sleep easy for a month."

"Did Mr. Delgato ever have visitors?"

"He never came in with anybody. Nobody ever came in and asked for him. He was a sad story, miss, ma'am, officer."

"Lieutenant," Eve and Koby said together.

"Sorry. He was sad. His wife gave him the boot, and he said his kids were pissed at him. He worked hard, he said, and he liked to ah, de-stress—by playing the horses. His wife didn't understand. He was a plumber, and he was a good one. I know because I had a toilet break, just bust, and he said he could get me a new one at cost and put it in and all. He did, and it's a fine-looking john, too. Best we got. He said maybe I could take the cost of it off the rent, and the cost of the install, at a discount, off, too. That's what we did."

"I'd like to see that john."

Jamal blinked at her. "You want to see the toilet?"

Koby elbowed him. "She's investigating, numbnuts."

She got the make and model and photo of the toilet, checked with the cousins—no help—and left to do the notification.

"Enterprising, entertaining, and interesting men, the Dell brothers," Roarke commented. "I'll wager their mother is a force."

"I wonder how many dollars she ended up collecting from them over the years. This notification could be messy, especially if you hit the mark, and I think you did, about her still being in love with Delgato."

"I expect it will be. And I expect, when you dig in, you'll find that very fine toilet fell off a Singer supply truck—metaphorically."

"Yeah, he was skimming, helping himself to supplies. And he was helping somebody else do that and more. Enough more it's worth two dead bodies."

Once she'd found a parking spot, and they'd walked a block and a half to the townhome, Eve paused again.

"If she gets sloppy, I need you to be Peabody again. You go soft."

"All right."

"You lean that way anyhow."

As do you, he thought as they walked up to the door, or notifications wouldn't be so hard.

Eve pressed the buzzer.

Angelina had shed her work suit for an oversize tee, leggings, and house skids. She sent Eve a molten glare.

"What now?"

"Could we come in and speak with you?"

"Why? Whatever Carmine's done has nothing to do with me. You see this?" She tapped on the glass of white wine in her hand. "I'm about to drink this halfway decent glass of chardonnay as a reward for a long day, and have a little dinner and relax. Tell him if he needs bailing out to call his bookie."

"Ms. Delgato, it's important we speak with you."

"Then freaking speak so I can drink my damn wine."

"It would be better if we came in."

"Oh for—" She broke off with a hiss, but waved her free arm as she stepped back. "Fine, you're in."

"Could we sit down?"

Angelina arched her eyebrows. "Want some hors d'oeuvres while we're chatting?"

"We'll try not to keep you long. If we could sit down for a moment."

She turned on her heel, marched into the sunny living area with the furnishings done in rich corals and tropical blues. She dropped into a chair, waved again at the sofa and its army of fussy pillows.

"Sit, say it. It took me over twenty-five years to accept Carmine wasn't ever going to change and shut him out of my life. And that's what I'm going to do the minute you're out the door again."

"Ms. Delgato, I regret to inform you Carmine Delgato is dead."

Angelina froze with the wineglass halfway to her mouth. "What are you talking about? You're not even real cops, are you? This is one of his ploys to get me to take him back, and it's just sick." She lurched to her feet. "Get out."

"Ms. Delgato. I'm Lieutenant Dallas with the NYPSD." Eve held up her badge. "You can contact Cop Central and verify my badge number. I know this is difficult, but you're Mr. Delgato's next of kin, and it's my duty to inform you."

"Why did you come here before if you're saying he's dead?"

"We were unaware Mr. Delgato had moved from this address, and wanted to interview him regarding an investigation. When we reached his current address, he did not answer the door, and the building super allowed us entry. Upon entry we found Mr. Delgato hanging from a rope in his apartment."

"You're saying he hanged himself?" Her face went dead white, then instantly, furiously red. "I know you're lying! Carmine would never commit suicide."

"I didn't state he had."

"You just said . . ." Now, breath hitching, Angelina lowered slowly into the chair. "You're saying somebody killed him?"

"We haven't determined self-termination or homicide."

Angelina closed her eyes, held up a hand to stop Eve from continuing. After an obvious struggle for composure, she opened her eyes. She drank half the wine in one gulp, then set the glass aside. Her eyes shined, but the tears didn't fall.

"I can determine it. I knew Carmine half my damn life. He'd never kill himself."

"Why?"

"Because he'd never have what he wanted if he's dead. Do you think this is the first time I booted him? It's not. I always caved and took him back. What he didn't get, would never get, is this time I meant it. I was done. He was never going to change, he'd never keep his promises. But he lived in a place where we'd just circle back, he'd come home, we'd try it all again. He loved me, okay? He loved me, and God knows I loved him. But he loved the horses more. He loved the thrill of betting, of winning, even the punch of losing. Because next time—always a next time with Carmine. No next time when you're dead."

She closed her eyes again, held up a hand again. This time a tear slipped down each cheek. "And hanging himself? Not in a million years."

"Do you know anyone who'd want to harm him?"

She let out a sharp laugh, inhaled a sob. "I told you before, didn't I, he'd get the snot beat out of him now and then. A good ten years ago—after I took him back again—I took control of the money in this household. He got an allowance. That was the deal, one he tried and tried to weasel out of, but I held firm."

She picked up the wine for another, smaller sip.

"A few years later, we go around again. This time I have the house account, but I open my own personal account, I put the investments and this house in my name. Just mine, all of it. That was what he agreed to five years ago to come back. So he'd find people to float him loans. Sometimes he won, plenty he didn't. He'd work side jobs to pay them off, but he got smacked around if he didn't pay them off fast enough.

"He denied all that, but I knew."

"Do you have names?"

She shook her head. Her hand trembled a little as she picked up the wineglass again. "I know his bookie's name's Ralph, but I never met him."

"Has anyone else come here looking for him since you separated?"

She shook her head again. "No one ever came around here. He'd meet them at one of his OTB places, or the track. Or, I don't know, but he knew if that type came around here, it was over."

"He didn't have a computer in his apartment. Did he have a home office here?"

"No. I kept the books, paid the bills. I ran the house. And

I kept my office door locked." Two more tears spilled out. "I knew I had to break that cycle, for good. You can't live a good life with a man you can't trust not to steal from you."

She pressed one hand to her mouth; in the other, the wineglass started to tip.

Roarke rose quickly, took it from her. "Ms. Delgato, could I get you a glass of water?"

"Yes. Yes, thank you. It's—"

"I'll find it. Would you like us to contact your children? Would you want your children here with you?"

Now she spread her fingers so her hand covered her face. And just nodded.

When Roarke slipped out, Angelina pressed that hand to her heart. "Where is he? I'm his wife. Whatever he did, I'm his wife. I need to see him."

"He's with the medical examiner. I'll make arrangements for you to see him as soon as possible."

"Because they have to . . . they have to . . . Oh God, Carmine."

"I'm very sorry for your loss. I know this is difficult, but I need to ask a few more questions."

"I don't know who'd do this. Nobody gets paid if you're dead. And he always paid the loans eventually. I'd tell you if I knew. I loved him. I couldn't respect the son of a bitch. I couldn't trust him, but I loved him. I couldn't help it."

"Was he a violent man?"

"Carmine?" She let out that laugh again. "Absolutely not. He was a liar. His addiction made him a liar, an asshole, and worse, but he was gentle and kind. I never knew him to raise his hand to anyone. He couldn't even bring himself to give one of our kids a swat on the butt when they'd earned it."

With her hand over her mouth again, she muffled a sob. "I loved that about him. I loved that sweet, kind, gentle part of him. Hardly ever raised his voice, even when I was shouting at him hard enough to blow the roof off. He didn't have violence in him. No meanness in him. Just that terrible sickness that ate away at everything good."

"You said you couldn't trust him not to steal from you. Would he have stolen from someone else?"

"Not from someone who'd suffer for it, but if he thought, if he'd convinced himself they could afford it, or not miss it? Sure. Because he'd know, you see, he'd just know, that next bet, that next tip on a hot horse? It would bring the rain."

When Roarke brought her water, she sipped it slowly. "I can't do this anymore right now. I was rude to you, and I apologize, but—"

"Don't. Don't, it's not necessary." Eve got to her feet. "Is there anything else we can do for you? Anyone else you want us to contact?"

"No, no. I just want my kids."

"I spoke with your oldest," Roarke told her. "They'll all be here as soon as possible."

"I'm going to leave my card." Eve dug for one. "If you think of anything, please contact me. We'll let you know when you can see him. We'll see ourselves out."

8

When they got back to the car, Roarke laid his hands on Eve's shoulders. "Would you like me to drive?"

"No, I've got it. I still want to talk to Singer." But when they got in, she sat a moment. "It would have been easier, I think, if she'd lost it, just fallen apart, than watching her fight to maintain."

She drew in, let out a breath. "Anyway. She was helpful. Here's what I think."

"Shall I tell you what you think?"

She shot him a look, then pulled out into traffic. "Okay, smart guy, what do I think?"

"You're thinking Delgato didn't kill Alva Quirk, but most likely witnessed the murder. Witnessed it because he was stealing from his employer. Or for his employer—that's to be determined. But stealing, you believe he was, and the one with him—one he was stealing for or who helped him steal—killed her."

"I might be thinking that. As a possible theory."

"And taking it to the next step, you're thinking whoever killed Alva Quirk let himself in Delgato's window, set up what would look like a suicide by hanging, and disposed of the witness."

"You may not have known me half your life, but that's a pretty good take on my current thinking."

"Who says we didn't know each other for half, and more, of another life?"

"Irish woo-woo." But she didn't object when he gave her hand a squeeze.

"So for this next part," she continued, punching it to get through a yellow light, "you'll stick with being Roarke."

"Excellent. I know that role well."

"Singer comes across as a decent sort, but that's not to say he isn't siphoning from the family business, and using a longtime employee with a gambling habit to help. Singer wanted to be a rocker, and he had to give that up to go into the family business. Could be he resents that and figures he's entitled to take what he wants."

"Scars and scabs from shattered dreams." Roarke considered. "If so, as CEO, he could find ways to conceal taking what he pleases."

"And if so, he'd have to have somewhere to put it. Hidden accounts. Or like spending it on a stolen Monet."

"A very fine way to wash ill-gotten funds."

"You'd know, so that's something we'll look into later. For now, I definitely want your take on Singer—and the family if they're around."

"I expect that fine dining and good bottle of red as my reward."

"Sounds fair."

"Perhaps I sold myself too cheap."

That earned a smirk. "That'll be the day."

The Bolton Singers had a double townhome on the Upper East Side, all rosy red brick and shining windows. It sat on a quiet, tree-lined street where Eve figured the nannies and dog walkers strolled the sidewalks with their charges more than their employers did.

Indeed, as she studied the house, a long-legged girl in a DOG'S BEST FRIEND T-shirt strolled by with a couple of dogs—more like mops with feet—on leashes.

Eve noted that the main entrance, and the door that led to a small grassy area boxed in with flowers and fencing, had cams and palm plates.

She chose the main with its glossy wooden door and pushed the buzzer.

She expected the usual computer inquiry. Instead the door swung open almost immediately.

Youngest son, Eve decided, as he looked early twenties and had his father's eyes. His hair, glossy and brown as the door, curled over his ears and collar in studied disarray.

He had a lean build in worn jeans and tee that asked: SAYS WHO?

Music pumped out of the house as he shot them a dazzling smile.

"Hey, hi. Thought you were Clem."

"No." Eve held up her badge. "Lieutenant Dallas, NYPSD, and Roarke, consultant."

His mouth dropped open for an instant, then he shot a finger at both of them. "Yeah, you are! Frosted! I saw the vid like three times, man. Clones. Up and out! We don't have any here, except I've always wondered about Layla. My sister."

"We're here to speak with your father, if possible."

"Guess it is. We're back there for an after-dinner jam. Clem's supposed to drop by." He gestured them in. "So, come on back."

The house had the feel of a family home, a wealthy one, sure, but lived-in. A lot of space, a lot of quiet colors with slashes of bolder ones. He led them through a sun-splashed living room where matted and framed family photos made up a gallery wall, through another space with a long bar and a fireplace tiled in a cheerful pattern that made her think of Italy.

The music gained volume—drums, a piano, maybe a guitar, something with enough bass to pump against the walls, and a lot of voices.

The tableau in the next room struck as cheerful as the fireplace.

A woman—that would be Lilith Singer, wife—banging it out on the piano, another—middle to late twenties, likely the older daughter, Harmony—beating a serious riff on a set of drums, another man—maybe thirty—standing hipshot as he worked the bass guitar.

Another female with blond-streaked hair curling halfway down her back executed a complicated and complementary series of notes on an electric keyboard.

And Bolton Singer—in jeans as worn as his youngest's—rocking it on a guitar and grinning at a toddler about Bella's age, to Eve's eye, who danced around with her—maybe his—arms waving.

The blend and enthusiasm of the instruments and voices told Eve this was hardly the first time for a post-dinner jam.

The one who'd let them in grabbed a sax and let it wail into the crescendo.

"Now, that's what I'm saying!" Bolton let out a laugh and started to bend down to pick up the kid. And spotted Eve and Roarke.

"Oh yeah, company, Dad."

Every head turned with expressions of curiosity—the friendly sort.

"Kincade, honestly." The woman at the piano shook back her hair—curly like her two youngest children's—with a combination of glossy brown and coppery streaks. She rose, walked toward them with her hand out.

"Roarke. You may not remember, but we met briefly several years ago at a benefit."

"I do, and it's lovely to see you again. I don't believe you've met my wife."

"I haven't, but I'm a fan. Everyone, this is Roarke, and Lieutenant Dallas. Our youngest, Kincade, Layla on keyboards, Harmony on drums, our son-in-law, Justin, on bass guitar, and our dancer, Marvi. Bolt?"

"Sorry. Caught me off guard." He set his guitar on a stand. "Roarke, it's been awhile." He offered his hand before turning to Eve. "You've had a long day, Lieutenant. Why don't we take this in my office?"

"We know what happened. It's all over the media, and we talked about it before dinner." Layla took a step closer to her father, but studied Eve. "Did you find out who did it?"

"The investigation's active and ongoing."

"That's what they always say, right, Justin? Justin's a lawyer."

"Almost." The son-in-law scooped up his daughter.

"I'd say that session worked up some appetites. Let's go have dessert. We'll just give you the room, Bolt." Lilith gave his arm a squeeze. "Come on, gang, that cherry pie à la mode won't eat itself."

The bell rang. "That's got to be Clem."

As Kincade dashed off, his mother called after him, "Bring him back to the kitchen. Sorry for the madness. Why don't I send out some pie and coffee?"

"We're fine," Eve told her. "We'll try not to interrupt any more of your evening than necessary."

Lilith ran a hand down Bolton's arm this time. "Let me know if you need anything."

Eve caught the older daughter starting to object—but so

did her mother. It only took a look, and Lilith herded the rest of the family out.

"You have a talented family, Bolton," Roarke began.

"We have a lot of fun. Please, have a seat. You must have questions that couldn't wait."

"Questions and information," Eve agreed. "Carmine Delgato."

"Carmine? Longtime employee. Chief plumber on the Hudson Yards project, and others."

"Were you aware of his gambling problem?"

Bolton sighed. "Yes, of course. I know he's separated from his wife again, and it seems to be sticking this time. I'm sorry about it. The company has offered to give him time off for rehabilitation, but . . . It doesn't affect his work, so we've kept out of his personal business."

He lifted both hands. "Surely you don't think Carmine killed that woman. I can tell you, without hesitation, he'd never hurt anyone."

"That may be, but someone hurt him. He's dead, Mr. Singer."

"He's . . . My God."

The shock looked genuine. He lost color with it. "Carmine? Dead? Are you saying someone killed him?"

"Unless I'm mistaken, yes. The ME will determine, but I believe his death was staged as a suicide."

"Suicide? Carmine?" Bolton had his hands in his hair like a man who didn't know what to do with them. "That doesn't seem possible."

"Why?"

"He . . . he's an optimist, Lieutenant. Often to his own detriment. He simply believes, absolutely, things will turn around, work out. His long-shot bet would pay off, his wife would take him back. A job that's run into serious problems will be fine with just a little work.

"But why would someone kill Carmine?"

"It's my job to find out. Mr. Singer, you knew Mr. Delgato for a number of years."

"Yes, he worked for us at least twenty years. Twenty-five is closer, I think. I can check."

"In your opinion, was he capable of stealing from the company? He may have thought of it as pilfering, or just skimming a bit here and there."

"No, I don't believe . . ." When he trailed off, Bolton stared over Eve's shoulder.

"You're rethinking the no."

"I . . . He had an addiction, and addictions cause good people to do bad things in the need to feed it. I can say I never suspected him of doing so."

"But you've had material, equipment, go missing from time to time."

"It happens. I'm sure Roarke would tell you the same. We're usually able to track that sort of thing down."

"Have you had that issue on the Hudson Yards site?"

"None that's come to my attention, no."

"On other jobs where he was head plumber?"

"I honestly can't tell you off the top of my head. I'd like to call Harmony in. She's been on parental leave, but she's our CFO. And if you don't object, I'd like my wife here, too. She doesn't work for the company, but she knew Angie, Carmine's wife."

"All right."

"I'll just be a minute." He rose, rubbed a hand over his face. "I'm having some trouble taking this all in. Two people are dead."

Eve watched him walk out. "If he's faking this, he's damn good at it."

"His greatest sin might be using too light a hand with the

company he runs. That may be because running it is duty, not passion or even true inclination."

"You have things walk off a job."

"From time to time. And if you let it slide, the ones doing the walking will not only do it again, they'll inevitably up the stakes. So you not only track it down, you let it be known you are. Now and again, things walk right back on—ah, look here, we found the missing items. Just misplaced."

He shrugged. "That's not always the case, of course, but it can and does happen."

Bolton came back with his older daughter. "Lilith will be right in. She's bringing coffee. She can't help herself."

"It's appreciated." Eve looked toward Harmony. "You're chief financial officer of your father's company."

"I am. And if you're thinking nepotism, I have a master's in accounting and degrees in finance and business management."

"Harmony."

"Just establishing my bona fides, Dad. A lot of people thought I was just the boss's daughter, indulged by her daddy. A lot of people found out differently."

"As that's the case, you could answer some questions."

"Happy to, once I know what this is all about. We all know about the woman who was killed, and we're all sorry. But I don't know what that has to do with the family, or the books. And if this gets too deeply into that, I'd like my husband to sit in as legal representation. He's taking the bar next month, but he can give us legal advice."

No pushover this one, Eve thought. Tough and pithy, with a no-bullshit air she admired.

"You're free to do that if you feel the need."

Eve glanced over as Lilith wheeled in a smart and efficient-looking stainless cart.

"If I recall from the Icove vid, you both take your coffee black."

"It's kind of you to trouble," Roarke told her.

"No trouble at all. Clearly, Bolt's upset, so I'm assuming you didn't bring good news."

"Lilith, Carmine Delgato's dead."

"What?" Her hands froze in the act of pouring coffee. "No, oh, Bolt, no. How, when? My God, I just spoke with Angie this morning."

"About what?" Eve asked.

"Open Hearts—I work with my mother-in-law in her foundation—we put on a fashion show every fall, a benefit. Angie's been cochair for the last five years. And she's a friend, we're friends. I need to call her. Should I go over to see her?"

"You should hold off on that," Eve said. "Her children are with her."

"She separated from Carmine—you must know. But she loved him. She couldn't live with him anymore, but she loved him. This will crush her. Oh my God, did he have an accident on a job site?"

"No."

"Sit, Mom. I'll do that."

Lilith sat, reached for and gripped her husband's hand. "What happened to him?"

"He was found hanging in his apartment in what appeared to be self-termination."

"No, no, no, that's somehow worse. But it can't be, it can't be. He loved her, too. He had a sickness, but he loved her and his children. He wouldn't do that to them. I don't believe it."

"There are certain factors that call the self-termination into question. The medical examiner will determine."

"You're very cool about it," Harmony muttered as she passed Eve and Roarke their coffee.

Ignoring that, Eve studied her. "Did you know Mr. Delgato?"

"Of course. I've worked for Singer in a full-time capacity for six years, and worked summers since I was seventeen. I know her better, as I also help run the annual benefit. I'm the numbers nerd."

"And as the numbers nerd for Singer, what sort of percentage goes into the lost or missing equipment and material column every quarter?"

"That would depend on the quarter, the nature of the jobs included in that quarter, but, in general, that figure ran about three percent when I came on. I had it down to one and three-quarters when I took my parental leave. When I come back, I intend to push it down to under one percent."

She passed coffee to her parents, then poured her own.

"How long have you been on leave?"

"Nineteen months. Marvi's eighteen months now, and Justin and I wanted to give her up to two years before we hired child care. I left in my last month of pregnancy, as I came under considerable pressure to do so."

She sent her parents the side-eye.

"You were exhausting yourself," her mother reminded her.

"Before that time, did any avenues lead toward Delgato?"

"I can't say, as my boss, the CEO, felt it more important to try to lower the percentage than point fingers."

"The cost of doing business," Bolton began.

"Shouldn't be allowing employees and subs to pick the company pockets," his daughter finished. Then smiled brightly. "The CEO and the CFO disagree on this point. You think Carmine Delgato was picking company pockets?"

"I do. But I don't have hard evidence as yet."

"If these avenues and information provide that hard evidence, or vindicate Mr. Delgato, we should find the information. And if it helps find out what happened and why to

Mr. Delgato, I know the CEO and CFO would fully agree to looking into it."

"Yes. If he did, it was to feed his addiction."

"While I'm interested in that data," Eve said, "if you find it, I'd like to know if Mr. Delgato increased his habit—as I believe he's been feeding his addiction in this manner for some time—since you went on leave. And most specifically as relates to the Hudson Yards project. Who's acting CFO?"

"We have two acting CFOs," Bolton told her. "It takes two to come close to managing what Harmony did."

"I'll need their names and contacts."

"Before you put the fear of God into them?" Harmony held up a hand. "I'd like you to give me a couple of days—at most—to dig down into this myself. I can do some of that from home, once I set things up, but I'd want to do the bulk of it in the office. Visible."

She smiled as she sipped her coffee. "Some who considered me daddy's girl have learned to fear me."

"I'm not surprised."

"You have a rep," Harmony said to Roarke.

"Do I?"

"You know you do. Fair, creative, involved, tireless. If you don't happen to be the smartest person in the room—though you usually are—you make sure the smartest person in the room is with you. And if someone tries to fuck with you—sorry, Mom, but sometimes it's the best word—you'll slice them to bits before they see the knife. So while you're admired and respected, fear has a role. If my family didn't have a business, I'd be working for you."

"You can't have her." Bolton managed his first genuine smile since they'd come in.

"A pity. The Singer organization is fortunate to have you."

"Damn right. I'll get that data if the data are there to get."

"She will," Bolton agreed. "And while I can't claim to be

the smartest person in the room very often, and certainly not in this one, I think I've started to connect the dots. I can tell you, with absolute certainty, Carmine didn't kill that woman, but I see now, if what you believe is true, he could have been up there, working with someone else. Someone capable of taking a life. And then taking Carmine's."

He brought his wife's hand to his cheek. "For money, Lilith. It all has to be for money, for profit."

"You have partners on the Hudson Yards project."

"Yes, Bardov Construction. My grandmother and my father both made connections there before I came on board. They go back. This is a very ambitious project. We're not Roarke Industries, and our resources aren't as deep. Do you think someone from that company is responsible?"

"I have no evidence of that, at this time." She considered bringing up Tovinski, but decided against it. Bolton Singer didn't possess any hint of a poker face. "I have to look at all angles, take all avenues. Did Delgato work or to your knowledge socialize with anyone from Bardov Construction?"

"He certainly would have known some of the employees, as we've done projects with that company before. I couldn't say on a social level."

"His gambling problems weren't a secret."

"No, not at all. And I understand what you're saying. Someone could have exploited him, pressured him, paid off a debt for him. Or threatened him. And even with all that, I don't believe he'd have killed because of it."

"We've kept you long enough." Eve got to her feet. "I want to thank you all for your time and your cooperation."

"Is it all right if I contact Angie? I won't discuss any of this," Lilith said quickly. "She doesn't need to hear any of this. She may need another woman to lean on."

"Of course."

"Even under the circumstances," Roarke began, "it was

good to see you both again, and to meet you, Harmony. I have a recording company, you know."

Bolton laughed as he rose to shake Roarke's hand. "Where were you forty years ago? I'll walk you out."

"I'll do that." Harmony popped up. "Go eat your pie—if there's any left. This way."

Harmony wove around her father, led the way back. She waited until they were well out of earshot. "I'd like to speak with you, Lieutenant."

"All right."

"I'm hoping my mother's schedule is clear in the morning so I can go into the office. Surprise!" She smiled a feral smile. "Anybody's been fucking with our company's going to know my wrath. But I can already verify there were shortages—before my parental leave—on some of the projects where Mr. Delgato worked as lead plumber."

"I could use the documentation on that."

"I'll send it to you. Dad didn't want me to look too deep, but I did. When I'd narrowed it down, I had a talk with Delgato—again on my own. He never admitted it, and that was as far as I could take it. My father feels sorry for him, my mother's friends with his wife, and I'm not in charge. Anyway, it eased off some after that talk."

"You never told your father your suspicions?"

"His instinct, his knee-jerk, his default is to take the blame or responsibility. He's slow to take credit, quick to take the blame. He's not to blame for this. And it's not all Delgato."

"Who else?"

Harmony glanced back over her shoulder. "You should take a closer look at the Bardov organization. I can't, or not too close, but I can say a lot of those shortfalls happened on jobs where they were connected."

"Your father continues the business relationship."

Annoyance flickered over Harmony's face. "The entanglement began before my father. Different times, different hands on the wheel."

"I appreciate the information."

Eve stepped out as Harmony opened the door. And Roarke turned back.

"Someone has killed twice. Be careful, won't you?"

"Believe me, I will. And I have to say it. I loved the Icove book, I loved the vid. I'm already halfway through Furst's *Red Horse Legacy*, and I think it may top it. It's got me by the throat. I'm not the risk taker either of you are. Have a good rest of your evening."

"It's never going to end," Eve muttered as they walked to the car. "The books, the vids. You know Nadine's going to write one about the Natural Order crap."

"I do, yes, and expect she'll do a fine job of it."

"That's the damn problem." Eve glanced back at the house. "She knows something or thinks she does. Bardov, her family history."

"They're a lovely, tight-knit family. And when her time comes 'round, she'll run that company with a great deal more passion, more vision than her father."

"And fear will play a role?"

"As it should," Roarke said as he got into the car. "I wonder if we have pie at home. Pie would be a nice complement to some fine dining and a good bottle of red." He took out his PPC. "I'll just push a bit more on Alva Quirk while you get us there."

"If it's not Tovinski who caved her head in and put that noose around Delgato's neck, it's someone like him." While he pushed on his PPC, she pushed through traffic.

She thought of murder and corruption and double-dealing.

And of cherry pie à la mode.

9

By the time Eve drove through the gates of home, her mind had circled from murder to pie and back to murder.

The house rose up, stone towers and turrets etched against a sky bright and blue with summer. Well, not quite summer, she thought, but nearly. Close enough.

Warm and bright enough.

Somebody—Summerset or some landscape guy—had set big stone urns to flank the front door. Flowers in bold reds and purples, flashes of bright yellow with trailing greens speared and spilled out of them.

They made her think of the pots of flowers on the Delgato stoop, so her mind tracked right back to murder.

"Morris should get me at least a prelim tonight on the body. Harvo will work that fiber in tomorrow. But I have to push on DeWinter if she doesn't come through by morning."

She pulled up, tapped her fingers briefly on the wheel. "And I have to write all this up, send Peabody a copy. She'll whine I didn't pull her in when we found Delgato."

He got out as she did, but she noted he still studied his PPC. "You've got something?"

"Maybe. Not quite there as yet, but maybe."

"We could just have pizza and—"

"No." He slid the PPC back into his pocket and took her hand. "A long, hard day deserves a meal."

"Pizza is a meal."

"Not tonight it isn't."

They walked in—more flowers, something as wildly blue as Roarke's eyes, speared out of a copper vase and sweetened the air.

And Summerset, the living cadaver in a perfect black suit, stood in the foyer with the pudge of a cat at his feet.

"You're quite late, but I detect no blood or bruising. What have you done to your boots, Lieutenant?"

Baffled, she looked down. Then remembered. Dumpster, remains in a rubble-filled cellar. "My job."

"Off with them," he ordered as Galahad strolled over to sniff at them.

"What?"

"No point in tracking whatever you've done all over the house. Take them off, and I'll see what I can do to salvage them."

She started to ignore him, but rethought because they were really comfortable boots, and simple ones. Just simple black boots—that had probably cost as much as six months' rent on a one-room apartment in Queens.

"I had to examine a body in a dumpster." She yanked one off.

"That would explain it."

"And remains in a busted-up cellar."

"Just your average day then." Summerset took the boots—delicately, with the tips of his fingers.

"I don't suppose we have pie."

Summerset smiled at Roarke. "As it happens, we do. I baked a cherry pie this afternoon."

Three steps up the stairs with the cat streaking ahead of her, Eve stopped. "You tagged him."

"I didn't, no."

"How'd he know to bake cherry pie?"

"The open market had some lovely cooking cherries today. I've had a slice, after my meal, and can attest the pie came out very well."

"Looking forward to it, thanks," Roarke told him as he started upstairs.

"After your meal. We have some excellent grilled pork chops."

"Sounds like just the thing."

Eve muttered her way up and toward her office. "I didn't trash the boots. They're just bunged up a little."

"He'll unbung them as much as possible." He gave her butt a quick pat. "I'm going to open that wine. I know very well you'll want to set up your board—or boards, in this case— and update your book and so on. But I'm having a glass of wine. You have twenty minutes to do as you must, and I'll take the wine with me and give this search another nudge or two.

"Twenty minutes," he repeated as he selected the bottle from the hidden cabinet in her office. "Then we're having chops."

She'd figured on thirty, and could probably squeeze him for the extra time—especially if he got caught up in the search.

Still, she got right down to it, opening the operations on her command center while the cat made himself comfortable on her sleep chair.

She wrote out the report, starting with the first interview with Angelina Delgato, attached the recording of the crime scene. She shot it to Peabody, who could whine all she wanted, because Eve didn't have time to bother listening. And because she wanted a consult, sent it and everything else she had to Mira, with a request for that consult.

Since that ate up the twenty, she was still setting up her board when Roarke came back.

"I'm almost done. Anything on your end?"

"We'll discuss."

He opened her terrace doors to the air before walking by her and into the kitchen.

"I didn't get anything from Morris yet," she called out as she worked. "I need to give him a nudge."

"Do you think he's lagging about?"

"No, but—"

"Leave it be, Eve. You've had three murders drop in your lap in one day. Take a breath, eat a meal, and let it process in that busy brain of yours for a bit."

"It's been processing."

"No." He came out with two domed plates. "It's been collecting, arranging, intersecting. Now let it sit there awhile."

He set the plates on the table in front of the open doors, then went back for the wine and another glass for her.

"Do you ever get tired of doing all that?" She gestured to the table. "And nagging me to eat something?"

"Yes. But we all have our crosses to bear, don't we?"

"I closed a lot of cases before I had fancy boots getting unbunged and fancy dining at regular intervals."

He poured her wine, poured a second glass for himself. Spoke very pleasantly. "Are you trying to annoy me so I'll say bugger it and leave you alone?"

She stuck her hands in her pockets, stepped back to evaluate a section of her board. "Maybe."

"Do you think it'll work?"

"I could make it work." But she turned around, walked to the table. "But then I'd spend time pissing you off instead of just eating the damn pork chops, then getting back to work."

"Aren't you the clever one?"

She sat, giving him the steely eye as she picked up her

wine. Because, damn it, she wanted some wine, and maybe a breather with it.

"You can be pretty annoying, too."

"Yet somehow we tolerate each other."

He lifted the domes.

"Crap."

And lifted his eyebrows at her snarl. "A problem with the meal I selected?"

"Yeah. It looks really good, and now I'm hungry. I could've done with a couple slices of pie—pizza and cherry. Now I want this chop and those whatever potatoes."

"Scalloped."

"Yeah, those. What is that green stuff? Broccoli?"

"Roasted sesame and ginger broccoli, according to the AC menu. That should disguise the green well enough for you."

"Maybe." But she went for the chop first. "I'm going to say I know you gave this a lot of your day. You did that, initially, because those remains—one an infant—turned up on your property. You may not take blame and responsibility like Harmony says her father does, but it weighs on you."

"It does. And on you."

"It's supposed to weigh on me. You kept giving more of your day because, well, you get a kick out of solving a puzzle in EDD, but then you gave more because I asked you. So I'll eat the stupid green stuff and won't bitch about it. This time."

"I accept the terms of your deal."

She took a small bite of the green stuff, which was surprisingly tasty. But she decided there was no need to sweeten the deal by mentioning it.

"If you want to wait until we eat before telling me whatever progress you made on Alva Quirk, I'm okay with it."

He took a roll, braided and golden and glossy, broke it in two. He passed her half.

"One of the multitudes of reasons I love you is because I know you mean that, even though it's brutally hard for you. One of the reasons I admire you is I know you'll work to the bone for Alva Quirk, and when you get her justice, you'll work to the bone for whoever lay in that cellar all these years. And you'll do the same for Carmine Delgato, even though he may have played a part in Alva's death."

He shook his head when she opened her mouth. "Don't say it's your job. Not to me. It's your calling, your passion, your bloody destiny. And I've found another part of mine is doing what I can do to help you. It matters to me that I can."

"It matters to me that you will."

"Then over this fine dining and good bottle of red, I'll tell you what I know of the sad story of Alva Quirk."

He knew how to tell a story, Eve thought. Even now, when he related essentially a report, he wove it his way.

"I can tell you Alva Elliot, known as Quirk, was born forty-six years ago in Stillwater, Oklahoma. She was the first child of Mason Elliot and Deborah Reems. She had two younger siblings, a brother and a sister."

"Any of her family living?"

"Both siblings. Mason, an electrician, and Deborah, an officer with the Stillwater police, separated when Alva was twelve. In reading the records, and between the lines thereof, it would appear Mason left Stillwater at that time. He joined the rodeo circuit."

"The rodeo circuit? Like . . ." She mimed twirling a lasso.

"Yes, that. He had limited success in that area, but pursued it for three years until injuries forced him to retire. He died at the age of forty-eight from the effects of long-term drug and alcohol abuse."

Eve considered as she ate. "So, though I'll look closer, from those between-the-lines, Mason had a substance abuse problem, which probably made family life difficult. Plus, he wanted to be a cowboy, so he took off, couldn't hack it, and drank and drugged himself to death."

"It would appear so. Meanwhile, Deborah had three children to support and raise. Ages twelve, ten, and eight. There were grandparents on both sides, and the maternal grandparents also lived in Stillwater. Deborah's father was a cop as well."

"Probably got some help there."

"As Deborah moved to a house on the same block as her parents after the separation, I would assume so. When Alva was nineteen, her mother was killed and her grandfather severely injured in what was called the Stillwater Riots."

On a swallow of wine, Eve pointed. "Wait, I know about that. Militia types and what they called sovereign citizen nuts stormed the city where one of their own was being held—charged with murder. A cop killing."

"Yes. They came heavily armed, drawing like-minded others or simply those who hungered for violence and chaos from across the state, across the region. What they claimed was a protest, a show of solidarity, sparked that violence and chaos."

"Bring a thousand or so armed nutcase civilians who think they're fucking soldiers together?" Almost viciously, Eve stabbed a bite of chop. "What could go wrong?"

"And everything did. By the time—it took three days—the violence was quelled, hundreds were dead, hundreds more wounded—those numbers included children, as businesses were burned out and looted, homes destroyed. Among the casualties, Deborah Reems, in the line of duty. Among the wounded, her father, who suffered a spinal injury that paralyzed him."

"Alva was nineteen?"

"In college at Oklahoma State, studying to be a teacher. She came home, one assumes to mourn her mother, help her grandparents, tend to her younger brother and sister. Her grandfather only lived another two years, and her grandmother had a breakdown. Alva's brother, then nineteen, studied criminal justice. Her sister went into nursing. Alva worked as a waitress."

Yes, he knew how to tell a story, and she saw the picture he painted clearly. "She gave up what she wanted to take care of her family."

"So it reads to me. At the age of twenty-four, with her brother now a rookie with the Stillwater cops, her sister getting her nursing degree, her grandmother living in a retirement community, Alva married Garrett Wicker, age thirty, and an officer with the Stillwater cops."

Roarke studied his wife. "For a brief time, only one term, she picked up her education in night school. She and Wicker relocated to a small town on the Oklahoma/Kansas border, where he took a position as a deputy sheriff. There's no record of her continuing her education or any employment during the eight years they lived there. During that time, five years in, her grandmother suffered a fall and died from her injuries. There were some local write-ups, as the woman had lost her daughter, and essentially her husband, during the riots. Alva was listed as too ill to attend."

"Bullshit." The fury of it, for it, pulsed in the back of her throat. "He'd isolated her. Wicker, the husband. Pulled her away from her family, her support network. Forced or badgered her into giving up any idea of a career in teaching. Knocked her around, that's what he did, physically, emotionally, every way."

As if to soothe, Roarke reached over, just brushed his hand over the back of hers. "I'm going to agree with that. From what I picked up on Wicker, he had a number of strikes in Stillwater for excessive force. He's now chief of police in the little backwater town of Moses, where he took Alva."

"She got away from him." Hadn't she thought something along those lines after seeing those old injuries? She got away, Eve thought. Ran.

"New York seems a stretch. She had a brother, a sister."

"Not oddly, to my mind, the brother was brutally beaten only weeks after the grandmother died. Set upon, the reports read, by three men. That same night, after the sister left her brother's bedside, she was also set upon, raped at knifepoint."

"Jesus Christ." She had to push up from the table, pace away, step out to breathe the air on the little balcony.

"That motherfucker. He set it up. I bet they took pictures. 'Here's what'll happen and worse, Alva, you stupid bitch, if you don't do what I say when I say it. If you try to tell anybody what goes on in my house. If you try running back home.'"

She closed her eyes. "'You're nobody, you're nothing. Nobody cares about you. I'm all you've got. I put a roof over your head. I put food on the table. Why do you make me punish you?'"

She came back to the table, sat again. "Her father—substance abuse. Maybe abusive otherwise. Deserted them. She married a cop—she admired cops. They keep the law, the order, they keep the rules. A cop raised her—probably protected her from harm—a cop helped her, gave her love and affection, safety, security. This cop, this husband, hurts her. She must deserve it. She broke the rules he set down, so she deserves it. Her siblings—she gave up her own dreams for them. She has to protect them, like her mother and grandfather."

Again, Roarke brushed a hand over hers. "I believe Mira will agree with your assessment. Alva lived that way for nine years. Then Alva Wicker disappeared. There were missing persons reports issued. Her siblings were interviewed, and from their responses I tend to believe she never contacted them."

"Protected them. He broke her, and she couldn't live that way anymore, but she had to protect what she loved."

"So Alva Quirk was born. The fake ID is well done, not perfect, but well done. A pro or someone with experience certainly. They laid a decent background from 2047 back."

"I didn't find any background."

"Washed, at a later time. In that, she changed her hair— very short and brown, where she was born very blond. Brown eyes, when she'd been born with blue. Quirk, two years older than actuality, and born in Dayton, Ohio, only child and so on. She listed her address, beginning in 2048, as Morgantown, West Virginia, and her employment as a housekeeper in a nearby resort. Enough time, I should be able to track down where the ID was made, but more importantly to you, I'd think, is she wiped it again in 2052. So Quirk ceased to exist."

"Something spooked her. She saw something, or someone, and got spooked. Wiped herself out again and went poof. But—"

"What you have on her? The ID? It's from a check-in at the Chelsea Shelter. Just bare bones, as is often the case. She gave them the name she'd taken, and nothing else. So she popped up again as Quirk, in New York. No background."

"I need to talk to her siblings."

"Both still in Oklahoma. I sent you the current contact information."

"Did Wicker ever divorce her?"

"He did, and remarried, divorced again. Remarried again. No children."

"Good." She grabbed her wine, took a quick drink. "Good. He doesn't get notification. What he will get is an investigation. DeWinter has to confirm the time line of those injuries. If

I can find Alva's place, where she kept her books. Maybe she wrote stuff down, maybe the rules she broke, the punishment he gave her."

"It's years ago, Eve. More than a dozen since she ran from him. And he's a cop."

Slowly, Eve shook her head. "No, he's an abuser with a badge, and that's the worst kind. He doesn't get to keep the badge. I may not be able to see that he's charged and convicted and locked up for domestic abuse, though I'm going to give it a solid try. But he's not going to keep the badge."

She looked straight into Roarke's eyes. "We're not going to let him. You've given me enough, you dug, you worked, and you gave me what I needed. I'm going to take that and do what needs doing. We—you and me—we're not going to let him hold a badge."

She picked up her wine again, sipped slowly. "We know what it's like—you and me—to live with someone who uses power and authority to hurt and terrorize us. I felt that from her. That's not woo-woo crap."

"Isn't it?" he asked her.

"No, it's instinct and training. It's following your gut and following leads. She lived with that. Nine years. I lived with it for eight, you lived with it longer. She broke. I broke. You never did."

"I'm not looking at a woman who broke."

"I broke," she repeated. "I mended. She'd started to mend, the way I see this. Got away, covered herself, protected her family, got a job. Then something or someone cracked the seal she'd put over the break."

She set the glass down again. "Wicker gave her near to a decade of abuse, and he's going to pay for it just like whoever bashed her skull in and tossed her in a dumpster's going to pay."

She felt her throat closing up, struggled against it. "I have a badge. And that's what I do."

Roarke rose, came around the table. He put his arms around her, just held her.

"I'm fine. I'm okay."

"You're more than both no matter how this upsets you and reminds you. And you're right in everything you said. You have the right of it." He drew back, cupped her face. "We won't let him keep the badge. And we won't let those who killed a harmless woman who'd already suffered get away with it."

She cupped his face in turn, touched her lips to his. "This is one of the multitudes for me."

With a light laugh, he kissed her back. "Good to know."

Her comp signaled an incoming. "Let that be Morris. Sorry, I need to see."

"Go. I'll see to the dishes before I see what else might have come through on Alva."

"I'll get to them later. Don't—"

She broke off as she called up the message and attached report.

Roarke saw her eyes narrow, saw the flat and yet fierce look of cop in them. And saw to the dishes.

When he came back, she stood at her board, added the report, the autopsy photos.

"A paralytic, into the throat. The pressure syringe mark would likely have been covered completely by the bruising if we hadn't found him so fast. He wasn't dead when we did, still had a heartbeat, so more bruising would have formed if he'd hung there longer."

"If you hadn't found the mark, Morris would have."

"Maybe. Probably, yeah, but if I'm the killer, I'm thinking who's going to bother to look real hard? Some mope whose wife booted him, who can't pay the rent on a flop, who's gambling his way into hell? Reads suicide. Especially since if we hadn't found him when we did, gotten him to Morris fast, the paralytic wouldn't have shown on any tox screen. Morris said it would have dissipated in another two hours, tops."

She stepped back. "Now it's murder, and I believe I have motive and means. I'll nail down the opportunity when I find out where Tovinski was. One way or the other, he's going to spend some time in my box."

"Do you want me to look at him more deeply?"

"No, I've got that. If you'd stick with Alva—anything else you can find. Then I want to start on financials. The elder Singers, Yuri Bardov, Tovinski—you can take that area on him. Anything hinky, anything I can use as a lever."

"A reward mixed in with the work. And pie to follow. I insist."

"Sure, pie to follow."

She programmed coffee, then sat to write it all up, sent the update to Peabody and to Mira.

Then she called Oklahoma. She started with the cop brother.

The cheerful blonde in her late teens answered with a wide grin. "Hello, New York City! What's happening?"

"I'd like to speak with Trent Elliot."

"Sure. He's just taking it chill in his burrow with a beer before he watches the game. I've never been to New York City. Is it frosty extreme?"

"I think so, most of the time."

"I gotta get there." The girl spoke on the move, crossed what Eve thought was a kitchen—light still poured in the windows—then started down some stairs.

Eve clearly heard pregame commentary—Yankee Stadium, Yankees versus the Oklahoma Buffaloes.

"Hey, Pops! Someone wants to talk to you."

"Is that Hank? Tell him to blow. I'm not biting."

"No, it's a woman, from actual New York."

The 'link changed hands. Eve saw a very blond—with some white sprinkles—man with a square jaw, annoyed blue eyes. "Who is this?"

"Detective Elliot, this is Lieutenant Dallas, New York City Police and Security."

"Did that asshole Hank put you up to this? You tell him the Buffaloes are going to kick some Yankee ass tonight."

"Detective, I'm contacting you regarding your sister."

"Chantal? What the—"

"No, Alva."

"Alva?" He came straight up out of his chair. "Alva's in New York? What the hell is she doing in New York? I want to talk to her."

"Detective Elliot, I regret to inform you—"

"No." He snapped it out. "Goddamn it. No."

"Pops? What's wrong?"

"It's okay, baby. Go on up. I need to talk now."

"I'm getting Mom."

"Not yet, Alva. I'll come up when I'm done. We'll all talk. My youngest girl," he said as he sat again. "We named her after my sister. My big sister. Oh, son of a bitch. What happened?"

She opted to talk cop to cop, and he listened as she took him through it.

"I want you to know, and I'm not bullshitting you, I have a strong avenue to pursue. I've made considerable progress already, and will continue. We were able to uncover her original ID, which led us to you and your younger sister."

"She was living on the street." His voice trembled, just a little, with both rage and grief.

"She was. She took care of herself, the cops on the beat

liked her. She used a couple of shelters when she wanted, and they liked her. She gave people origami flowers and birds and animals. She kept a book so she could report to the cops if somebody littered, for instance."

"Crime and punishment," he murmured.

"Yeah, you could say."

"No, it's from our mother. When we were kids, she kept a chart—the crime, the punishment. Little shit, you know, kid shit. Hit your sister—crime—punishment—lose thirty minutes' gaming time. Don't eat your vegetables—no dessert. Like that.

"Alva, she was always the rule follower—used to piss me off sometimes. She was always the responsible one. She didn't tattle on me or Chantal, unless it was major, but she started keeping a notebook. Kid stuff. I guess she went back to doing that."

His eyes went glossy with tears, but he let out a long breath until he had them under control. "She ran from that son of a bitch she married. That's what happened. We hardly ever saw her after they moved, hardly ever got to talk to her. She always said how everything was fine, was great. How happy she was. I didn't half believe her, but she kept saying it, and how she loved her house, and living in the country, having all the room. And—and—how there was so much sad back home. Mom, Grandpap, Grandma, all gone."

He had to take those deep breaths again. "Was he hurting her? Chantal worried about that, but whenever I asked her, asked Alva, she just laughed it off. He was the sweetest husband in the world.

"Fuck that, he had a rep here in Stillwater. *Sweet* didn't apply."

"I'm verifying old injuries with a forensic anthropologist. She had several."

"I knew it, part of me knew it. Goddamn it! Why didn't she come home? We'd've taken care of her like she took care of us."

"Shortly after your grandmother died you were attacked and badly beaten."

"Yeah, that's right. Laid me up good for . . ." He came out of his chair again. "He set that up? Bastard had friends on both sides of the law around here back then. He set me up. And Chantal, Jesus God, she was raped while I was in the hospital. He did that to keep her quiet. Alva . . . She'd have died to protect us."

"Detective. I need you to listen to me. To stay calm and listen."

"He's not going to sit on his fat ass and get away with what he did to my sisters."

"No, he's not. You have to leave it to me."

Those blue eyes went molten. "My sisters, Lieutenant New Fucking York."

"He's not going to get away with it, but if you go after him and do what I know you want to do, he will. You can beat the hell out of him, end up losing your badge, doing time for assault, and he'll come out of it a victim."

"Not if he's dead."

"I'm ignoring that. You're a cop, a solid cop like your mother, like your grandfather. He's scum, and he's not going to keep the badge he doesn't deserve. I'm asking you to give me time to get Alva justice. For what happened then, for what happened now."

"And if you don't?"

"I helped lift her out of that dumpster this morning. I stood over her when she was on the slab in the morgue. I've spent the day finding everything I could about her and for her. Finding you, so someone who loved her would know, would come, would take her home again. There is no *don't* for me. I'm standing for Alva, and I'll make certain she gets justice."

His eyes teared up again. "She wanted to be a teacher."

"I know. She gave it up when your mother was killed and your grandfather was injured. She gave it up for you and your sister. Don't let your very justifiable rage and grief stop me from taking down Garrett Wicker for what he did to her for nine years, what he did that set her on the path to that goddamn dumpster."

He swiped at his eyes. "I have to talk to my sister, to Chantal."

"Do you want me to notify her?"

"No, no, that's for me. I'm sorry I took a punch at you."

"Forget it."

"I'm sorry for it," he repeated. "I know you're right. I know what my mother would say, my grandpap. Hell, what Alva the rule follower would say. I know you're right. I'm going to give you all the time I can stomach. Let's say a week. If by then you're not any closer to taking down Wicker for what he did, I'm not making any promises."

"It won't take a week."

"Can I use this number to contact you when we've made arrangements to come out there? To come for Alva."

"Yes, anytime."

He rubbed his face. "Later there, right. Like an hour?"

"Yeah, something like that."

"Thank you, Lieutenant, for looking out for her. I expect I'll be in touch tomorrow."

"I'm sorry for your loss, Detective."

"I think you really are. Good night."

10

After the conversation, Eve rose and walked to the board to study Alva.

"Somebody knew you, loved you. They'll take you home."

No one had known her, Eve thought, or loved her when she'd wandered the streets, a child bloodied, broken, traumatized.

But someone had helped her.

"I'm not finished helping you."

The hell with the time, she decided, and went back to her command center and contacted DeWinter.

"Are you ever off duty?" DeWinter demanded.

"I need a time line on Alva Quirk's previous injuries. I'll take your best guess."

DeWinter lifted a glass of straw-colored wine, sipped delicately. "I don't guess."

"Listen, we've ID'd her. I have a name. I have a history that includes what reads clearly as a nine-year abusive marriage to a cop. Her mother was a cop, and went down in the line. Her grandfather was a cop, and he went down in the line. Before she hit twenty, she gave up her own ambitions so she could take care of her younger siblings. She trusted cops, she did everything right, and he broke her bones, blackened her eyes, isolated her from everything she loved and valued."

Annoyance fought a war with distress over DeWinter's face. "Dallas—"

"He's still a cop, head cop in some podunk town in Oklahoma."

"Do you believe he came to New York and killed her?"

"No. I believe he broke her, mind, body, spirit, and she'd be alive today if he hadn't. I want his badge. If her injuries occurred during the time frame of those nine years, I'll make him pay."

"I set aside other work to prioritize this case. You'll have a full report in the morning."

"I just got off the 'link with Alva's brother." Keep saying her name, Eve thought. Make it personal. "I had to tell him we found her, and she's dead. Their father was a drunk, a junkie, and took off when she was twelve. Their mother went down in the Stillwater Riots when she was nineteen. Alva wanted to be a teacher, but she gave it up. Gave it all up. And when her family was settled, she married a cop.

"He broke her."

"Damn it. Give me a minute."

The screen went to holding blue.

"You have a way," Roarke told her, and so deep was her focus, Eve jolted.

"Jesus, make some noise."

"I have more for you when you're finished badgering Garnet. I'll tell you over pie."

DeWinter came back. "I haven't organized this into a report as yet."

"Just give me the time line. The report can wait."

"I determined that the victim was forty-six years of age at TOD. The earlier, nonfatal injuries occurred over a period of eight to nine years. The victim would have sustained these injuries after the age of twenty-four and before the age of thirty-five, with the earliest, the fractured rib, occurring at approximately age twenty-five and the severe orbital injury and the later break on the finger of the right hand at approximately age thirty-three. I have more specific data on each injury, but any and all ages will be approximate and within a small margin of error."

"She was twenty-four when she married the son of a bitch. She'd have been twenty-five when he relocated her across the state from her family. The orbital and other facial injuries? That would come in shortly before the ID wash and replacement."

"Then you have what you need. And you'll know he very likely abused her before they relocated. Slaps, intimidation, shoves, and so on that wouldn't show."

"Yeah, I know how it works, like I know it wouldn't show up now how many times he raped her."

"No." DeWinter took another small sip of wine. "It wouldn't. I hope you'll succeed in making him pay. I hope our work here helps you do that."

"Get me the report. I'll do the rest. Thanks—when he pays, you get part of that, so you earned the wine."

"I already earned the wine by convincing my daughter that despite not having school tomorrow, she still has a bedtime. And now I'll drink it. Good night."

"You have what you needed," Roarke said as he came back in. He set a slice of pie beside her before taking a seat at her auxiliary with his own.

"Yeah, I do." She took a bite. "God. Really good pie."

"Are we going to Oklahoma?"

"No." Unless she had absolutely, totally, and completely no choice.

"Town chief of police, that's an appointed position. I'll do a run on the mayor, the town council, whoever, see if I get a sense who'd back him, who won't. I get that started, and I contact the fuck, tell him about Alva, get him to come to me."

"Your turf, your box."

"Damn right. I send a copy of DeWinter's report, which will have pictures of the injuries and be all scientific and inarguable, to whoever's in charge back there. And I'll let them know big, bad New York cops are going to be talking to people out there, getting the county and state boys interested in talking to people. People like the second ex-wife, neighbors, voters."

She took another bite. Angled her head as another thought occurred. "And I've got a way to spread the word on him, spread it far, spread it thick. After I get the report."

He let out a short laugh. "I believe I know how you intend to spread that word. Nadine's on book tour, you know."

"She's a reporter right down to the soles of her fancy shoes. Spreading the word's what she does." She ate more pie. "I may not be able to nail him for Alva—think I can, but if not? Abusers like that don't change. There'll be plenty of others with stories to tell once the door opens. He'll lose the badge and have civil if not criminal charges up to his ass before I'm finished."

"I may be able to help you with that."

"You know any muckety-mucks in Oklahoma?"

"Most likely, but I found someone who may be able to speak for Alva. I found the source of the ID."

"That's quick work."

"I was nearly there, and it fell into place after a thought and another conversation I had."

"What thought? Who'd you talk to?"

"Shelters create official IDs—quite legally, through a process. But when you look at abuse shelters, those who seek shelter there aren't always looking for that. They may often want to disappear, just as Alva did. And so it occurred to me there might be some willing to help with that."

"With fake IDs? Who'd you talk to?"

"Someone I thought might have some knowledge of a network that helps provide this service."

"You're not going to tell me."

"I'm not, no, but the conversation narrowed the search, particularly when one of the names I had founded a women's shelter in Dayton, and did so five years before Alva's Dayton ID. This name interested me in particular, as this woman did time."

"For what? Shit, for forging IDs?"

Amused at her instant irritation—such a cop—Roarke enjoyed more pie.

"She doesn't hide the fact, and founded the shelter after she served that time. Because, it seems, she learned many of the women inside with her were also victims of abuse. From lovers, johns, spouses, parents. It changed her, so she said, made her want to do something that could help, that could break the cycle. The Home Safe Women's Shelter is highly regarded."

"You can stop playing her legal rep."

"Now I'm a lawyer? How many ways can you insult the man you love?"

"I've got more when I need them. Do I get that name?"

"Of course. And a contact number." He handed her a mini-disc. "All the data and background's on there. And this is very good pie."

Eve plugged it in. "Allysa Gray, mixed race, age sixty-one. One marriage, one divorce, no offspring. You didn't mention the assault charge."

"Dropped, wasn't it? If you glance through, you'll see her husband—they were estranged—came at her outside her house. He got two punches in before she wailed on him. They were both charged. His stuck, hers didn't, particularly after her history showed multiple nine-one-one calls prior to her moving out and filing for divorce."

"Yeah, I see it. Got popped for the ID forgery three years later."

"And served her time. A year afterward she opened Home Safe."

"Yeah, yeah."

He just smiled. "You've learned to live with a former criminal, haven't you, darling Eve?"

She smiled back. "It's a process." She picked up her 'link.

"You're contacting her now?"

"That's right, and don't give me the time and Earth-rotation crap. I don't care what time it is there."

Rising, he picked up the empty pie plates. "Put it on the wall screen, would you? I'd like to observe."

Since he'd found the woman, Eve couldn't think of any objection. She switched the communication mode, swiveled to face the wall screen.

"Allysa Gray," the woman announced as she came onscreen.

Her hair, bold, bright red with a lot of gold streaks, fell in fluffy disorder around her narrow, foxy face. Eyes heavy-lidded and deep brown looked straight into Eve's.

Eve noted she sat at a desk, and now picked up a mug, put her slippered feet on the desk, and smiled.

"Well, look at this. I know that face. What can I do for you, Dallas, Lieutenant Eve?"

"Do we know each other, Ms. Gray?"

"Never met, but I've seen your face, read about your work. Liked that book and vid, too. What would New York's top murder cop want with me?"

"Do you know an Alva Quirk?"

Now there, Eve thought, was a poker face.

"Why do you ask?"

"I'm the primary investigator on her murder."

That poker face vanished into shock. Anger and sorrow came on its heels. "Alva? She went to New York? She's dead? He killed her? How did that bastard find her after all these years?"

"Which bastard would that be?"

"If you found me, you know damn well I'm talking about that wife-beating son of a fuck Garrett Wicker."

"I don't believe that particular son of a fuck found her, or killed her."

"What happened to her? Goddamn it. Give me a second, would you? Tea, my ass." She shoved up, crossed the room—home office to Eve's eye—opened a cupboard. A lithe calico cat leaped down from the top of it, sauntered away while Allysa poured what looked to be a glass of bourbon, neat.

She sat, lifted the glass. "To sweet Alva." She knocked back a swallow. "What happened?"

"She suffered a severe and fatal head blow in the early hours of this morning, and was found in a dumpster on a working construction site at start of shift."

"Aw, Jesus. How long had she been in New York?"

"I can't say for certain. She was living on the streets."

"On the streets." Allysa bolted up straight. "Why? Oh, bullshit, why ask why? Fear's why. Are you sure he didn't find her?"

"I believe the motive for her murder wasn't personal in that way. I will be speaking with Wicker before I'm done."

"He tormented and beat and told her she was nothing, for years."

"How did she get away? She told you."

"He broke her fingers on one hand, burnt her other hand on the stove because she didn't have dinner on the table fast enough. Then he blackened her eye for good measure. So bad she was afraid she'd never see out of it again.

"Then he raped her, and told her, like always, he hated the way she made him punish her. She told me she couldn't think straight the next morning. That it felt like she was dreaming."

Yes, Eve thought, she understood that. She'd lived that.

"After he went to work, she stuffed her purse with whatever money was in the house. She got in the car—she had one for running errands, and he kept track of her mileage. She drove and drove and drove. She didn't remember how far, until she ran out of gas. Then she left the car and started walking. She didn't remember much of that, either.

"Anyway, a woman in a pickup came by, stopped, saw the state she was in. Alva got hysterical when the woman wanted to take her to the doctor or the sheriff, so didn't. She took her home—a ranch—and she fixed her up as best she could. She was afraid to stay, so the woman gave her a hat, sunshades to hide the eye, packed food for her, and drove her for an hour or so to a bus station. She remembers changing buses in Missouri. She had family, but—"

"I know about that. I've spoken to her brother."

"Then you know what he did, how he had her brother beaten, her sister raped, and used that to keep her in line. She wasn't thinking when she left, or she wouldn't have. She didn't go to them when she started thinking again because he'd find her and hurt them. In any case, a couple days later, she ended up in Dayton. She didn't have much money left. As fate would have it, she was sitting on a bench, not sure what to do, and I walked by. She was only a few blocks from the shelter. I knew what I was looking at. I'd seen it too many times."

She paused to drink again. "So I sat down beside her, and I told her I could help her, that I had a place she'd be safe.

She was exhausted, every part of her. She went along with me like a little puppy. She was badly damaged, Dallas. Not just physically."

"I know it."

"So damaged, but she had this sweetness. When she healed up—her hands—she pitched in. Nobody had to tell her to help with the washing or the cooking, or give a tired mother a break and rock a baby. One of our ladies did origami, and she took right to it. Loved sitting there making little animals and flowers."

"She kept up with that."

"Did she? I'm glad. It gave her some joy. Are you going to ding me about the ID?"

"No. I'm not recording this, and it won't go in the file, not that part of it. You can record what I say next as insurance."

Allysa pursed her lips, leaned forward to manually go to record. "Okay."

"You won't be charged or prosecuted for any fraudulent identification you've generated, assisted in generating, have knowledge of, possess equipment for. None of that information will go beyond this room. If I break my word on that, you have the means to bring me up on charges."

"Why are you doing that?"

"Because she deserves justice. Because the ones who hurt her, last night, years ago? Those sons of fucks need to pay. I'm going to see they do."

For a long moment, Allysa said nothing. Then she gave one short nod. "I believe you, and I'm deleting the recording. Trust for trust. She was here six, seven months, and she knew enough about the shelter to know we always needed the room for the next. When she was ready, I made her ID, worked with her on the background. I had some contacts and I got her a job in housekeeping at a resort in West Virginia. Pretty place, nice country, good, honest work. She'd check in pretty regular. She was happy. She was never going to be all the way right again, do you understand?"

"Yes."

"He'd broken something in her, and it just couldn't mend all the way through. But she was happy, productive, safe. And one day she called, full panic. She was on the run. They had a big law-and-order-type convention at the resort. She saw him. I calmed her down as best I could, but she'd already bolted, sure he'd found her, he'd come for her, and begged me to wipe her ID again. I told her she could come back here, or I'd make arrangements at another shelter for her, but she just said she had to run. And that was that. I never heard from her again."

"Do you have any documentation of her injuries when she came to your shelter?"

Allysa's lips spread in a thin smile. "You really will go after the fucker. Yeah, we'd have photos and a medical report. We had—and have—a doctor who comes to the shelter when and if a guest is too afraid for a hospital or health center."

"I'd appreciate a copy."

"I'll dig it out when I'm at work. I'll go in early. If you need it sooner, I'll go in tonight."

"The morning's fine. Do you remember if Alva kept a notebook?"

"Alva and her famous notebooks. Yeah, she did. She told me how she started keeping one when she was a kid. Law-and-order thing, mostly a record of sibling infractions, or classmates. Around here, she modified it. She called them her Support Reports. When somebody needed a hug or somebody else to listen. When somebody went out of their way to help with a kid or some of the domestic work, that kind of thing.

"Damn it." Allysa paused, pressed her fingers to her eyes. "Another second."

"Take your time."

She dropped her hands, took another drink. "She hid them away during her marriage because she kept a record of what he said she did wrong—a lot of guilt there, a lot of self-blame we tried to work through. And she kept a record of the hits, the breaks, the rapes."

Eve felt the lift in her chest. "She wrote down what he did? When he did it?"

"Lifelong habit. She documented all of it. Do you want me to send you the notebooks?"

Eve's spine snapped straight as a ruler. "You have them?"

"She left them behind. She said she was leaving all of that behind and starting a new life. New name, new Alva. I kept them because you just never know. I can ship them to you in the morning."

"No." She didn't want to trust them to a shipping company. "I'm going to ask you for a solid, Allysa."

"It's for Alva. Ask away."

"I can have a couple cops from my department on a shuttle and to your shelter within a couple hours."

"I've got the books here. I kept them here, in my home office. I'll have them ready, and the medical report and photos when your people get here. I'd like a solid back."

"What do you need?"

"Keep me in the loop—I want to know when you nail that Wicker fucker. And when you cage up whoever killed her. One more? If her family's going to have a service or memorial, I'd like to know. I'd like to go."

"I'll do all of that."

"It's hard to lose one, I guess you know. She had a sweet heart. A lot of hard breaks through her life, but she kept that sweet heart."

"Her brother, possibly her sister as well, are coming to New York for her. I'd like to give them your name and contact."

"Yes, please. I'll wait for your people."

"Thanks for all of this."

"Back at you, Dallas." Now Allysa lifted the glass in a toast. "Hunt them down."

"That's the plan."

"A shuttle's being prepped," Roarke told her when she ended the call. "Who are you sending?"

"They can take a public . . ." Quicker, easier, she admitted as Roarke just waited. "Uniform Carmichael. He'll probably take Shelby. Thanks."

She turned back to contact Carmichael, give him the assignment and information he needed.

"Seal and label it, on the record. Take it straight into Evidence when you get back. I'll pull it out in the morning."

Because she hadn't switched modes back, Officer Carmichael nodded on her wall screen. "Yes, sir. I'll notify Shelby, pick her up on the way to the shuttle."

Rather than his uniform, he wore a red T-shirt, buff-colored khakis. "You can go in soft clothes. Is that the game?" she asked, because she heard the distinctive *thwack* of bat to ball, followed by cheers.

"Long foul," he said. "We're bottom of the eleventh, Lieutenant, tied up at six each. It hasn't been what you'd call a pitcher's duel."

"I'll say. Text when you have the evidence in hand, Officer, and when it's been checked into Evidence."

"Yes, sir."

"Dallas out."

She swiveled back to Roarke, who sat on the sleep chair with the cat sprawled over his lap. Eve ran both hands over her hair. "She wrote it all down, and the woman who gave her a fresh start, a new life—at least for a while—kept the books."

Roarke kept stroking the cat, who purred like a jet shuttle. "I heard."

"I'm going to crush Garrett Wicker."

"I know."

"I need to write this up. In the morning, I have to check with Harvo on the fabric trace, check in with Morris. I want that consult with Mira. And I guess I'm going to tap you for a goddamn jet-copter to make it easier for me to push on Yuri Bardov."

Coming together, she thought. She could feel it coming together.

"And since they're in the same area with their big-ass country estates, I'll talk to Elinor Bolton Singer. I'll round up J. B. Singer. That'll be like a flock of birds with the one rock, and it'll overlap both cases. It should give me some sense, some information to pull from once I close Alva's case and move to Jane Doe's remains."

"I have more for you on the plans and specs and blueprints on the original building where we found those remains."

"I'll want them as soon as I close this one. I'm sorry, but—"

He shook his head. "Your investigation needs to be logical and focused. You know her." Roarke gestured toward the board. "And though she didn't die first, she comes first."

"That's it, but there's going to be that overlap. There's already a connection point with the Singers. Why don't you give me an overview or a couple of highlights if anything applies? I can keep it working in the back of my mind. You're not the only one who can multitask."

"Well then, I can tell you something I found very interesting when the analyses confirmed it just a bit ago."

"Which is?"

"After you left this morning, and we went about shutting down the project, both Mackie— You'll remember him."

"Sure."

"Both he and I noticed a few things. One, already mentioned, is the proposed wine cellar's dimensions were off—which I've confirmed from the original plans. The inner wall, though designed to appear as an exterior, was, in fact, three feet in from the actual exterior wall."

"Yeah, I caught that. To hide the body."

"A logical conclusion, yes. But what we noticed was quality and material. And so, to satisfy our curiosity, we took a few samples."

"What do you mean you took samples? It's a crime scene."

His tone marked a cool contrast with her instant outrage.

"And you've, no doubt, taken your own and you'll do your own lab tests, but it remains my property and I bloody well wanted to know. So I went down—"

"You went down there?"

"Appropriately sealed, though, Lieutenant, you and I both know there had already been considerable activity in that area since the murder. The remains had been removed by then, and the evidence collected. I took a few moments to take samples from the floor, what had been the ceiling, the exterior wall, and that inner wall."

"You weren't cleared for that. Damn it, Roarke."

He met her angry glare with a careless shrug.

"Neither had any official document been served, at that point, to prevent me. Would you like to argue about it, or would you like to know what we found?"

"Both."

"Multitasking." After giving Galahad a last rub, Roarke hefted him up, set him aside, then rose. He walked over to sit on the leg of her command center. "To, perhaps, hold off the argument, let me say you had, rightfully, left the scene to go back to Alva Quirk. We had, cooperatively, begun the process of shutting down the work, relocating the workers in anticipation of the official paperwork."

"If you'd seen something, you should have reported it to the primary investigator."

"And so I am, though we've both been very busy for, what is it, sixteen, seventeen hours now? And the results verified what I saw while you were speaking with the brother of your victim."

"Fuck it. What the hell did you see?"

"As you're aware, we razed what was left of that building, and continued demolition on the concrete, into that cellar because it was unsafe. Substandard materials. That's not unusual, as again you're aware, for post-Urban construction, not for the three years or so before regulations locked back into place. But that inner wall, you see—or I could, Mackie could—it hadn't crumbled as easily or in the same way. It had a different texture to the brick. And while the ceiling above the wine cellar was low-grade preformed concrete, the section, that three-foot section between the brick interior and concrete exterior wall? Top grade, poured and formed on-site to my eye, and Mackie's."

"Done to hide her body."

"These weren't discrepancies we found important prior to finding the bodies. Just idiosyncrasies of the era, the builder, or so we thought. So I took the samples, and as we suspected, everything else used, substandard. But not that single wall, not the span above it. That was built with good, solid brick—very costly at that time—and top-grade mortar, and poured concrete."

"How come she wasn't buried in the concrete?"

"It was formed up, you see, to the exterior wall. And then that section—and only that section—poured, leveled, left to set. The work we could see—as, if you remember from your trip down, that wall wasn't fully down—that was on the sloppy side, with uneven joints, too much mortar or not enough. Not the work, I'd say, of a professional bricklayer or stonemason, but superior material. That single wall."

"Needed it to hold up, willing to spend more—or steal better material—to make sure it would."

"Precisely. You'll have the report, or you can do your own."

"The sweepers would have taken samples. We're not idiots."

"I would never think, much less say, you were. But I could, and did, expedite mine. You have necessary priorities, as does your lab. I wanted to know. The child, Eve. The woman was bad enough, but those tiny bones . . ."

"I want to be pissed. I am pissed, but not as much as I should be, or want to be. Because . . . I went down there, I looked at them up close. Tiny bones," she repeated and had to get up, had to pace.

"It made me think about what's going on inside Mavis, which creeps me out, sure, but . . . It hits cops, too, no matter how long you've been on the job, it hits when it's a kid."

She shook it off, had to shake it off. "I'll bribe Dickhead to push on our analysis. It has to run through the chain, Roarke, to make sure it holds up in court when we have who did it."

"Understood."

"They're not going to get away with it. I don't care if it's Singer's hundred-and-whatever-year-old grandmother who built that wall, I'm tossing whoever put them behind it in a cage."

He smiled a little. "She wouldn't have been a hundred and whatever at the time."

"Don't know how old, exactly, she would have been until DeWinter does her work. But nothing in the background shows she knows any more about laying bricks than I do.

Maybe sloppy work, but I'd think more rushed, nervous, had to do it at night, right?"

Hands in her pockets now, she wandered the room. "At night when nobody else is on the site. You can't have a bunch of construction guys around when you're walling up the body of a pregnant woman. Can't have them around when you put bullets into her."

Frowning, she circled around to the other side of her board. "It has to be at night, all of it, the kill, getting the good materials, using them. All the same night.

"Had to put the ceiling in, too, or someone would see her, someone would notice the three feet and a body. They had to have the—what, boards, beams?"

"Support beams—the steel. And joists."

"Those, she falls between them. They hadn't done the floor yet, hadn't cleared all the rock because she fell on rocks. Get the wall up, cover at least that three feet of floor. Doing the form, you said. Forming it up, then pouring the concrete. A lot to do, a lot to do fast."

She stuck her hands in her pockets again. "The floor of the main part—the restaurant part—that was concrete, like the wine cellar."

"The plans were for an industrial look—an upscale industrial ambiance."

"So how do you put that in, form it so you're not just dumping the stuff so it goes down to the lower floor?"

"Supports—those joists—form it out, install the subflooring, the base. Layer the cement over the subfloor. Pour, level, smooth."

"Got it. They didn't have to worry about the rest as long as she was covered, all sides. They could use the other stuff for the rest. Wanted the higher grade for the fucking coffin they put her in."

He walked over to her, slid his arms around her from

behind. "And I've pulled your focus away from your priority."

"It's just something I can let simmer around. Plus, I can work it into my interviews tomorrow."

"Let me know when you need the copter to go upstate."

"Yeah, yeah. Now I'm going to write up what I got from Gray, and let all that simmer."

11

Once she accepted she couldn't do anything more until morning, and kept covering the same ground, Eve shut down.

She walked over to the adjoining door to Roarke's office.

He sat at his own command center, hair tied back, jacket off, sleeves rolled to his elbows.

The cat, she noted, had deserted them both, and was unquestionably stretched out across their bed.

"I'm closing up shop," she told him.

He didn't glance up, certainly didn't jolt as she had earlier, but finished whatever he had on his desk screen.

"Without me finding you asleep at your desk or nudging you to give it a rest?"

"You want me back in pissed mode?"

"Not at all. Just pleasantly surprised. I'm happy to close down as well, in just one minute."

"What are you working on?"

"I had some business of my own, then I thought to turn to the fun of sliding into the financials of other people."

"Like who?"

"I've the Singers going in one area, and so far I believe the family has very clever, very enterprising financial managers.

Nothing you could deem illegal, just close to a shade of shady, but not over the line.

"So far," he added, and finally looked at her.

"Yuri Bardov, that's another matter. Very complex, very layered—also clever, but I'll wind my way through. A smart, experienced man is Yuri. His wife's nephew isn't quite so smart."

She heard the smug, very clearly. "You've got something on him."

"He apparently thinks that by setting up some of his shell accounts in the Caymans and Russia as well as New York, he doesn't need to bother with all the layers—and what those layers cost—as his uncle does. He also spends lavishly. I can't say if his wife—who lives very well—and their children—who are receiving an excellent private school education—are aware he keeps women."

"Side pieces? Plural?"

"Three, and kept women seems the right term in this case, as he pays for the lovely villa on Corfu for one—along with the minor female child, whose expenses he covers."

"He's got another kid."

"That would be my conclusion, as he transfers funds, monthly, into an account for her education, her clothing, her ballet lessons, and so on."

He leaned back, gestured to the screen, where Eve saw the ID shot of a woman in her early forties and a minor female, age fourteen. "It's the same for the woman in Prague, and the two minors—male and female—whom he supports."

The screen split, showing three more IDs. Adult female, middle thirties, two minors, ages eight and six.

"More recently he opened yet another account after purchasing a home in Vermont for a third woman. Going by medical records she's about thirty weeks pregnant."

Eve studied the next photo. "Busy guy."

"He is, and one who apparently insists on spreading his seed. A man in his position and with his, let's say resources, could easily pressure a woman to terminate a pregnancy—and one would think would use some standard caution to prevent same in the first place."

Hands in her pockets now, Eve rocked back and forth on her heels. All three women, she noted, were dark-eyed brunettes.

So he had a type.

"All of this paid for out of hidden accounts?"

"Hidden, and not very well, and not legal."

"I need to—"

"You'll have it all." Roarke rose as he spoke. "All tidy and clearly drawn in the morning so you can use it as a hammer when you get him in the box."

"It's a really big hammer. No, it's a bunch of hammers. Hidden accounts? Wife doesn't know. Maybe she knows he cats around, but I'm betting she doesn't know her kid has a bunch of half sibs or her husband's shelling out all that money, every month."

"And a very tidy sum it is." Roarke took her hand as they walked, brought it to his lips. "I have to thank you for giving me such an enjoyable task to end a long day."

"I wonder if his uncle knows."

"Now there's a thought. I imagine Bardov might think boys will be boys about the catting about, although one hears he doesn't do the same himself. Never has."

"Is that what one hears?"

"It is. Regardless, those particular accounts aren't set up through the business, or through the financial firm that Bardov uses, and that Tovinski uses for all the rest."

"Where does he get the money for those accounts? All that extra dough?"

At the doorway of their bedroom, Roarke turned her into

him. "Aren't you the clever one? And now I wonder if all the funds come from Bardov-sanctioned jobs and tasks."

"Huh." She circled her arms around him. "That makes you a clever one, too. He could be moonlighting so he can pay all that out without his wife, his uncle knowing."

"I'll scratch through more in the morning. Now, why don't we find something enjoyable to end our long day?"

"Yeah." Because she needed it, needed him, she rested her head on his shoulder. "I could use some enjoyable."

In something close to a dance, he circled her to the bed.

Fatigue? Yes, she felt it, knew her energy hit low ebb. But she needed to be held, to be touched, to be loved. She needed to give him the same.

When they reached the bed, he released her weapon harness. She lifted her head from his shoulder as he slid it off.

"How come your shoes didn't get bunged up like my boots, since you went down there?"

"Once a cat burglar."

He toed off his shoes, then eased her back on the bed.

The cat rolled over in visible disgust, then leaped off the bed.

When they lay together, she drew the tie out of his hair so she could comb her fingers through it. "You need to go back to your own stuff tomorrow."

"Is that an order?"

"Like anybody gives you orders. But who's going to buy Lithuania?"

"Lithuania?" He lowered his head to brush his mouth over hers.

"That's a place. Somewhere." Rolling, she reversed their positions, then just turned her cheek to his chest. She could hear his heartbeat, feel it.

It soothed and calmed and helped her believe everything could be all right. At least here. At least now.

Her communicator signaled in her pocket. "Crap. Sorry."

She shifted, dragged it out. "It's good. Uniform Carmichael. They have Alva's books, the medical reports. They're heading back."

She set it aside on the bedside table, added her 'link.

"Now, where were we?"

He sat up, pulled her to him, and took her mouth.

Not calming and soothing, just the here and now.

She let the day, the work, the worries, the rest of the world evaporate with the kiss. And locked herself around him as she answered it with all she had.

He brought her home. Every day, no matter what she faced, he brought her home.

His hands slid up her back, down again. No, not soothing. Possessive. Those long, skilled fingers knew how to take what they wanted, and how to give her what she needed.

She could all but hear him think: Mine. And that, only that, brought a quick thrill that banished fatigue.

Wanting him to share that thrill, she unbuttoned his shirt. Her fingers, quick and determined, shoved the material aside, spread over the hard planes of his chest.

She wanted to touch him; wanted him to feel her touch. Wanted to know his heartbeat quickened with it.

And when he tugged her shirt aside, she pressed against him, skin to skin, so those heartbeats merged.

So right, he thought, the shape of her against him. Long and lean, angular and agile, the tough muscle under soft skin. He yearned for her, endlessly, and here in the dark with the world and all its sorrows shut away, she was only his.

Hands rushed now, yanking at belts. Wanting more.

He thought the *more* they craved from each other, always the more, would never be fully filled. Her body, so familiar to him, remained a source of wonder, and would always be, he knew, if they loved a thousand lifetimes.

He pleased himself, letting his hands roam and possess, his lips taste and feed. And felt her pleasure in that freedom with the rapid kick of her pulse, heard it in her quickened breath.

He drove her up, slowly, steadily, barely clinging to his own control as he sought to shatter hers. When she broke, quaking under him, the thrill of her release spilled from her into him.

Greedy, still greedy, she rolled—cat-quick—to straddle him. Still shuddering, still riding, she took him in. Her body bowed, her head fell back as, swamped in her own needs, she dragged him with her to that edge.

Held him there, held them both in that impossible rush of sensations. So the here and now spun out, spun out, spun out to saturate them both in the desperate rush of joining.

Then with a cry of triumph, when pleasure shook and shattered, she whipped them both over.

She slid down to him like water, once again rested her cheek on his heart. Its wild beat made her lips curve.

"Even better than pie," she murmured, and made him laugh as he shifted her so she could curl against him.

She felt the cat leap back onto the bed, then settle himself against the small of her back.

Sated, sleepy, satisfied, she dropped straight into sleep.

"That's right, *a ghrá*." He brought her hand to his lips to press a kiss to her palm. "Rest that busy brain."

The moon was up, a bright white ball in a starless sky. It spread ghost light over the construction rubble, glinted off the dull metal of the security fence.

Alva, her face bruised, her eyes blackened, swollen, walked beside Eve.

"I liked it here," Alva said. "You can see so far. I wish they hadn't made a fence so nobody could sleep in the apartments, but I still liked it here. I thought I was safe here."

"I'm sorry you weren't."

"Some people are mean." Alva brushed her fingers— crooked, broken—over her bruised face. "Some people are mean. They like to hurt you. Even when you try to be good and do what you're supposed to do, they like to hurt you."

"I know."

"He was supposed to love me." Alva let out a sigh as she looked out at the city, at the lights. "He made a promise to love and cherish me when we got married. He broke his promise. He broke it lots of times. And it broke me."

"You got away from him."

"I don't remember too well because everything hurt, and I was scared, and I couldn't go home because he'd do terrible things to my brother and sister. I'm the oldest. I have to pro- tect them."

"You did." Even in the dream, in the dream she knew was a dream, Eve's heart hurt. "You protected them."

"Nobody protected you, so you know it's important. I ran away, but I had to protect them. Then I was safe, and I learned how to fold paper and make it pretty and sweet."

She offered Eve an origami cat.

"Thanks. It's great."

"I liked giving people presents because they'd mostly smile when I did. He found me again, so I had to run again, and I couldn't stop being scared. I had to forget, you know, like you did. I had to forget what came before so I wouldn't be scared all the time. You know."

"Yes, I know."

"Do you think she was scared?"

Eve looked down and saw they stood at the other site, the other scene. That same moonlight washed over the remains below.

"I don't know. I'm going to find out."

"She was going to have a baby, and somebody was mean to her. I'd write it in my book and tell the police, but somebody was mean to me, too."

Eve looked over, saw the blood sliding down over Alva's face.

"I'll find them."

"They've been alone a long time. They should have something." Alva held out cupped hands full of paper flowers.

As she let them fall, they drifted down like little birds. In that strange moonlight, Eve saw those tiny bones move and shift, heard a kind of mewling echo up.

"Baby's crying," Alva said.

With that sound still echoing in her ears, she shot awake.

Roarke sat on the side of the bed, one hand gripping hers while the cat bumped his head against her shoulder.

"I'm okay. I'm okay. Not a nightmare." Still, she couldn't quite catch her breath. "Just a really weird dream."

With her free hand, she stroked Galahad to reassure him. "A little creepy toward the end, I guess. I'm okay."

When Roarke leaned over to press his lips to her brow, like a test, she sat up. "You're already dressed. King-of-the-business-world suit. What time is it?"

"It's half six. I had an early 'link conference."

"Lithuania."

His lips curved, but his eyes stayed watchful on her face.

"Not this time, but I'll be sure to look into it, as you seem to want it. Take a minute, and I'll get us both coffee. You can tell me about this weird, ending-on-creepy dream."

He rose to walk over, open the door to the AutoChef.

"It was one of those deals where you know you're dreaming. You're asleep, but your mind's spinning."

She told him while he again sat on the side of the bed, and she let the coffee jolt her fully awake.

"What does it tell you?"

"Nothing I didn't know. I don't need Alva's books from back then to know what Wicker did, and to follow her from what Allysa Gray told me. I'm working with those elements. And I know—knew—I relate to her on some level because of Richard Troy.

"I think or want to think, or find it's just the most logical conclusion, that she blocked her past out. Maybe deliberately, maybe not. Doesn't apply to her murder anyway."

"And the others?"

"I'm not giving them what they need. Just—well, figuratively—leaving them in a hole in the dark."

"Not at all true." He cupped her chin in his hand for a moment. "Not approaching true. You're prioritizing Alva, which is entirely right, but you're already laying the groundwork for the second investigation. Tell me, would you have passed the second case on if it hadn't been on my property?"

"No. There's no need, at least not at this point. Even though we have a pretty good time line for when she went into that hole, because she fell or was pushed in there, as the trauma to certain bones tell that tale, the science has to catch up."

He was right, she assured herself. But the echo of that tiny, mewling cry haunted her.

"We need confirmation on a date of death," she continued, "her age and anything else DeWinter can pull out of the bones. With luck we get a sketch and a holo simulation of her, and I ID her, go from there. It's in DeWinter's area first."

"Exactly, and still you're talking to and will talk to people who cross both sites. And may have crossed both victims."

Eve looked down into her coffee. "It was the baby crying at the end. It was creepy, and sad."

She blew out a breath, finished the coffee. "Anyway, I need to grab a shower and get started."

"Eve," he said as she started toward the bathroom. "You started the minute you saw the remains. The minute they became yours."

"So did you."

So had he, she thought again as she stepped into the shower. That formed a united front. Whoever had killed, no matter how long ago, would pay. Because they'd never beat that united front.

She let the hot jets pummel the dream out of her, and used her shower time to line up the most efficient order for her day.

When she came out, Roarke sat on the sofa, the wall screen scrolling indecipherable stock reports while he studied his PPC.

The cat sprawled next to him, probably trying to soften Roarke up so he got a shot at whatever was under the warming domes on the table.

Not a chance.

To prove it, Roarke gave Galahad a nudge. "Off you go. You've had your breakfast."

The cat slid down, strolled a few feet away before sitting down to wash. But Eve noted he still had one bicolored eye on the domes.

When Roarke removed them, Eve sat down to a golden omelet, hash browns, and fat berries.

Suspecting spinach hid inside the eggs, she took a careful forkful. Her day started out on an up note when she found nothing but cheese and chunks of ham.

"Good deal."

"I thought you'd earned one."

"I bet you've got a full plate today—besides this one."

"It's an expansive menu. You don't ask me if I've dug up any more on Tovinski because you don't want to add to it."

"You gave me plenty already. I'm going to enjoy sweating him today."

"I'll be sorry to miss that. But the overnight did unearth a few more interesting nuggets."

"Really? Like what?"

"Like transactions into those hidden accounts I told you about. Amounts the search tracked back to the sources, in most cases. The bulk, as one would expect, come from his employer, or investments. Some from his employer are generous—bonuses. But interestingly, in the past thirty-six to forty months or more, there have been others, and in the past eighteen to twenty-four, those amounts have increased. Considerably."

"Others—like individuals? Repeat amounts? Like black-mail?"

"No, though he'd likely insist on cash for an endeavor like that. Individuals, yes, and they repeat, but not the amounts. I'd say the amounts depend on how much material Tovinski can siphon off, or what percentage he charges to switch top grade with cheaper."

"From the Singer project?"

Roarke spread a bit of jam on toast, passed it to Eve.

"Oh, from their Hudson Yards project most definitely. But not only, and not only with projects where Bardov is part-nering with Singer. Averaging amounts over these last two years? Tovinski's adding about forty-five thousand a month to his income with his side deals."

"Forty-five," Eve repeated. "A month?"

"For the last couple years, yes. It started off smaller—eight to ten thousand—but it's grown. And I'd say more, as some would be cash deals. The old fell-off-the-truck sort of thing."

Roarke ate some omelet. "I doubt his uncle will be pleased to find out the boy he took under his wing is cheating him."

"He could be following Bardov's orders."

Shaking his head, Roarke lifted his coffee. "I rolled it back to study a few invoices—spot checks, if you will—and the outlay from Bardov's company, accounts received from certain vendors. A jump from there to the individuals who work for or own the companies—then had a quick glance at Tovinski's books—which, again, he didn't hide very well. Not well at all."

"How did you get into all of that? Invoices aren't just laid out there, not without a court order and—"

"Trade secret," he said easily. "You can't use the details of what I've found, of course, but it should be easy enough for a clever woman such as yourself to . . ."

He gestured with his own slice of toast. "Intimate. To, if it helps your cause, give Yuri Bardov a reason to take a look himself. Or to simply make Tovinski sweat harder."

The united front, she realized, already had some cracks along the fault line.

Damn it.

"You weren't authorized to do all that."

"Oh dear." Taking a bite of toast, Roarke looked at Galahad. "She's going to scold me now."

"Hacking into a competitor's books to pull up invoices—"

"Do you see Bardov Construction as my competitor?" He sighed a long, exaggerated sigh. "Well now, that stings a bit."

"Screw that." Part of her wanted to punch him for tantalizing her with data she had no business knowing. "The information's tainted, as it was accessed illegally."

"Technically illegal," he agreed.

Now she wanted to punch him and pull her own hair out. "Bullshit on your 'technically.'"

"It's as innate for you, Lieutenant, to hold that legal line as it is for me to slip a toe over it. Then again, one could argue, if one must, I . . . stumbled upon some of the information while conducting an authorized search."

"Stumble, my ass. When it comes to cyber shit, you wouldn't stumble if somebody shoved you over a trip wire."

"That's sweet of you. We'll say one thing led to another."

She started to snap back, but he held up a hand for peace.

"What I would have told you, through those authorized means, is Tovinski's outlay and expenses far exceed his recorded and legitimate income. Being a clever woman and an experienced investigator, you would wonder where that additional—and considerable—income comes from. I expect you would see about that court order and a forensic accountant."

She ate in silence for a moment because that's exactly what she'd have done. Would do. "You could have kept it at that. Damn it, Roarke, you could've stopped at that. Should have."

"You have me on the could. The should? It's more problematic for me." He looked at her then with eyes calm and clear. "I see a woman who'd escaped from years of beatings and abuse. Who overcame it. And died, brutally, because she never lost her need to do the right thing, to follow the rules."

He rubbed his hand over Eve's. "So, more problematic for me, darling Eve."

Because you see me, Eve thought. And hadn't she seen herself in Alva? How could she blame him for doing the same?

"It's not the same. We both know it's not the same, what happened to her, what happened to me."

"And we both know there are disturbing echoes."

There would always be a few cracks along their line, she decided. It didn't undermine the foundation. Love had pushed him over the line—this time—as much as his own insatiable curiosity.

She couldn't punch him for loving her. Even if part of her still wanted to.

"Forty-five large a month?"

"As I said, he started out with a few thousand here, a few there, and increased it. Last month, he skimmed just over forty-eight thousand."

"Got greedy, got sloppy."

"In this area, he was always sloppy."

"Bardov doesn't know about the women and kids, not all of them anyway, or he'd know about the additional income to cover those expenses. Tovinski keeps banging babies into these women, keeps setting them up with houses and all that. He needs more money.

"It takes balls or stupidity to cheat a man like Bardov."

"He may believe the family connection keeps him safe." Roarke continued to eat. "It won't. I'd have a care letting too much slip to Bardov until you have the nephew sewn up. Otherwise, you're unlikely to find what's left of the body."

"Being a trained investigator, I already figured that."

"And so trained, you'll use that to help push the truth about Alva Quirk and Carmine Delgato out of Tovinski. Being alive in a cage is far better than ending up in pieces and dumped in the Atlantic.

"The sharks took the rest. Classic line," he told her, "from a classic vid."

"I can work with this. But next time—" She cut herself off. "Forget it. Beating my head against the wall of you just gives me a headache." She rose. "I'll contact Reo on my way in, and work it."

Knowing the cat, Roarke covered the breakfast plates so Galahad couldn't lick them clean. "I'll do that."

"Do what?"

"Get your clothes for the day. Your head's already working out what to tell Reo."

"I can think and get clothes."

But he beat her into the closet. "We may get some rain, so you'll want the topper, I'd say. Considering that."

He pulled out stone-gray pants, slim ones, with a strip of leather down the sides. Then a crisp, businessy, mannish white shirt—no frills.

"As you'll have a Russian gangster in your box if all goes your way, we'll go for the vest." Stone gray like the pants, with the back in leather.

"I could've done that."

"Mmm-hmm. Stick with the monotone for the boots and belt—the white shirt keeps it fresh. You'll look efficient, and with your weapon harness, intimidating."

"I am efficient and intimidating."

"Which is why you'll wear the clothes. They won't wear you."

Since it saved her time—and his choice hit simple—she didn't argue.

She heard the crash, recognized the sound of the dome hitting the floor.

Roarke turned on his heel. "Bloody hell."

She snickered as she dressed and her efficient, intimidating, and brilliant husband rushed out to argue with a cat.

Fifteen minutes later, with the cat banished, he walked with her to their adjoining offices.

"Let me know if you decide to go to the Singer and Bardov estates. I'll arrange for the jet-copter."

"I've been thinking I can drive it."

"Eve, the copter can get you there in ten minutes or less as opposed to the ninety you'd need to drive through traffic."

But it would be ninety minutes of annoyance and frustration against ten minutes of abject fear.

"I'll let you know."

When she'd put together a file bag, he took her by the shoulders. Kissed her.

"Depending on the timing, I might be able to pilot you and Peabody myself."

"Can't say yet, but I'll let you know." She kissed him back.

"Do that. And take care of my cop."

"Russian gangsters are just thugs with accents and tats." She started out, paused at the door. "And thanks—sort of— for the lever. Even if I can't use it, I know it, and knowing it, I know him before I sit across from him."

He won't know you, Roarke thought as she left, and again found himself regretting he'd miss that particular meeting.

Her topper lay across the newel post at the bottom of the staircase. Her car waited outside.

It always amazed her.

She texted Peabody.

Want to stop by the morgue re Delgato. Just meet me at the lab. Sent more reports. Read and familiarize.

As she drove, she tagged Reo. When the assistant prosecuting attorney came on-screen, Eve watched her putting fussy stuff on her eyes.

"Don't you just want to rub the crap out of your eyes once you put that stuff on there?"

"No." Reo gave her image in the mirror a serious study, then started on the second eye.

"I do. I'm sending you files and reports. Alva Quirk."

"Homeless woman. Dumpster. About this time yesterday."

"Yeah, so you got that much."

"We got your report on her identification, yes. You have more?"

"I got a shitload more. I got the sort of more that's going to need a warrant. Alexei Tovinski—nephew of Yuri Bardov's wife."

Reo's hand paused. "The Russian mob killed a homeless woman? Who was she really?"

"Nobody important to them. Also on the dead list is Carmine Delgato—head plumber for Singer. It's all in there, Reo, including Morris's report, the tox report. Look at Tovinski's finances: hidden accounts, lots of women—and children—that aren't his wife. A lot of money that doesn't add up to what he's spending on them. Delgato—gambling issues."

"A little embezzlement going on?"

"You're smart. You'll see it, and get that warrant to take a nice deep dive into his money pile. You're going to be issuing another with his name on it before much longer. For Quirk and for Delgato. And, just maybe, for the unidentified, as yet, woman on the second Hudson Yards site."

"Have you dated the remains?"

"I'm going to see DeWinter. Read the reports. It's a lot, and I'm going to give you more."

"Are you going to make me smile really, really big, and tell me we're going to nail Yuri Bardov?"

"Can't say. Yet."

"I'll start reading, and I'll let you know about the warrant on the financials. How many women?"

"Three—that showed up. Three kids, and another in the hopper."

"Jesus, when does he have time to kill people?"

"You don't find time, Reo. You make it. Later."

Satisfied Reo would come through, Eve tagged Nadine Furst.

Far from the hotshot, camera-ready reporter, bestselling

true crime author, and Oscar winner, Nadine answered with a groan.

And dragged the covers over her head in a room lit only by city lights out a window wall.

She said, "Why, God, why?"

"Where the hell are you?" Eve demanded. "Why is it dark? That's not New York out there."

"Because I'm not in New York, I'm in Seattle. I think. And it's the middle of the damn night here."

"Not my fault you're somewhere the Earth hasn't turned toward the sun. I need a favor."

"This is a really bad time to ask me for a favor."

"Do you know any solid reporters in Oklahoma?"

"Why would I know anybody in Oklahoma?" Curiosity, Eve deduced, pushed Nadine's head out of the covers. She frowned, streaky blond hair tangled, foxy eyes heavy, as she held the sheets up over her breasts with one hand. "Why?"

"It has to do with the favor, and a dead homeless woman, the fucker who beat the crap out of her years back in Oklahoma, where he's now chief of police in someplace called Moses."

Nadine rubbed her eyes just the way Eve always wanted to when she had to put stuff on them.

"Did he kill her?"

"No. It's looking like a Russian gangster and the gambling plumber who were embezzling took care of that. But I want the ex-husband, too. That's where you come in. A favor, Nadine."

"Who was she?" Nadine demanded.

Before Eve answered, she heard a rustling, then saw Jake Kincade, rock star and Nadine's bedmate, prop his chin on Nadine's shoulder.

He had purple streaks through his midnight waves, and a sleep crease in his left cheek.

He sent Eve a sleepy smile.

"Hey, Dallas."

"Hey. Ah, sorry to wake you up or interrupt."

"Avenue A had a gig out here," Nadine said, "so . . ."

"And it looks like your workday's starting early, Lois." Jake kissed Nadine's shoulder. "I'll order breakfast."

When he rolled out of bed, Eve had a very clear view of his excellent naked ass backlit by Seattle.

"Huh. Nice," Eve decided as he moved out of frame.

"This feels like a dream. Hold on." The 'link went screen down on the bed. When Nadine snatched it up again, she wore a plushy hotel robe. "What do you need?"

"First, I need you to contact people you can trust, reporters who'll hold on this until I give you the go, and you give it to them. I want it hitting all over hell and back at the same time."

"Seriously, Dallas, who the hell was she?"

"Nadine, she wasn't anybody important. This isn't a big story. He's a cop, and he beat, raped, broke his wife until she got away from him. And he's still a cop, and I need—I want," she corrected, "him to pay. So it's a favor. I want you to help me see that he pays."

"Let me get my notebook."

"Thanks. I mean it. It's not necessary. I'm going to send you everything you need, and you'll know what to do with it. I may not be able to give you the green for a couple days, but—"

"I'll be ready. And I know people I can trust to hold the story. Just give me his name, so I can get myself some background. In Oklahoma? Moses, Oklahoma?"

"Yeah. Garrett Wicker. I'm on my way in. I'll send you what I can when I get to Central. I owe you."

"Hell." On a yawn, Nadine dragged her fingers through her sleep-tousled hair. "It's the middle of the damn night, practically, but I'm going to get breakfast in bed, and I'm going to get laid by a rock star. We can call this a wash."

Relieved, grateful, Eve shoved her way downtown.

12

After a quick stop, she made her way to Morris's double doors. He stood, the protective cape over a suit of molten blue, a pale pink shirt, and a tie that merged both in minute checks.

In one hand, he held a scalpel in preparation, Eve concluded, for making his Y-cut in the young female on his slab.

His music today had a soft voice singing over harp strings.

"I wasn't sure you'd be in yet," Eve said.

"Death doesn't end our day, it starts it. It ended hers at the tender age of twenty-three."

Eve stepped forward. The dead's hair was a tangle of gold with emerald streaks. The body itself was thin to the edge of bony—which made a sharp contrast to the overenthusiastic boob job with the tat of a blue butterfly spreading its wings over the heart.

Eve noted the navel, nose, and eyebrow piercings, the multiple ear piercings.

Under the pale gold tan—no tan lines—the skin read gray.

Blue-and-green polish covered the fingernails in diagonal stripes. On the toes, green on the left foot, blue on the right, with the second toe of each sporting an artfully painted flower.

"Rich," Eve concluded. "Either born that way or she found a generous daddy. The piercings, the tat, the nails, those aren't low-rent or home jobs. Those cost."

She considered.

"Where was she found? What was she wearing?"

"On the floor of her dressing room in her Riverside Drive penthouse—family money. A party dress—just the dress—at about two this morning."

"Going, coming, or at a party?"

"At. Hosting. One of the party guests stumbled over her, and according to his statement thought she was passed out or sleeping."

"Probably because he was as wasted as she was before she OD'd. I'm betting there were lots of illegals and plenty of high-dollar booze at the party."

"You'd win that bet."

"She's been using a long time. Looks like she had an eating disorder on top of it. Her arms are toothpicks, and the faint, circular bruising says ingesting and/or inhaling wasn't doing the job for her anymore. She needed the syringe."

"On the visual, and from the statements, I agree. I'll need to confirm."

She looked at him then. "Why are you on a rich junky's OD? Who is she?"

"The only child of Judge Erin Fester and her former husband, the attorney general of New York. Judge Fester asked for me."

"Fester's solid, and the media will crawl all over this. She knew you'd be respectful and discreet."

"Youth is often tragically foolish. But you're here about your newest victim."

He gestured to his wall of drawers before walking over to open one. "His wife and children are coming in this morning. We'll have him ready."

"You found the paralytic in his system before it had time to dissipate."

"Another sixty to ninety minutes, there wouldn't have been a trace of it. His killer obtained a high-grade, controlled medical substance. Dexachlorine. It's used in conjunction with an anesthetic during surgery so the patient is not only asleep but immobile, which is equally important. Dexachlorine doesn't require a counteragent post-surgery to restore mobility."

"It just goes away."

"In surgery, the anesthesiologist would monitor the patient, administer more if need be. Its effects are immediate but relatively short in duration. Two and a half to three hours at most, depending on the dosage."

"Can't be easy to come by for a layperson."

"If whoever administered it didn't manage to steal it himself, he would have paid dearly for it."

"Or he had a medical source he could lean on, threaten, blackmail. Anyway, your quick work screwed the killer's plans for Delgato to go down as a suicide."

They stood on either side of the drawer tray, with the corpse on it. Eve held out the glossy bakery box.

"And what is that seductive smell?"

"A couple of cinnamon buns. I've got a source."

"I should point out that if you hadn't found Delgato on the line between life and death, it would've been very unlikely for me to find the paralytic.

"But I'm taking the buns."

"If this place runs anything like my department, you'd better have a good place to stash them."

Morris brought the box closer to his nose, inhaled. "I have my ways."

"If I have mine, I'll have Delgato's killer—who damn well killed Alva, too—in a cage by end of shift. Her siblings are probably going to come in for her in the next day or two."

"I saw in your report you'd found next of kin. We'll take care of her until then."

She knew he would, and left him with his soft music and harp strings.

She hit the lab next, and made her way through the cubes, around the counter, by the glass enclosures manned by the lab geeks.

She spotted the head geek's egg-shaped skull as Dick Berenski worked at his station. He hunched, skinny shoulders bent as he slid from one end of his counter to the other on his rolling stool.

Eve walked to the far end, waited while he ran his spider fingers over a keyboard.

"We got your tox back on the hanging guy." He kept tapping, and his voice already sounded aggrieved. "Harvo'll get to your fabric trace when she gets to it. I got drones going through the contents of the dumpster on your other victim. Not going to find squat, but you gotta look. Got her tox back—zip and nada there, like it said in the report. Only blood on her or the tarp's hers. Tarp came from the roll in the storage shed inside the fence on the construction site."

He rolled back in her direction, and Eve saw he was trying to grow a goatee. He'd worked on a mustache once that had resembled a skinny caterpillar with mange.

She doubted this would be any more successful.

"Just because you're stacking 'em up, Dallas, doesn't mean we don't have other cases, other work without your name on it."

Eve said nothing, just held up the bakery box.

His beady eyes went nearly as glossy as the box.

"What's in there?"

Since this was a bribe instead of a gift—they didn't call him Dickhead for nothing—Eve had increased the amount.

"A half dozen of the best sticky buns in the city. Possibly the state. Maybe the Eastern Seaboard."

He wet his lips. "Whaddaya want?"

"I had three crime scenes yesterday. The second, unidentified female and fetus."

"Yeah, yeah, DeWinter's got the bones. We got the shoe, some jewelry, bullets. We'll get to them."

"The sweepers sent you samples. Dirt, brick, concrete, block, wood."

"Yeah, yeah, yeah. So?"

"I need a full analysis on the brick from the inner wall, the materials in the outer wall, the ceiling between the inner and outer wall, and the floor and ceiling outside the inner wall."

He gave her a sneer she found severely compromised by the attempted goatee.

"I want a pair of frosty blondes and a pitcher of vodka martinis all served up on a tropical beach. Naked."

She refused to let that terrifying image into her head. "I get the analyses, you get the buns."

She heard Peabody's pink boots clomping her way, but kept her eyes on Dickhead's.

"Lemme see 'em."

She untied the cord, opened the lid a few inches, tilted the box toward him. The scent streamed out, and could have made a grown man cry.

Peabody gave a yip from behind her. "You went to Jacko's!"

Dickhead's long fingers reached; Eve shut the box.

"Did you get any extra?" Peabody all but bounced in her boots. "I'll work out a full hour for half a sticky bun from Jacko's."

"Keep me waiting, Berenski, she gets one and you're down to five."

"Hold on, just hold the hell on." He snatched his station 'link, stabbed at it, rolled a foot away from Eve. "Taver? You got the samples from the Hudson Yards construction site, the Jane Doe remains?"

He slid his eyes toward Eve, hunched his skinny shoulders. "Move it up. That's what I said. Do a quick prelim on—"

"Full and detailed," Eve corrected. "Brick from the inner wall is priority."

He curled his lip at her, but turned away, muttered into the 'link. Then he rolled back. "I've got Taver and Janesy on it. It's going to take awhile."

"Define 'awhile'?"

"Maybe half a day."

"Brick's first. How long for that?"

"Maybe a couple of hours. You said you wanted the whole shot."

"I do." She set the box on his counter. "Don't make me come back here."

"You do, bring me a latte—extra shot!"

Okay, Eve thought as she walked away, she had to give him sarcasm points for that one.

"You let him have the whole box." Peabody sighed, deep, wistful. "Probably for best. I don't think I have an hour to sweat off that sweet, cinnamony goodness tonight. The decorator's bringing samples. Tile and countertops and cabinets and—"

"I'm taking DeWinter," Eve interrupted. "Go back and see if Harvo's had a chance to start on the fabric traces I got from the Delgato scene."

"Okay. I can't believe you hit another murder after you left Central." Peabody looked up the stairs that led to DeWinter's area. "She probably hasn't had time to do much on the remains."

"Then I'll incentivize her."

"With sticky buns?"

"She's not the bribe-me type. I'll just harass her."

Eve turned, headed up the stairs.

She expected to find DeWinter in her lab in one of her co-ordinated lab coats using some of her strange equipment on human bones.

She found the bones, the woman's precisely arranged on a worktable and the fetus's on another.

But the only living being in the area sat crossways on a chair, legs dangling over the side while she did something on a tablet.

A kid. DeWinter's kid. Eve knew she had a daughter-type kid.

This one wore bright green high-top kicks, jeans with turned-up cuffs, and a shiny belt with a green tee tucked into them.

Her hair, like DeWinter's when it wasn't sleek and tamed, exploded in dark curls, these with some caramel worked through.

Flower pins scooped it back from her face, a face with skin the color of that caramel with just a dollop of cream.

She turned her head to study Eve out of almond-shaped eyes as green as her kicks.

Eve didn't know much about kids, but she knew when one had a face destined to break hearts. Plus, those eyes. They looked as if they knew entirely too much.

More than an actual human should.

"I know you." She didn't smile when she said it, but swung her legs off the chair to stand. "You're Lieutenant Dallas. My mother worked with you on the Lost Girls—that's what I call them. I read *The Icove Agenda*. They were misguided men who twisted science for their own ends. I'm reading *The Red Horse Legacy* right now."

She tapped the tablet, then set it aside. "I have a lot of questions."

"I've got one. Where's your mother?"

"She had to talk to somebody, but she'll be right back. On the Icove investigation, do you think the clones who got out of the school, most were just kids, do you think they scattered? Or do you think they found a way to regroup, that they found a haven?"

Eve thought of the girl with the infant she'd released herself. Because it wasn't right. None of it had been right. "They've got no reason to cause any trouble or be any threat."

"That's not what I meant." The girl rolled those compelling, farseeing eyes. "Like I'd be scared of kid clones. There were babies, too. Someone has to take care of them, to feed them, educate them, socialize them. I feel the Avrils—and it's wrong to take a life, but in a way, a very real way, they were defending their own and others—had a place, a safe place. And a way to help the others."

"I couldn't say."

Now she did smile. "Because you think I'm too young to understand. A lot of people make that mistake."

DeWinter's heels clicked toward the lab. "That took longer than I thought. Sweetie, if you want to . . . Dallas."

"Lieutenant Dallas and I were discussing Avril and the clones."

"You'll need to save that for another time, Miranda. The lieutenant has her hands full with her current investigation."

"The woman and the fetus. It's very sad."

Miranda studied the bones with the sad mixed with fascination.

"It's good you have my mother working on finding out who she was, and when and how she was killed. The way you collaborated on the Lost Girls. In that case, the man who'd killed them and hidden their bodies had mental and emotional defects. From what Mom's told me, that doesn't seem to apply here."

DeWinter slid an arm around the girl's shoulders. "I don't think you've met my daughter, Miranda. Her school has a professional day today, and her sitter—"

"Who I don't need."

"Her sitter had to cancel."

"I like coming here. There's so much happening."

"Why don't you go see what's happening with Elsie? She's working on the sketch and holo of the adult victim."

"You want me out of the way while you talk to Lieutenant Dallas."

"Yes." DeWinter bent down, kissed the top of her daughter's head. "Yes, I do."

Miranda tilted her face up. "Can I get a fizzy?"

"Fine. Use my code. And don't wander off downstairs."

The girl rolled her eyes again. "It was nice meeting you," she told Eve. "I'd like to talk to you about the Red Horse investigation when I've finished the book. A lot of people think, and say, there isn't real evil in the world. But there is. I have to decide if I want to work on the science end or the investigative end of stopping evil, and the misguided, and the ones that fall into other areas."

She went back for her tablet, tucked it under her arm. "Did it take you long to learn how to use your service weapon?"

"Miranda."

"All right, all right, I was just wondering. I'm going."

Eve frowned after the girl as she left. "How old is she?"

DeWinter just laughed. "She still wrestles with the dog and bargains for ice cream. But her mind? She's scary smart, and sometimes it exhausts my brain trying to keep up with hers."

"You talk about cases with her?"

"She offers interesting perspectives. I can't shut what I do away from her, so we talk, and I explain. Often that sparks something, shows me another approach." DeWinter's eyes turned cool. "You don't approve?"

Eve lifted a hand for peace. "I don't know anything about kids. She threw me off, that's all. Maybe part of that's because she had the same take I do about the clones. About the Avrils and the rest."

"She wants a happy ending for them. Or at least a just one. I'd imagine you'd hope for the just as well."

"Hope's not enough."

DeWinter nodded as they shifted to the tables. "But it should factor in, shouldn't it? Especially when you're still a child. I can tell you these remains were weeks away from full term, from the chance to be a child. My analysis puts him at thirty-two weeks. Viable, and just over six pounds, and seventeen inches. I found no defects or indications of medical issues. He died inside his mother, cut off from oxygen and nutrition."

"Forty weeks is full term, right?" She knew that from Mavis. "So eight weeks to go."

"Which would have made him premature, but again, viable. He would have lived outside the womb."

"What about the woman?"

"I've only gotten started. Elsie has taken measurements, done a 3D replica of the skull, and is working on the reproduction. I can tell you she was between twenty and twenty-five at TOD. Five feet, six inches in height. We were able to extract DNA, but have just begun an analysis and a search."

"If she went in that hole when the building was going up, that's a long shot on the search."

"We can analyze the DNA, and will. Her injuries, the breaks, the dislocation of the shoulder are consistent with a fall. The damage to the ribs is consistent with gunshot wounds. They recovered three thirty-two-caliber bullets."

"Yeah, I got that report."

"She wore a size seven shoe, narrow. You likely saw that report, and the report that the ring size was a five. It's consistent again with the remains. A delicate build. If she gained normally, given the week of pregnancy, the weight of the fetus, she would have been between a hundred and forty to a hundred and forty-five pounds at TOD. Most likely a hundred and fifteen to a hundred and twenty pre-pregnancy."

"A hair over average height, slim build, small-boned, narrow feet and fingers."

"Long, slender fingers. A bit short-waisted, as she had long legs for her height. The bone structure of the skull? Delicate features. A narrow nose, strong but not prominent cheek-bones, a heart-shaped face, wide eyes, well spaced. Her teeth are perfectly even, and while we'll run tests, I found no visible signs of decay."

It didn't give her a name, Eve thought, but it gave her quite a bit.

"So she had dental work—perfectly straight—and good nutrition and hygiene."

"We'll run tests, but yes. I see healthy bones. Nothing to indicate she lived on the street, used illegals. Everything to indicate, at this point, she had good nutrition and good health care, good prenatal care."

"That's helpful."

"I think she would have been very attractive. Early twenties, so on the young side for marriage—if the ring she wore is a wedding ring—and motherhood."

"The jewelry looked like the real deal to me, and the shoe was leather. I'm waiting on those reports, but if they confirm, she had some income or someone who paid for that sort of thing."

"I'll be working on this today, and Elsie will continue with the reproduction."

"Okay, this is a good start. Anything you get, anything, send it to me. I'll take it in bits and pieces."

"You haven't closed your initial case."

"Working up to it."

Eve started out and down. She spotted Peabody just outside Harvo's domain, leaning against the glass wall while she scrolled on her PPC.

"That better be work and not home improvement."

"It is. I skimmed when I got up this morning, but I'm catching up. Harvo had to finish something, but she's on ours now. Jesus, Dallas, we've got Alva's books. We're really going after her fuck of a husband."

"Damn right we are. But he can wait."

She stepped through the doorway.

Harvo looked through a microscope while she tapped her blue-tipped fingers on a mini pad. Over her head, codes and symbols, maybe equations—who knew?—covered a screen.

She wore white baggies and a white sleeveless tee—tame for her, if you discounted the figure of a woman on the back of her shirt flying through what appeared to be a meteor storm above the planet.

She tapped her feet, one, then the other, so her glittery blue toes sparkled through the clear boots.

Blue, Eve assumed, ranked as color of the day, since Harvo had gone for it with her short, spiky hair.

She shifted, swiveled. Eve caught the bold red lettering on the front of the shirt.

GIRL GEEKS SAVE
THE WORLD!

"Yo," she said to Eve as she made an adjustment on the microscope, then tapped something else on the pad.

On-screen the fabric traces popped, magnified. The screen split with the right side full of symbols.

"Sorry I couldn't get anything interesting from your dumpster DB, but I hit solid on the shoe in the wine cellar."

"You took the shoe?"

"Dezi or Coke would've run it usually, but they went and got married. They're honeymooning this week. Anyway, my baby's working on your fabric from the hanging man, but I can give you the lowdown on the shoe."

"What's the lowdown?"

"High-quality Italian leather." She swiveled again, worked a keyboard to bring the shoe on-screen. "European size thirty-seven, narrow, and exceptional workmanship. A classic low-heeled pump in your classic black. Prada."

"Where it was made?"

"No, the designer. It's a designer shoe, and they carried that classic pump, with that heel height and width, that toe shape 2022 to 2025. Before '22, they had a slightly thicker heel, after '25, a thinner with a more narrow toe shape."

"That's good data, Harvo."

"We live to serve. The bad news is, classic black Prada pump. You're never going to narrow down where she bought it if that would apply. Plus, thirty-five, forty years in the deep, dark past."

"It's not the where so much, but the what. Designer shoes, good jewelry. Classic pump. You'd call that . . ."

Harvo arched her eyebrows as Eve gestured to the screen. "Boring, and way, way conservative. Even for back then. A conservative, no-risk, no-statement lady shoe for a lady who could afford a grand for boring shoes."

"A grand. Okay, yeah, it's all giving me a picture."

Something went ding-ding-buzz, and Harvo swiveled back again.

"Okay. First, good eye on the fabric trace, Dallas. You didn't get much, but I don't need much. I could nail it as wool—the good stuff—just eyeballing it."

"Seriously?"

"Sure. How it looks, and the texture. Good wool. Italian again, as it turns out. Very finely combed Italian wool."

"Sounds expensive."

"You betcha. This is ult-grade fabric. And I'm going to give you a ninety percent probability the garment this came from is new. No chemical remnants from dry-cleaning—and you gotta with this fabric. Got your dye lot, and that tracks back to Italy."

"It's going to be a male. The trace came from a suit jacket or pants. Had to. I can use this to track designers or tailors or vendors who used this fabric from that dye lot."

"Or . . . I could've programmed that in. Geek, not a cop, but—"

"Girl geeks save the world."

Harvo spiraled a blue-tipped finger in the air. "Exacta-mundo. Now, the fabric and in that color, which is a medium sort of gray, probably sold to a whole bunch of high-class designers and tailors. Like the bespoke kind. My uncle's a tailor."

"Your uncle?"

"Actually my great-uncle. Uncle Den's in Chicago, has his own shop and all that. He's probably worked with this fabric. But the specific dye lot narrows it down." She toggled the symbols off, and a list came up.

"I'll take that list. If we go with the probability of new, he got it in New York. Most likely."

"Got that. Hey, baby, display New York City recipients only." Seconds later, the list shortened to three.

"Better."

"Hey, Leonardo's on there. I got to get myself over to see the new digs in progress. Anyway, I can run it for—"

"I got it from here. You never fail, Harvo."

"Geeks accept no failures. Sending all data to you now. Copy Peabody?"

"Do that. I owe you a sticky bun."

"I like sticky buns."

"You'd be crazy not to. Thanks."

"Get the bastard, Dallas, save our world. Cha."

Peabody continued to scroll on her PPC. "It's still work, I swear. And I was listening, so I got that we got."

"We got a lot. Tag Leonardo, since that one'll be quick and easy. Have him check what he used the fabric for—that dye lot of it."

Eve paused because she'd scanned the lab and saw Dick-head standing, waving an arm in the air.

"The bribe paid off. He's got something."

Once again, she wound her way to his workstation. "Were you waving or having a seizure?"

"Funny. You got lucky."

"Did I? I'm not the one with sticky bun breath."

He grinned at that. "Those bastards are awesome. But you got lucky. Full analysis isn't complete, but the concrete—and that's floor, ceiling, outer wall—it's substandard and pre-formed shit. Wouldn't have passed code pre-Urbans, wouldn't pass it now. Only passed it during that period because they relaxed the codes. But . . ."

He went for the dramatic pause.

"The area from the approximately three-by-eighteen-feet area between the interior and exterior walls is high-grade poured concrete."

So Roarke, and Mackie, hit that one, Eve thought.

"Tell me about the brick, Berenski."

"I'm going to tell you, for Christ's sake. Brick's top grade. Natural clay. You got barium carbonate in there for adding resistance to the elements, and your colorants added to sand for the shade. Samples we got are uniform, so they were molded, fired, cooled, and whatnot. They weren't slapped together. The mortar samples are top grade, too.

"Had to cost, especially back then, see? A lot of money for one wall when the rest of the place went up on the cheap."

"Yeah, I see." She saw very well. "Send me what you've got so far. I'll take the rest as it comes in. Tell your lab rats I appreciate it."

"Hey, I got it done."

"You already ate some of my appreciation. It's coming together, Peabody," she said as they walked away.

"Leonardo's going to check on the fabric. He's weirded out, because he's Leonardo, that he might have designed something for a killer."

"Then he'll feel better, if that's the case, when we lock said killer in a cage. Start contacting the others on Harvo's list. They won't be as quick and easy, but we'll nail it down."

"Dead Delgato? It plays for me like he didn't do the killing—it doesn't give him a pass. But it plays like since he was on that job, he probably saw her around sometime, and the statements from the super, the wife paint him as nonviolent. A loser, a cheat, a gambling addict, but like somebody who'd have tried talking his way out of it. Making up a story she might have even bought. Then he ends up dead because he freaked."

"It plays like that," Eve agreed. "But if he hadn't been a loser, a cheat, a gambling addict—add thief and liar—he wouldn't have been up there with someone who killed Alva, then killed him."

When they got in the car, Eve picked up a small white bag, held it out to Peabody.

"You didn't! You did! I can smell it!" Bouncing in the seat, Peabody opened the bag and inhaled lavishly. "Jacko's sticky bun!"

"Don't make me sorry. And don't make me sorry I'm giving you five minutes—five—to blather on about tiles and counters and the rest of that crap. Five."

"Best partner ever." Peabody sighed. "You have to take half of this. I'll hate myself later if I eat it all. They're huge."

If she hadn't smelled them most of the morning, Eve could've said no. "A third. I'll take a third. And your five minutes starts now."

With the care usually reserved for cutting diamonds, Peabody tore a section off the bun, passed it to Eve. "We're going sort of soft in the kitchen. I thought I wanted strong and bold, but when I saw the soft, I fell for it. So the cabinets are going to be this soft, but deep, sage green. I didn't want wood tones or white. But two-toned because we're going cream on the lower cabinets of the island."

She took a tiny bite of the bun, made a yummy noise. "And we're reversing that on the counters. Creamy white, except the island top will echo the green."

Eve drove, ate her portion of the bun while Peabody rhapsodized about backsplash tile and cabinet hardware, kitchen sinks, faucets and pot fillers.

Eve had always figured a faucet was a pot filler.

"Time," Eve called in the middle of an ode to walk-in pantries. But she added, "It sounds nice, Peabody. It sounds like you."

"It feels like me, and McNab's all about the sound and security systems, the lighting, so we're merging it all really well. At least right now."

She ate her last bite as Eve pulled into Central's garage.

"You should see what Mavis and Leonardo are doing in the main house."

Eve thought about it. "I can definitely wait."

"It's going to be a showstopper."

"It's Mavis. What else could it be? Start on the designers. Reo ought to have a warrant on Tovinski's financials by now. Or soon. And when we have that, we'll bring him in."

13

Eve decided to take a chance and jumped off the elevator at Mira's level. The NYPSD's top profiler always added some insight. She expected to get pushback from Mira's admin and started working on a pushback to the pushback that would get her by the dragon and into Mira for ten minutes.

Instead of the dragon, she found a young, chirpy sort behind the admin's desk.

"Good morning! May I help you?"

She all but sang it.

"I need ten minutes with Dr. Mira."

"Do you have a session or appointment?"

"No. I have dead bodies. Lieutenant Dallas, Homicide."

"Oh, oh! Of course! I'm reading *The Red Horse Legacy* right now! It's amazing. I was still on Long Island when that happened, but I heard all about it. Let me see if Dr. Mira has a free slot."

She tapped her earpiece. "Dr. Mira, Lieutenant Dallas is here. She'd like a few moments. Yes, ma'am, thank you."

She tapped again. "Dr. Mira can see you now. She does have an appointment in fifteen minutes."

"I'll keep it short." Eve stepped to the office door. "What happened to her usual admin?"

"Oh, her daughter went into labor early this morning. It's so exciting! I'm filling in for her for a few days."

Too bad it wouldn't be longer, Eve thought. The chirp would get annoying fast, but the new one was an easy mark.

Inside, Mira sat behind her desk. It was rare to see the calm and elegant Mira frazzled, but that's what Eve saw now.

"Sorry to add to your day. You must be busy."

"I'm scattered. My temp is adorable, but not efficient. Or not what I'm used to." Mira pushed back her rich brown hair, then shook her head. "We thought we had another week, but babies will come when they come. And a new life's about to come into the world, which is a lovely antidote to what you and I deal with every day.

"So I need to stop whining."

"That sounded like frustration, which is way different than whining."

"I'll take it." Rising, Mira walked to her AC, and Eve knew flowery tea was coming. "I've read your reports—not as thoroughly as I'd like. Alva Quirk—or Alva Elliot Wicker Quirk."

Thorough enough, Eve thought.

"Actually, I know your time's short so I'd rather focus on the unidentified remains. I've got a solid line on Alva's case."

"The Russian gangster."

"Evidence is circumstantial so far, but it's piling up."

"Sit," Mira said, and took out two delicate cups of girly tea.

She settled in one of her scoop chairs. Though Eve knew appearances deceived, Mira looked as delicate as the china in a suit of pale pink that showed off admirable legs. The shoes with heels like wicked stilettos mirrored the shade.

"I'm not sure how much I can help you there," she began.

"I have additional data. I know she was between twenty

and twenty-five, in good health. Odds are she'd had excellent dental care—straight teeth, no decay. She was wearing—as we found one with her and the sizes match—designer shoes. Classic Prada pumps, according to Harvo. Black leather. I haven't gotten the report on the jewelry yet, but it didn't look like costume to me. Subtle stuff, but the real deal. Gold band on the third finger of her left hand, gold earring, a gold neck chain with like little swans forming a heart, a gold analog watch. Watch brand, Bulgari. That's another high-dollar brand."

"Yes, it is. So a young woman of means and taste. Nothing overt, but conservative and classic."

"The fetus was thirty-two weeks, and again in good health at TOD."

"We can assume the victim had good health care, was seeing a midwife or OB. She was married, or wore a symbol of marriage. Young. Clearly she wanted to deliver a healthy baby, whether she intended to keep it or she was a surrogate for someone else, or she intended to give it up for adoption."

"Or sell it."

"Yes, certainly possible. The jewelry and so on may have been down payments. Although—"

"Why go subtle—or boring, as Harvo sees it?"

With the saucer perfectly balanced on her knee, Mira sipped from the cup. "A matter of taste, perhaps. If so, I'd tend to see her as someone who aspired to the subtlety wealth can buy, or who had experience with it. The shoes. I know they were in your report, but can you refresh me?"

Eve took out her PPC, brought the photo of the shoe onscreen.

Mira studied it. "They are a bit boring, aren't they? You'd expect something with more flair from someone that young. But they're very practical."

"That's debatable."

Mira laughed, sipped more tea. "A low-heeled pump—practical for a meeting, for instance. Low enough for a woman in her last trimester of pregnancy. Certainly not practical for a visit to a construction site."

"She dressed up. Subtle, tasteful, low-key, but she dressed up. That pulls me back from the probability she worked on the site. She could have been part of the design team, or part of the architect's firm. I need to run all that down when I close Alva's murder. So, maybe she came from work, but she met someone on the site."

Setting her cup aside, Eve leaned forward. "Substandard materials—but if she threatened to blow the whistle there, nobody would give a damn. Regs and codes had been rolled back. Nobody'd kill her over it. But there's been a steady stream of pilfering and stealing, doctoring invoices going on at the Singer site. Maybe that's got a history."

"Singer owned this site at the time." Mira nodded. "She discovered, as you believe Alva did, this activity, threatened to report it?"

"She went to the wrong person—maybe. Agreed to meet the wrong person on the site. Bang, bang, you're dead. Whoever killed her knew enough to know where to hide the body. Knew where to get good brick—not substandard—and build a wall, and the form thing, pour the form over her with concrete. Seal her up."

"Cold, killing a woman, a pregnant woman, and walling them up. It takes cold calculation, planning, and, as you say, the ability to access the materials and use them to conceal the bodies."

"I don't see how it could be someone on the level of Delgato—he wasn't employed by them then, I'm just meaning at his level. Why wasn't the wall, the work, questioned? Even if it was all so rushed, nobody noticed the wall was three feet farther in—and I understand construction often was rushed and cheap and disjointed post-Urbans, but nobody questions the work?"

Dissatisfied, Eve pushed up. "The murder had to happen when nobody was working. Probably at night. Crew comes back to work in the morning, or say after the weekend, and nobody goes, 'Hey, somebody poured this section of floor in this building'?"

"A good question. Then again, if anyone at a higher level answered that question by claiming they'd done it over the weekend, that would likely suffice. People were hungry for work," Mira pointed out, "for paychecks, for housing, for normality."

"So they might not question it in the first place." Eve sat again. "She may have been married, may have been in a relationship, may have carried the baby as a surrogate. If any of those are true, someone should have looked for her. I've been running missing persons from a three-year period, to cover all the possibilities, but I haven't come up with any record of a woman in her early twenties in the later stages of pregnancy."

Eve shook her head. "It feels like someone killed her and sealed her up, and everyone just forgot her. She had bottles of wine stacked up in front of her, on the other side of that wall. People ate and drank and worked over her head."

It didn't seem right. None of it felt right.

"Didn't anybody go to where she worked, where she lived? Didn't she have family or friends who filed reports? But I don't find any."

"It may have been a friend or family who killed her."

"Yeah, I'm working with that, too. Have to ID her to go there. But . . . what if she wasn't from New York? She could have worked at one of the suppliers, seen the problem. She comes in to meet with someone to report it, to offer what she knows. Bang, bang, you're dead. But the missing persons don't show up because she wasn't from here. She might not have told anyone she was coming. She could have been told to keep it quiet. 'Don't want to alert the bad guys, don't let on what you know, where you're going. We'll look through everything and go to the authorities.'"

Mira nodded, sipped tea. "It's a theory, and a good one. Given her age, she may have been naive enough to believe all that and follow those instructions. And I'm not helping you."

"It helps to talk it through. I haven't been able to give her much time. I wanted to give her this, talk it through. I need a face, I need a name. But I've got this picture."

She looked back at Mira. "Young, pregnant, proper. Do you know what I mean?"

"Yes. Proper."

"Probably well brought up, so either married or planning to be. Because pregnant. Healthy—no signs of abuse. Good, practical shoes, good, subtle jewelry—including the ring. She probably wore a dress or a suit—that's long gone. She went up there to meet someone. Maybe she was coerced, maybe she was deceived, but it was important enough for this young, proper woman to go up to a construction site, at night, either alone or with her killer. She couldn't have believed she was in danger. She hadn't carried the kid that long, taken that much care, to risk it, or herself."

"Someone she knew?"

"I keep circling to that when I can give it five minutes. Maybe the husband or lover. Maybe he was married and promised her the usual bullshit. She believed him, and now he's in a box. So he had to get rid of her."

She rose again, shook her head again. "But that doesn't hold strong for me. She goes poof, somebody's going to ask questions. Somebody knows about the relationship. So that doesn't play all the way through.

"Anyway, thanks for the time."

"If it really did help, I'm happy to give it."

It did help, Eve thought as she made her way back to Homicide. Some consults with Mira, like this one, pushed her to pick through her own brain, study the angles she'd pushed. See the strengths and weaknesses of embryonic theories.

And with Mira's help she was forming a picture of Jane Doe.

And now she had to put her aside, again, and focus on Alva.

As she stepped off the glide on Homicide, the elevator doors opened. Reo stepped out.

"Took you long enough."

"Hey." Reo gestured. "Let's talk."

"You got the warrant."

"Yes. But we need to go over some things."

She breezed into the bullpen, then arrowed straight toward Eve's office.

Deceiving appearances, Eve thought again. With her fluffy blond hair, pretty-girl looks, and faint southern drawl, she presented a picture of female sweetness, and that often came off as weakness.

Inside that pretty package lived steel and sharp brains and cunning.

In her straight-lined red dress, Reo flicked a glance at the murder board.

"I'm not sitting in that vicious chair. Everybody knows it'll bite your ass, and everybody knows that's why you have it in here. It's outlived its purpose."

Eve studied her miserable visitor's chair. "I like that chair."

"Then you sit in it."

Reo slid into Eve's desk chair, set down her briefcase. Crossed her legs.

Maybe she still had shoes and their hidden meanings on the brain, because Eve studied Reo's.

"Why are you wearing those shoes?"

Reo lifted her foot, turned it right and left as she studied her heels—high and thin and red to pop against the more somber gray of the body.

"What's wrong with my shoes?"

"They can't be comfortable."

"Actually, they have a very nice cushion and excellent arch support."

"Yeah, right. Why those particular shoes?"

"They go with the dress, add a nice polished look. They say I'm a serious, professional woman, but I also have style."

"Huh. They say all that?"

"They do. Why the interest?"

"Just trying to get a picture on another case. What about the warrant?"

"The boss and I went over the financial data you already found. Obviously we can charge him with tax evasion, fraud, and all the connected goodies. Now, while going after one of the Bardov family would be satisfying, it's also a bit deflating to do the dance over relatively small potatoes."

"There are going to be bigger potatoes. And why is it potatoes? Why isn't it small apples, or elephants?"

Reo tilted her head as if giving that serious thought. "I have no idea. But we tend to agree there may be bigger potatoes—or elephants. Even a cursory study indicates his outlay is considerably larger than his income—even the unreported income. So this leads the cynical mind toward the possibilities of money laundering and/or cash transactions, which may involve blackmail, force, intimidation, or other nefarious means."

"*Nefarious.* That's a word for it."

Smiling, Reo swiveled left and right in the chair. "And

since I know, the boss knows, everybody in my world knows you don't want to sweat Alexei Tovinski, Yuri Bardov's favored nephew, over his financial machinations, we want all the t's crossed before he's picked up."

Reo gave Eve her big, southern smile. "Wouldn't it be nice if we had coffee?"

Eve walked to her AutoChef. "I'm going to use those machinations—and his habit of knocking up women he's not married to—to sweat him for two murders. Alva Quirk and Carmine Delgato. I suspect, as you do, those aren't his first. Wouldn't it be nice if they were his last?"

She handed Reo a mug of coffee, then, since she wasn't about to use the visitor's chair, eased a hip down on her desk.

"Yes, it would. It very much would. So let's talk."

Eve leaned over, hit her interoffice. "Peabody, my office."

After a brief pause, Peabody responded, "I need five minutes! I've got something!"

"Bang," Eve murmured.

"Bang what?"

"The fabric I found on Delgato's windowsill. Harvo tracked it down to type, dye lot, manufacturers, venues in New York. Peabody's working on finding out where Tovinski bought the suit, pants, whatever, made from that expensive Italian wool. How do you figure he's going to explain snagging his fancy pants on the windowsill of a dead man's flop?"

Reo sipped coffee. "I can't wait to find out. That sort of physical evidence adds weight to the circumstantial. It connects the two men—though Tovinski won't be the only person in the city of New York with a garment made from that fabric."

"Dye lot narrows it—and Harvo says it's new, not yet dry-cleaned. It's weight."

"It's weight," Reo agreed.

"They both needed more money than they earned to feed their addictions. Women for Tovinski, the horses for Delgato. They worked together to defraud the Singer company, by straight theft, by doctoring invoices, by changing orders to cheaper material. I'm betting Tovinski's skimmed plenty from his favorite uncle."

"The thought crossed my mind. And if so, favorite or not, Tovinski will be lucky to live long enough to go to trial."

"I don't want him dead; I want him in a cage. I'm going to have a chat with Bardov. I just have to put enough together to convince him not to order a hit. I think—"

She broke off as Peabody's boots sounded a double-time clomp toward the office.

Her partner's face shined bright, her smile spread wide. "Got the fucker! Hey, Reo."

"Hey, Peabody. I completely love the potential of your new house."

"Isn't it just the maggiest of mags? We just settled on the colors and materials for the kitchen and—"

"Shut up, both of you, shut up about houses and kitchens, or you'll have to arrest me and Reo charge me for punching both of you. How did you get the fucker?"

"It wasn't Leonardo, thankfully, because he got shaky over it. Leonardo was one of the designers who ordered the fabric and the dye lot," she added for Reo. "But Casa Della Moda—that's house of fashion in Italian—ordered the same fabric—for one customer."

"You got him."

"Oh yeah. Tovinski has all his suits made there—custom. Picks out the fabric from samples, the buttons, the design, all of it. They make his shirts, too. He picked up this particular suit four days ago. I was curious enough to ask. Eighteen thousand. Add two more for custom silk lining."

"Harvo hits again. And good work, Peabody."

"Good enough for coffee?"

Eve jerked a thumb at the machine. "We're going to get a forensic accountant to start on the finances. With what we have so far, they'll have a head start. We're already authorized to go into Singer's business accounts. There's going to be discrepancies, and they're going to point to him and Delgato. Could be others in on it and, if so, we'll find them."

Eve pushed up, moved to the board.

"Consider this, consider a possible connection between Alva Quirk and the woman whose remains we found on another site previously owned by Singer. Both of them almost certainly killed at night, when the site was closed. The use of substandard materials. Yeah, common on the old site, but who's to say there wasn't skimming and theft and fraud?"

She tapped a finger on Tovinski's photo. "Who's to say he wasn't there?"

"He'd have been a teenager, right?"

Eve tapped the photo again before she looked back at Reo. "Born to kill. And we both know you don't have to be an adult to kill. I do believe it's going to come up in conversation when he's in Interview."

"He'll have a lawyer on tap. A good one."

Eve smiled. "Are you afraid of a mob lawyer, Reo?"

"Not even a little."

"Me, either. Peabody, get the warrant and the files to the best accountant we've got, then write up the statement from the fancy-pants house."

"I've got it."

As Peabody rushed out, Eve leaned on the desk again. "He's weak," Eve began. "He thinks he's tough, feels invincible because he's always had protection. He's always been inside the club with his uncle patting his head. But he's weak. The women, and the way he sets them up, the way he hides them. From each other, too, I bet."

"I tend to agree with that," Reo said. "I can't see those women, or his wife, tolerating the others. Or not well."

"He struck Alva from behind, he lay in wait for Delgato and took him out with a paralytic. He's used to giving orders, being feared. He's not that smart. Roarke said his financial—what's the word you liked?—machinations were sloppy. I'll break him."

"You wouldn't know about any bigger elephants in those sloppy financials, would you?"

Eve glanced over, eyes cool. "Smaller ones generally grow into bigger ones, don't they?"

Reo just nodded. "We'll leave it there. Now, let's take the next fifteen—because I have to get back to the office—to make sure we're approaching this upcoming interview from the same angle. Then I'll come back when he's ready for the box, and we'll sweat him together."

When they'd finished, Eve updated her board, both sides, then sat to do the same with her book.

She wanted that sit-down with Yuri Bardov, but knew it had to wait until she broke his nephew, until she had that wrapped. And the day was already clicking away.

She needed the accountant to find what Roarke had. Since it wasn't something she could push, she went down to Evidence for Alva's books.

She hadn't expected to cart back an evidence box holding more than two dozen.

But Alva, the rule-follower, had each one dated. For expediency, she started with the last, opting to work her way back.

When she realized that book detailed Alva's time at the shelter, she set it aside, took out the previous.

It was a nightmare from the start.

It twisted in her heart, in her guts, the despair, the self-blame, the fear, the loneliness.

She'd known all that, could still feel it if she let herself.

> Trying isn't enough. I overcooked dinner and
> wasted food. Three slaps. Garrett hates to yell at
> me, so I have to do better. Accidents don't happen.
> Saying they do is a lie and a weak, whiny excuse
> for being careless. I broke the glass. Two slaps. I
> tried to hide the broken glass and that's deceitful,
> disgusting, and dishonest. I deserved the broken
> finger. He hates when I make him punish me, but
> the pain will remind me to be careful, to value what
> he works so hard to give me.

She read page after page of vicious, systematic, sadistic abuse. Day after day, with few respites.

And though the writing was nearly illegible, she read the last day Alva spent in that prison, read of the beating. She hadn't felt well—he cited lazy, ungrateful—so hadn't cleaned the house to his standards, didn't have the evening meal ready, embarrassed him by not weeding the flower bed in front of the house so the neighbors could see how stupid and lazy she was.

The rape followed the beating, though he called it his right, her duty.

"Dallas."

She looked over, saw Peabody. She hadn't heard her. How could she have heard her when she'd been living a nightmare?

"Alva Quirk's—or Alva Elliot's—brother and sister are here. They just got on a shuttle and came."

"Take them to the lounge. Stay with them. I'll be right there."

"You okay?"

"Yeah. I'm, ah, I'm going to text Morris to expect them. Get them settled in the lounge."

Alone, she sat back, breathed it out. Should she tell them about these books? No, she didn't think so. Not now.

But she very deliberately printed out Garrett Wicker's ID shot and, rising, added it to her board.

"Once I put her killer away, you miserable, sadistic fuck, I'm coming for you."

She got a tube of water, drank half of it to relieve her dry throat. She looked back at the books, then picked up the last one. The one Alva had filled with peace, happiness, growing confidence.

They could read some of it now, maybe take some comfort in their sister's words. Eventually, when it was done, when justice was served, she'd send it to them.

14

Eve gave them as much time as she could spare, told them as much of the progress as she felt necessary. In the end, she arranged for them to be taken to the morgue.

"They won't be able to take her home yet," Peabody said as they walked back to Eve's office.

"No."

"Before you came in, I found out they hadn't even booked a hotel or anything, so I gave them a couple of recommendations. They just wanted to get here, just wanted to see her."

"Morris'll take care of it."

"These are her books, from before." Peabody looked at the stacks on Eve's desk. "A lot of them. Do you want me to take some?"

"No, I've got this, and she's very detailed on the abuse. So there's that after we close this end of it down."

"Are we going to Oklahoma?"

"When we close the investigation of her murder and Delgato's, the timing of that depends on how quickly DeWinter gets us what we need on our other victim. But we won't be going to him. Not his turf, Peabody. We'll get him on ours."

"I wouldn't mind seeing Oklahoma—you know, cowboys—but I like that better." She looked at the stacks again. "How bad was it?"

"As bad as it gets. He'd have killed her eventually. In a way, he did. I've got Nadine on tap for this, and she's getting other reporters on tap. I'm feeding her what I can."

"She'll dig up the rest."

"Exactly. When we've got him in the box, when we start sweating him, I'm giving her the go. He deserves that," she murmured. "He deserves having his officers, his neighbors, absolute strangers know who he is. What he did to her."

"I'm hungry."

"What?"

"Let's have some lunch."

Sincerely stunned, Eve watched Peabody go to her Auto-Chef and bring up the menu of choices.

"Hey, you've got grilled rosemary chicken sands with pepper jack cheese. We should spring for fries with that."

When she punched through the shock, it hit her.

"Are you playing Roarke?"

"I can't match the accent or the mmm sexy, but being your professional and platonic partner, I'm taking his lead. You need the boost if we're going to kick some Russian gangster's ass, and follow it up—soon—by kicking that fucking abuser's ass. And I get one, too. That's a good deal for me."

Peabody took out the plates, passed one to Eve. Taking her own, Peabody looked at the visitor's chair.

"I'm sitting on the floor."

Once she'd ordered two tubes of Pepsi—diet for herself—she did just that.

Eve sat, ate a fry. "Reo's getting a search warrant for Tovinski's residence and his office—or will when the accountant comes through. I hit Feeney up for McNab and Callendar to take the electronics."

"His uncle's going to hear about all this."

"Counting on it. It just might bring him to our turf."

"No trip to the Hudson Valley? Big sigh!" Peabody nibbled on her sandwich. "I'd love to see the Hudson Valley."

"You may yet. The elder Singers need to chat with us. Singer senior might have a hand in the skimming. He was a crap CEO."

Eve, no nibbler, bit into the sandwich and her incoming signaled.

"Accounting," she said with her mouth full. "I told them to send me an alert if they found anything. Very preliminary," she read. "Discrepancies re invoices, material, and equipment changes. Unaccountable income stream. This is good."

"The sandwich or the data?"

"Both." She took another bite, then copied the report to Reo.

Get the search warrants. We're picking him up.

She hit interoffice for Officer Carmichael. "I want two of your biggest, baddest uniforms to pick up a suspect. I'm sending you the information."

"Copy that, Lieutenant."

"I'll send it," Peabody told her. "I've got it right here."

"Accountant says it could take a couple days to cover everything." Eve smiled. "And that's before we get to Tovinski's electronics, and his second set of books. We're going to grill him, Peabody. Just like this chicken."

Then she frowned at the visitor's chair again. "I like that chair."

"You like what the chair represents," Peabody corrected as she sent the data.

"Same thing."

Eve ate another fry, then picked up her plate and sat on the floor across from Peabody.

"Aw."

"It's not sentiment. It's weird looking down at you when we're working out how to go at Tovinski."

"I'm good cop." Peabody made an O with her mouth, slapped a hand on her heart. "Surprise!"

"Not exactly. Women are his bad heel."

"Achilles' heel?"

"Isn't that what it means? He's got that weakness. You could get a little flirt on—not overdone, just a little."

"Flirt?"

"You've got the tits. Plus, you're his type. I ran his wife, his other women. He goes for brunettes with the tits. Reo's got the girly looks and knows how to use them so dumb-asses underestimate her. But you have the tits."

Peabody looked down. "Why is it always about the tits?"

"I figure men don't have them, so they want them. Add the last one he knocked up is young. You're younger, but she's still in her twenties. He's going younger and sticking with tits, so a little flirt on's a good angle."

"I can do a little flirt. Can I giggle?"

"Don't overdo it. And shut it down when you feel it's time. Shut it down hard."

"I like that part."

"We start with Delgato—nothing about Alva unless it opens. Delgato—the fabric, the finances, that connection. And the other women. I want to know if his uncle knows about them. If he knows about the skimming."

"You don't think he does?"

"I don't, but I could be wrong. I'm right, we play it that way. I'm wrong, we play it the other."

She looked back at the next signal. "That's the search warrants. Let's get this party started."

It took time to bring Tovinski in, for him to contact a lawyer, for the lawyer to arrive and consult with his client. Eve gave them plenty of time and used it to prepare for the interview, to drag more updates from the accountant.

She had her file ready to go when Reo walked into her office.

"Tovinski and his lawyer are about finished. He's got Dima Ilyin, Yuri Bardov's personal attorney. I assume you already know that."

"Pays to know."

"So we go with Plan A."

"It's a good plan."

"I'll be in Observation until. Interview A, correct?"

"Yeah, Santiago and Carmichael are working one in B."

"Okay then, God bless us, every one."

Eve finished loading her files, gathered them up. When she walked into the bullpen, Peabody rose from her desk. "Good timing. They're ready for us."

"They think they are." Revved and more than ready, Eve walked to Interview A.

She opened the door. "Record on. Dallas, Lieutenant Eve and Peabody, Detective Delia entering Interview with Tovinski, Alexei and counsel. State your name please, sir, for the record."

"Dima Ilyin."

"Ilyin, Dima, representing Mr. Tovinski in this interview regarding case number F-26451 and case number H-45180, and related matters."

Eve sat, set the files on the table as Peabody took the seat beside her. "Mr. Tovinski, were you read your rights and, if so, do you understand your rights and obligations in this matter?"

"My client stipulates that he was read his rights and understands them."

"Great." Eve opened the first file, and saw out of the corner of her eye Peabody execute a not altogether subtle hair flip.

"While my client is prepared to fully cooperate with your investigation into this unfortunate death, he further stipulates that he had only the most peripheral and occasional working relationship with Mr. Delgato.

"Lieutenant." Ilyin folded his well-manicured hands.

As he paused with what Eve took to be a sober smile on his face, Eve folded her own hands, looked directly at him.

A hawkish face, she thought, with the beaked nose, the jutting jaw, the prominent black eyebrows over eyes nearly as dark. He wore his hair in a snow-white mane.

He had no trace of an accent in his deep, almost throaty baritone.

"It wasn't a secret that Mr. Delgato had a serious, one could say debilitating gambling addiction. This addiction had cost Mr. Delgato his marriage, the respect of his adult children, and caused him to live alone in a small apartment in a building patronized by street LCs and indigents."

"That's a lot of information about someone who was only a peripheral and occasional coworker."

Ilyin lifted the fingers of his folded hands. "Mr. Delgato's difficulties and predilections were common gossip among the crews. As is the information that Mr. Delgato was found hanging in his apartment in what would strongly appear to be a suicide. While tragic, I fail to see how this involves my client."

"I hope to make that more clear. We'll start with the fraudulent financial accounts, which violate U.S. tax and investment laws."

"Lieutenant." That smile again. "We're all aware you and the detective work in Homicide. If we could—"

"Is your client refusing to cooperate re these violations?"

"I believe we can discuss those with the authorities so assigned. Meanwhile."

"I'm the authority so assigned," Eve snapped back. "Two of these fraudulent, tax-evading, illegal accounts are in New York, and the funding of same applies to the investigation of Carmine Delgato's death. If your client wishes to remain silent on those matters, I can have him taken back to his cell."

Tovinski muttered something in Russian and earned a sharp look from the lawyer.

"My client is an engineer, not a financial expert. Clearly, he mistakenly and inadvertently signed papers that opened these additional accounts, and was unaware he was in violation. He will, of course, immediately rectify that mistake and will pay any and all fines attached."

"Would that include the accounts set up in Grand Cayman, in Moscow, and in Kiev?"

Ilyin's interlocked fingers tightened, just a little. "Of course."

Didn't know, Eve concluded. Somebody's client isn't being fully open and honest.

"There's a question of the funding thereof. How did you come up with one million, two hundred and eighty-four dollars over and above your earned income in the last twenty-four months, Mr. Tovinski?"

"My client receives cash bonuses."

"Cash, unreported, of over a million dollars in the past twenty-four months?"

"Again, my client admits to some mistakes, as he is not fully educated on tax law and codes. He wasn't aware he needed to report the cash."

"Strange. You'd think his lawyer, his accountant, his financial adviser would be fully educated."

"Lost in translation."

"Oh? Do you speak English, Mr. Tovinski?"

"I speak English."

At the accent, Peabody let out a soft sound, like a woman who'd just taken a bite out of something decadent and delicious. It earned her a warm look.

"And Italian and, of course, Russian. I am an educated man, but with money matters . . ." He lifted broad shoulders, giving Peabody another eye-flirt. "I am not so much."

"Are you married, Mr. Tovinski?"

"My client is a happily married man, and a loving father to his son and his daughter."

"Son and daughter, singular?" Eve nodded as she looked through the file. "I see here you have a joint account with a Nadia Tovinski, that would be your wife. And there's an account, a trust fund for your son Mikael and your daughter Una." She looked up and straight into Tovinski's hard, handsome face. "I assume these other accounts, the hidden ones, are in your name only, as you preferred to keep them from your wife, son, and daughter."

"My client's marriage isn't relevant."

"Have to disagree. It's relevant when the accounts in question are used to provide funds for . . . Let me find the list. Here we go. Elsa Karvell and the two minor children Gregor and Alise. For Pilar Sanchez and the minor child, Elena, and for Masie Franks, who is currently thirty weeks pregnant."

She looked up, noted Tovinski's stony face and the glint of anger in Ilyin's eyes.

"I see a pattern there. Don't you, Detective?"

"I . . ." In Peabody's eyes, Eve saw dazzle, which her partner struggled to erase. "I, yes, sir."

"Do your son and daughter with your legal wife know they have half siblings, Mr. Tovinski?"

"This is not your business."

"I take that as a no. You've cheated on your wife a minimum of three times, impregnating these women—one of them twice—and have these accounts to pay them off, ensure their silence."

"I pay no one off!" Outrage sparked, had him pounding a fist on the table."

"Alexei—"

"No!" He shoved the lawyer's hand aside. "She insults me." He turned his gaze to Peabody. "Do I look like a man who must pay women?"

"No." Peabody let out the giggle, then quickly covered her mouth with her hand. "I mean to say . . ."

Eve barely flicked Peabody a glance. "You went to a lot of trouble to set up hidden and illegal accounts to conceal them from your wife."

"It's not illegal for a man to have needs outside of marriage. I do not pay them off. I do my duty and see that the children have good homes, the best education and care. This is what a man who is a man does."

"It's a great deal of money."

"These children are my blood."

"If your wife were to learn of these accounts, the funds in them, and how some of those funds are used?"

"There is no reason for her to know."

"And your uncle. Yuri Bardov."

"There is no reason. This is my business only." He turned to the lawyer, eyes hot. "This is attorney-client privilege."

"Maybe Carmine Delgato found out."

Tovinski made a *pfft* sound. "The man is a plumber. He's a plumber. I barely know him. How would he know my private business?"

"Maybe you had a drink with him after work. I'm told some of the crews do that sort of thing."

"I am not crew. I am an engineer."

"Right. So you and Delgato never sat down over drinks."

"No. I barely know him. Knew him."

"You never had personal conversations or conversations that didn't apply to the work itself?"

"No."

"You never went to his apartment, visited him there?"

"Why would I? I don't know where he lives. He matters nothing. I don't know him."

"So you never went to his apartment on West Twenty-sixth? Apartment 2B?"

"I said no. No, I have not been there."

"Okay, let's move on." Eve pushed through the files. "Detective, there should be water in here. Go out and bring in some water."

"Yes, sir. Um. Peabody, exiting Interview."

At the door, she turned, shot Tovinski a quick smile. When he smiled back, she only half muffled a giggle.

"Lieutenant."

Even in the single word, Eve heard the change in Ilyin's tone. He was angry. Oh yeah, he was pissed. But he'd continue to do his job.

"We've answered your questions regarding the mistakes made in my client's financial accounts. We will agree to rectify those mistakes and pay appropriate fines. My client's personal . . . behavior regarding his marriage and extramarital activities are private matters."

"Look at that. We disagree again. It goes to motive."

"My client has stated, repeatedly, that he had no relationship with Mr. Delgato. He would certainly have no reason to share this personal and private information with a plumber with the Singer organization."

"Maybe, maybe not. But he shared other business with him. I'm going to believe you're crap at financials, Tovinski. Just like you're crap once someone with working brains goes beneath the surface of invoices and orders and material inventory."

She pulled copies out of the file, shot them across the table. "And I'm betting your uncle doesn't know you've been dipping your hand in his pockets. I wonder if he knows you've been dipping it into the pockets of companies he's partnered with on various projects. Like Singer."

"This is bullshit! This is made-up!"

"I'm betting your lawyer has a working brain, and it won't take him long to see the bullshit's on your side of the table. Or to see that a good many of these invoices, order and inventory sheets are signed off by you and Carmine Delgato."

"Then he was a cheat as well as a gambling whore."

"Oh, agreed. But you're a cheat as well as—in my personal opinion—a man whore."

He lunged up, his face infused with rage as he reached over and dragged Eve out of her chair. She punched him in the throat—pulled it, as she wanted him to be able to talk. He flung her across the room.

Her shoulder hit the wall, but she sprang up as Ilyin struggled to pull Tovinski back.

Ilyin shouted in Russian, wrapping his arms around Tovinski as Eve rolled her shoulders back. "We'll add assaulting an officer to the rest. Sit your ass down, and now."

"I take that from no woman."

"You'll take it from me or sit in a cage until I'm ready to bring you back."

"Alexei, Alexei, you must sit. You must be calm. Lieutenant, my client is overwrought. You clearly goaded him. I need a few moments with my client."

"You want a few minutes?" She started gathering papers

that had scattered when he attacked her. "That'll give me time to put all this back together. Including the records from your client's comp in his home office. Search warrant, counselor, a copy of which is in this file. The records that list just how much he stole from his own uncle. Bardov projects accounted for more than seven hundred thousand in the last twelve-month period. It's not a cash bonus, Alexei, when you steal it."

"Lies. She lies."

"Fact. Documented. Your own records. Uncle Yuri's going to be very disappointed." Eve gathered up the files, headed for the door. "Interview paused by counsel's request. Dallas exiting Interview. Record off."

She pulled open the door, glanced back. "I wonder how Yuri Bardov handles someone who disappoints him."

She shut the door, then gripped a hand on her screaming shoulder and said, "Fuck!"

"You hit hard." Peabody hurried down to her. "I was going for the door when Reo said to stop, you had it under control. I got you a cold pack."

"I figured him for a puncher and I could block most of one, just let him catch a piece of me." She pushed the files at Peabody, then slapped the cold pack on her shoulder. "Well, we got violent temper on the goddamn record."

She nodded as Reo came out of Observation and started toward them. "How're we doing?"

"Plan A's a very good plan. Ilyin's off his game because his client lied to him. He's certainly known Tovinski for years, but he didn't know. Not about the women, the other children, and he sure as hell didn't know about the skimming. My take? Right now, he's getting as much out of Tovinski as he can and it's likely Tovinski will give him some because he's counting on privilege."

"But?"

"As we discussed, unless Tovinski's a complete idiot, once he calms down, clears his head, he'll start thinking about who Ilyin's real client is. How's the shoulder?"

"Hurts like a mother."

"If it's any consolation, it's going to make an excellent visual on record. I'm going back. I say I stay where I am until the next reveal."

"It'll be coming right up."

While Reo walked back, Peabody turned to Eve. "How's my flirting?"

"It's revolting, which means it's good. He thinks you're an easy mark. Plus, you're feeding his considerable ego. You should keep it up until—"

She broke off when Ilyin stepped out. "Lieutenant, I'd like to apologize again, but I believe the record will show you goaded my client into an unwise reaction."

"Looks like we disagree again. Is he ready to continue the interview?"

"Yes, or in a moment. I appreciate the water, but I'd prefer coffee."

"Oh." Peabody handed Eve back the files, juggled the four tubes of water. "I'll get that for you."

"No need. I'd like to use the washroom. I'll just be a moment."

"Down the hall, on the left," Eve directed. "We'll hold outside the room until you're ready."

Eve started back toward Interview, glanced back to see Ilyin pull out his 'link. "He's contacting Bardov."

"He could be disbarred for breaking privilege."

"Who's going to tell on him?"

Eve tossed the cold pack in a recycler. "Give it another minute. I'm dressing you down for acting like a girl in there."

"Got it." Peabody lowered her head.

"I want to give the lawyer time to hit the high points

before we go in. Okay, he's gone into the john. He's going to make it quick, but Tovinski's going to have time to sit and stew. And start thinking."

She took out her communicator, set up the next step.

When she slid it back into her pocket, Ilyin came out of the restroom, stopped by Vending for coffee.

"Thank you for your patience," he said when he joined them. "If we could continue, without histrionics, I believe we'll resolve this entire matter quickly."

"Sure." Eve went in. "Record on. Dallas, Peabody, and counsel for Tovinski reentering Interview."

Peabody actually flushed and fluttered her lashes as she set the tube of water in front of Tovinski.

"Thank you. You're very kind. I am to apologize, Lieutenant, for allowing my emotions to rise."

"Is that what you call it? Let's continue. Regarding these invoices, inventories, order sheets."

"I can think only someone forged my signature. It may be this Delgato did so to feed his gambling habit."

"And did Delgato somehow create the set of books, clearly showing—in detail—what you stole, how you did so, and when, on the passcoded computer locked in your home office?"

"It's not unheard of for the police to manipulate such matters. I know this, my uncle knows it well."

"Really?" She looked back at Ilyin. "That's the line you're going to take? Did your counsel mention what's going to happen when we check with your uncle regarding these extremely generous cash bonuses you claim? Is he going to back you up there?"

"Why would he not? It's truth."

"And, of course, he'd have records of those bonuses in his personal or company's accounts."

Hadn't thought of that, she noted.

"He'll also testify that he issued those cash bonuses without reporting them. So, anyway, you're stating that the money you used—unreported income of over a million dollars just in the past two years— Oh, and we're going back to previous years as we speak. You're stating the money you used to support two women and three children, another woman who is currently pregnant in what many would call a lavish lifestyle is all from cash bonuses earned through your work with Bardov Construction?"

"I have made that clear."

"And that someone—likely Delgato—forged your signature to sign off on fraudulent invoices, on material that was substandard rather than what was originally listed, and on amended inventories as material and equipment went missing. In addition, someone—the police, in your opinion— manipulated your records, created records that document the fraud and thievery—that somehow come out to the same amounts deposited in your fake accounts over the same twenty-four-month period."

When Tovinski said nothing, Eve just smiled.

"Yeah, when you hear it spelled out like that, it just defies logic, doesn't it? What's logical is you and Delgato worked together to do all of the above. He didn't get the lion's share, but enough to keep him playing the horses, sure he'd hit that long shot and everything would be fine again.

"But he knew too much. He had to go."

Tovinski spread his hands, appealed directly to Peabody. "A man has loyalty to his family. Didn't my uncle bring me to this country, to this city, give me a home, give me food, give me education and work? Loyalty and gratitude in my heart."

Sympathetic tears shined in Peabody's eyes as Tovinski laid a hand on his heart.

"He is a father to me. You understand?"

"Yes."

"This Delgato, I say again, I barely know him. And he killed himself, which is a sin. I'm sorry for him. But he is the cheat, the thief. I think the guilt drove him to take his life."

"If you barely knew him," Peabody asked, timidly, "why do you think he used your name? Just yours?"

"He would know I'm important. No one would question my signature."

"That makes sense. Plus, you never went to his apartment."

"No, I was never there. I have pity in my heart for a man so desperate and lost he would take his own life."

"Mr. Tovinski," Eve continued. "Can you explain why you withdrew ten thousand yesterday morning, in cash, from the fraudulent account you have in New York under the name of New York Opportunities, the shell company you created for same?"

"A man needs cash."

"That's a lot of cash. Did you make a specific purchase?"

"I have expenses." He executed the shrug and dismissive hand wave of an important man. "I tip generously. My wife and my children, they have expenses."

"So this wasn't for a specific purchase, such as a syringe full of Dexachlorine?"

Nothing showed in his eyes, but a muscle twitched in his jaw. "I don't know what this is. A medication? I take no medication."

"It's the paralytic found in Delgato's system—as we found him seconds before he died and the chief medical examiner of New York performed an autopsy, including a tox screen, immediately and expediently."

Eve pressed a finger to her throat. "The neck bruising didn't quite hide the pressure mark. Homicide," she told Il-yin. "Not suicide. Your boy here broke into the apartment.

He installed a hook in the ceiling. You should've left the tool behind, Alexei. Delgato didn't have one in the apartment that could have drilled that hole, and the paint and drywall flaked. Fresh flakes on the floor."

"Lies, lies. Desperate lies now."

"And all yours." Eve rose at the knock on the door. She took the suit from Officer Shelby. "Thank you, Officer. Freshly back from the lab," she said as she held the suit up in its sealed bag.

"Is this your suit, Tovinski?"

"How do I know? I have many suits."

"Well, it was taken from your closet, in your home, hung in the section you use for garments to be dry-cleaned. Plus, it's custom—bet it fits like a glove. And you have your name monogrammed inside the jacket."

She broke the seal, removed it, opened the jacket to show the name embroidered on the black silk lining. "Again, is this your suit?"

"Yes, so what?"

Eve took a small evidence vial out of her files. "See this?" She showed the tiny fabric traces. "This came off the suit—right here." Now she showed the portion on the inside upper leg marked by the lab. "The slight snag, the tiny bits of fabric. Too bad. It's terrific material. You snagged it when, after you jimmied the window on Delgato's flop, you climbed in to lie in wait."

"These are lies."

"This is science. You broke in, installed the hook, waited for him. And when he got there, you jabbed the paralytic into him so he couldn't fight back. He'd be aware and, oh, he'd feel, but he couldn't fight back when you put the noose around his neck. When you stood on the chair and pulled him up.

"You didn't wait for him to die. Nobody cared about him,

that's what you figured. You climbed back out the window, but only seconds, I'm thinking, before his landlord started pounding on his door. Maybe a minute or two before I walked to his door, hoping to question him."

"It's threads, threads in a bottle." Though he let out a short, hard laugh, a single line of sweat ran down his left temple. "It proves nothing! The plumber, he did the stealing. Why would I kill him for what I didn't do?"

"You did it—and there's ample evidence, which is why your lawyer's quiet. But you didn't kill him over that. Hell, he was useful there."

Rising, Eve circled around the table, leaned in over Tovinski's shoulder.

"You killed him because you couldn't trust him to keep quiet. Not after Alva Quirk saw the two of you up there, taking materials from the site. Not after she told you to stop, started writing in her book. Not after you went into the storage shed, got a crowbar, and slammed it into her head. Not after you killed her, and, with Delgato's help, because he was terrified, wrapped her in plastic and tossed her in the dumpster."

She circled around again and looked back at the lawyer, whose face showed nothing.

"He killed two people to cover up the fact he's a thief, one who'll steal from his own family. And we've got him cold."

Tovinski must have sensed it, in the silence, in the cold look in Ilyin's eyes.

"You would let them do this to me?"

"I will speak with my client alone, please."

"No, no, no. You think I can't see? You think I don't know? You're not my lawyer now. Get out. Get out."

"We'll talk. Alone."

"No. You don't stand for me. You don't represent me. He's not my lawyer now," he said to Eve. "He must leave."

"Sir, Mr. Tovinski has terminated your services, on record. This is his right. I have to ask you to leave the room."

"This is a mistake, Alexei. Take some time," he said as he rose. "Tell them you want time to think, to calm. Do this for yourself. If you contact me, I'll come back."

"Former counsel for Alexei Tovinski exiting Interview. Mr. Tovinski, do you wish to contact different counsel at this time?"

He leaned forward. "We will make a deal. I want a deal."

"Are you waiving your right to legal representation at this time?"

"Fuck the lawyers. We will make a deal. And you will be head of the whole police with what I give you with this deal."

"Well, wow. You must have something really big to offer."

Eve glanced over as Reo came into the room. "And here's handy Assistant Prosecuting Attorney Cher Reo entering Interview. Reo, Tovinski wants to play Let's Make a Deal."

Reo sat, set her briefcase aside. And smiled. "All right, Mr. Tovinski, let's play."

15

"I can offer you anything you could want."

As if fascinated, Reo propped her chin on her fist. "You're going to offer me a villa in Sorrento?"

His lip curled. "You think this is a joke? What I have in here?" He tapped his temple. "With this, you could buy a dozen villas. Now you're only an assistant, but with what I can give comes power, and with power comes money and fame."

He shifted to Peabody. "A young, pretty woman such as yourself has dreams. I can help you reach them. You're three attractive women. You want more than to work all day, every day, taking orders from someone else."

"Goodness, it's like he can see inside our souls." Reo tossed her hair. "Or, no, that's not it, is it, Dallas?"

"No. More like a mirror. Is that how this started, Tovinski? You got tired of taking orders from Uncle Yuri?"

"You don't make the deals." Dismissing Eve, he turned his body toward Reo. "You do. I can give you Yuri Bardov. Think of that."

"Okay, I'm thinking of it. And what do you want in return?"

"I want immunity, full immunity. And I want—"

"No. Do you have a second option?"

"You think we'll play games here?" Voice rising, he banged his fist on the table. "You'll give me what I want, and I'll give you enough for you to take down my uncle and his organization. You're an underling. Your boss will want this."

"The prosecutor's office isn't much interested in Yuri Bardov at this time. While we believe he's a very bad actor, his influence and activities have waned, considerably, over the last several years. He's an old mobster, Mr. Tovinski, who's been more interested in his gardens and fruit trees than expanding his network for quite some time now. We prefer leaving him to the feds."

"Must've been frustrating for you," Eve said. "Always believing you'd inherit this wide, organized criminal enterprise, only to find your uncle slowly getting out of the game. Why take orders from an old man when you could pay him lip service and steal from him?"

"Add the women," Reo put in.

"Oh yeah, the women. Yuri Bardov once may have been a criminal kingpin, but he's remained married—and faithful, according to all agency reports—to his Marta for nearly sixty years. He brought you to America, into his business, treated you like a son because she asked him to. And . . ."

Eve shuffled through her file until she slid out a media photo of Tovinski's wife, his aunt, and another woman in formal dress beaming at the camera. "Your wife is the daughter of your aunt's oldest, closest friend."

"Cheating, stealing, lying?" Reo sighed, then ticked a finger back and forth in the air. "And against family? Uncle Yuri's going to be very upset."

"He knows nothing. He's become a fool. A weak man who forgets what made him great. But there's money, much money in what I know."

Eve glanced at her wrist unit. "By this time, I'm confident in saying he knows everything. Who sent his top mouthpiece to represent you, Alexei? Buy a couple clues."

"He would be disbarred if—"

"They'll both deny it," Reo cut in. "And how are you going to prove Ilyin broke privilege?"

"That'd be a tough one," Eve agreed. "Especially since you'll be dead before the sun comes up tomorrow. He may have stepped back, but he's still Bardov, and you insulted him, betrayed him and your family. You betrayed your wife."

"You can't let him have me killed. You must put me in witness protection."

"You're not a witness," Reo reminded him.

Quickly, he turned to Peabody, held out his hands in appeal.

"He will pay someone to murder me. My own uncle will do this. He's heartless, ruthless. He'll do this because I have too much heart, and I gave it to women not my wife—a wife he chose for me. He'll do this because I wanted to give all my children a good life, and a good life takes money. It was only money, and he has so much. It was for my children, and he'll kill me, and they'll have no father.

"You understand. I can see you have a heart. You have to help me."

"You want me to help you?"

Peabody started to reach her hands toward his. Then she slammed her palms on the table as she lurched up. "You want me to help you? You spineless prick of a slug stain. You greedy, brainless ball of pus. You smashed a harmless, helpless woman's skull in, exploited a desperate addict, then pumped a drug into him so you could string him up without getting your pampered hands dirty."

While Eve watched with pride swelling in her heart, Peabody rounded the table to push her face in his. "How many others have you killed so you could buy your fancy suits and screw around on your wife? You're going down, you whiny asshole fuckwit. We've got you cold, and you're going down. Help you? You bet your miserable murdering ass I'm going to help put you in a cage for the rest of your ugly worthless life."

Eve let the silence hang for a beat. "What she said." Since Peabody's outburst threw him off balance, Eve pushed hard.

"We've got everything we need to put you away for Delgato. Everything we need to prove you used him to help you steal from your uncle's company, Singer's, others. We have what we need to take you down for the murder of Alva Quirk."

Eve leaned back as Peabody came around the table, dropped down in her own chair.

"We know you killed Delgato because you were afraid he'd talk, he'd tell someone how you killed Alva Quirk."

Fear, genuine fear, flickered in Tovinski's eyes before he cut them away.

"You can't prove it. Maybe he killed the old woman. Then himself."

"He couldn't fricking hang himself pumped up with a paralytic, Alexei. Pay attention. You were there. You climbed in the window. Went up the fire escape, went in. Do you think nobody notices some guy in a custom-made suit climbing in a window of a flop?"

She had nothing there, but he didn't know that, she thought. And she watched the idea of a witness strike him.

"We'll be rounding up all your associates and accomplices on your skimming scams and we may be making some deals there, right, Reo?"

"Absolutely. I believe I have the list the forensic accountant so kindly provided." In turn, Reo shuffled through her file. "Yeah, here it is. Small change." She beamed across the table at Tovinski. "I love making deals with small change to rake in the bigger bucks."

"But we don't need them for Alva Quirk. We have her books."

Eve smiled when she said it, continued to improvise as she saw fear bloom.

"Yeah, I figure you trashed the book you grabbed after you smashed Alva's head in. The thing is, she's been keeping those books since she was a kid. She had a hell of a collection. Do you really think the night you killed her was the only time she'd seen you on the Singer site? The only time she'd noted down you were there, where you had no business being?"

"You're lying."

"Test me," Eve invited. "If you live to go to trial, manage to get another lawyer and risk a trial, picture me on the stand reading from one of this sweet, harmless woman's notebooks. Imagine the chief medical examiner describing the killing wounds—back of the skull. Back of the skull, Alexei, and testifying when our APA here shows the crowbar you didn't quite clean thoroughly so it still had traces of her blood and brain matter on it."

"If you put me in prison, I'll be dead. You'll be murderers, the three of you. I want a deal."

"He wants a deal," Eve said to Reo, and Peabody snorted.

"Here's how I see it," Reo began. "We go to trial with evidence so profound I expect the jury would come back with a guilty—all counts—in under an hour. Could be a record. You then spend whatever's left of your life off-planet. We could keep you in isolation—from now and until."

"He'll pay for my death, and my blood will be on your hands."

"How much blood's on yours?" Peabody shot back. "You murdering shitbag."

"Or . . ." Reo let the single syllable sit a moment. "You make a full confession, a full and detailed confession, on both murders, and we immediately transfer you, under another name, to an on-planet facility. You'll be provided with another identity, another background. Think of it as witness protection in prison."

"My children."

"Would Yuri Bardov harm or cause harm to be done to your wife, the women you're supporting, or your children? Lies," Eve added coolly, "cut back on the terms of any deal. Test me," she invited again.

He met Eve's steady gaze for an instant, then shook his head. "No, I have no fear for them. He would never harm a child or the mother who tends them. But I provide for them. I visit them. Children need their father."

"You should've thought of that part before you screwed with your uncle, before you murdered two people to cover that up," Eve said flatly. "You heard the deal. Take it or leave it. Either way, you're spending the rest of your life in a cage. How long a life, and where that cage is, that's up to you."

"I did it for my children. I want the best for my children. The best costs. My uncle, he knows about the oldest in Corfu. He was very angry. Nadia is his goddaughter. He said he would keep this secret as not to hurt her. I would continue to support the child and her mother. It would never happen again. If it happened again, I would no longer be welcomed in his home, I would no longer be part of his family, in any way."

"But it happened again."

"This is my business, not his. It's my private business. I take his orders. He wants me to be an engineer, so I study to become an engineer. He wants to . . . persuade someone to fall in line. I persuade them. He wants me to marry Nadia, I marry Nadia. I give her a good life. But I have my life, too. He wants to control me, and all the while I see him get weaker, draw back from what made him great. From the man I respected. So I took what I wanted. I took what I needed."

Disgust covered his face. "The man I respected? It wouldn't have been so easy to take from him as I did. He plays with his flowers, his trees. But he still holds the wheel, and won't give it to me. So I took more. What I wanted, what I needed. What I deserved after all the years of doing what he said to do."

"Did he order you to kill?"

He sneered at Eve. "I don't give you that now. Fuck you for that now."

"Move on then. Alva Quirk."

"Crazy old woman with her book and paper flowers. She's nothing. A little mouse in her hole, nothing more. We have business, me and Delgato. To move some material out—we have a buyer, we have the invoices marked as we need. A small shipment, so it's very quick for the buyer to remove and pay and take away."

"Who's the buyer?"

"Fuck you."

"Fine. The invoices and your records tell that tale anyway. What then?"

"We talk, me and Delgato, and arrange for the next shipment, and there she is at the fence with her book. She's sorry, but she has to report us. We broke rules. Delgato goes over, talking to her, talking about how we're just doing our job. He's wasting time, convincing this mouse. I have the crowbar we had to check the shipment, to open the box. I use it."

"You struck her with it?"

"I did what had to be done."

"You struck her with it," Eve repeated. "How many times?"

"Once—no, twice. To be sure. Delgato loses his mind. I

think he might faint, he's so weak. I slap him to calm him down. He cries, like a baby, but he does what I say. He gets the plastic and we roll her up, carry her to the dumpster. I take her book—that was before we rolled her in the plastic. I think it should be a day, maybe two, before she's found. And who will care?"

He shrugged that off. Even now, Eve thought, he shrugged off the murder of Alva Quirk like it was only a small inconvenience.

"You were wrong there, on both counts. When did you decide to kill Delgato?"

"Then, but it's not the time, the place, the way. I'm not stupid. He's a miserable man, a weak man, a crying man. I have a source for the Dex—and fuck you on that. I know he'll break. He'll tell his wife, or maybe go to the police, claim he saw it happen, but wasn't part. So I took care of it."

"How?"

"You said how. I took the drill, the syringe, the hook, the rope. His window lock is flimsy."

He flicked a hand in the air. Dismissing it all, Eve decided. Because it had been just another job.

Born to kill.

"He lives in a dump because he's weak and tosses his money away on horse races. I put the hook in the ceiling, make the noose. He's a failure of a man. They will say he killed himself. The Dex only lasts a few hours at most. No one will find him before it's gone. No one should have."

"You've had a real run of bad luck," Peabody commented.

Tovinski ignored her. "When he comes in, I push the syringe to his throat. The bruises should cover the mark."

"You've done this before," Eve said.

"Fuck you on that. His eyes are so wide—he can fear. He knows. I make it quick, and I leave. No one should have found him so soon."

"Okay, let's go over a few details." Eve paged through her file. "Before that, I have another question. Singer, not long after you arrived in the U.S., owned a second site, had started construction. Also Hudson Yards—they called it South-West. It's about a block from the site where you killed Alva Quirk. Did you ever visit or work on that site?"

"My uncle was invested, but he wanted me to get my education, to study the business, yes. But on Bardov projects. We were only invested."

"You never went there?"

He looked genuinely puzzled. "Why would I? If someone there had to be persuaded, or needed a lesson, maybe he would have sent me—like an apprentice. But it wasn't a Bardov project."

"All right. Let's go back over the night you killed Alva Quirk."

When it was done, Eve turned the record off. Two U.S. Marshals came in to escort him out.

"Do you think Bardov will find him?" Peabody wondered. "Or even try?"

"He may try." Reo shrugged. "But I think Tovinski—or whatever name he'll have now—is going to live a very long life in a cell. Only a finite group of people know where he's going, the name he'll have, the background created. And no, I'm not one of them. All I know is my boss and yours signed off on it.

"We did our jobs. The job's done."

"He didn't know about the remains—the woman," Eve said. "I'd've seen it by the time I pushed that. Bardov, maybe, but Tovinski didn't know about it, and he's killed plenty more than Alva and Delgato."

"Let's take our win, Dallas." Reo rose. "We've put a—what was it, Peabody? A spineless prick of a slug stain away, for a couple of lifetimes."

"I'm taking it. I liked the 'whiny asshole fuckwit' myself. Good job, Peabody."

"It felt good."

"Let's write it up, close it out. We'll take Bardov and the elder Singers tomorrow. Let's see if we can pry out anything on our Jane Doe."

In her office, she studied the board before she sat at her desk.

She contacted Alva's brother.

"Detective Elliot, it's Lieutenant Dallas. I wanted to inform you that we've apprehended the person responsible for your sister's death."

She told him what she could, then contacted Angelina Delgato and did the same.

She closed the book, cleared the board. She sealed and labeled the box holding the case files. Instead of calling to have them taken to storage, she lifted the box.

A walk, she thought, just walking it all down herself felt like putting an end to it. And taking a breath.

As she walked out to the bullpen, Yuri Bardov walked in with what she assumed was his bodyguard.

He'd gone a little soft in the middle and carried some extra weight there under a fine suit of apricot linen. The bow tie made him look like someone's dapper grandfather—especially if you didn't know he'd run a murderous and merciless criminal empire for a number of decades.

His hair had gone to silver, and he kept it cropped close. He offered a charming smile. His eyes were as cold as January.

"Ah, Lieutenant Eve Dallas." His voice held only the barest trace of an accent, and came rich and full. "I recognize you. What a treat to meet you in person. I'm Yuri Bardov."

"I know who you are." She stepped over to set the box on Peabody's desk in a bullpen that had gone silent. "I'm wondering if this is the first time you've walked into a cop shop voluntarily."

Those eyes, ice blue, bored into her for five thrumming seconds. Then they brightened as he laughed as though he meant it.

"Just as I expected. You don't disappoint, Lieutenant. I was told, after our very thorough scanning, to address any inquiries I had about my nephew to you. It seems Alexei's gotten himself into some trouble. I'm hoping he's allowed visitation so I can speak with him."

"Peabody," Eve said without taking her eyes off Bardov or his companion. "See about a conference room."

"Yes, sir."

"I hate to take up any of your valuable time."

"You've gone to the trouble to come in, I can spare the time."

"We have room one," Peabody told her.

"Want any backup, boss?"

She glanced over at Jenkinson, who was currently sending Bardov the hard eye. She did her best not to react to a tie swirling with a series of rainbows that might arc across the sky after a nuclear disaster.

"We're fine, Detective. This way, Mr. Bardov."

She took the lead and caught a whiff of Bardov's aftershave. Something citrusy that suited the butter-yellow bow tie.

"May I say, Lieutenant, how I'm looking forward to Ms. Furst's new book and reading about your exploits. A terrifying time that was. My wife and I, and some of the family, were in Europe during that episode. I can confess, I was grateful to be an ocean away from New York."

"Right." She opened the door to conference room one. "Have a seat." She glanced at Peabody.

"Would you like some coffee?" Peabody asked. "Tea?"

"I would love some coffee, extra cream. No tattling, Roger," he said to the bodyguard, who cracked the faintest of smiles. "My Marta is doing her best to wean me off caffeine."

He took a seat—the head of the table—and Roger stood at parade rest behind him.

"My wife, my Marta, is very upset about Alexei," he continued. "Her sister's boy, you see, and like a son to both of us. Dima—that is, Mr. Ilyin—would only tell me Alexei dismissed him. Very rash. I'd very much like to speak with him and make sure he's properly represented.

"Ah, thank you," he added as Peabody set the coffee on the table. After one sip, he laughed again. "Some things don't change. Police house coffee is dreadful. And yet . . ." He took another sip. "Still coffee. Now, about Alexei."

"Alexei Tovinski was charged and has confessed to the murders of Alva Quirk and Carmine Delgato."

"I must insist on seeing and speaking to him immediately. I'm his family."

"You can insist, but you won't see or speak with him. Mr. Tovinski, on record, signed a deal with the prosecutor's office, by this time will have been arraigned and sentenced and transferred to the prison where he'll remain, without possibility of parole, for the rest of his life. Times two, consecutive."

"Under duress a man might agree to anything."

"The only duress he may have felt came from your direction, Mr. Bardov, and his fear you would take action to punish him for systematically stealing from your construction company, your partners."

"You expect me to believe that Alexei, a man as close to me as a son, would steal from me?" He waved a hand in the air—a calloused hand, Eve noted. A working hand. "You're mistaken, and if there is action—legal action—it will be taken against you."

"I'm assuming a man of your contacts and experience would have verified the facts by now. You trusted him; he betrayed you. And killed to cover it up. He betrayed his wife and stole to keep the other women and children secret."

She leaned forward a little. "If he'd rolled on you, if he'd given us anything on you, trust me, Mr. Bardov, you'd be in cuffs right now."

"You're a bold one," Bardov stated.

"I'm a cop. We're the cops that took the man who betrayed you, betrayed his wife, stole from you, stole from your partners, and killed two people so he could keep on doing it."

"You ask me to believe terrible things about a cherished member of my family."

"You already believe it. You know it or you wouldn't be here now. You wanted a last look at him, a last word. You won't get them. He's out of your reach—and you'll find that's solid truth. We made sure of it because death is too easy. It's the end. He's going to pay for a very long time. That's justice."

He studied her as he drank more coffee. "Perhaps we view justice differently."

"No doubt. He refused to implicate you in any crime or illegal activity. Take that for what it's worth. He worried about the other children and their mothers. How they would get by."

"The children are family, however they came to be. Their mothers are their mothers. They will be supported properly."

He paused a moment, frowned into his coffee. "I wasn't aware before this time he had killed the woman, the homeless woman. You may think what you think, but I don't approve."

"What about a young woman, a young pregnant woman at another time, in another place?"

His shoulders drew back, and that cold look in his eyes

went fierce. "Are you saying Alexei took such a life? For money? To hide his thievery?"

"Someone did."

"I?" He tapped a fisted hand to his chest. "A woman with child is sacred. Sacred. For all my many sins, as you would see them, this is one I would never, never commit. The life that holds life? Sacred. What does this have to do with me?"

"Another time, another place," Eve repeated. "You can waste your time, money, and resources trying to find Tovinski, seeking your sort of justice. Even I don't know where the cage he'll stay locked in is, but I do know I'll hear if he meets a fatal accident, or gets himself shanked. I'll hear, then, as much as I think he's scum, he'll be mine. And I'll come for you."

"A bold one," he repeated.

"He fears you, and that fear will live in him every day, every night. He'll never stop looking for your revenge. I think that's plenty of justice, even your kind."

"You may be right." He set the coffee aside. "I'm older than I was. I take pleasure in simpler things than I once did. And as the years accumulate, I have less to prove."

He got to his feet. "Thank you for your time, and a very stimulating conversation."

"Detective Peabody will escort you out."

Alone, Eve sat, thought through that stimulating conversation.

She expected Bardov would at least put out feelers to try to find the nephew. He'd do that for form, or from habit. But she doubted he'd expend much time or energy. As he would have if she'd told him his nephew would have rolled on him for immunity.

And he'd told the truth about a woman with child being sacred.

He hadn't put those bullets in her victim, nor had anyone done so on his orders.

More, he hadn't known about the body behind the wall.

So until DeWinter came through, she had nothing.

16

As Eve started back to her office, Peabody hurried in her direction.

"Wow. I have to say wow! Maybe Bardov looks like your great-uncle, the friendly librarian, but you know he's a criminal overlord and you so totally handled him."

"Did I?"

"Oh yeah, you did. Wait. Wait." Catching the tone, Peabody snatched at Eve's arm. "You did. Sure, maybe he'll do a little poking around to satisfy himself, but he listened to you, Dallas. I watched him listening, taking it in. And maybe it's not the straight line, but you telling him Tovinski's going to live a long time not just caged up but living in fear? That hit the right mark with him. Because it's true, and he knows it. Just like he knows it's true you'd go after him if he takes Tovinski out.

"That's handling," Peabody insisted, "and that's keeping Tovinski alive, that's nailing down justice for Alva and Delgato. That's a fucking win."

"Well." The fire in Peabody's eyes burned away the weight on Eve's shoulders. "I'll return the wow."

"Fucking A!"

"Do me a solid and write it up. I want a copy in the case

file I left on your desk and another for the unidentified remains. Then contact Bolton Singer and let him know his site's clear."

"Got it. He was telling the truth about the sanctity of pregnant women. Or he doesn't remember making an exception in this case."

"Oh, he'd remember. Whoever she was, however she ended up behind that wall, it wasn't on his orders."

When she stepped back into the bullpen, she caught Jenkinson's long stare. Despite the tie, she walked to his desk. "Do you figure I can't hold my own with an eightysomething-year-old gangster, Detective?"

"You hold your own, LT. Some of us are old enough to remember when Yuri Bardov wouldn't have shown his face in a cop shop unless he was in cuffs."

Jenkinson looked around the detectives' bullpen. "Well, one of us is old enough."

"Did you ever tangle with him?"

"Not directly. When I was still in uniform, back when you were still in diapers, I had a weasel. An asshole, liked to play big shot, but he had his ear to the street. So he tells me he's hearing about a big one coming up. Weapons deal. Now, back then, Bardov was all over the weapons trade, had a pipeline going up and down 95. Weasel says he's got a meet on it and he'll pass on what he gets, how it's going to cost me big. Next day, he's floating in the East River, throat slit with a dead rat tied around it.

"Guy was an asshole."

"But he was your asshole."

"Yeah. His hands look clean, Dallas. They ain't. Never have been."

"No question of that. What's his deal with women and kids?"

"Never touched the sex trade. Word was he felt it was beneath him. Gunrunning, cybercrime, booze, the protection racket, all that, but no sex trade and no kiddie porn or exploitation."

"Okay, so he's got a code, or a line he won't cross."

"You could say," Jenkinson agreed. "I remember—my gold shield's still shiny—there was a task force working on a child porno ring. Getting close, that was the buzz. Before they nailed it down, every one of the ringmasters ended up dead.

"Organized hits," Jenkinson said, "coordinated, professional hits. It had Bardov all over it, Loo. Couldn't pin it on him."

Now he shrugged. "Maybe they didn't try so hard."

Jenkinson gave her that long stare again. "You would've. You don't have to mourn the fucking perverts to do the job. Are you looking at him for something?"

"He doesn't fit. Pregnant woman, shot, maybe thirty-five to forty years ago, as yet unidentified. Walled up in the wine cellar of an old building—old restaurant."

"The other Hudson Yards case. Yeah, I heard some of it."

Absently, he fiddled with his tie. Eve's eyeballs vibrated.

"Not going to be Bardov. Not a pregnant woman. The bastard has a code, like you said. And he loves kids. Doesn't put a fucking halo on him, but he loves kids."

"He's got four." Eve reached back to the backgrounds she'd run. "Two of each, and no criminal on any of them—or their kids. No connections I found to his organization."

"Wouldn't be any. The story goes he fell for this Russian girl—like a friend of a cousin—and fell hard. He was already taking over—who the hell was it?—Smirnoff—like the vodka—Smirnoff's territory. Had a rep, wasn't afraid of doing his own wet work. This is before my time. I ain't that old."

"He's been married close to sixty years," Eve pointed out. "That puts you in the diapers."

He smirked. "Yeah, well. Story is, she laid down conditions to marry him. He kept the business outside the home, and when they had kids none of them would be part of it. She wouldn't interfere in his business, but she didn't want it in the home, didn't want it passed to their kids. So that's how it is."

"Not her kids," Eve noted, "but her nephew. This is good to know, Jenkinson."

"He may not like putting a target on women, but you being a cop changes that. Cop's first."

"He's got no reason to put a target on me. Yet."

She walked over to Peabody's desk. "When you're finished, have the files picked up. Then go home. Or wherever."

"We had a good day, Dallas. Are you heading out?"

"Just about."

One more thing, Eve thought as she went to her office, sat down at her desk. One more.

She contacted the police department in Moses, Oklahoma.

"Moses Police Department, how can I assist you?"

"This is Lieutenant Dallas, New York Police and Security Department. I need to speak with Chief Wicker."

"All the way from New York?" The man on-screen looked more like a cowboy than a cop to Eve's eye. Ruddy face, faded blue eyes, crooked smile, and sun-bleached hair. "Can I tell the chief what this is about?"

"I'll tell him."

"All righty then. Hold on a sec."

The screen went to waiting blue; the audio to some drippy music.

It didn't take long.

"This is Chief Wicker. What can I do for you, Lieutenant?"

No cowboy this one, Eve noted. He had a square face with a hard jawline that was tanned rather than ruddy. With skin that looked pampered to her. He wore his dark brown hair in a buzz cut, adding a military tone.

She could all but feel the starch in the collar of his tan uniform shirt.

"Chief Wicker, I have some difficult news regarding your ex-wife."

"Genna?"

"No, sorry, I should have been more specific. Your first ex-wife. Alva Elliot."

His brown eyes widened. "Alva. She took off for who knows where years ago. She's in New York?"

"She was. I'm sorry to tell you she was killed, two nights ago."

"I'll be damned."

No grief, no regret. Just what Eve saw as mild interest.

"I've got to tell you, Lieutenant, I figured she'd been dead years now. That Alva, she had a flighty nature. I'm real sorry to hear she's passed on, but I don't know why you're notifying me. I wouldn't be her next of kin."

"I've notified her siblings, Chief. I want to say she didn't simply pass on. She was murdered. I'm Homicide."

That got his attention. Narrowed those eyes, stiffened those shoulders.

"How the hell'd she get herself murdered? If you're doing some fishing here, looking at me—who hasn't seen or heard from her since she took off—"

"The individual responsible for her murder is in custody. She was a witness to his illegal activity. As her former husband, as a police officer, I'm sure you're satisfied justice is done."

"Of course."

"Of course," she repeated. "I felt obliged to contact you, Chief, as during the course of our investigation we recovered a number of notebooks—handwritten notebooks."

"She picked that up again?" Like a man pitying a wayward child, Wicker shook his head. "She had a strange habit of keeping those books—rule books—before we got married."

"We recovered a considerable collection. I haven't been able to read them all. Fortunately, the case broke quickly, so I've had no need. But as your name was mentioned in one I skimmed, I felt I should let you know."

"I'm in there?"

"Some of them are dated during the period you were married. As I said, the case broke and the investigation ran in other, more immediate avenues, so there was no reason to read the older notebooks. While we'll turn over the victim's effects to her next of kin, I felt you might want to have those that applied to the years you and the victim were married.

"Just as a courtesy," she added. "Cop to cop."

"I appreciate that." He pumped a little warmth into his voice. "She was young and foolish back in those days. But I loved her. She broke my heart when she took off that way. I've carried that a long time, to be honest about it. I'd like to have them, have that memory of her."

"I understand. As a fellow police officer, you know this is a little irregular. Now that the case is closed, I expect the next of kin to make arrangements to transport the body and retrieve her personal effects. Still, I'm sure they'd agree to turn over the ones written during her marriage to you."

She watched annoyance, then calculation come into his eyes.

"You're talking about her siblings, I expect."

"That's right, Chief. Her brother and sister."

"I'm not sure they would agree, to be honest. The fact is, a lot of blame got tossed around when Alva ran off and that caused some hard feelings on all sides. I've made peace with that, but . . . I'd like to have that part of Alva, those memories of her, to help put the rest of my heart at rest. If you could send them to me, I'd be grateful."

"It's one thing to hand them off to you, Chief. I can justify that. But to ship them out, well, I'd need to have a record of that, paperwork. My boss is a stickler."

"How about I come to you then?"

"I know it's a long way to travel."

"She was my wife once. This is all I'll have left of her. I can fly out there first thing in the morning, pick them up, then head right on back."

"I'll have them for you. We will have some paperwork, but I can slide that through."

"I'm grateful to you."

"I'm at Cop Central. Lieutenant Dallas. Morning's best, as I had another case fall in my lap, and I have to get on it."

"Big-city busy." He flashed a smile. "I'll be there by nine."

"That works. I'll see you then. And I'm sorry for your loss."

Big-city busy, Eve thought when she sat back. You have no idea.

Driving home, she let the noise of the city wash over her. She didn't bother to separate the blasting horns from the rumbling maxibuses, the rumbling from the overhyped shouts of sales and more sales from the overhead ad blimps.

She didn't bother to fight the traffic, to dodge and weave, but simply adjusted to its fits and starts, its snarls and stops.

And let her mind empty.

She wanted home. Wanted the cool, the clean, the quiet, but just didn't have the energy left to push for it.

It would be there, she told herself. Beyond the endless river of pedestrians, the smoking glide-carts, the yellow flood of Rapid Cabs.

It would be there.

And when she drove through the gates, the world shut itself on the other side.

Before Roarke, she'd never had that, that demarcation, that line between everything else and home. Even when she brought the work, the blood, the death, the despair through the gates, she still had home.

And now, when her head ached from the blood, the death, the despair, with work yet to do, she thanked God for home.

Summerset waited, and the cat pranced away from his side to ribbon between her legs.

"Did you lose your topper?"

It took her a minute to understand what he meant. And to realize she'd forgotten to grab it when she left her office. "I left it at work. It didn't rain."

"Thunderstorms likely tomorrow afternoon. You'll want it then."

She didn't want to think about tomorrow afternoon. She didn't want to think about tomorrow morning, so she walked up the stairs.

Summerset watched her go, then took out his 'link, sent a text.

Boy, the lieutenant has exhausted herself.

The reply came quickly.

Leaving for home shortly. I'll see to her.

Because she was exhausted, more in mind than body, Eve went straight to the bedroom. Without bothering with her weapon harness, her boots, she flopped facedown on the bed.

When Roarke came in some thirty minutes later, she lay where she'd dropped, with the cat stretched over her butt.

"Worn herself out, has she now?" he murmured to Gala-had. "Well then, we'll tend to her as best we can."

He gave the cat a light scratch between the ears before he tugged off his tie.

He was ready, more than, to shed the day himself.

He loved his work, as his cop loved hers, but Christ, there were times it left you knackered.

His thoughts ran right alongside where Eve's had as he changed out of his suit. Home. He'd had the building, and the beauty, the space and the quiet of it. But he hadn't had home, not the full of it, before Eve.

He left her sleeping to see to some details. When he came back, he stretched out beside her and let himself fall away.

Still, when she surfaced, stirred, opened her eyes, his looked back into them.

"Hi," she said.

"Hi to you." He laid a hand on her cheek. "You rested well."

"I needed to get out of my head. I guess I did. The cat weighs a ton."

"He's been on guard."

"Damn good cat. Did you actually nap?"

"For a bit. I wanted out of my head as well. What do you say to a walk on this fine spring evening?"

"I could take a walk. Do you have work?"

"Nothing urgent. Do you?"

"We closed it." She put her hand over his, squeezed. "Alva and Delgato. I'm sorry there's not much movement on—"

"Stop." He brought her hand to his lips. "The Russian, was it? As you thought."

"Tovinski, yeah."

"You'll tell me about it, if you like, while we take that walk." He sat up, picked up the cat, stroked him. "I don't think you'll need your weapon."

"Right. It was a good day," she said as she pushed up, released the harness. "We did the job."

"And still you're unsettled."

"Some, I guess. Yeah. It's not time to walk away."

He rose, reached for her hand. Satisfied he'd done his job, Galahad stretched across the bed to take his own nap.

They went out the front door and walked the lush grounds through the long tunnel of roses. They bloomed elegantly and scented the air while little diamonds of sunlight sparkled through.

Another world, she thought. A separate world from blood and death and petty cruelties.

"He was sloppy," Eve began, "just like you said. Reo got a warrant because I had enough—the correct way," she added. "And the forensic accountant found what you found pretty quick. Not Roarke quick, but quick."

"Well, after all, the accountant would have to do it the correct way."

"Reo and I came up with a plan—and an alternate if that didn't fly. Peabody and I worked out strategy . . . Over lunch. Over lunch on the floor of my office, because she decided to be you."

He shot her a bemused look. "I don't recall ever having lunch with you on the floor of your office."

"She cornered me into eating, which is you."

He took a long, winding, meandering way as she filled him in.

"Not to disparage your considerable skills—or Reo's, or Peabody's—the man broke quickly for a veteran gangster."

"Fear for his life." They walked through the orchard, where tiny green peaches replaced the fragrant blossoms of May. "He could take lives without a second thought, but the idea of his own death terrified him. Bardov terrified him. Living in a cage is still living."

"A kind of living, I suppose. And you don't know where he'll do that kind of living?"

"No. They're not going to read us into that. I figure the PA knows, Tibble and Whitney, whoever coordinated with the Marshals Service. I'm going to bet the warden wherever they stick him doesn't know. It's smart, and I'm good with it. He'll never get out, never wear a twenty-thousand-dollar suit again, bang another woman. It closed the book on Delgato, and most of it on Alva."

"The ex-husband."

"Yeah, but first I should tell you about Bardov. He came to see me."

Roarke turned his head toward her. His eyes went ice-floe cold. "He came to you?"

"Came to, not at, so stand down, pal. Very polite—old-school—and . . . it's natty, right? Why do people say *natty* for somebody who wears bow ties and linen suits and shiny shoes?"

"I expect because it fits."

"But what does it mean? Gnats are annoying little bugs. Spelled different, but still . . . Doesn't matter. He comes in—nattily—with his bodyguard. Tried the concerned uncle routine, hoping to get a chance to talk to Tovinski. And put the fear of God into him."

"Which you'd already done."

"Yeah. I used a conference room."

She told him, straight through, pausing only when she saw the pond, the bench. And the wine bottle and glasses on it.

"The pond fairies left wine."

"So they did. Well now, it wouldn't do to insult them, would it? Let's go sit and have a glass while you tell me the rest."

"Not much more, really. He didn't like it, then you could see him starting to consider the advantages. Kill him, it's just over. Life in prison, afraid, never quite sure the shiv's not going to slide between your ribs? It's a lot more."

"And he's getting soft," Roarke added as they sat.

"So I keep hearing."

"His name once struck fear in just the saying of it—I know from before I came to New York and in the circles, we'll say, I ran. Now, though he's not one I'd easily turn my back on, he's considered more of . . ." He thought it through as he took out the wine stopper, poured two glasses. "An elder statesman in his milieu."

"Milieu." She rolled her eyes, took the wine. "He didn't kill the pregnant woman, or order it. He says, and he means it, a pregnant woman's sacred."

"Hmm. I can believe that. I don't know a great deal of him, not in the last decade, we'll say, as he's been moving toward that elder statesman for some time. But it's definitely well-known he's a family man—not just the mob family. His family."

"I won't have any trouble with him, and he won't have any from me unless he crosses my line."

"No need for the jet-copter then."

"I still need to talk to the Singers—the father, the mother, the grandmother. They may know something. Hell, they may have shot the woman, built the wall, poured the concrete."

Roarke smiled, tapped his glass to hers. "Good luck there."

"Garrett Wicker comes first. He's coming to New York, meeting me at Central at nine sharp. He thinks, to pick up Alva's books from when they were married. One cop doing another cop a little favor."

"Is that how you played him?"

"Didn't have time to read the books, case broke fast, blah blah. Feels like he should have those. Siblings are entitled to her personal effects, but and so on."

She took a long drink. "He was easy to play because it's

all about him. Just him. He never asked how she was killed. He's a cop, the ex, but he never asked how she died. Never asked what she was doing in New York, nothing. Not a single question about her."

She drank again, looked at the fat white flowers floating on the water. "I'll close Alva's book tomorrow. Then I'm going to hound DeWinter until she gives me something on Jane Doe."

"Oh, I'm sure that'll make her work faster."

"Shut up." She elbowed him, then leaned her head on his shoulder. "I met her kid today—DeWinter's."

"Did you?"

"She's a little scary. I mean, most kids are, as I see it, but this one bumps it up a few levels. She's beautiful—I mean like wow, is-that-a-real-kid beautiful. And she's full of questions. She read the Icove book. She's just a kid."

"As I remember her from the few times we met—some time ago—some of that scary comes from brains. She's terrifyingly smart and, with the work her mother does, I imagine understands much of the world already. The Icove story would likely fascinate her."

"Tell me about it." She sipped more wine. "This is nice. It's nice to just be here."

He joined their free hands. "Let's just be here awhile longer."

After a while longer, they took the wine with them as they walked back to the house.

And Eve thought of the Marriage Rules.

"You should tell me about your day and stuff."

"No, I really shouldn't."

"Why?"

"Because it consisted of meetings, negotiations, progress reports, a small, easily fixable manufacturing glitch out of Cincinnati, a less easily but still fixable data drop in Tokyo, considerable revisions to the Sea and Space Museum on the Olympus Resort, a preview of the presentation for the roll-out of the remodeled and redesigned Typhoon All-Terrain and other '62 vehicles, some key staff adjustment issues in Detroit—and on Vegas II—and so on."

He paused a moment. "Which is why I didn't find the time to buy Lithuania."

"Well. There's always tomorrow. Where is Lithuania anyway?"

"On the Baltic Sea." At her stony stare, he laughed. "Baltic is here," he said, holding up the wine bottle. "Sweden and Denmark here, Belarus here, Poland here, and . . . yes, Latvia up here. So sits Lithuania." He circled a finger at the point in his invisible air map.

"How do you know that? Seriously. I could go out, grab twenty strangers off the street, and, unless they're Lithuanian, odds are low I'd find two who know that."

"It pays to know when you have business interests there and in the region. How many people did the Traveler murder?"

"Jacob Ainsley—I hate when they have a nickname. Traveler because he stayed mobile, using mostly campgrounds, national parks, cheap motels in his quest to murder at least one person in every U.S. state and territory. He used various means—shooting, bludgeoning, stabbing, strangling—but preferred the knife for the close-up work and the blood. Blood he kept labeled by date of kills in a collection of vials.

"Between 2037 and 2043 he killed fifty-three—that's known kills. He'd have made it fifty-four, but the woman he targeted in Juneau, Alaska, Marian Moon, former U.S. Army Special Forces, kicked his ass. Ainsley was the first convict transferred to off-planet prison Rexal when it was completed in 2053."

"I'll wager I could grab twenty strangers and so on."

"I see your point. Where's Mirvinastan?"

"Somewhere on the north side of your imagination."

"Just checking."

As they approached the house, she saw a table set on one of the patios. Summer-blue linen, scattered tea lights, cheerful flowers, silver heating domes.

"You had a plan."

"I did."

"It's a good plan."

He poured more wine and, prepared for anything—even spinach—Eve removed the domes.

"Pizza." She felt a ridiculous surge in her heart. "You must really love me."

"I must."

She sat, reached for his hand one more time. "After dinner, we could walk around the other way, work off the pizza. And we could watch a vid."

"Now who loves who? What sort of vid would you like?"

"Let's do one of those ancient ones you like so much, where the men all wear hats and the women dress like getting out of bed's a formal event."

"I can make that work."

She took her first bite of pizza and thought again it was good to be home.

17

In the morning, she woke refreshed and satisfied. Hard not to, she figured, when you had a pond, pizza, popcorn. Add in a pretty entertaining vid followed by a round of lazy sex, and how could you complain?

And she woke with the man she'd shared all that with sitting across the room, the cat curled in his lap. The stock reports scrolled by on the wall screen, but he appeared to pay more attention to whatever he studied on his tablet.

"They insist we'll have storms with heavy spots of rain this afternoon," he said without looking up.

"They do?"

"They're very confident, so you'll want your topper if you go out into the field."

"Check."

Right now she wanted coffee. But when she glanced at the time, she saw she could squeeze in a solid thirty-minute workout.

"I'm going to hit the gym. I've got thirty to spare."

"Take twenty, and use the other ten for a swim. That's the way I started my day, and it's set me up nicely."

"Your day starts in the middle of the night."

But she considered it as she rode the elevator down and decided it was a damn good idea.

Thirty minutes later, system pumped and ready, she came up to grab coffee and to shower. And he still worked the tablet.

"What's on there?"

"The security system McNab and I are designing for the new house. Plus, the other business—sound and entertainment, lighting, communications, and the like."

She took her first life-affirming gulp of coffee. "I gave Peabody a time-limited opportunity to gush about her kitchen stuff yesterday."

He looked up, smiled. And God, that smile could drain recently pumped muscles into putty.

"It's a warm, lovely palette she's chosen, good materials, an efficient but not stagnant design. Or they've chosen, as Ian's very involved."

She shrugged, grunted, then went to shower.

Under the jets, she let her mind open to the work again. Garrett Wicker, and she looked forward to that one. Now, if storms and crap really were happening, she wanted to get to the Singers in Hudson Valley before they hit.

Especially if getting to Hudson Valley and back involved a jet-copter. Which, sadly, made the most sense.

But she had to hit DeWinter. Lab first, she decided. And if she got to Central a little later than nine, the son of a bitch could wait.

Since she'd pushed it off her plate the night before, she needed to contact Reo about Wicker, set that up. Have Peabody set up the meet with the Singers.

She stepped into the drying tube, closed her eyes as the warm air swirled, and laid out a mental agenda.

She grabbed the robe on the back of the door. When she

stepped back in the bedroom, she saw the covered plates and the pot of coffee waiting.

The cat, she noted, had chosen to stretch out in the sunlight under the window. She poured more coffee, then considered the plates he'd uncovered.

The yogurt stuff with the healthy tree-bark stuff that the fat berries made reasonably okay. And she'd get through that because . . . waffles.

She immediately coated them with butter and drowned them in syrup.

"Have a look here."

She scooped up some of the yogurt to get it out of the way, and glanced over at the kitchen layout on his tablet. She remembered the design Peabody had rhapsodized over, the soft greens and creams.

"That's Peabody's?"

"It will be."

"That evil science lab–looking kitchen is going to turn into that?"

"The science lab is no more. Demo's all but finished, both sides. There was some back-and-forth there, as on the Mavis side, they said do Peabody's first, and on the Peabody's, it was do Mavis's first. And I finally stepped into that to remind them you wouldn't allow Mavis and her family to move in without the cops, and it would be not altogether pleasant for the cops to move in while construction crews were swarming all over the place."

Nodding, she stuffed in waffles. "Damn right on reason one, probably true on reason two."

"In any case, the demo's all but done, so we'll start on those internal systems very soon. Then we have this."

He swiped the screen. Eve let out a laugh.

"Jesus, that's Mavis all over. No, it's her and Leonardo, and the kid. It's all of them. Who knows about the one that's still cooking, but that's the three of them."

Color, color, and more color, but not, she thought, crazy. Not Jenkinson's ties crazy. Cheerful and bright and happy and maybe right up to the edge of crazy so it came off artistic.

"It's going to work," she said. "Because of who they are— all of them. And because you're helping. You're helping them make a home. Peabody and McNab, they grew up in one. Now they're really making their own. Mavis and Leonardo, they made one, made one with the kid, but it was always temporary. This is the real deal."

She'd finished off the yogurt without realizing it, and happily attacked the rest of the waffles. "It strikes me, a lot, what a difference it makes when you've got one. I had the job, but I've seen cops burn out when they didn't have the home to fold into. How you can lose your edge, or lose what you need to keep that edge from going too sharp.

"It's not just waffles and sex."

He leaned over to kiss her cheek. "They don't hurt."

"Don't hurt a bit. But it's knowing you can go there, that you're going to get there no matter how hard and ugly the day. It's not the color schemes and all that, but they make you feel at home. That safe space. Alva had one, then she didn't. In the end, not feeling safe broke her, so she made her home on the streets."

She looked at the cat stretched out in the sunlight.

"I think she let herself forget the safe spaces as much as she did the prison Wicker locked her in. Delgato, he lost home, because his addiction dragged him down so far he couldn't climb out."

"And let himself forget making and keeping a home takes work and care."

"Yeah. Did she have one?" Eve wondered. "The woman

behind the wall? Did she think she'd go home that night, or the next day? Into that safe space, take what was inside her there? Did she have someone waiting for her? Did they just forget her when she didn't come back?"

"She has you now."

"I need more. She's basically a ghost at this point. I have an age range—young twenties. Basic height and weight—right about average, but small-boned. I've got shoe size. I know she had long, narrow fingers. She probably had money. Designer shoes, good jewelry. Had conservative lady tastes or wanted to project that image—the shoes and jewelry again. And I know she was thirty-two weeks pregnant, or thereabouts, when she took the bullets.

"Three shots, thirty-two caliber. I got that lab report mixed in with everything else yesterday."

"Lieutenant."

The quiet patience in his voice made her stop eating to look at him. "You learned of the remains less than forty-eight hours ago. And in that time, closed two murders. I'd say you have quite a lot."

"I'm not giving myself grief. Really." But. The *but* struck her hard and clear. "Alva's case broke because Tovinski's name popped in the first interviews, and Delgato's murder was so damn sloppy. We did good work, but we had things fall on our side fast. And I know DeWinter's not scratching her ass on the remains. I just need more."

"And you hate depending on someone else to get it for you."

"Maybe." She polished off the waffles. "Oh hell yeah, I do. I can't see her. I can't put her up on my board and look at her face or read her background and piece together who she was. Can't interview her friends, family, coworkers if she had any. Was she married, or was the ring a blind to keep people off her back because she was pregnant? Who was the father? Too many questions I can't begin to answer until I know who she was."

"You plan to talk to the Singers today," he said as she rose to go to her closet.

"It sounds like the grandmother had her hands on the wheel during that period. The father was supposed to, but my take is he was more interested in flitting around the world than getting his hands dirty."

She poked her head out. "Know anything about that?"

"Well before my time, but I can ask around."

"Couldn't hurt. It bugs me, the wall bugs me. Superior material there, crap on the rest. Where'd they get it? From another site? Had to be a quick, fast, in-a-fucking-hurry job, so you can't, you know, order a bunch of bricks."

"A great deal of construction in that area at that time," he pointed out from the doorway of her closet.

"Yeah, yeah, yeah, I've got that. Like I've got Singer was a player back then, too—and Bardov either partnered or invested in Singer projects. Which tells me there wasn't much problem with the big shots on hooking up with a mobster. Yeah, yeah, yeah again, post-Urbans, desperate times and all that, but that connection's still there. So."

She wanted to grab black, just whatever in black, but he stood there in the damn closet.

"Okay, fine. I'm going to take down another cop—fucking wife-beating, smug, bullying bastard. And I'm going to interview Elinor and J. Bolton Singer—as long as I can get to them today. And since I'll be in the area, I may give Bardov another push, see if I can talk to his wife."

She threw up her hands. "What in this vast labyrinth of clothes do I put on, and why?"

"First, power and authority are what you project. The clothes only confirm what you already are. The Singers are wealthy, and so are you."

He held up a hand before she could object. "Which means you speak to them on the same level, and you show you're on the same level. Money and status matter to Elinor Singer. That much I know."

He chose slim pants in smoke-gray leather, passed them to her. Then a T-shirt—on the silky side and several shades lighter. Like the topper, she remembered.

"Go with a vest again—three-button style." He handed her one the color of the pants but with a thin stripe in the lighter gray.

"The tee shows off your very-well-toned arms, and projects power and strength, but the material's rich."

He turned to the wall of boots. She figured he'd go with the lighter gray and what she thought of as a girlier style.

Instead he lifted a smoke-gray pair, thick soled, that laced over the ankle.

"Add the edge. Military style. Authority."

"Okay, I like it."

"Then suck this up. Diamond studs—very small, barely noticeable. They'll be noticed, believe me, by the women."

"Shit." The idea actually brought on a twinge of pain. "A bullpen full of cops'll notice, too."

"I'm sure you'll all deal with it." He toyed with the fat diamond she wore around her neck. "You might wear this over your shirt instead of under for the Singers."

"I'll think about it."

He cupped her face. "It matters to me you wear it."

"You got that stupid button in your pocket?"

He reached in, drew out the gray button that had fallen off her ugly suit the first time he'd met her.

"Same thing." She lifted her shoulders. "It's the same damn thing, which makes us a couple of saps for each other."

"There's no one else I'd rather be a sap for." He kissed her, stepped back. "I'll get the earrings."

"Really small, right?"

"Practically invisible."

She rolled her eyes, but dressed. And dressed, decided she looked like a cop—vital to her—and a woman who could handle herself.

She took the earrings. Not practically invisible, she thought, but they were pretty small.

But it all felt better—more her—when she strapped on her weapon.

"And there you have it," he said with a nod of approval. "Let me know if and when on the copter. I'd pilot you myself, but I'm a bit crowded today."

"I'm hoping for ten, maybe eleven. It all depends on how quick I can wrap up Wicker."

"Just tag me. And don't forget your topper when you leave for Hudson Valley. And these."

He handed her sunshades with smoke-gray lenses.

"I'm going to lose them."

"Probably, but before you do, they add another edge."

She glanced toward the mirror to see. "Man, they're excellent. I'm going to hate losing them. Gotta go." She kissed him hard. "Got APAs to push and scientists to nag."

"Good luck on all of that, and take care of my cop."

"Look at her." Eve waggled the sunshades. "She can take care of herself and anybody else she needs to."

He counted on just that.

Eve tagged Reo, coordinated with her on Wicker. It involved some legal maneuvers—which she happily left in Reo's lap.

She texted Peabody, gave her the outline.

And with renewed energy and purpose, fought her way through traffic.

She appreciated the sunshades, as the sun beamed like a

laser. And its strength in a solid blue sky made her think the infamous "they" missed the mark again on rain.

Once again, she walked through the lab and up the steps to DeWinter's area.

The bones, the woman's, the fetus's, lay on the tables as they had the day before.

This time, no kid full of questions lounged in the room. And no DeWinter worked with those bones.

A little steamed, she checked DeWinter's office—empty—then made her way to the next section.

She found Elsie Kendrick working on the sketch, with the computer-generated version on-screen while she used a large sketch pad.

Not complete, not yet, but for the first time Eve had an image.

Delicate features, yes, but sharp. Slender nose, a bowed mouth, high cheekbones, long, almond-shaped eyes, very deep-set, and ears small, close to the head.

A striking face, Eve thought, the sort that would have stayed striking had she been allowed to live decades longer.

"Middle East heritage," Eve said, and Elsie jolted.

"You gave me a start! And good eye. Yes, from her tests and studies this far, Dr. DeWinter's determined Middle Eastern genetics. Most probably Lebanese."

"What about the fetus?"

"I can't tell you. I've focused on her. I don't have enough for the holo or for running facial rec, but I'm getting close."

"I can see her."

"Yes." Elsie smiled a little. "It's a strong, memorable face even with its delicacy. Maybe because of it. I haven't added it yet, but going by genetics, she'd have had dark hair, likely true black. And extrapolating from the era when she died, the profile of her personality you and Dr. Mira provided, I see her with long, straight hair, simply styled."

"Yeah, I can see that, too. Where's DeWinter?"

"On her way in. She ran a little late this morning. Her usual child care provider's still down, so she went with her backup." She smiled again. "Miranda had some objections. She should be here any minute."

"Okay. Can you make me a copy of what you've got so far?"

"I could, but if you give me a bit more time, I should have her finished. A few hours more, I'll have the full body—best probability pre-pregnancy and at TOD."

"Send me the complete as soon as you have it, but I'll take what you've got now. I can add in the confirmed data points, run it through any missing persons for the time frame, try facial recognition. I could hit there."

She turned as she heard the click of heels.

"Elsie, I'm sorry—" DeWinter hurried in, stopped when she saw Eve. "Dallas. We're not going to get this done any faster because you're hovering."

"I needed an update." She gestured to the sketch. "And I've got one."

"You'll get more if you let Elsie work." She waved a hand in a commanding come-along, and clicked out.

Eve just turned, gave Elsie and her careful poker face a nod. "Thanks," she said, and went after DeWinter.

"Again," DeWinter began the moment Eve stepped in, "the victim was a female between the ages of twenty and twenty-five. Highest probability indicates earlier rather than middle twenties. She was in good health before sustaining three gunshot wounds, one in the sternum, one on the left side, which cracked the rib as discussed, and one in the left shoulder."

"The shoulder?"

"The dislocated shoulder we project sustained that injury when she fell, yes."

As she spoke, she opened a closet and took a pink lab coat—that matched her shoes—from a forest of others. "She also sustained a head blow—again, from the fall in all probability. The ballistic report, as you know, identifies the recovered slugs as thirty-two caliber."

As DeWinter swung on the lab coat, she circled to the other side of the table. "The full panel DNA confirms my belief the victim was of Middle Eastern heritage."

"You didn't mention that belief yesterday."

"Because it wasn't yet confirmed. Now it is. Both parents were Middle Eastern. Lebanese is, again, the highest probability. She had a hairline fracture, well healed, on her right ankle. A childhood injury, at about the age of twelve. There's no sign of abuse, addictions, serious illnesses. Everything indicates excellent health care, excellent dental care and hygiene."

When she paused, Eve pushed in. "What about the fetus?"

"Healthy, approximately thirty-two weeks. The DNA is Middle Eastern—maternal—and paternally, European—that is, primarily Britain. Also Germany and some northern Europe."

"Don't tell me Lithuania."

DeWinter looked baffled. "No, why?"

"Stupid joke. Nothing."

"Scandinavia, likely Sweden. Anglo-Saxon, Caucasian."

"Interesting. So, thirty-seven years ago—"

"Between thirty-five and forty, more likely on the lower end," DeWinter interrupted.

"Plans and building permits, such as they are, say that cellar went into construction thirty-seven years ago, in the fall. That's when she went in."

"You assume."

"Jesus, DeWinter, it lines up. That's 2024, and the damn restaurant opened for business in the spring of the next year.

She couldn't have fallen through a goddamn concrete floor. Did she fall or not?"

"Yes, she sustained a fall of between eight to ten feet."

"Thirty-seven years ago, she's early twenties and a few months away from having a baby. A baby she, this young, conservative woman of means, steps out of her race and culture—"

"You don't know culturally where—"

"No mix. None. The baby would have been. Even the father had some different countries in his DNA—all WASP—but she doesn't. You didn't say most likely Lebanese with some Iranian and/or Sudanese, whatever. Her family, her ancestors stuck to their own. And the father of the fetus, his family stuck to the WASP."

"That's a fair point," DeWinter conceded, "but—"

"Don't *but* me," Eve snapped back because—finally—she could see her victim. "Why did she come to New York—or America? Did her family immigrate, did she come to study, to work? She meets this guy, this white guy, and she steps out, and so does he.

"Maybe it's love—even just passion—or maybe he was a hit-and-run sort. But the ring . . ." She shook her head. "Odds lean love, however transient. Not everybody wore wedding rings, and not every woman who got knocked up worried about it. She might have, but if he was a bang-and-blow sort, would she want to be reminded? Anyway . . ."

"That's a lot of supposition."

"It's making a picture, it's building a theory. Different races—who cares? Except some did, some still do."

"Such as the Natural Order cult you just exposed."

"Can't have a cult unless some people want to join in. Different religions, too, right? She'd most likely be Muslim—probabilities," she said before DeWinter could object again. "Not fringe, not hard-line, she's too conservative for that. But that would be strike two for some people—say, family who's traditional, who sticks with their own kind."

"Enough to kill her over it?"

"Enough to object, to make things difficult. And people kill people, including family, for all kinds of ugly reasons. Three shots. Someone wanted her gone, her and the kid inside her. Gone and forgotten."

They may have hard lines on their individual processes, but on this, DeWinter absolutely agreed.

"She won't be forgotten now."

"No, she won't. I've got to get to Central. I have to take Alva Quirk's ex apart, and take him down."

"The one who beat her? How are you going to— Never mind. I'm already late getting started and I'd really like to get out of here on time today. I have a date."

She smiled slowly, meaningfully. "With the sweet, charming, stunningly built Mackie."

Eve very nearly goggled. "The construction guy?"

"That's right, and you're thinking he's not my type."

"I don't know your type, but okay. You're standing there in hot-pink skyscraper heels and a matching lab coat over a white dress. He's work boots, coverall, and calluses."

Face just a little smug, DeWinter examined the hot-pink tips of her fingers. "Did I mention he's sweet, charming, and built? It's just drinks, but I like his smile. And his delts."

DeWinter set one pink-tipped hand on her hip. "You never fully believed I didn't have designs on Morris."

"*Designs on* is a bitchy phrase, and I didn't think that. Not like that."

"That's appreciated. The fact is, Morris came into my life when I was in flux—new city, new job, new people, and all that new for my daughter. Hell, for our dog. And I came into his when Li was at his lowest. Not quite lowest, because you'd been there for him when he lost Amaryllis. We gave each other someone to talk to, who shares interests. We still do. He's my closest friend.

"Now, Mackie," she said with another smile, and patted a hand on her heart.

"Well, good luck with that."

"Good luck with the wifebeater."

"I'll take it," Eve said as she walked out. "But I don't need luck on this one. He's finished."

She checked the time as she wound her way out of the lab, calculated she'd be a few minutes late for the nine o'clock. And she was fine with that.

She tagged Peabody. "I'm just leaving the lab. We have a face, not complete, and not the holo replica, but enough to start facial rec. I want you to go back to April and through the end of 2024, adding she's Middle Eastern and the wedding ring. We'll see if anything pops on that. We'll start the full run after we're done with Wicker."

"Reo just got here."

"Make sure she's in Observation before he gets there. Which is any minute. You just tell him how I got held up and I'm on my way. You know the rest."

"I've got it, and looking forward to it."

"We're not supposed to count our ducks, but—"

"It's chickens," Peabody corrected automatically. "You don't count your chickens, but you have your ducks in a row."

"Whatever. Stupid. And I'm counting all the damn bird rows on this. Get Reo set up."

Why would anybody count chickens anyway? she wondered as she got in her car. And no way ducks would just stand in a row.

What she had was everything and everyone lined up. And she'd damn well make sure it worked.

She didn't rush. Let him wait. When she parked at Central she took her time, suffered the endless stop and go of the elevator, and didn't push off until the floor below Homicide.

From there she jogged up the glide like a woman late for an appointment, then hurried into the bullpen.

Peabody had him sitting in a chair beside her desk. It didn't surprise Eve in the least to see he'd worn his uniform—all spit and polish.

He rose when he saw her, offered a polite, restrained smile and a hand to shake as he crossed to her.

"Lieutenant Dallas."

"Chief, sorry I'm running late. Detective, didn't you offer Chief Wicker some coffee?"

"I—"

"Never mind. I'll get you some in my office. If you'd come with me."

"Sir?" Peabody, the meek and mild, chewed on her bottom lip. "I'm sorry, sir, but your office is still closed off."

"What? They said they'd be finished by last night."

"Yes, sir, but they ran into a problem. They said by noon."

"Damn it. Fine. I'm sorry, Chief, Maintenance isn't always reliable."

"I hear that."

"We'll take Interview A. Private, quiet. Detective, I need the evidence box on Quirk and the paperwork secured in my office. Bring it to A."

"Sir, the Elliots aren't due to come in for the victim's effects until this afternoon."

"I'm very aware." Eve matched the cold tone with a cold stare. "The evidence box I clearly marked for Chief Wicker. Please come with me." Tone changed, brisk, but welcoming. "How was your flight?"

"Smooth enough. It's been a long time since I shuttled out East."

"You've been to New York before?"

"No, first time. Wish I could spare a couple days to see some sights. Atlanta, Georgia, a few years ago, and West Virginia, lord, years before that. Work conferences."

"I hope you have an opportunity to come back to New York. Be sure to let me know if you do."

She opened the door, gestured him inside. And turned on her lapel recorder.

"So this is where the magic happens?"

"I like to think so. It happened yesterday when we sweated a full confession out of the man who killed your ex-wife. Again, I'm sorry for your loss."

"I very much appreciate that. And I appreciate you letting me have this piece of her to take with me. In my mind, she's still the girl I married. Young and charming with her silliness, and with a sweet heart."

"And she just walked out on you one day."

"Her father walked out on her, so I guess it's in the blood. I don't think she ever got over it. Abandonment issues. And she never got over her mother's death. Her mother was a cop. Took one too many risks. A woman with no husband and three kids at home, but she kept taking those risks."

In his world, Eve concluded, women belonged where he'd boxed Alva—in the house, where the man ruled.

"You and Alva didn't have any children?"

"No, we weren't blessed. Just as well. She tended to be forgetful, just lose herself in her daydreams."

Eve nodded as if she understood, then looked over as Peabody came in with an evidence box.

"That'll be all."

"Lieutenant." Peabody looked close to tears as she clutched the box. "I'm sorry, sir, but the new directives and protocols are very clear."

"For Christ's sake, Chief Wicker is a LEO."

"I know, sir, but it's mandatory. And—and—and, I had to sign for the evidence box."

Eve let out a long sigh. "Another stickler," she said to Wicker in a tone dipped in annoyance. "Any transfer of effects from a homicide—this comes from upstairs—has to be on the record. And the recipient of same must be Mirandized and asked a series of routine questions."

"That's ridiculous."

"I hear that," she said, echoing him. "And it's a time suck. But it's from upstairs. I apologize for this, and I'll make it quick." She sent Peabody a scalding look. "Record on. Dallas, Lieutenant Eve, Peabody, Detective Delia, following protocol in the transfer of certain personal effects of Quirk, Alva—aka Wicker—to Wicker, Garrett, chief of police of . . ."

He smirked. "Moses, Oklahoma."

"Right, sorry, Moses, Oklahoma. In order to turn over these items, Chief Wicker, as they were evidence in a homicide investigation, now closed, I need to read you your rights."

He waved a hand and sat patiently while Eve recited the Revised Miranda. "I have to ask if you understand your rights and obligations in this matter."

"Sure do. Read them off plenty of times myself."

"I bet. Let me just ask the required questions. What was your relationship with the deceased?"

"We were married. I divorced her about twelve years ago for abandonment."

"Have you had any contact with the deceased since that time?"

"None at all. Fact is, I didn't know where she was until you contacted me yesterday."

"Do you know or do you have any knowledge of an Alexei Tovinski?"

"Never heard of him. Russian-sounding name, isn't it? Is he the one who killed Alva?"

"He confessed to her murder from the chair you're sitting in right now. Satisfied, Detective?"

"Yes, sir. I'm sorry, sir, but the commander issued the directives."

"You're dismissed. Peabody, Detective Delia, exiting Interview."

Eve rolled her eyes. "He issues directives like that because he rides a desk instead of riding suspects."

He laughed while she picked up the thick file on top of the box. Eve used her penknife to cut the seal on the box, then sat again.

She smiled. "You said Alva was flighty and forgetful."

"That she was. Sweet, but in another world half the time or more. I don't know where she picked up the name Quirk, but it suited her. She was a quirky one."

"Flighty, forgetful, quirky." Eve nodded. "Is that why you, routinely, beat the crap out of her?"

18

The humor—at his dead ex-wife's expense—didn't just drain out of his eyes. They went feral.

"You've got no business saying such a thing to me."

"Sure I do. It's all written out—in details, with dates—in her books." Eve patted the box. "And those injuries and dates match the conclusions from the chief medical examiner of New York, and our forensic anthropologist. And I have photos as well as medical reports."

She opened the file. "Like these pictures—also dated, as you see—of Alva's facial injuries, her broken fingers, the burned fingers, the bruising on her ribs. You'll note they're time-stamped, two days after you filed a missing persons report on her. The medical—a Dr. Grace Habit—certified the injuries as approximately seventy-two hours old."

"I don't have to listen to this." He started to rise.

"Stay in your chair or I'll cuff you to it."

"You and who else?"

"I don't need anyone else. And I'd be delighted to add assaulting an officer to the charges."

"What charges? There's no proof of anything in a half-crazy woman's scribbling in some book. Some pictures? She could have gotten her ass whooped after she took off, and you can't prove different. And you're talking to a cop, you stupid bitch. There's a statute of limitations on domestic abuse."

"There is, but there isn't on rape, there isn't on felony rape."

"We were married. A man can't rape his wife."

"I bet you believe that, but the law disagrees. Strongly disagrees. You'd beat her next to unconscious, then rape her. You'd break her fingers, then rape her. On the night before the morning she ran away from you, you did this." She shoved the pictures across the table.

"Then raped her. And to the many counts of rape documented in her books, I'm going to shoot for enforced imprisonment. You wouldn't allow her to visit or be visited by her family—under threat of more beatings. You had her brother beaten, her sister raped, to prove to her you could hurt them if she didn't toe your line. It's all in here."

He shoved the photos away. "None of this is going to hold up in court. None of this. I've got better than twenty-five years on the force. I'm the fucking chief of police. I've got a wife who'll swear I've never laid a hand on her."

"She might. But, hey, your second ex-wife's going to be a different story. I'm betting a lot of it'll hold up. A long, ugly, humiliating trial for you, but if you've got a smart lawyer, you'll probably get some of it tossed. Not all though."

She sat back. "No, not all. Especially when we send investigators to Oklahoma. Someone like you? They don't just pound on a woman half their size. Give them a badge and a weapon, they like to use it. I'm betting you've tuned up more than a few suspects in your day, guilty or innocent, and done the same with someone who just pissed you off."

She gazed up at the ceiling. "Add it all up, I'm betting we could get you twenty years. Twenty to twenty-five. With good behavior—which I don't think you can pull off—you could, maybe, get out in fifteen."

She smiled at him, fiercely. "Want to try it?"

"What do you want? And don't tell me this is about Alva. You didn't even know her. You looking for a score? Looking for something under the table?"

"A bribe? Are you offering me a payoff for tucking all this away?"

"I asked what you want."

"I'll tell you. Hold on a second." She took out her 'link. "Hey, Nadine. Locked and loaded?"

"You bet."

"Pull the trigger."

"Consider it done."

"Thanks." She put the 'link away. "I'll tell you what I want. What I want right down to my bones. I want you to spend the rest of your life in prison for what you did to Alva, for the shit you've smeared on your badge. That's what I want. Now, what I'll take?"

She folded her hands on the file. "You own up to what you've done, sign a statement thereof. You resign—immediately—and we'll deal it down to five years inside. If you can keep yourself in check, you'll probably get out in three, maybe three and a half. But you'll never carry a badge again."

"Fuck you."

"That's your answer? Let me tell you why you're going to take that back, and the time inside just went up to seven years. Right now, as we speak, Alva's story, those photos and documents, pages from her books, they're all over the media. Not just in New York, Wicker, all over. All the way out to Oklahoma. I expect your 'link's going to start blowing up really soon now."

"You're lying."

She just smiled again, made a gun out of her index finger and thumb. "Bang. Trigger pulled. How fast do you figure the cops who've worked under you will take to turn on you? The mayor of your little cop kingdom, the council members who are going to have the media beating down their doors?"

His 'link signaled.

"You wanna take that? I can wait."

He yanked out his 'link, set his teeth when he read the display. He turned it off. "I can beat this. Then I'll sue you for the skin off your ass."

"Documentation, photographs, scientific data, and witnesses. Do you think nobody knew what you did to her? Do you think nobody ever noticed the black eyes, the splinted fingers? The county sheriff has men out right now, interviewing neighbors."

His face flushed with rage. "I'm not doing seven years."

Eve leaned forward. "Wanna bet?"

He punched out, but she was ready for it. She wanted to punch back, more than she could say, but she just shoved his bunched fist back. "Make that ten years."

Reo opened the door.

"Cher Reo, assistant prosecuting attorney for New York, entering Interview."

"And by 'link conference," Reo said as she sat and set up a tablet, "Marvin Williams, prosecuting attorney for Beaver County, Oklahoma. Mr. Williams and I have observed this interview, have read over the file. At this time, Mr. Wicker, we are prepared to offer you a plea bargain. A full confession, your permanent resignation from your current position as chief of police, and your sworn agreement to never pursue or hold another position in law enforcement. Which includes prison guard, security guard, hell, crossing guard positions, or any position of authority."

"Go to hell."

"Jesus Christ, Garrett." On-screen, the Oklahoma prosecutor dragged at his hair.

"And you go with her, you simpering fuck."

"Ten years," Reo said flatly. "Or we go to court, drag it all out—adding your second wife, from whom I have a statement—the attempt to assault an officer, every Tom, Dick, and Mary we find that you used excessive and/or unnecessary force on, and every other thing we can and will dig up. I'm betting it's a lot. I'm betting it's going to add up to fifty before we're done with you."

"Take the deal, Garrett. Take the ten, because I'm telling you as someone who's known you—or thought he did—for eight years, you'll do twice that or more if this goes to trial."

"She's fucking dead!" He shouted it, pounding the table. "Why do you give a shit about any of this? She's dead."

Eve pulled out her badge, slapped it on the table. "That's why. Because it's meant to protect and serve, not hurt and terrorize. Because she mattered."

She rose. "Take the deal or don't. I don't care about that, because you're done. You're finished." She picked up her badge. "And when you're inside a cage where you belong, and they will put you there, I'll still have this. Because it's got to matter. Because of people like you. Dallas, exiting Interview."

She stepped out, took a couple of breaths.

Garrett Wicker wasn't her father, she reminded herself. But he and Richard Troy ran the same vicious, violent road.

And she'd beaten them both.

"Okay then." She breathed out again. "Now it's done."

She saw Peabody come out of Observation, and recognized the cautious concern on her partner's face.

To eliminate it, she held out a fist for a bump. "Good job as the whiny, stick-up-the-ass subordinate."

"I thought so. You're not staying in for the finale?"

"He's finished. Sometimes you have to leave it to the law-yers. He'll take the ten, figuring he'll get out in maybe six. He figures he can do six."

Eve shook her head as they walked back. "But he won't get through the first year without screwing it up, going at one of the guards, getting into it with another inmate. He'll do the full dime, and maybe more."

"He never saw it coming."

"He wouldn't. He's not wired to believe he'd pay any price—especially because of a woman."

"Not just that, Dallas. You had it ultrafine. The timing, the media storm, the whole ball of 'tude. I thought you were go-ing to punch him when he took that swing at you. But really, you did. Complete beatdown."

"We did." She pointed to her office so Peabody went with her. "Now it's done, so we move on."

"No hits on the missing persons search, citywide, state-wide, nationally," Peabody told her. "I started a global, but—"

"She went missing in New York, so there should be some-thing. Still, it's possible nobody but her killer knew she was here. Thin, but possible. Or any record's been lost in the fog of time.

"Coffee," she said, then walked over to look out her win-dow.

"We can start a facial recognition for her ID," Eve began. "The likeness isn't complete, but we start it, it starts elimi-nating."

She took the coffee Peabody held out.

"A young Middle Eastern woman, maybe Muslim—and during a period when there were still some loud echoes of bigotry—in New York. A woman college age or just beyond . . . Grad school? She's got means—jewelry, shoes—superior health and all that, so higher education feels probable. Did she go to college in New York? It's an angle. Pregnant, and the remains indicate good prenatal care, so a doctor, an experienced midwife."

"The wedding ring," Peabody put in. "So most likely married."

"Most likely, but a young, attractive, pregnant woman might put on a ring to avoid questions or issues. If she had a purse—and her type would—it didn't fall in with her. Or the killer got it out when they built the wall.

"The wall, the brick, the timing, that's why we're going to Hudson Valley."

"Hot damn!"

"Start the facial recognition. We'll update when we have the completed sketch. I'll contact Roarke for the copter."

"Double hot damn!" Peabody executed a butt and shoulder wiggle. "Like mega burning damn."

"We just closed a two-pronged case. I don't want to hate you right now."

"When I contacted the Singer estate earlier, they said the Singers would meet with us. Briefly."

"Tag them back. Tell her we're coming. Make it all routine."

"Isn't it?"

"We won't know until we get there. When we're done there, we'll drop in on Bardov."

Peabody's eyes went to big brown moons. "Really?"

"Routine follow-up. I want to see if his memory matches theirs. Get going. I'll write up Wicker."

"I can take care of it."

"I want this one."

Understanding, Peabody just nodded. As she started out, she gave a butt wiggle. "Jet-copter ride!"

* * *

Eve weighed two choices whenever she faced air travel. She could pretend she remained on the ground by concentrating on something else—anything else—for the duration. This required never looking out a window of any kind, and convincing herself any and all turbulence was just the rumbling of traffic over a pothole.

In the street.

On the ground.

Because the size and amount of glass in a two-passenger jet-copter took this option off the table, she had to count on Plan B and focus every cell in her body on keeping what she considered a flying insect aloft.

She didn't like the constant, low-level buzz reminding her she rode in the belly of the insect. And insects often ended their short, annoying lives being swallowed up by a larger flying thing, or getting swatted flat.

As Peabody loved every minute of buzzing around in the air like a mosquito, when flying with her partner, Eve had to merge both options.

Eve hunched over her PPC, studiously reviewing data she'd already committed to memory. Peabody plastered her face to the porthole in the door Eve imagined could burst open any second and suck them out so they pinwheeled screaming over the scenery Peabody rhapsodized over.

"Oh, it's so pretty! The hills! The trees! I bet it's super-ult-mag in the fall. All kinds of vineyards and orchards!"

"Go sit up with the pilot."

"Is it okay? I can see through here, but—"

"Go."

Peabody hopped up and all but danced the short distance to do her rhapsodizing in front of the wide windscreen until they dropped, mercifully, on the helipad.

The minute Eve got behind the wheel of the waiting car, everything inside her settled. She put the return trip firmly out of her mind and programmed the Singer estate.

"That was so quick." Still flushed with pleasure, Peabody strapped into the passenger seat. "McNab and I talked about taking a day trip up here, but decided we'd spend too much of the day getting here and back."

Eve gave her the next ninety seconds to chatter—"The hills! The green! The river!"

"Since we're not here to cozy up together in some quaint bed-and-breakfast, maybe you could focus on the people we're about to interview."

"I bet they have mag-o B and B's up here. Anyway, J. Bolton and Marvinia Singer are in residence, as is Elinor Singer. That's how they put it anyway. 'In residence.' So we can talk to all three of them in one place."

"Bardov's only a few miles from their estate, so we'll see if he's 'in residence' when we're done at the Singers'. I want to get a better sense of that relationship. It goes back decades."

"I can see why they all built up here. It's peaceful, and you can really spread out. And the scenery's the total. But it feels like, especially in Elinor Singer's time at the helm, she had to spend more time in the city than here."

"And it had to cost to maintain a country estate," Eve added. "Tough going in the couple years before the Urbans, a lot tougher going during."

"So you hook up—on a business level—with the deep pockets of a mob boss."

"A calculated business decision," Eve concluded. "But here you are, decades later and still hooked. And did that initial hook have anything to do with killing a pregnant woman and walling her up?"

"I gotta say, Dallas, it feels like Bardov would've been too smart for that. You don't hide the body, you get rid of it."

"Agreed. And I don't see him condoning that kind of hit. But it's time for these people to reach back in their memory banks."

She drove along a wall of white brick to an arching white gate. And rolled down her window to speak into the security intercom.

Good morning. Rosehill is a private estate. If you have an appointment, please state your name.

"Lieutenant Dallas and Detective Peabody." Eve held up her badge for the scan. "We're expected."

Welcome to Rosehill. Please proceed through the gate and continue directly to the main house. You will be met. Enjoy your visit.

The gates swung soundlessly open.

The drive ran arrow straight to the house. They'd gone with white brick there, too, in a three-story structure that struck Eve as more big and sturdy than elegant.

Generous windows, yes, and plenty of plantings to soften those straight lines, but no balconies or terraces, no gracious front porch or veranda.

"It's impressive," Peabody commented. "But it's not, you know, welcoming. It looks really stern and strict. Our house isn't going to look stern and strict."

"No chance of that."

"The front garden's nice, but there's just the long, long lawn up to it. No trees or anything. You've got some over there, way to the side, and they probably have a garden in the back, but otherwise, there's like this big blank green slate."

She shot Eve a look. "I'm paying a lot of attention because

I've got landscaping on the brain, but inside that, it kind of speaks to who lives here."

"Agreed. It looks more like an institution than a home."

"That's it! And you get the feeling that everything inside runs on schedule. Or else."

Eve pulled up at the end of the drive. Since she didn't spot any other vehicles or a specified parking area, she left the car where it was.

The door, six feet across and twice that high in steel gray, opened as she and Peabody got out.

A man of about fifty, wearing Summerset black stood militarily straight. "Lieutenant, Detective. I'll show you where you may wait."

When she crossed the threshold, Eve's sense of an institution didn't fade. A well-endowed one, she thought as she scanned the grand foyer. A lot of dark, heavy furnishings, a lot of paintings of dour-looking people scowling out of dark, heavy frames.

A thick rug in red and gold tones spread over the floor to the straight-as-a-ruler staircase.

The man in black led them to a room off the right, where the generous window looked out over the foundation plantings and endless sea of green to the wall of white.

"May I take your coats?"

"No, we're good." Because it's cold in here, she thought. Not temperature-wise, but in every other sense.

"Please make yourselves comfortable. The Singers will join you shortly, and you'll have a tea and coffee service."

More dark, heavy furniture, more—to her eye—depressing art. More white brick in a fireplace framed by dark wood. The white walls were done in stripes—one matte, one gloss, one matte, and so on—in a style she found disorienting.

"Antiques," Peabody said, studying a deeply carved table.

"Really valuable antiques, but too heavy for the room, you know? And you just want to strip off the decades of lacquer to get to the gorgeous wood under it."

"Why are you whispering?"

"It just sort of feels like you're expected to."

"Got your dust catchers here and there, but no family photos. Not a single one. And what's growing all over that couch?"

"Cabbage roses. It's really old-fashioned and, again, just too much. And the millwork's gorgeous, but with the white-on-white walls, it's all wrong. I mean the walls are wrong. I'm taking mental pictures so I know what not to do."

Eve heard the approaching footsteps—quick, female—and turned to the doorway.

Her first thought—though she'd studied Marvinia Singer's ID shot—was the woman looked completely out of place in the cold, institutional air of the house.

Her hair swung in rich brown, chin-length curves around a pretty face warmed with a smile. She wore a bright blue shirt with a long tail over simple black leggings. Blue-and-silver twists dangled from her ears with a small diamond stud winking from the left cartilage.

Her voice rang like a bell. "Oh, I'm so sorry we've kept you waiting. I'm Marvinia Singer." She stuck out a hand, gripped, and gave Eve's a hearty shake before doing the same with Peabody's. "My husband and his mother will be right along. Please, please, sit down. I'm delighted to meet you. How is Roarke, Lieutenant? I haven't run into him in months."

"He's fine, thank you."

"I'm sure he is. I'm hearing really wonderful things about An Didean. Such a brilliant and generous undertaking. I'm hoping to arrange a tour of it very soon."

She gestured to two chairs of the same rusty red as the enormous couch roses, then settled in the corner of the couch.

"My son tells me you found the person who killed that poor woman. I know it's a relief to him, to all of us, to know that man's been caught."

"Yuri Bardov's nephew."

The smile left her eyes. "Yes, so I heard. I'm sorry to hear it. I'm very fond of Marta."

"You're friendly with Mrs. Bardova?"

"Yes. She's been very generous to my foundation. And we're neighbors, women with some common interests. I haven't spoken with her since I heard. It feels wrong, even for a friend, to speak to her of this right now. I know she and Yuri treated Alexei as one of their own."

"You know him?"

"Not well, no. His wife, Nadia, has again given some time to my foundation and I'm grateful. I can't conceive she knew he was capable of doing what he did. I can't believe Marta had any idea he was stealing from her husband, from us. Am I correct you're here to ask us about all of that?"

"In part, yes."

"It may seem biased for me to say, as a woman, a mother, that neither of these women, these mothers, were aware. But I believe it, absolutely. I've known Marta for—God—nearly fifty years."

"And Yuri?"

"He's less . . . knowable. I have talked to him more in the last few years than previously, as he's actually a very skilled gardener, and I've asked his advice in that area."

She glanced toward the doorway before she continued, "I'm not unaware of Yuri's reputation, but can tell you I haven't seen that side of him, if true, in the years I've known

Marta. Alexei . . . the phrase is *a lean and hungry look*. I would have applied that to him."

"He and your son are about the same age," Peabody said.

"Yes. Different interests, different circles. And Bolt was a few years older when Alexei came to the country, and already had his established friends, and then was off to college. They never clicked."

Eve heard more footsteps and noted Marvinia's glance at the doorway. "And here we are."

Eve turned her head to watch the entrance.

J. Bolton, trim, tanned, tall in his pearl-gray linen suit, his hair a shining wave of golden blond, had his mother's hand tucked in his crooked arm.

His smile was all charm and dancing eyes.

Elinor Singer wore a white long-sleeved dress all but cracking with starch. Her hair, gold like her son's, slicked back from her face to form a hard knot at the base of her neck.

She'd gone with a suite of rubies: bloodred orbs at her ears, another at her throat, a circle of them on one wrist, another on her finger.

On her left hand the bright white diamond cut the air like a knife.

Her eyes glinted, hard blue. Eve wondered how many treatments it took to get every line and wrinkle stretched and erased out of century-old skin.

"What a treat!" Singer patted his mother's hand as they walked. "The famous Dallas and Peabody in our parlor. I'm J. B. Singer. Lieutenant Dallas, Detective Peabody, let me introduce you to my mother, Elinor Bolton Singer."

Elinor took the corner of the couch opposite her daughter-in-law. Singer sat between them.

"Isn't this lovely?" Singer began.

"Don't be a dolt," Elinor snapped, and, like her skin, her

voice was drum-tight. "They want us to gossip about the Bardovs. You're wasting everyone's time. We don't gossip in this house."

Strict and stern, Eve thought, came from the top.

"No point in wasting time," Eve said in return. "So how about we talk about murder?"

19

Elinor's expression didn't change—then again, Eve wasn't sure it could.

"As you've arrested Alexei Tovinski and the thief Carmine Delgato is dead, we have nothing more to say on the subject. The woman was trespassing, but her transgression exposed crimes against our company. We will, of course, take steps to ensure such difficulties don't happen again."

"Will you continue your association with Bardov Construction?" Eve asked.

She lifted an eyebrow a fraction of an inch. "That association is legal. The Bardov organization, like ours, was victimized. I would assume they, as we, will take all necessary steps to prevent any future thievery or exploitation. If you've come here to intimate that the Singer organization or any member of my family played a part in this thievery, exploitation, or the death of a trespasser, I would suggest you leave now. You may address your remarks to our attorneys."

"Now, Mother." Singer reached for Elinor's hand. She swatted his away.

"Our victimization continues with honking media gossip and innuendo. I will not have it. An employee, one who should not have been trusted, stole from and conspired to steal from us. From the very people who provided him with employment, with the wherewithal to make a good living. And we're to be questioned?"

"This is a very upsetting time for you," Peabody began.

"You know nothing of it. Our reputation has been smeared by this. Our efforts to create a space of beauty and function will be forever besmirched by this woman's death."

"Her name was Alva Quirk," Eve said, voice cold. "And I'd say her family's finding this a pretty difficult time."

"Perhaps if her family had done more to preserve family, she wouldn't have lived on the streets, nor ended up dead in a dumpster."

"Elinor, please!"

Elinor spared her daughter-in-law a glance. "You will make heroes of them. Your downtrodden and underserved. I have nothing more to say on the subject. So if that's all—"

"It's not," Eve said as Elinor started to rise.

The butler and two women—also in black—filed in carrying trays. A coffee service, a tea service, china.

Without a word, they arranged it all on the table between the sofa and chairs. One of the women poured tea into a cup, passed it to Elinor.

"I'll do the rest, thank you." Marvinia rose. "Coffee, tea?"

"Coffee, black," Eve said. "My partner takes cream and sugar. The Alva Quirk case is closed. Of course, if more information comes to light, we'll reopen it. We're here about another murder."

She took the coffee from Marvinia, but she watched Elinor.

"A woman, early twenties, in the last trimester of pregnancy, murdered on another Singer construction site."

"Nonsense," Elinor decreed. "What site? We've heard nothing of this, and surely would have."

"You no longer own the site. Roarke Industries does."

Elinor managed a smirk. "Then I would suggest you look to your own."

"That would be a waste of time."

"I'd expect you to say so. But one does hear what one does hear about Roarke."

Eve just sipped some coffee. "Since gossip isn't allowed here, we'll skip over that."

She heard Marvinia choke back a laugh.

"But it would be a waste of time because the murder occurred thirty-seven years ago. And Singer was the owner and developer of record."

"I did hear something about this." Marvinia spoke again. "Something about human remains found on another development project in Hudson Yards. A woman, you said. And pregnant?"

"That's right. We're in the process of identifying her."

Eve took out her PPC, brought up the sketch. Held it up.

"Oh, poor thing. So young!"

"Does she look familiar?"

"I can't say I recognize her," Singer said. "Thirty-seven years. A very long time."

"She could be anyone." Elinor dismissed it. "Likely a squatter, one who came to a bad end."

"We recovered certain items that indicate she wasn't squatting. My questions, at this point, center on the time frame, her identity, and how her body was concealed."

"Concealed?" Marvinia shook her head. "I assumed she'd been buried."

"Not exactly, no. Mr. Singer, you were running the company at that time. Though, of course, Mrs. Singer, you were still very much involved. Do either of you recall an employee or subcontractor going missing?"

"No," Singer said immediately.

"It was difficult to keep good employees during that time,"

Elinor added. "To find and keep the skilled and responsible. Many were transients, or simply unskilled and looking for any kind of work. Most of those didn't last. We could hardly, considering the circumstances, remember who came and went."

"It seems a young woman about thirty-two weeks pregnant would be more memorable than most. She was Middle Eastern, in excellent health."

Singer stared. "How could you know all that? You said you hadn't identified her."

"Our forensic anthropologist has examined the remains. As has the chief medical examiner. This woman was shot, three times, with a thirty-two-caliber weapon."

"Oh my God." Marvinia pressed a hand to her mouth as her eyes glistened. "The baby. How horrible."

"Part of your project on this site was a restaurant. The plans included a wine cellar, which required some excavation. We've established at the time of the murder, the foundation and the exterior cellar walls were in place. We haven't located records of the specific work or the building inspections."

Elinor let out a dismissive huff. "Study your history, girl. There was still considerable turmoil, and the building trade was rife with corruption. Those of us trying to rebuild the city the mobs had done their best to destroy did what we could and how we could. Most building inspectors expected cash payment if they troubled themselves to come to a site. It took months, years, for the system to right itself."

"But you remember this project? Bardov was, again, a financial partner."

"If you believe Yuri Bardov had some pregnant girl killed, speak to him."

"I have, and I will again. Now I'm speaking to you. You remember this project, Mr. Singer?"

"I do, of course. We were more focused, and further along with the River Park project, the signature tower—which we're proud still stands. The site you're speaking of was more of a mix of quickly constructed affordable housing and commercial spaces. All making use—on both sites—of what we'd begun before the Urbans.

"But, as Mother said, post-war was a complicated, chaotic time." With a sorrowful smile, Singer spread his hands. "In the end, the South-West project simply wasn't profitable enough to continue. We sold off a considerable portion of it and, again, focused on River Park and other projects."

"But before you sold a portion of the property, this restaurant—which opened spring of 2025 as the Skyline—and several other buildings were completed."

"Oh yes. Several of the commercial spaces were occupied, if memory serves, and several of the low-rise residential buildings as well when we sold."

"Who was in charge of the restaurant's construction? The job boss, the foreman? The mason and so on?"

"Oh my goodness." With a half laugh, he sat back. "Nearly forty years? Longer than either of you have been alive and nearly half my own life? My memory isn't nearly that good."

Eve turned to Elinor. "How's yours?"

"As I said, it was difficult to find and keep skilled labor at that time. J.B. and I struggled over that very issue. But I do recall we decided to promote Joe Kendall—a longtime employee—to foreman on several buildings on that site. You remember Joe Kendall, J.B.?"

"A blast from the past," he said with a laugh. "Yes, I remember Joe. Big as a house, smoked like a chimney. He may have handled the restaurant—the one with the wine cellar. We had several buildings earmarked for restaurant use, I think. I know Joe took on a few of the commercial buildings.

"God, I haven't thought of Big Joe in years."

"He no longer works for Singer?"

"He's been gone twenty years—or nearly. Smoked like a chimney, loved food—especially fried—and carried at least thirty extra pounds."

"I remember him," Marvinia murmured. "From the holiday parties. He had such a big laugh. He always called me Miss Marvinia. He had a wife and a couple of children. He wouldn't have hurt anyone, Lieutenant."

"That's not for us to say," Elinor corrected.

"There was a discrepancy in materials."

"Of what sort?" Elinor demanded.

"The exterior walls are concrete and block—substandard."

"Material was hard to come by, and there was considerable price gouging. The goal was quick, and with hopes updating would be done at some point. As it is being done now."

"An interior wall was constructed about three feet inside that exterior wall. Brick. Good-quality brick and mortar were used. The ceiling—or the floor of the main restaurant over just this area—was formed and poured using good-quality concrete."

"She was . . ." Marvinia rubbed a hand over her heart. "They walled her in? Her and the baby?"

"Yes. They had to access the brick—much higher quality than anything on that site at that time. Where would they access it, and so quickly? You had other projects."

Singer held up a finger. "I see! Someone who worked on, or perhaps even a supervisor on that site could have—would have—known where we had a supply of brick. Either warehouses, or on another site. But, dear, if you're asking me to try to remember missing material from that time, a shortfall? I couldn't possibly."

"That's what they counted on." Marvinia turned to him.

"Darling, that's what they counted on. Someone stole it, they'd say, or like with Alexei, they doctored an invoice, or amount. Oh, this is just so sad. Think of that girl's family. What they've gone through. Not knowing. All these years."

"Stop fancifying," Elinor ordered. "For all you know she had no family. Or they booted her when she got pregnant."

"If they did, shame on them," she bit back, and from the look in Elinor's eye, Marvinia didn't bite often. "And that doesn't change what happened. J.B., you have to think back, look back."

"Of course I will, my sweet. But honestly, nearly four decades. Sketchy records, lost records, workers coming and going. And I confess, my focus was much more on River Park at that time. The other?"

He looked at Eve, lifted his hands. "It was get it up as best we could. Businesses, ours included, were bleeding money. So we took partners, did what we could to increase revenue while trying to build. To give people some normality again. We did our best in a difficult time."

"I'm sure you did. But if you would think back and if you have any records from that time we've so far been unable to access, we need them.

"Peabody."

"Yes, sir. We have a warrant for records, invoices, inventory lists. I'll print that out for you now."

"A warrant." Singer held up his hands again. "Hardly necessary. We're more than willing to cooperate."

"Even so." Eve rose as Peabody used her PPC to print out the warrant. "We expect to have the victim's identity verified within the next forty-eight hours. Employee records are also included in the warrant. She was on your property when she was killed, so she may have had business there."

"Or she was trespassing."

Eve nodded at Elinor. "We'll find out. Trust me. This case is as important as Alva Quirk's. Thank you for your time, your cooperation, and the coffee."

"I'll show you out." Marvinia rose, walked them to the door. "I'm so sorry I can't be more help. I've never taken an interest in the business. But I'll do what I can to nudge J.B.'s memory."

"And your mother-in-law's?"

"Well, Elinor remembers what she chooses and how she chooses. But the company's reputation is everything to her. She'll do whatever she can to end this and move on from it."

"I'm sure she will. Thanks again."

As they walked to the car, Peabody glanced back at the house. "It must be hard."

Eve got behind the wheel, took one last look herself. "What's that?"

"I'm guessing in a house this size, they each have their own wing, but still, it must be hard to live in the same house as your mother-in-law when you really don't like her."

"And knowing the person you really don't like is top of the food chain." Eve did a three-point turn to head out. "They travel a lot, have a couple other homes in other places, but they use this as home base. Why do you figure?"

"Well, Elinor might have had her skin stretched so tight you could bounce a five-dollar credit off her cheek, but she's still over the century mark. That's one."

"That's one, but my take is it's mostly habit. J.B. was never really head of the company, and didn't want to be. All that shows in his background. She's ruled right along. And when he took on a project, he was mostly crap at it. She let him be. That's indulgence. He married money and status, so points in his favor. But Marvinia has her own life and interests."

"I looked into her foundation a little, and they do good work."

"Good work, and she's not just a figurehead. She's involved—and not involved in the Singer family business. Probably points for her on Elinor's scale. So they maintain a polite if cool relationship because they both indulge J.B."

Eve made a turn, following the computer's prompts for the Bardov estate. "Even though he's weak, spoiled, and a liar."

"I felt like he was lying, but I couldn't catch it."

"Taps his foot—right foot—when he's lying. Looks you straight in the eye, doesn't evade or hesitate, but that foot tapping? Major tell."

"I missed that! I hate when I miss stuff like that."

"His mother's a better liar. No tells there. Just icy contempt. Anyway, they knew the victim was down there, so they didn't sell off that section of the property. I'm wondering now if Bolton Singer sold it to Roarke before they could stop him."

"Or maybe they thought, after all this time, it wouldn't matter."

"Maybe. Whether they walled her up or not, that's for us to find out. But what I know is they walled her right out of their minds. She didn't matter. Forget her, move on."

"If they killed her or had her killed . . ."

"That's an if, but one way or the other, they knew. I don't care how much chaos or corruption was going on, Elinor Bolton Singer damn well knew if a freaking truckload of bricks went missing. And she knew a wall of high-quality bricks went up in a cheap build. I'm saying she knew why. She knew."

Peabody shifted as Eve pulled up to another gate, gleaming black in the opening of the stone walls.

"Young, pregnant woman—pretty woman. J.B. has a little roll there, and oops. She decides to have the baby. Maybe he tries to pay her off, but as it gets closer to the time, she wants more. More support, acknowledgment. Maybe she loved him, or he promised the usual. Leave my wife, and all that bullshit."

As her thoughts had run the same, Eve nodded. "Makes her a threat. He lures her up there. Maybe he planned to scare her, or threaten her back, or offer her more money. Whatever, it didn't end well. He panics, or loses his temper, or he planned to get rid of her all along."

"He gets the brick. It would be easy for him. I guess he could build a wall. I mean he grew up around construction."

"Sloppy build. Solid enough, but sloppy. Yeah, he could've done it. Then he tells Mother all—or he tells her before and she tells him how to handle it. That works for me because they knew. They knew her face when they saw the sketch. They knew she was down there."

She rolled down the window.

"Lieutenant Dallas, Detective Peabody to see Mr. Bardov."

Instead of a computer-generated response, Eve watched a man—big and burly—walk to the gate.

She got out of the car, approached from her side.

"You're not expected."

"No." But she expected he had a weapon under his suit coat. "We conducted an interview in the area and hoped Mr. Bardov would be available to speak with us. A follow-up to our conversation yesterday."

"Wait."

When he walked away, Eve took the time to study the view through the gate.

Trees, green and leafy with early summer. A winding drive, a green lawn with groupings of flowering shrubs, some sort of stone structure where water tumbled.

All dominated by the big house of dusky blue with its generous terraces, glass rails, tall windows, and wide, covered porch where flowering vines wound up thick columns.

No strict and stern here, she thought. Inhabited by a mob-

ster, yes, guarded by armed security, no doubt, but with a fa-
cade, at least, of welcome.

The guard came back. "Mr. Bardov is pleased to meet with
you and offer you refreshments in the garden. You may go to
the house, and Mrs. Bardova will show you the way."

"Thanks."

She got back in the car.

"It's beautiful," Peabody said. "And I know it's probably
built on the crushed bones of his enemies, but it still looks
sort of like a mansion in a fairy tale.

"That water feature. I wonder if I can build something like
that."

Eve nearly stopped the car. "Build?"

"It would be a fun project—maybe next spring. I've never
built anything like that." Peabody craned her neck as Eve
drove past it. "I think I could."

"You baffle me, Peabody. Sometimes you just baffle the
crap right out of me."

Before they reached the house, a woman came out on the
porch.

Like Marvinia, Marta Bardova wore simple leggings
and an overshirt, hers in bright red with some frills down
the front. Tendrils of silvery-blond hair escaped from the
loosely bundled knot on top of her head.

"Welcome to our home," she said when Eve got out of
the car. "I'm Marta Bardova. I'm starstruck." She laughed
as she pressed a hand to her heart. "I so loved *The Icove
Agenda*, even though I wept for the babies. Oh, those babies
broke my heart."

She held out her hand to shake. A ringless hand, Eve noted,
of a woman who smelled like . . . sugar cookies.

"Detective Peabody." Marta shook again. "I have to ask
you a personal question."

"Um. Okay."

"McNab. In the book, and now in the new book, he's your love. Is he?"

"Ah, yes. We're . . ."

"I'm so glad!" Beaming, Marta clapped her hands together. "He's adorable. In the books, he's adorable. I wish you many happy years together. Please, come in. Yuri's working in the garden. My granddaughter brought her twins to visit."

"We're sorry to interrupt," Eve began.

"No, no. We're baking, so you'll have lemonade and cookies. They'll be thrilled."

Here was color, Eve thought as Marta led them through the house. Lofty ceilings, open space, happy colors, and floods of light, vases everywhere filled with flowers.

And the smell of sugar cookies.

"You've beaten the storms they say are coming," Marta continued. "It should be nice to have a talk in the garden while the sun shines."

Eve heard squealing, a female voice order someone named *Nicholas Michael Cobain!* to *Stop that right now*, followed by laughter.

Marta rolled her eyes. "Our great-grandson is a handful."

Eve spotted the handful—around four, she guessed, all curly headed and caramel skinned and wickedly gleaming eyes—squeezing some pink stuff out of a tube onto a girl—obviously his twin.

"I make a flower on Tasha, Mama!"

The girl, a near mirror image of her brother, squeezed something green out of a tube. It shot out in a stream, hit him right below the left eye.

Hilarity ensued.

"My charming and perfectly behaved family."

The woman currently refereeing looked over, sighed. "We're a mess, Mama. So sorry."

"Messes clean up. But how will the cookies get decorated if you decorate each other?"

The girl offered an angelic smile. "We taste good!"

"Let me see." Marta walked to the wide kitchen island, bent down, made smacking noises on the girl's arm, the boy's face. "Good enough to eat. Now pretend you're good children and say hello to our guests."

"Hello!" they chorused.

"Well done. Just this way," she added, and gestured to the wide opening where the glass doors had been folded back to let in the June day.

Peabody actually gasped, and had Marta pausing to look at her.

"It's—it's just glorious. Your gardens. And another water feature, the arbors! Oh, and the play area for the kids. The flagstone paths, with moss. It's the good witch's garden. I have to steal these ideas. We're going to start gardens and landscaping."

"You garden?"

"When I can. But not like this. I haven't worked in a garden like this since I came to New York. Smell the peonies! I'm sorry." She caught herself—or Eve's bland stare caught her.

"Yuri will be delighted. And you must talk to him about your gardening. I dig and plant where he tells me, but this is his."

She led them down one of the paths, beyond a knoll buried in flowers, through a screen of slim trees to where the mob boss, in dirt-stained baggies, a faded blue shirt, and a straw hat, sat on a low, rolling stool, doing something to what even Eve recognized as a tomato plant.

"Yuri, your guests."

"Yes, welcome, yes. One second."

"Epsom salt mixture," Peabody said. "For the magnesium."

He looked over in approval. "You know."

"Your gardens are amazing, Mr. Bardov."

"They're work, and the work is my pleasure." He rose, dusted his gloved hands on his pants.

"You'll talk," Marta said. "And when you're ready, there will be lemonade and strangely decorated cookies on the patio."

"Thank you, *lyubimaya*."

Eve recognized the look in his eye as he watched his wife walk away. And wondered if she'd still see the same in Roarke's for her when they were eighty.

"So," he said. "There's more for us to discuss?"

"We came to the area to speak with Elinor, J. Bolton, and Marvinia Singer. And thought we'd conduct a follow-up with you, as we're here."

"Ah, Marvinia. A lovely woman. She and my Marta are good friends."

"So she told us."

"I fear Elinor will be displeased with me, for Alexei's sins. What can you do? So, Alexei, he's on his way to his new life?"

"I'm sure you know he is."

Bardov smiled. "You and your associates have done an excellent job. I don't believe I'll waste time, any more time, on Alexei. He's hurt and disappointed his aunt and, for me, this is a bigger sin than the theft. She shed tears for him, but they're done now. Our granddaughter brought the twins to make her happy. They do."

"They were decorating each other more than the cookies," Peabody told him, and now he flashed a grin.

"Children are the light that cuts through any shadow. You don't ask, but I'll tell you. We've gone to see and reassure

Nadia. She's family, her children are our children. As are the others. They'll be cherished and tended as children should be.

"Now." He gestured and began to walk. "Tell me why you came. You don't worry I'll hunt for Alexei. The woman he killed, I know, is to be laid to rest by her family, in her home. As I know the man who once beat her, treated her cruelly will now be punished for it."

"You know quite a lot."

He nodded at Eve, stopped to pull small snippers from his baggies. He cut a fat red peony and offered it to Peabody. "You enjoy the scent."

"Yes. Thank you."

"I know quite a lot because I have an interest. You and Detective Peabody are of interest to me. At one time of my life, this interest would have had a different purpose. But these days, I enjoy my gardens, I think to get chickens. The children would enjoy them. I think a puppy. It's time, as old Boris died in his sleep last winter. I think I have years ahead and will spend them with the gardens and the children, the chickens, the dog. Two dogs," he said with a nod. "We'll get two puppies."

The idea seemed to please him as he took off his gardening gloves.

"The . . . pursuit?" he continued. "The interest in such things wanes. I wonder if your husband would like to buy my company."

"I'm sorry, what?"

"I have no one to leave it to now. It would have been Alexei's. How foolish he was to steal what would have been his own in only a few years. My children have other lives, and are not involved in this part of mine. I'm grateful for that now. I see Marta was wise to insist. So, I think I am retired."

He nodded again. "I'll be speaking to Roarke. But that's

another world from this, from you coming to see me. This is about the woman, the one with child. I have thought of her since I learned. I've asked some questions, but I don't have any answers for you."

"Would you tell me if you did?"

"Yesterday, ah, perhaps, perhaps not. Today, I'm retired." He smiled, radiating charm. "Yes, I would. I would accept your way of justice today. And I hope, tomorrow. She haunts me. I have no face to give her, but she haunts me. I ate in the restaurant with my family, many times, with her and the child trapped under our feet. I would help you if I could."

Eve pulled out her PPC. "Let me give you her face."

20

Bardov studied the sketch, then crooked his finger.

He sat on a bench and, when Eve sat beside him, studied the sketch again.

"A man in the line of work from which I have retired must remember faces. I remember faces. I don't know hers. Didn't know hers," he corrected. "I'm sorry I can't tell you who she was. But I know I'll remember her face now.

"Will you find her?"

"I will. We will."

"Good." He put his hands on his thighs. "She had a mother, perhaps my age now. Her mother should know."

"How closely was your business aligned with the Singers when the woman in this sketch died?"

"They had more trouble than me. I had ways to profit from the . . . unrest. Some still call it unrest. Ways I won't detail to cops on such a pretty day. We can say my interests were more diverse, and not so bound up in building and development. So during the time this young woman died, and the push for building ran hot, the Singers, and others, required backing. Loans or influence."

"Such as knowing which inspectors to bribe, what official to blackmail?"

"Such as," he said with a smile. "Though Elinor still pulled most strings, J.B. was the titular head and he would have his vanity project."

"The Singer Tower."

"Yes. It had survived the unrest, but hadn't been completed and, as many buildings did, had damage—from the unrest, from squatters. He had a vision, and not a bad one for all that. For the tower, for the lesser buildings to accent it. He poured the company into that, and gave less to the—ah, what did they call it?"

"South-West, or Hudson Yards Skyline, depending on the records."

"Yes, yes, I remember. I like better Roarke's Hudson Yards Village. Be that as it may, J.B. overweighted his outlay—he's a poor businessman—and they needed backing. I—my company—made them a loan, taking a ten percent interest. On both sites. Elinor was not pleased."

At his satisfied smile, Eve spoke her mind. "You don't like her."

"She's a dislikable woman, as I'm sure you found her. But business is business, and it wasn't my problem, was it, if J.B. accepted the terms so quickly, and without fully informing her. So we became partners of a sort, and that's continued on a few projects over the years. Such as the River View project—the renewal of it—where Alexei killed the woman."

He sat back. "You wonder if they knew of my other . . . my diversity at the time we made this partnership. Of course, but business is business. You wonder if they ever came to me for a favor. This might be true. It might be true I granted that favor and took one in return. Business."

He gestured toward an emerald-green bird that hovered with a blur of wings at a red flower.

"Hummingbirds are so industrious. And such a bright

sight in any garden. They're very territorial, and will fight off their own kids to drink their fill."

He smiled again.

"You wonder if favors continue. If the grandson now in the big office asks for favors from me or seeks my influence. And I can say he doesn't. I can say he's not the businessperson his grandmother was, but a far better one than his father. This is a low bar," Bardov added with a laugh.

He looked at Eve. "This is why you're here. For the gossip."

"Yeah, you could say."

"I like gossip. It adds some spice to the bland."

"Did J.B. have affairs? Were there other women?"

Bardov's eyebrows winged up. "Juice as well as spice. Some men can love with their heart, but their body wants more, and their mind allows this by believing it doesn't matter. Or count. Or hurts no one. The mind lies. But what J.B.'s faithfulness matters in this . . . Oh, oh, I see."

He went silent a moment, brows drawn together now.

"You wonder if J.B. indulged himself with this young woman. A much younger woman than his wife, as many men look for. We're not friends, you see. I'm not a confidant or someone he'd speak to about his infidelity."

"But you know he had affairs."

"It pays to know a partner's weaknesses. I know that for a time and, during this time, there was dispute, tension. As I said, Marta and Marvinia are friends. They are confidantes."

"Tensions because he cheated?"

"No, not that precisely. Tensions that may have allowed his mind to justify breaking his vows. Their son didn't want the business. He wanted music, the freedom of it. The fame from it. He has talent, and his mother very much wanted him to pursue his dreams. I know she and Elinor fought over that and Marvinia, outnumbered as J.B. won't stand against his mother, made a bargain. They wanted the boy safely out of New York during the troubling times, in any case, and so he was allowed to go to the school he wanted and study his music. But he had to take business courses as well."

"Seems reasonable."

"Yes, it was a good bargain, but the getting there caused trouble. And their son's passion for the music caused more. For a time, Marvinia lived separately and there was talk—she talked to Marta—about divorce. The son stayed away—somewhere in the South, I think. Marta would remember. And J.B. traveled, and enjoyed a single man's lifestyle, for that time."

"But she didn't divorce him?"

"No. The bargain—which she might have broken—was kept, as J.B. went to her, romanced her, asked her to try again. So the bargain—that they would not support the son financially—was kept. I have reason to know J.B. didn't fully honor his vows for a longer time, but the son finally came home, tail between his legs, his dreams turned to smoke. And now he sits in the big office."

"Did she know he had other women?"

"She knew there were others when they lived separately. She forgave him. I don't believe she knew he had others after they reconciled. He learned to be discreet and, eventually, learned to be faithful."

"Was she his type?"

Bardov looked at the sketch again. "Younger women were his type. I don't know if this girl was. I never heard of J.B. having a liaison that resulted in a pregnancy. I would have tucked that away for use in any future negotiations."

He let out a short laugh. "This isn't what I expected we would discuss today."

"Could he kill?"

The humor faded, and his eyes latched on hers. "You

know, as I know, all and any can. Is he a violent man? No. I would know. But he's a weak man, dominated and indulged by turns by his mother. And perhaps indulged, yes, by a wife who prefers not to look at him too deeply."

"You don't like him, either."

Now he pursed his lips in thought. "I can't say J.B. is a dislikable man, but he is, under the polish, a contemptible one. He all but frittered away a company and fortune his grandfather and father had built, one his grandmother had steered successfully through difficult times. Then rather than allow his son dreams of his own, he pressured him to accept a legacy the son didn't want.

"I'll sell what I built to your husband, if he wants it. I would never demand any of my children accept what they don't want. Could he have killed this woman and the child he'd planted in her if that part's true? Yes, a man can do anything, can do evil things, out of fear, anger, greed, envy. Did he?"

Bardov shook his head. "This is for you to learn. If it's true, I'll be sorry, for it will hurt Marta and the good woman J.B. married. It will make them weep."

He pushed up. "Come, we've talked of this enough. We'll sit on the patio and have lemonade."

"We appreciate your time. We'll let you get back to your family."

"One glass, two cookies." He wagged a finger at her. "You can give that time in return for mine. Marta will be disappointed if you don't."

"Mr. Bardov?" Peabody fell into step with him. "Some of your children would be about the same age as Bolton Singer. Did they socialize?"

"Not much, no. As I said, they traveled considerably, and Elinor would not have approved. Now, I would say Marvinia would have overruled her—or attempted to—if my children and their son had struck up a friendship. I do recall, now that I think, my younger daughter sighed over him a bit one summer—but he barely noticed her. His music was all."

"He didn't have girlfriends?"

"I suppose he did, but nothing serious—or I would have heard. His music, Detective, was his passion and only love. Until he met his wife. They have a beautiful family. And no, he does not break his vows."

"You'd know?"

He glanced at Eve. "I would. Of course, now I've retired and have no purpose in knowing. There, see?" He pointed to where the twins swarmed over some sort of outdoor play deal with a slide and bars and a kind of fort. "There is the future. Let's have cookies and talk of pleasant things."

Eve decided having cookies with a Russian gangster (retired) on his patio while he bounced a couple of kids on his knees went down as one of the strangest interludes of her career.

As they drove back to the heliport, Eve pushed forward.

"Find out if any of the Singers have a gun collector's license."

Peabody shifted the little container of cookies as she pulled out her PPC. "You have to take these cookies. I had three damn cookies, and that's it. You take them. A gun collector's license?"

"If we treat this theory as fact, there had to be a gun, a thirty-two. Maybe they kept it after the gun ban, got licensed as a collector, then we can at least try to find out if any of them had a license for the weapon thirty-seven years ago."

"That's a stretch, plus plenty of unregistered and illegal possession of firearms back then."

"We look, then maybe we know. Like we asked, and now we know—because that's a credible source—J. B. Singer had affairs and liked younger women."

"Men always like younger women."

The sour tone had Eve glancing over. "McNab's only got a couple years on you."

"Because we're both young. But say when we hit like fifty, he could start eyeballing twenty-year-olds. Of course, if he does, I'll spoon out his eyeballs and keep them in a glass box on the mantel. That'll stop that shit."

"I like that one. I'm keeping that one in reserve."

"Happy to share." Peabody looked up from her PPC. "No collector's license for any of them."

"Okay, that was too easy anyway. They could've gotten rid of it, or reported it stolen, or it was never registered so they've still got it somewhere. Start searching for incident reports, involving any of them. Intruders, theft, domestic disturbance, vandalism, anything that involved a police report."

"All the way back, thirty-seven years?"

"Go forty."

"Once I go back over twenty, twenty-five, it's going to get murky. Can I pull McNab in to help?"

"Do that. Prioritize anything that involved violence or a weapon, but get it all. Global."

"Jesus, Dallas."

"Yeah, yeah, but they traveled. After that, it's civil suits. Let's start putting their history together. And how big a financial hole did J.B. dig back then? Our profile says the victim was Middle Eastern, and from a solid background. Maybe he hoped to squeeze some money there. Rich parents, potential investors, romance the daughter. Oops."

"It's a big oops."

"It wasn't piddly shit that put her in that cellar. Yeah, Bardov's right. People will kill for all sorts of reasons, but not the way this went down. Too much purpose."

As she pulled into the heliport, she comforted herself that

at least on the return trip she had work. Plenty of work to get her through.

She intended to dive straight back into the work when she got to Central. Armed with coffee, she read Reo's roundup of the Wicker deal.

He took the ten.

She checked the facial rec on her victim and found the problem wasn't a lack of matches, but a bounty of them.

Not enough detail, she reminded herself, and started to contact DeWinter when she got the word Alva's siblings had come in for her effects.

She took them to the lounge, spent the next twenty minutes with them. On the way back through the bullpen, Peabody hailed her.

"I've got a handful of incidents on J.B."

"Really?"

"Nothing recent yet, and nothing in New York. What I did was do a run through global media for, well, gossip, and when I hit, cross-checked. What we've got is mostly in Europe, and mostly two or three decades back. So far."

"Such as?"

"Reckless driving, disorderly conduct, trespassing, creating a disturbance, an assault—assault with a martini. He tossed his martini in this guy's face, and the skewer of olives hit the guy in the eye."

"You're not making this up?"

"Hand to God." Peabody put one over her heart. "This one also led to a civil suit, settled out of court for an undisclosed amount. It's all partying related. McNab's giving workplace incidents a shot."

"Huh. Good idea."

"Yeah, he figured if Singer had a history of screwing around, he maybe screwed around in the office, or tried to.

Maybe some sexual harassment. Nothing's popped yet on anybody but J. B. Singer."

"Keep at it."

"The Elliots?"

"They're going to be shaky for a while, but knowing their sister's killer's put away, knowing Wicker's doing ten will go a long way to steadying them up."

"That's good."

"I want any hits on the workplace incidents. One of them might have been our vic."

She went back to her office, sat to contact DeWinter. Her comp signaled an incoming.

She studied the completed sketches of her unknown victim.

> To Lieutenant Eve Dallas from Dr. Garnet DeWinter:
> Attached is the completed reconstructed images of
> Jane Doe based on our analysis. Holo-imagery is
> available now in the lab, or can be sent to an autho-
> rized holo-portal on written request.
>   Also attached is my final report on the remains
> of Jane Doe and Baby Doe.
>   We will secure the remains until such time as the
> victim is identified and/or the disposition or transfer
> of said remains are authorized.

Eve updated her board with the sketches, the reports. She considered ordering the holo, but didn't think she needed it.

"Damn good work," she muttered and wondered if her go-to police artist, Yancy, ever talked shop with Elsie Kendrick.

She saw a young woman, a pretty—edging toward beautiful—face made up of delicate features. High forehead, long, wide eyes—dark eyes in a heart-shaped face. Defined but not prominent cheekbones, a small bow-shaped mouth.

Not quite petite, but small-boned, slender—in the full-body pre-pregnancy reproduction. Long fingers, long, narrow feet.

In pregnancy, the belly ballooned to accommodate a life that would never be.

She went back to her desk, programmed a global facial recognition search.

It would be harder, she thought, considering the search had to go back nearly four decades. But.

"We'll find you."

She tried another angle. Given her age, the victim could have come to New York to work or go to college. For that, she'd have needed a visa. Taking a leap of faith DeWinter hit on the country of origin, Eve started the process of searching for visas issued to females from 2020 through 2025 from Lebanon.

It took her under a minute to hit the bureaucratic wall.

She considered going to Whitney and asking him to cut through it, then decided to make use of a contact.

She hit on Agent Teasdale, formerly Homeland and now FBI—and, in Eve's opinion, on track for the top slot there.

Ten minutes later, she had Teasdale on board and the assurance she'd have the information by morning.

Morning would have to do.

Had she been Muslim—had she been religious enough to go to a mosque? A couple of uniforms could show the sketches around—but then again, she had no guarantee the victim had lived in New York.

Still, another angle to work.

She walked out to the bullpen.

"Peabody, I sent you the completed sketches on the Jane Doe. Grab a couple uniforms, have them take copies around to mosques in the city. Look for older, longtime members who might have seen her."

"It's a line to tug," Peabody agreed. "Is OT authorized?"

Frowning, Eve checked the time, saw it was nearly end of shift. And she weighed the benefits against the budget.

"Have them start in the morning. You can hook up with McNab—"

"Every chance I get."

"Funny. You can put the searches on auto at home. I want to know when you get hits. Just put them together and send them to me. I'm running facial rec on the sketches, and I'll do the same. Teasdale's working on getting me data on work and education visas within our parameters."

"Another good angle. We'll keep them running on porta-bles. We're going by the house, doing another walk-through with our landlords, then grabbing some dinner together. We can skip the dinner part."

"No, go ahead. Just keep it running."

"Can do. Are you heading home, too?"

"I will be."

"Got a second first, boss?"

She looked over at Baxter. "I have a few of them."

He made an eye slide toward her office, added a little head nod.

"Let's take it in my office so I can get my things."

When he followed her in, he took a look at her board. "Pretty young thing, and a baby, too."

"Yeah. Problem, Baxter?"

"Not really. Trueheart and I are clear, so if you need any legwork, we're available."

She edged a hip on the corner of her desk. He hadn't needed her office to volunteer. "We're covered, but I'll let you know if that changes."

"The boy and I, we're heading out for a brew, maybe some

chow. There's a mosque a couple blocks from where we're going. We could take that one on the way."

"All right. Computer, print out sketches A, B, and C from current file."

Acknowledged. Working . . .

"And you wanted to come in here to tell me this?"

"The reason we're heading out for a brew, maybe chow, isn't just because we're clear. Trueheart's girl's taking a transfer to East Washington—comes with a promotion."

Baxter slid his hands into the pockets of his perfectly tailored suit pants. "He's bummed about it. They're making noises about long-distance relationship, but that's not going to fly long. It's not everlasting love, but he's bummed. He could use a little busywork."

"Tell me he's not thinking about following her down there."

"Oh hell no. His job's here, his mom's here, his life's here. That wasn't ever on the table."

"When does she leave?"

"Left this morning. It's why he's low right now. So busywork."

She handed him the sketches. "Get busy. You were a good trainer to him, and you're a good partner now. Don't get him too drunk."

Baxter grinned. "Just a little drunk. Trust me, it doesn't take much with my boy."

She'd been right, Eve thought, to assign the green, earnest, upright Trueheart to Baxter. And Baxter had the way of systematically rubbing off the green without losing too much of the earnest and none of the upright.

Eve looked back at the board. "I'm right about you, too. Just need a little more time."

She gathered what she needed to take some of that time

at home. The rumble of thunder and the lightning flash outside her window reminded her to grab the topper on her way out.

She ran into Mira on the glide.

"Leaving on time?"

"Looks like it. You, too."

"Sternly scheduled. I'm meeting Dennis and some friends for drinks. Just a few blocks from here, so I planned to walk."

She smiled as more thunder rolled. "Not anymore. I'm calling my car service. I'd never get a cab in this."

"I'll give you a lift."

"Are you sure? Do you have time?"

"Yes, and yes. Plus, I can run something by you on the way."

They switched to the elevators for the garage levels, and Eve found the downside of leaving on time when they squeezed in.

"Interviews in Hudson Valley on my Jane Doe. Elinor Singer and J. B. Singer are both lying."

"About your victims?"

"They both know something. I'm not sure about Marvinia Singer. She struck as straight, but some lie better than others. I think they both—mother and son—knew about the body, the wall, the cover-up. And may have been part of the murder."

"Motive?"

"J.B. liked, at least for a stretch of time, young side pieces."

"Ah."

"A marital separation, likely more about his mother—she's a piece of work—went down during the period my victim would have been pregnant, would have been killed."

"Can't trust a guy who'll step out on you," came the opinion of a female uniform behind Eve. "Take my word."

"There's that." Relieved, Eve muscled off on her level,

waited for Mira to exit more elegantly. "He's got some minor dings—party style. Reckless, stupid shit. The 'I'm rich so I can do what I want' shit. It fits him like a tailored suit."

"Violence?"

"Not really, unless we count a martini olive in the eye. But he's a liar, he's a cheat, he's—what's that word?—feckless."

"So." Mira slid into Eve's car. "The theory is, a rich older man with a history of extramarital activity has a fling, an affair, a relationship with a young woman—one young enough to be his daughter—resulting in pregnancy. From the personality profiles of the two of them, I'd say fling on his side and the illusion of a relationship on hers."

"Agreed. Where to?"

"Oh, Du Vin. One of Roarke's—and one of your earlier crime scenes."

"Yeah, I know where it is. Maybe she worked for Singer, or he met her at a party, a bar, whatever. Then she's knocked up. Maybe he makes some promises, gives her money, makes some threats—whatever he thinks will cover him. Covering himself would be priority."

She pushed out into the hard rain and insane traffic.

"She was nearly full term," Mira said. "Why would he wait so long?"

That one kept circling around in Eve's brain.

"Maybe she believed the promises, took the money, or believed the threats. But now reality's setting in. Pretty soon the baby's going to be that reality, and she's practically a kid herself. She wants him to make good on the promises, cough up more money, or she's going to hit him with threats of her own. Meanwhile, he's trying to get back with his wife—the timing works. He can't afford some, you know, indiscretion to get in the way."

She braked at a light, watched the stream of pedestrians splash by.

"Maybe he told himself he was taking her up there to just scare her, but if so, he lied to himself. He had the weapon, he had the bricks. He had to have those bricks waiting."

"He would have known the status of that building, the cellar," Mira continued. "He was in charge of the company—at least in name—and, yes, could have ordered bricks."

"So he covers himself by getting rid of her, walling her up. But his mother had to know."

She streamed through the green light, made her turn where a skinny guy in a hoodie hawked cheap umbrellas for inflated prices.

"I'm not sure he could've done it if she didn't give him the nod. And she'd have known about the order of bricks, the wall, because he was mostly name only."

"It's very tidy, actually." After using the vanity mirror to check her face, Mira took out a tube of lip dye. She painted it on with experienced precision.

"If she didn't have family or close friends," Mira continued as she took out some sort of compact and blotted what Eve considered a pretty perfect face with invisible powder, "or that family and friends didn't know she was in New York at that time, if she didn't reveal the name of the baby's father, tidier yet."

"I need to shut down those ifs."

"There was always a reason the remains were found on a Singer property—or what was a Singer property."

Once again Mira reached into her bag that apparently held all things, took out a little tube, and uncapped the rolling ball at the top. Eve caught a subtle whiff of spring as Mira dabbed it on pulse points.

"Your theory proposes a very solid reason."

"Just have to prove it." Eve pulled up in front of Du Vin. "I've got her completed sketch now, so I'm running it, and we'll find her. Once we do, I'll find the connection."

"Send me the rest of what you have. I'm interested. I'll read it over later, see if I can add anything."

"Thanks. I appreciate it."

"A fair trade for a ride on a very stormy night. Dennis would love to see you if you want to join us for a drink."

"I want to keep on this, but tell him I said hi."

Mira reached into the Bag That Held All Things, pulled out a collapsible umbrella. She opened the door, popped the red-and-white-striped umbrella, and shot back a smile.

"Best to Roarke," she said as she dashed out on her red-and-white-striped heels.

"Her umbrella matches her shoes." Eve shook her head. "I mean, who thinks of that?"

Pondering it, she inched her way home in the deluge.

21

Since she didn't have a Bag That Held All Things, or an umbrella that matched her footwear, Eve sprinted through the rain to the front door of home.

She slammed the door behind her on the next boom of thunder, then raked her fingers through her wet hair.

"You have an umbrella in the storage unit in your car," Summerset informed her.

Did she know that? Had she forgotten that? Either way.

"It's only water. Actual humans don't dissolve in the rain like zombies."

"Don't put that there, it's damp." He snatched her topper from the newel post. "And, in lore, zombies don't dissolve in the rain."

"They should."

She jogged up the stairs with the cat keeping pace.

In her office, she checked the facial recognition run. With no results as yet, she programmed coffee before updating her board and book.

When Roarke came in, Galahad took a moment to go over and greet him, rubbing his pudgy body against the leg of Roarke's perfect suit.

Eve noticed Roarke's hair remained dry.

"I bet you remembered an umbrella."

"It's a night for one." So saying, he pulled open the doors to the little balcony. The room filled with the sound of driving rain and a crackling snap of thunder. "And a fine storm it is."

Then he walked over, pulled her in, and kissed her like a man going off to war.

When her brain stopped spinning, she drew back. "Okay."

"It puts me in the mood to cuddle up with my wife and have wild sex." He looked at the board over her shoulder. "Which I see isn't a current option."

"It could be later."

"Mmm." He shifted so they stood hip-to-hip, his arm around her waist as he studied the sketches. "So there she is. No name to go with her yet?"

"Working on it."

"She's lucky to have you. As am I. We'll have some wine while you tell me about it."

She watched him as he went over, chose a wine. "You had a good day."

"I had a fairly brilliant day, which ended with a verbal agreement to buy Bardov Construction."

"He really did it. He really wants to sell out to you."

"He does." Roarke poured wine, rich and red, into glasses. "He admires you."

"Step off."

"No, I believe he does, and sincerely. Just as I believe he's quite sincere about retiring. There may be at least a minor connection between the two."

He handed her a glass, tapped his to it.

"You'll have to do some house cleaning there."

"He'll be doing some of that before the sale. We discussed. It's a good company and, after some adjustments, it'll be a better one. Many details to work out, lawyers and accountants to weigh in, but we'll come to terms."

"Okay," she said again. "Congratulations. How will this affect the partnership with Singer on any of their projects?"

"One of the details to work out. You've updated and adjusted your board and, knowing how you work, I see you've moved Elinor and J. Bolton Singer up your list."

"They're in the lead right now."

"I'd love to hear why. How do you feel about a steak dinner?"

"I always feel very pro about steak dinners."

"Let's see to that, shall we? Then we can sit while this storm rolls out and the next—they're promising another— rolls in, and you can tell me."

She did, over a long meal, and an oddly relaxing one considering the subject matter and the rain.

"You'd suggested I ask around about J.B. Easy enough to bring it up in conversation with the murders. What we'll call the old guard speaks of him as an entertaining sort, well-traveled, impeccable taste—a bit light on the business end of things, but game, if you will. I did get whiffs of a roving eye, which fit with what Bardov told you."

Eve sat back with her wine. "I'm really glad I'm never going to have to scoop your eyes out and keep them in a glass box on the mantel."

Roarke sat back with his own. "I'm trying to decide if I'm relieved or mildly disturbed to hear that."

"You don't take promises lightly. Number one Marriage Rule? It's a promise."

He reached over for her hand. "Why would my eye rove when everything I want's in front of me?"

"You really do want the sex."

"Well, yes, but that doesn't make it any the less true. What I know of Marvinia shows a steady sort of woman, one who recognizes her privilege and uses it to help those who don't have the same. She's chosen her causes, and she works them. Diligently."

The eyes she wouldn't have to scoop out flicked over to her board.

"I realize that doesn't take her off your board, but it's difficult for me to reconcile the woman I know, however superficially, with someone who would take a part in any of this."

"My take's the same, but we'll see."

"Men like Singer? They always, always look beyond what they have. I have all this, why shouldn't I have more? More money, more fun, more women. And in looking for more, they don't really value what they have. Bardov? He's no doubt done more wicked deeds in his life than Singer. But he's a man who values what he has. Bardov has a code—however that falls short of yours. But Singer has none."

"And the mother?"

Considering the rainy night, Roarke poured more wine. "The terms that come up, depending on the person speaking, are *formidable*, *regal*, *cold*, *ruthless*. She's credited with keeping the company alive during a very difficult period."

"Seems to me the company might have gone down, or certainly suffered some losses, if the CEO got caught in a scandal like having a kid with a woman half his age while still married. And say that woman half his age worked for him."

Roarke nodded. "The possibility of an ugly, public divorce, of paternity and civil suits. It would have shaken the foundations a bit. I don't think it would have taken the company under, but there would have been repercussions—and a lot of money to stanch wounds."

"It plays for me," Eve said. "I can almost see it. He tells her to come with him to the site, to see what he's trying to do. Trying to build. Let's just keep all this quiet, private.

Don't destroy what my family's worked for. He could tell her he needed to stay married because they needed the money to help make the city whole again."

Roarke nodded, sipped his wine. "Trying the 'This is so much bigger than you and me.'"

"But I don't think he meant to let her live. He had to have done the prep. He did need money, and had already tapped Bardov. He couldn't afford the scandal, the loss of revenue, the piles of legal fees."

"And it would make him as cold as his mother."

"Steel rod up her ass," Eve commented. "And she's proud of it. Plus, I get vanity, okay? But it seems to me when you're a hundred and whatever, you might want to ease up on getting your skin stretched so tight it could split open if you sneezed."

"That's an image," Roarke replied.

"I didn't like her," Eve admitted. "But that, the steel rod and the stretched skin, doesn't make her a killer. It was the attitude, and the dynamic between her and her son. I'm betting she helped, or encouraged, or even told Singer what he had to do. What I know, absolutely, is neither of them are going to enjoy their time in the box, even with their fleet of fancy lawyers."

"My money is, as always, on you."

"Wicker didn't enjoy his time. I haven't told you about that one. Reeled him right in when—"

She broke off as her computer signaled.

"Son of a bitch, we got a hit."

She leapt up, bolted over. "On-screen. Put the match on-screen. That's her." Eve smacked a fist into her open hand. "That's her. Split screen with sketch of Jane Doe's face."

"It is her, yes." Roarke walked over, laid a hand on Eve's shoulder. "You've found her. Johara Murr."

"Look at the DOB. She was twenty-two. DeWinter hit."

"She was lovely."

"Yeah, Kendrick hit, too. That's a solid match. And on the Lebanese citizenship, one more hit. I'm not seeing a marriage. Give me more," she muttered. "Here you go, a London address. Singer liked Europe. I bet he played in London plenty. Occupation, student. Okay, here's another address, a residency in the States."

She read the address, and both hands balled into fists. "Savannah, Georgia. Goddamn it. I've been looking at the wrong Singer."

"Ah, I see." Now Roarke's hand trailed down Eve's back. "She went to college with Bolton Singer. They were the same age."

"He wants to be a rock star, but he gets this girl pregnant. She wants the baby, wants to get married—she wore a ring. He doesn't have time for that. He's damn near broke anyway."

"She died in New York," Roarke pointed out.

"Yeah, yeah." She began to pace. "'Let's go to New York. You need to meet the family. Hey, let me show you what they're building.' Maybe the father was in on it, but I'm still damn sure the grandmother was. They shouldn't have used good bricks. He goes back to Savannah—maybe claims it's just to establish an alibi, but he wants the rock star. Fails, comes home."

She whirled around to stare at Bolton Singer's photo. "Family man, loving husband and father. Jesus, he had me with that. I didn't even get a whiff."

She drew in a breath. "Well, he's about to have a really bad night."

"I'll drive, but if we don't see to those dishes, the cat will be all over them."

"Fine, fine, fine. Deal with that, will you? I'm going to put this photo, the sketches together. I want him to look at her, to see her, then try to fucking lie to me."

She was still steaming when Roarke got his topper, and hers, from the closet.

"You're pissed you believed him. Pissed you saw what he wanted you to see."

"I bought it. I bought it all, so, yeah, I'm pissed. But I'll get over that. He'll have a hard time getting over doing life in a cage."

She used the drive to cool off, and to work out strategy.

"Sorry to disturb his evening," Eve began. "Some follow-ups, and didn't want to ask him to come into Central. Spoke with his parents, his grandmother, blah blah."

"Friendly." Roarke drove though the quieting rain. "Personable."

"Exactly. We'll probably have some coffee, and I can explain we have more information about the victim. How we have a sketch. I show him the sketch, gauge his reaction, his response. It goes from that."

"Understood. I'm sorry it's turned this way," Roarke added. "In my dealings with Bolton I found him interesting, and committed to his family, his company. In that order."

He glanced over at Eve's set profile. "You'll want his wife in the room."

"Oh yeah, I do. No reason I can see she'd know about any of this. I want to see how she reacts to his reaction. Then we'll see how he explains, when I pull out her photo, how it is they went to the same college—a pretty small college—at the same time."

"Do you need Peabody? Reo?"

"Not yet. Let me corner him. When I take him in, he'll

lawyer up fast. Then I bring them in. I looked away from him because he loves his wife, his kids. That's not fake."

"You looked away from him because he was, as far as anyone believed, in Georgia when she was killed in New York. Because you had no connection between them. Because he was open and honest about his onetime dreams and failures. I've a good measure for bollocks, Eve, and I never saw it either."

All true, Eve admitted.

"I'm getting over it. Somebody out there in Hudson River Valley knew about all this. Maybe all of them did. And if they did, they're all going down."

She had herself under control by the time they reached the double townhome. Eve hitched the file bag on her shoulder as they walked to the door in what had gone to a soft, drizzly mist.

Bolton answered himself—jeans, T-shirt, worn-out kicks.

"Lieutenant Dallas, Roarke. Come in out of the wet." He poked his head out as they did. "Looks like the storm's over."

"For now," Eve said with a careful smile. "I'm sorry to disturb you at home again, but I have more information and a few more questions. I thought it would be more comfortable for you here than asking you to come into Central."

"I appreciate that." He gestured them into the front room, one slightly more formal than where they'd talked before. "Hey, Lilith! Roarke and Lieutenant Dallas are here!"

Not a flicker, Eve noted. Just smooth and warm.

"Can I get you a drink? Lil and I had some nice wine with our very quiet dinner—our son's out with friends. There's plenty left."

"I'm still on duty."

"Coffee then. How about some coffee, Lil? Let me take your coats."

"We're fine. We hope not to take up much of your evening."

"All you like." He gestured again for them to sit. "I can't believe how quickly you found the person responsible for Alva Quirk." He sat himself, crossed a leg over his knee. "And for Carmine. Lilith's spoken to Angelina. She's going to go over there tomorrow, help her and their children with some of the arrangements.

"I know it doesn't excuse what he did, but I think he was a victim, too. Of his gambling addiction, but of that man. Tovinski. Tovinski didn't only kill him, he ruined him first. And now Carmine's family has to live with that."

He looked over, then popped up when his wife carried in a tray with four white mugs. "I'll get that, babe."

"I remember you both like it black." Once Bolton set down the tray, Lilith passed two mugs to Eve and Roarke. "Thank you, so much, for all you did to find Alva Quirk's killer. I wanted to ask if you think it's all right that, in a few days, we contact her family. Offer condolences."

"I'm sure they'd appreciate it. Meanwhile I have more information about the remains we found on what's now Roarke's property."

"Really?" Bolton looked surprised, and pleased with it. "That's amazing. I have to admit I wondered if you'd ever find out anything about her. But you did."

"Our forensic artist has a sketch." Eve opened the file bag, drew it out. "We believe it's very close to what she looked like when she was killed."

"I can't imagine what it takes to . . ."

He'd taken the sketch with one hand. The one holding his coffee went limp. The mug bounced on the floor, splattering the contents. His face went dead white.

"My God. My God. It's Johara."

Lilith had already jumped up to go to him. She froze with

an arm around him and stared at the sketch. "That's Johara? Bolt, are you sure?"

"It's Johara." Eyes glassy with shock stared into Eve's. "Her name. Her name's Johara Murr. Lil. Lil."

"It's all right. It's okay. I'm going to get you some brandy."

"I spilled the coffee."

"Don't worry. I'll clean it up. Don't worry. Give him a second, please. Give him a second. I'll be right back."

Eve jerked her head.

"Let me help you." Roarke followed her out.

"You knew her."

"Yes. Johara. I'm sorry. I can't get my breath." He lowered his head between his knees. "I can't get my breath."

"Stay down. Take it slow." And if he was faking, Eve thought, he was in the wrong line of work. "How did you know her?"

"College. We were together. Oh Jesus." Trembling, he lifted his head. "We were together nearly two years. We— I loved her."

Lilith rushed back with a towel. Roarke followed with a snifter of brandy.

"Lil, I'm sorry. I'm sorry."

"Stop." She rubbed his leg with one hand as she mopped up the spill. "Roarke's got your brandy. Slow sips now. It's going to be all right. You'll have answers, Bolt. After all these years."

"I'm going to need some answers first," Eve stated.

"Yes. You want to know about her. I need to tell you about her. I don't understand. I don't understand how this could be."

He sipped some brandy, then closed his eyes for a moment.

"We met in college. She was a brilliant pianist. She was nearly as brilliant with the violin. She came to study, transferred from London. We were about nineteen when we met. It didn't take long, not long at all. It should have—we were so different."

"How?"

"She was shy—oh, steel under it, but a little shy. Very proper, too. She seemed older than nineteen, twenty. She'd grown up very strict, sheltered, I guess you'd say. Her parents were very devout Muslims, very traditional. But her talent persuaded them to let her come to study music at the conservatory. Classical music. I wasn't much on classics, but when she played, you were transported. I think I fell in love with her when she played."

His hand trembled a little when he picked up the sketch again.

"I was her first. She'd never been with anyone, so we took that part slow. Well, slow for me at nineteen. And we just . . . fell. Crazy about each other, wrapped up in ourselves and our music."

Carefully, in a room crowded with regrets and grief, he laid the sketch down again. "After about a year, we moved off campus, got a little apartment together. If her parents had known, they'd have yanked her back, or tried. She'd say she couldn't tell them. And I'd say, you're an adult. You can make your own decisions."

He sat back, eyes closed again. "Arrogant, so arrogant. I didn't understand how hard it was for her to stand up to her family when I was so busy pushing away from my own. But we were happy, we made it work. We were so young, and we were careless. She got pregnant."

He straightened, reached for his wife's hand as she perched on the arm of his chair.

"I was terrified and saw my life going up in smoke. We talked about choices, but in her heart, from her upbringing and beliefs, she didn't have a choice. So, we're going to have a baby."

He pressed his wife's hand to his cheek.

"What did your family say?" Eve asked him.

"Nothing. They didn't know. I never told them about Johara. My business and fuck them."

"Bolt."

"That's how I felt about everything back then. They wanted me back in New York, working sites or a desk. Carrying on the Singer legacy."

He dragged his hands through his hair. "I wanted none of that. I wanted music, the stage. And Johara.

"We were going to get married. She said she needed to go back to London first. She needed to talk to her parents. She needed their blessing. I needed their blessing, after she'd spoken to them. I can tell you I didn't want that. I fought that. We fought."

He blew out a breath. "We made up long enough to exchange vows—not legal, which I didn't want anyway. Who needs a contract? That's all bullshit."

He breathed out, then scrubbed his hands over his face. "Young and stupid, and selfish. I was so goddamn selfish. But we had a little ceremony, just the two of us. I didn't realize she'd done that to soften leaving. She left me a note and said she had to do the right thing for her family, for the baby, for our future."

"When was that?"

"Ah . . ." He set the brandy aside, pressed his fingers to his eyes. "In April. April of 2024. She was, um, about four months along. Just starting to show. And I don't know, maybe she panicked a little. We weren't going to be able to keep it just our thing much longer."

"What did you do?"

"I was so mad. I tried calling her, but she didn't answer. I thought about going after her, but, Christ, I didn't have the money. And I didn't know where her parents lived. I waited. I worked, took gigs, wrote really bad songs. I didn't hear from her until June, more than a month. I was out of my mind, pissed off with it, and I get a letter. An actual letter."

He took another moment, leaning in when his wife stroked his hair.

"She told me she was sorry and she loved me, but our love was selfish. She'd disgraced her family and I'd cut myself off from mine. How could we give a child a good, loving life? She had to do what was best and right for the baby, so she was going to a quiet place where her parents wouldn't be disgraced, dishonored. And she was giving the baby to a loving family so the child we made so recklessly would have a good, safe, and happy life. She asked me to forgive her, asked me to reconcile with my family as she had with hers. Not to give up my music, to be true to myself but find a way to respect and honor my parents."

He looked back at Eve. "What did I do? Nothing. She broke my heart, but more, she closed the pieces of it off. I got drunk—a lot. Missed gigs, lost work, wallowed, and raged. I pulled it back together after a while, telling myself the hell with her. I got work and I wrote, but I couldn't get it back. By the next summer, I was dead broke. Seriously broke, mostly busking for loose change. When I pawned my guitar, I knew it was over, so I stuck out my thumb and I rode it home."

"You never told your family about Johara?"

"No. I'd had the pride kicked out of me, my heart broken, but that was mine. That part of my life was mine. I fell in line, went to work for the company, learned the ropes. I guess it's in the blood, because I had a knack for it. But I stayed sad and mad—really clung to that sad and mad—under the show. Until I met Lilith."

"Sad eyes." She leaned over to kiss the top of his head. "You had such sad eyes back then."

"You knew about Johara," Eve said.

"Bolt told me everything before he asked me to marry him. She was wrong to leave the way she did, but . . ."

"Do you still have the letter she wrote?" Eve asked.

"I kept it a long time. Years. To remind me love was a lie, dreams were illusions. That's how I felt until Lilith. I showed her the letter when I told her about Johara, the baby, then I balled it up and threw it away."

"I . . . I have it. I'm sorry, Bolt, I pulled it out of the trash and kept it. I thought maybe one day, when the child grew up, they might want to know you, find you. And I know the letter hurt you, but it was loving toward the child you'd made. She was so young and trying to do what she believed was best. So I kept it."

"You kept it." He pulled her down into his lap, pressed his face to her shoulder. "I loved her, I loved the baby we'd started, but Lilith, you're the world."

"Could I have it?" Eve asked. "Make a copy of it?"

Lilith stroked Bolt's hair. "Will it help?"

"It may."

"I'll get it. I'm so sorry." She lifted Bolton's face, touched her lips to his. "We're going to get through this, but I'm so sorry."

Still holding him, Lilith looked at Eve. "It wasn't his mother. I know her. I met Bolt because I worked for her foundation. She would never have been a part of this. If she'd known, if she'd found out after it happened, she would have gone to the police."

Bolt shot his wife a baffled look. "What are you talking about?"

Eve kept her eyes on Lilith's. "You don't say the same about his father, his grandmother."

Bolton's face went from puzzled to stunned. "You can't think—They didn't know about her. I never told them."

"Bolton." Lilith cupped his face in her hands. "Think. Do you really believe your grandmother didn't keep tabs on you back then? Didn't know about Johara? Didn't know everything?"

She rose, but kept a hand on Bolt's shoulders. "Elinor Singer is a cold, calculating woman."

"Lil—"

"I will say it," she snapped. "You know how I feel, and I know you feel the same. Status and reputation are her gods, and she's ruled this family with an iron fist."

"Not you," Bolton muttered.

"No, not me. She thought she could, and so approved of me. She was mistaken, and we coat our dislike for each other in manners. It wouldn't surprise me in the least if she'd found some way to pressure or intimidate a girl barely into her twenties, emotional, fragile, to give up her child. But Johara never got the chance to do that, did she?"

Tears spilled out of eyes hot with anger. "She loved, too. You can read it, read her own heartbreak in the letter. She came to New York, that's what you think, isn't it? She came here to tell Elinor, to tell J.B. she was keeping the baby, she wanted to make a family with Bolt, she wanted their blessing. For the sake of the child. That's what you think, isn't it?"

"What I know is she came to New York, and she was shot three times on a site owned and run by Elinor and J. B. Singer, and she was walled up there, left there for thirty-seven years."

"You can't possibly think my grandmother, my father would have . . ." Bolton trailed off. The color drained out of his face again. "Who else?" He whispered it. "Who else could have?"

"She was coming back to you, Bolt." Lilith dashed tears away from her cheeks. "I'm sure of it. They couldn't have that, couldn't allow that. She didn't meet the standards. I did—a few years later when you'd fallen in line, I did. Or so they thought. A well-educated, well-brought-up young woman from a wealthy, prominent New York family. An all-American family. Marvinia met those standards in her day."

He dropped his head in his hands. "Oh Jesus, Lil."

"If she had her way, Kincade will be obliged to select a woman by those standards—because it's the sons that matter to her." Lilith's face went feral. "She'll never get her way with mine, with ours. It eats at her to know that."

Then her eyes filled again, and she pressed a hand to her mouth. "Oh God, I hate her. I didn't realize just how much. God, Bolt. Oh God."

He got up, shakily, but wrapped his arms around her. "We'll get through it. You're right, we'll get through this. Lieutenant Dallas, do you think, do you believe, my grandmother and my father killed Johara and our child?"

"I need to follow through with this information." She had two people very much on the edge, Eve thought, and needed to be very careful not to tip them over. "We're going to pursue every avenue to find out who murdered Johara Murr, to bring them to justice. Whoever they are."

Now Eve got to her feet. "I can't stress enough how vital it is you have no communication with your family until I tell you otherwise."

"Do you think I'd warn them?"

"I think you're upset and angry and confused, and may feel the need to confront them. You need to stay back and let me do my job."

"We will. Johara deserves that, Bolt. From both of us. I'll go get the letter."

"Lil," Bolt said as she started from the room. "We were so young, and each of us so sure we were right. Not much compromise between us. I can look back and see we probably wouldn't have made it. We'd have tried for each other, and the child, we'd have tried. But love isn't enough without understanding, real respect, and a hell of a lot of compromise. We wouldn't have made it. You and me? We always will."

"Damn right we will."

He sat again. "I don't know what to think, what to feel. If my grandmother did this, if my father . . . He can't stand up to her. Few can. I tried, all those years ago. I failed. And I never really tried again until Lilith, until the kids."

He turned to Roarke with the faintest of smiles. "A strong woman will make a man of you."

"Truth. We're fortunate in ours. I'm very sorry, Bolton, for your loss. I'm glad to see you've made a family who'll let you grieve that loss."

"I only knew her surname. She didn't like talking about her family, it made her feel guilty. We had some friction about that, too. I know she had a brother—in medical school. In London, I think, but I'm not sure. Her family needs to know. I could hire investigators to find them."

"Let me use my resources for that," Eve said.

"If you find them, any of them, I'd like the chance to speak with them, if they'd agree. And if you can't find them, or something happened to them over the years, Lilith and I would like to—to make the arrangements."

"I'll let you know."

"Can you tell me? You must know. We, ah, Johara and I, weren't going to find out before the birth, but you must know."

Eve started to say the fetus was male, but saw his eyes. "A boy."

"A boy." His lips trembled, then firmed. "Thank you."

After Eve took the letter Lilith had folded in an envelope,

they left the Singers and stepped out into the quickening rain.

"You trust them not to make that contact."

"Yeah, I do. Especially since we're going to move fast now. Get us a copter." She looked up at the boiling sky as she got into the car. "There's more than one storm coming."

22

While Roarke drove, Eve tagged Peabody and snapped out orders. "Don't ask questions, just listen. Contact the local LEOs in Hudson Valley and inform them I'm on my way there, to arrest Elinor and J. B. Singer on suspicion of murder."

"Holy—"

"Shut up. The warrant will include bringing Marvinia Singer in for questioning. There will be a search warrant. As the murder took place in New York City, I will transport the individuals and any evidence found to New York City. They are to do nothing, I mean nothing, until I arrive. They are not to approach, not to enter, not to do anything. Whoever's in charge can contact me for details if deemed necessary."

"Got it. Should I meet you at the heliport?"

"No time. Get to Central, set things up there. I'll write up what I can on the flight there—God help us all. Shit, contact Mira. I want her in Observation. I may need a shrink on this. Contact Baxter, tell him and Trueheart they're on the search. They can drive. Give them the particulars. And have them pick up McNab for the electronics."

"Got it."

"Good. Go." She clicked off, tagged Reo. "Warrants, now. Listen."

She banged out details, continued to bang them out as she ran through the rain to the waiting copter.

She heard the helipad guy say, "It's going to be rough up there, sir."

"Too rough for clearance?" Roarke asked.

"No, but rough enough."

"I'll see you at Central, Reo. I have to keep a jet-copter from crashing with the strength of my will."

"You're taking a chance—with the arrests, and the flight. Let's have good luck on both."

"Yeah, let's." She strapped in. "This is a bigger machine than Peabody and I took this afternoon."

"I assumed you'd be transporting prisoners on the return."

"That's right." She tried not to think about what he did with switches and monitors or who he talked to on the headset. "It's not raining that hard."

"Not here."

She closed her eyes as the jets wound up. "Oh shit."

"I've got you, Lieutenant. Reo meant you're taking a chance, as you don't have hard evidence so much as circumstantial."

"Piles of circumstantial now. And I'm betting on a seventy-five, maybe eighty percent chance the gun that killed Johara Murr's in that big, ugly house."

"Is it ugly? And why do you think they kept the gun?"

He was keeping her talking as they rose into the air. Good idea, she decided.

"Strict and stern, Peabody said. She's right. You'll see for yourself." Everything shook, including the contents of her stomach. "And the gun's power. I didn't find a collector's license or any record of a license in the past for that weapon. It probably came down through the family."

"Licenses, bugger licenses. We're too important for that."

"Yeah, that's it." She saw lightning flash in a giant five-pronged fork in the distance. The shake and roll of the answering thunder made her seriously consider curling into a whimpering ball.

"You see Elinor pulling the trigger."

Talk, talk, keep talking. Why wasn't she on the ground somewhere, battling a rampaging horde of chemi-heads hopped up on Zeus?

"J.B. could have done it if his ass was on the line—the way I had it playing out. Knocked her up, get rid of her. But for this? He wouldn't have the guts. Oh, fuck, fucking fuck, there's another one."

"We're fine."

She risked a glance at him. He looked calm—calm, determined, and focused. Which meant more than the strength of her will kept them aloft.

"I know what I saw in Elinor Singer today." It wasn't easy to keep her voice as calm as his, but she worked on it. "But I got a look through Lilith's lens. She's a tyrant. On top of the rest. What Lilith didn't add on the standards? White and Christian. Johara fell short on those, too. Maybe you don't have to be really religious, or totally pure, but a young, Lebanese, Muslim pianist? That would never do. She's not going to be able to pull Bolton back, get him firm under the thumb if he makes a life with that substandard girl and their illegitimate child."

She pulled in a breath, let it out slowly. "I have to ask. How much longer before we land?"

"About five minutes." He reached over, gave her hand a squeeze. "We're coming into the rough part now."

"Coming into? Fuck me sideways."

"Let's try that one once we're home again."

They bounced, swayed, jittered. She heard Roarke swear—lightly, and under his breath, but she heard it. They dipped, they danced, and a line of ice-cold sweat slid down Eve's spine.

The world outside the windscreen rolled thick and dense and dirty gray. All angry clouds snarling, booming.

Peabody would pick it up, she told herself. If they ended up a smoking, smoldering tangle of body parts and twisted copter in the river, Peabody would see it through. Justice would be done.

That was something.

Then a few tiny tears ripped through the solid gray, and through them she saw the flicker of lights from the heliport.

Roarke communicated with somebody, got clearance, and, after a couple of final, nasty shakes, they landed.

"There now."

Eve held up a finger, then dropped her head between her knees. "Not gonna boot. Just need a second. Need my warrants, too. Need my goddamn warrants."

"And there, she's rounding back already. You're a bit pale yet," he told her when she straightened. "But you'll do."

She got out, resisted kissing the wet ground, and slid into the waiting all-terrain.

"Big enough for transporting." She nodded. "I'll guide you in."

"I had them program the address. Have some water. Settle yourself the rest of the way."

"Yeah, maybe. Come on, Reo. I expect some mild resistance," she continued. "The grandmother's over the century mark, and he's a coward under it, but some. Probably threats and insults, which will hurt my delicate feelings."

"You'll muddle through."

"I tend to agree with Lilith's take on Marvinia, but we don't take chances. I'd peg her as in the best shape, physically, of the three of them. We'll be sexist here. If it comes to it, I'll deal with the women, you deal with him."

"As necessary."

"You're carrying, aren't you? You're always carrying. Don't pull a weapon, for Christ's sake, but they've got security, a gate. I don't want them to know we're coming until we're there. With the warrants. Cams on the walls, about every five feet. And alarms, scanners on the gate."

"No worries."

"Got none there. Yes! And Reo scores."

"I don't like to go on auto in this weather, so . . ." He pulled over, took out his 'link. "Just under a quarter mile."

"What are you doing?"

"Scanning their system. Ah well, it's not absolute shite, but they can afford better. I'm just going to deactivate cams and alarms. If they notice, they'll likely blame the storm. There we are."

Though pleased, the cop in her frowned. "You can do that with your 'link?"

He shot her an easy smile. "It has a few handy accessories built in."

He continued to drive and when he reached the gates, hit vertical and sailed over them.

"It is very ugly. I've seen prisons—from the outside of course—with more charm."

Lights glared against the window glass, but didn't add welcome or cheer. Eve walked through the rain to the door. "Are the door cams down?"

"They are, yes."

She rang the bell. Moments later a flustered Marvinia opened it. "Oh! Hello. I thought you were the driver. The storm's taken out the security."

"Going somewhere?" Eve asked.

"Me? In this?" On an eye roll, she shook her head. "No.

But J.B. is determined to head off to Capri for some sunshine. Elinor's up there trying to talk some sense into him. I've left them to it. So sorry, come in out of this horrible rain."

She stepped back. "Roarke, it's lovely to see you. I didn't expect to see anyone on a night like this. Let me take your coats."

"We're good. I need to see your husband and mother-in-law."

"Yes, of course. Come, sit down. I'll go get them. I assume you have some resolution on your investigation, and coming out on a night like this shows you're even more dedicated than I believed."

"If you could use the house 'link to ask them to come down," Eve began, when she heard J.B.'s voice.

"I don't want to wait until morning, Mother! I need to get away from all this stress."

He appeared at the top of the staircase, and froze when he saw Eve.

"I wouldn't." She saw flight in his eyes. "Nowhere to go. Come down, Mr. Singer, or I'll come up and get you. And tell your mother to get down here."

"What is this?" Marvinia put her hand on Eve's arm. "What's wrong?"

"Okay, I'll come to you." Eve started up the staircase. "James Bolton Singer, as you already know, this is the police. I have a warrant for your arrest for the murder of Johara Murr and the viable, healthy fetus she carried."

"What? What? That's crazy. Who is she talking about?"

"Marvinia." Roarke spoke softly. "Stay here."

As Eve reached the top of the stairs, turned Singer around to restrain him, Elinor strode down the corridor to the right.

"Take your hands off my son. Get out of my house."

She lifted the gun in her hand and fired.

The bullet pinged off Eve's topper. The impact—a solid punch with a sledgehammer—jerked her back, spun her to the left. As she reached for her own weapon, Roarke flew up the stairs.

The second bullet struck closer to her hip.

The pain stole her breath, had the edges of her vision blurring. Eve set her teeth, held her weapon steady.

"Fire again, you crazy bitch, and I'll drop you. I've got it on low, but at your age, it'll put you in ICU, I swear to fucking God."

"You broke into my house. I will defend myself."

"I'm a police officer. I have a warrant. Drop that weapon, or I drop you. Last chance."

Eve held out her free hand to stop Roarke from shoving in front of her, and for five humming seconds they faced off.

Elinor let the gun fall to the thick rug. "I should have aimed for your head."

"Yeah, your mistake."

She walked over, put a boot on the weapon as she cuffed Elinor's hands behind her back.

She muttered a curse as, restraints aside, Singer ran.

"I've got him," Roarke told her and had him in hand, face against the wall, in under four feet.

"Elinor Bolton Singer, you're under arrest for the murder of Johara Murr and the viable, healthy fetus she carried. You are further charged with the attempted murder of a police officer. Additional charges will include possession and use of an unlicensed firearm."

Marvinia sat on the floor at the base of the stairs, arms wrapped tight around herself, eyes moons of shock as she rocked back and forth.

"What have they done? What have they done?"

"Shut up, you foolish twit. Contact my lawyer immediately."

"Go to hell, you evil witch. Who was she? One of J.B.'s dalliances? Did he get some poor girl pregnant?"

"Johara and your son were in love, met in college," Eve said as she walked Elinor down the stairs. "They lived together, hoped to get married."

"He— But he never told me."

"It was your grandchild they killed."

"Oh, please don't say that. Please no. Oh, J.B., no. No."

"It's insane, of course this is all insane," J.B. babbled as Roarke walked him down. "A terrible mistake. Call the lawyer now, Marvinia."

She got slowly to her feet. "Oh my God, you're lying. You're lying."

"I need you to come with us, Ms. Singer."

"Don't call me that," she snapped at Eve. "Use Kincade. Am I under arrest?"

"No, ma'am, but I need you to come with us."

"Marvinia, darling—"

"I will never speak to you again." She turned away from him to Elinor. "If there is one positive note to this horror, I never have to speak to you again."

"Let's move them out. I'll start with Mother. Elinor Singer, you have the right to remain silent."

Eve read them their rights, one at a time, as they loaded them into the all-terrain.

"I need to take the weapon into evidence. I need something to put it in."

"Field kit in the cargo area," Roarke told her.

"You never miss."

As Eve pulled out the kit, Elinor spoke coldly. "You will pay for this."

"Sister, I get paid for this. But for this one, I'd do it for free."

As she walked back in, she pulled out her communicator. "Suspects in custody. Female suspect fired an illegal weapon during the arrest—two shots at the arresting officer. I'm bringing the weapon, a handgun, which I believe is a thirty-two caliber, into evidence."

"Whoa!" Peabody shouted out. "You got shot?"

"Magic topper. I'm five-by-five. On our way to the heliport."

"Safe travels. It's cleared up here."

"Thank Christ."

She went out to where Roarke waited.

"You're going to have a couple of bruises blooming like flowers under that topper."

"Yeah, I feel them."

He gripped her chin, gave it a little shake. "Mild resistance, my ass."

"Yeah, bad call on that."

"I'm surprised you didn't stun her."

"At her age, even on low, she could stroke out. I want her alive for the ten, maybe fifteen or so years she's got left."

Those bruises sang an ugly song by the time she turned the Singers over for booking and escorted Marvinia up to an interview room.

"If you'd give me a couple minutes? I'm going to leave the door open, and Roarke will stay with you. You're not under arrest. Can I get you something to drink?"

"Water, please. Just water."

"I'll bring it back."

She stepped out as Peabody walked down with an ice pack. "Even with the coat, it had to hurt."

"She caught me twice. Bitch."

"I'll get another."

"No, I'd pretty much have to sit on the other. Are you caught up enough?" She slid the pack under her topper, pressed it to her chest.

"Yeah. Reo's talking to the PA. She's using your office."

"I figure we'll take the Singers—him first—in the morning. They're lawyering, as expected, and given the time, her age, blah blah, they're going to want to wait."

"Copy that."

"But I want to talk to Marvinia, get anything we can. Then release her. She's not in this."

"Yeah, I got that, too."

"Here." She started to take off the topper, winced. "Fuck, shit, bitch! Okay. Take this back, will you, and ask Reo to join us. Damn, and bring in some water."

"No, don't toss the pack. Keep it on. It's not like she's a suspect you have to intimidate. She saw what happened, right?"

"Yeah, yeah, you're right. Okay."

She kept the pack, walked back to the interview room. "My partner's bringing you water. She and the APA will join us. Roarke, if you'd like to wait in my office."

"Can he stay? He's someone I know, at least a little. Is it all right? Would you stay?"

"Sure, he can stay." She buzzed Peabody. "We need another chair."

"She—she shot you. With a gun. I saw . . ."

"I'm wearing protective gear."

"I've never seen anyone shot. It was horrible. They, they shot that poor girl. You said she was . . . was Bolt's girl."

"I think he should tell you the details there."

"Does he know what happened now?"

"Yes."

Tears began to slide. "He may never want to see me again. How could I blame him?"

"That's not at all true." Roarke spoke up, soothing, kind. "Your daughter-in-law, nearly the first thing she said when they learned what happened is you'd never be a part of it."

"I wouldn't. I swear to you, I didn't know. She was pregnant. My grandchild." She took a breath. "She didn't meet Elinor Singer's standards, did she?"

"I don't believe so. Ms. . . . Kincade," Eve remembered. "You met Detective Peabody. This is Cher Reo with the prosecutor's office."

"I'm sorry for your loss," Peabody said, and Marvinia burst into tears.

"I'm sorry, I'm sorry. This isn't helping. Tell me how I can help. I need to help."

"If you could think back, probably late August, early September of 2024."

"That's when it happened? Yes, I remember that time very well because J.B. and I had separated, had been separated several months. I was seriously considering divorce. We'd been fighting all the time, over Bolt, mostly, and what he was doing with his life. I wanted him to be happy, to do what he loved. They—or Elinor—wanted him back in New York, in the company. His duty, his legacy, all of that. We argued about Bolt, we argued about his mother. Even when we traveled, he spoke to her every single day. And when we came back, it was to that house."

She cracked the seal on the water, drank.

"I hate that house. Hated it from the first moment I saw it. We fought about how J.B. lived his life. He wasn't responsible back then. Or ever," she added after a moment. "Charming, sweet, romantic, but never responsible. Even when he took over Singer, Elinor ran it, or covered his irresponsibility, his mistakes."

With a murmured thanks, she took tissues Peabody offered, then mopped at her face.

"It's not love with her. It's the Bolton-Singer name, it's how it's perceived. And it's bloodline.

"I was going to ask for a divorce, try to mend fences with Bolt, and J.B. came to me, he asked me for another chance. He seemed so contrite, so eager to try to make our marriage work again. We'd take a long trip—no partying, just the two of us. We'd reconnect. I loved him, so after some time, I gave in."

She closed her eyes. "And now I see he came to me after they'd done this. He wanted me back, that cushion, wanted to get away from what he'd done. Just bury it. I let him."

"You didn't know," Eve said.

"No, but I wanted everything he said to me then to be true, so I made it true. He even promised we'd leave Bolt alone, let him try to make a go of it with his music. At least another year."

"Can J.B. lay brick?" Reo asked.

Marvinia pressed a hand to her mouth and nodded. "Certainly not very well, but his father would have insisted he learn the basics. But they spoiled him, you see. Her especially, and his father died so young really, so it was all her. That doesn't excuse him, and I won't excuse him, but she dominates him. In the last ten years or so, I've let her dominate me far too much and too often. She's a hundred and five years old. I could justify living in that house for duty. My husband's mother, my son's grandmother."

Eve took out Johara's photo. "Did you ever see her?"

"Oh, oh, is this her? Oh, she's lovely. Lovely. Bolt never told me about her."

"He will now. He told Lilith everything before they got married."

"Good, that's good." Gently, very gently, Marvinia brushed her fingertips over the face in the photo. "They have a strong marriage, they have a strong family. Wonderful children. I would have had another grandchild.

"I'll never forgive them. No punishment the law allows is enough for what they destroyed. Did she have family?"

"We're going to look into that."

She nodded. "He's weak." She cleared her throat, drank more water. "You know how to do your job, obviously, but I want to tell you because it might help you. He's a weak and selfish man. It's not love with him, either, for his mother. It's dependence, and some fear. He'll tell you everything if he's afraid, or if he thinks you'll give him something he needs. He lies. I can tell, almost always, when he lies."

"He taps his right foot," Eve commented.

"Does he?" She laughed a little. "I've never noticed. It's his eyes. I can see the lie. We've known each other almost sixty years. I can almost always see a lie in his eyes. Will I have to testify?"

"It's possible," Reo told her.

"I don't want to speak to them. Ever. I'll testify if it helps. But I won't speak to them. And God, I don't want to go back to that house."

"You should go to your son's. Stay there for now. They'll want you," Eve added when she saw the hesitation. "I'm going to have Peabody contact them, tell them you're coming. We'll have you taken there."

"They need you now, Marvinia," Roarke told her. "As much as you need them."

"Do you really believe that?"

"I know it." Roarke took her hand. "I saw it."

"Peabody, go ahead and fix this up. Reo, any more questions?"

"Not right now. We'll contact you when we need to talk again. I know this is hard for you," Reo added. "Thank you for your cooperation."

"I'll wait here with you," Roarke said.

When they stepped out, Reo looked at her 'link. "Give me

a minute," she told Eve. "Elinor Singer's lawyer's demanding to speak with me."

"You want my office?"

"No, I'll take it in the lounge. It's Michael C. Breathed."

"Breathed? Why would she have a criminal attorney on tap?"

"I'll find out."

They peeled off, Reo to the lounge, Eve to her office.

Eve hit the coffee and sat to start the paperwork.

When Roarke came in, he went straight to her AutoChef, programmed more coffee. "It's difficult to watch a woman's world fall apart."

"She'll get through it." She shook her head at him when she saw the gleam of annoyance in his eyes. "I'm not being cynical, especially. I know death when I see it. It may be the first time I've watched love die, just stop breathing, but I saw it. I saw just that on her face when she understood what he'd done. She stopped loving him and she has her son, her son's family.

"She'll get through it."

"You're right about that, but it won't be easy for her."

"No, nothing's going to be easy for any of them for a while. If the Singers push this to trial, it's going to be a lot harder."

"You think they will?"

"She hired Breathed, and he's damn good at this. Not good enough," she added. "Nobody is. She shot me, twice. That gun and the bullets—from me, from Johara—are in the lab right now. They're going to match. And in the morning, I'll break J.B. So Breathed's going to want a deal. We'll see how she feels about that."

She looked over as she heard rapid heel clicks. "Here's Reo now."

Reo pointed at the coffee. "I want that." She waved Roarke away before he could go back to the AC. "I'll get it. Elinor

Singer's on some committee with Breathed's wife, and Breathed and J. B. Singer golf together."

"Explains the quick turnaround," Eve said.

"In any case, Breathed's trying the we're-all-in-a-huff routine. Centenarian client dragged from her home in a storm, in the middle of the night."

"The storm was done, and it wasn't twenty-two hundred."

"I said 'trying.'" Reo gulped coffee. "She should be immediately released on her own recognizance, would even suffer the humiliation of wearing a tracker."

"No and no."

"And when he got no and no, he insisted we go tonight."

"They want to do this tonight?"

One more unexpected turn, Eve thought.

"Mira's on her way in. I was going to dump all this on her, apologize, and send her back home."

"Are you up to go tonight?"

"Abso-fucking-lutely. But she waits while I have a round with her son first."

Reo toasted with her coffee. "We're drinking out of the same pot. He's got Indina Cross—junior partner in Breathed's firm. She's good."

"Junior partner. Mother took the top cream for herself. Let's get it lined up. This is going to go long," she told Roarke.

"And should be quite a show. One I wouldn't miss. There should be popcorn in Observation."

Now Reo tapped her mug to his. "I can't tell you how many times I've said that."

23

They took a conference room, and Roarke sat back and watched the four women discuss evidence, strategy, psychology.

Singer didn't have the slightest clue what he was in for.

They would, Roarke had no doubt, simply dismantle him.

Eve pushed back, came to attention when Commander Whitney strode into the room.

"Sir."

"Sit, sit." Rather than his usual suit, he wore a casual shirt in thin blue-and-white stripes and, a little to Eve's shock, jeans and high-top kicks.

And still looked every bit in command.

"Doctor, Lieutenant, Detective, Assistant Prosecutor, Roarke." He moved straight to the AutoChef. "I don't suppose this is your coffee in here, Dallas."

"No, sir. We can get that for you."

"This'll do. I'm here to observe. I haven't asked for face-to-face reports on these cases, as you not only had them well in hand, but they moved rapidly. Yet this?"

He took a hit of coffee. "When I'm informed we've made arrests within days of an investigation of remains more than three decades old, and those arrests are individuals of some status and repute, I like to study more details. Which, considering the time, I would have done from home."

He sat, drank more coffee. His wide, dark face went to stone. "However, when those details include one of those individuals firing a handgun on one of my officers, striking her twice, I'm damn well coming in. Have you had medical attention, Lieutenant?"

"I was wearing protective gear, Commander."

"A considerable number of years ago, I was wearing protective gear when I took two hits." He tapped a fist just below his breastbone. "Knocked me flat. Dr. Mira?"

"After considerable nagging, browbeating, and guilt-tripping, I convinced the lieutenant to allow me to examine the areas involved. She has severe bruising, but the portable scanner detected no fractures or internal injuries."

"All right then. Is my information correct that you intend to start the interview process on both suspects tonight?"

"At their insistence, sir," Eve told him.

He smiled. "This should be interesting. Are you observing, Roarke?"

"I am, yes, and it'll be very nice to have your company, Jack, as well as Charlotte's."

"I promised to keep Anna informed. She despises Elinor Singer. An incident twenty, maybe twenty-five years ago involving table decor at a gala." He studied his coffee. "My wife holds a grudge."

Then he smiled broadly at Roarke. "But as she's not here, we'll get snacks. And enjoy them," he added, scanning the women. "Because I have every confidence in my officers, our prosecutor, and the doctor to wrap these two up and serve them a very large, very unpleasant platter of justice."

He rose, turned to Roarke. "I want chips. There should be some salt and vinegar chips in Vending, which are now banned by Anna's decree from our home and my office. I'm buying. We'll get you a share, Dr. Mira."

"We should have fizzies with that." Roarke shot Eve a wink as he left with Whitney. "Do it up right."

A little bemused, Eve watched them walk out. "Well, that was unusual."

"He's angry," Mira said to Eve. "He's furiously angry. You were shot. He wants payment for that. He's angry, but he also trusts we'll get that payment. But trust aside, he needs to see it done."

"Peabody, have them bring J. Bolton Singer into Interview A. And let's get it done for the commander."

Singer didn't look so stylish in his orange jumpsuit. Beside him, his lawyer appeared very buttoned down, very ready to go. Indina Cross, a mixed-race female of forty-eight, wore a navy suit, a crisp white shirt, and tiny gold balls in her ears as her only jewelry.

Currently, her wide, thin mouth pressed into disapproving lines as Eve ordered the record on, read off the names, case numbers, and charges.

She pushed off first. "My client wishes to get this ridiculous interview over and done so he can return to his own home. The charges are without merit. There is no evidence supporting them or involving my client with the death of the woman purportedly identified as Johara Murr."

"First, she has not been purportedly identified, the victim's identity is confirmed, and her relationship with your client's son has been confirmed. The paternity of the fetus has been confirmed by the father—your client's son. So don't sit there and insult the victim, counselor."

"We will have our own forensic scientists examine the—"

"Fine, you do that. When we go to court. Meanwhile, she is Johara Murr and your client is the grandfather of the fetus who died with her. You're going to want to move off that one, Ms. Cross." Eve's warning filled the room with frost. "You're going to want to move off that one real quick or your client's going to be escorted back to his cell for the night, and this interview ends."

"Indina."

"The identity of the victim doesn't change the lack of evidence as applies to my client." As she spoke, she reached over to pat Singer's hand.

Indulgently, Eve noted.

"She was murdered, shot three times, in early September of 2024 on a property owned by your client and his company. She was concealed by a hastily built brick wall in a building under construction on property owned by your client. She was in a serious, committed relationship with your client's son, and carrying a child from that relationship.

"These are facts."

"As it's impossible to establish the exact date this unfortunate incident occurred—"

"Between September seventh and September twelfth, according to the records of the building under construction. It's the wall, J.B., it's all about the wall. The bricks. When they were ordered, delivered, used."

"And you have job reports, invoices, and so on from this time?"

"Your mother's a sharp businesswoman, isn't she? I bet she kept records. And I bet the search team, the very skilled e-man on it, will find those records in her files. They're searching right now."

"They can't go into our home!" Singer snatched at Cross's arm. "They can't just go into our home, go through our things. It's insulting."

"Warrant." Reo opened her file, slid it across the table.

"I didn't order any bricks. You won't find anything about them."

"But you laid them. You built that wall."

He smiled, held out his soft, pampered hands. "My dear girl, do I look like a bricklayer?"

Eve smiled back. "I'm not your dear girl. And no, you don't. That's why you did a sloppy job. Did it bother you at all as you laid those courses? Did it make you just a little sick seeing her lying there, knowing what was dying inside her? Part of you, dying inside her, did that trouble you at all?"

"My client categorically denies knowing the victim, knowing of the victim, of having any knowledge of her death. All you have is innuendo and circumstantial."

"I've got the thirty-two-caliber handgun, the two bullets that hit me tonight from said weapon, and the three recovered from the remains of Johara Murr."

"And the ballistic reports?"

"Waiting on that."

Cross let out a soft sound of dismissal, but Eve looked at Singer. "You know they're going to match."

"I know no such thing."

She nodded as she heard the quiet tap of his foot on the floor. "You know they're going to match, just as you knew, and feared, we were going to find out who the woman you and your mother murdered was, her connection to your son. The son who wept for her tonight."

"I don't know anything about it." Tap, tap, tap. "I imagine Bolton had relationships, as any young man might, with any number of women he met in college."

"I didn't say they met in college."

"I assumed."

"You don't care about him, either," Peabody put in. "Your own son, his pain or grief. That's just sad."

"You know nothing about it."

"You haven't asked about him at all, or about your wife." Peabody jabbed a finger at him. "You haven't shown any concern for Johara or the baby. Nothing. Because you don't feel anything for any of them. That's why it was easy for you to kill her."

"I didn't kill anyone!"

"You were running," Eve reminded him. "When we arrived at your home tonight, you were packing to fly out, to run."

"My client planned to take a trip, a break from the stress of the last several days. It's not a crime."

Eve ignored the lawyer. "You tried to run. Your mother tried to kill me, and you tried to run."

"You burst into our home. You frightened her. Obviously, she believed you were an intruder and put hands on me. She tried to defend me, and herself."

"Left your wife off that one, too. Your wife, who opened the door for me. My partner and I had been in your home only hours before. You and your mother knew who I was, a police officer. I announced same, informed you and your mother you were being arrested and why. And yet she fired on me."

"We were confused, obviously. It happened very quickly. In any event, I didn't have a weapon. I didn't fire a weapon."

Time to toss Mother aside, Eve decided.

"You knew about Johara, about the baby, because your mother holds on tight. Johara came to you, didn't she, desperate to have you accept her, the child, so she could have a hope of making a family with your son. She needed your blessing, your support. Maybe she couldn't get that from her family—we'll find out. But as she came closer to term, she wanted family for the child. She wanted a father for the child, so came to you for your blessing."

"Nonsense."

This time he couldn't meet her eyes as he lied.

"So you and your mother had her come to the site—a

handy place to kill and conceal the body. No one would know. Everyone would forget her. Bolton wanted music, and he refused to take his place in the business. So you told her to come there. Look at what we do, what we build, what we want for Bolt. That would be a pretty good way to lure her there.

"Then you shot her, watched her fall."

"I did not. I did not."

"And built the wall, poured the ceiling. Gone, forgotten, finished. But here's the thing about the walls, J.B. You're no bricklayer, you're right about that. Sloppy work. I'm betting you were pretty shaken while you built it on top of being crap at it. How many times, I wonder, did you scrape your knuckles? Work gloves? But even with those, you banged your hands, maybe an elbow. You bled a little here and there."

He thought about that, Eve noted. Sweat started to pool as he tried to think, to remember. "We're testing every brick, and we're going to find your DNA. And when we do, what happens, APA Reo?"

"What happens is Mr. Singer does two consecutive life sentences in a small, unpleasant cage in an off-planet facility. The fetus was healthy at the TOD, the fetus was viable outside the womb at TOD. Two life sentences and your attorney knows when we find that DNA, and we will, that's a slam dunk."

"His attorney is very confident her client's DNA will not be found, as Mr. Singer had no part in constructing the aforesaid wall."

"Did Mommy help you?" Peabody wondered. "Or did you do it all by yourself?"

Singer leaned over, whispered in Cross's ear.

"Of course. I need a few moments with my client."

"No problem. Dallas, Peabody, and Reo exiting Interview to accommodate counsel. Record off. Anybody want a snack?" Eve said, deliberately carefree as they left. "Peabody, use my code and get us some chips."

"Really?" Peabody said when the door closed.

"Actually, yeah. And something to wash them down. This isn't going to take as long as I thought."

Mira came out of Observation, hurried toward them. "He's lying, of course, but even in the relatively short time of the interview his skill for lying is eroding."

"The DNA on the bricks did it," Reo concluded. "Good call there, Dallas."

"It might even be true. He's worried it's true. He's afraid of prison."

"He should be. And he's sure as hell going there."

"But you'll make the deal."

Reo spared Eve a glance before she put her hands together for Peabody and her armload of chips and sodas. "Yes! I want!"

"I started to get veggie chips for me, then I thought, screw that. I've earned these calories today."

"You'll make the deal," Eve repeated as she opened her bag of chips.

"Twenty to twenty-five, minimum, on-planet. We discussed this, Dallas."

"I'm not giving you grief over it. We both know it's the mother pulling the strings. He rolls, he lays it all out, he can have the deal. He'll probably die in prison anyway." She crunched into a chip. "I'm not sorry about that. I don't know if he pulled the trigger—I lean, especially after tonight, toward her on that. But he's just as responsible."

"You should take a blocker," Mira told her.

"No. Feeling the hits keeps me mean. How's it going in Observation?"

"Jack—the commander—is enjoying himself—and the chips. He liked your sad outrage, Peabody."

Peabody lit right up. "Really?"

"I wonder what this grudge is Anna Whitney has on Elinor Singer?" Eve turned as the interview door opened.

And saw, immediately, Cross's mouth had gone thin again.

"My client has certain information he's willing to share, on record, for a dismissal of charges against him."

"That's a no. Cross, don't waste my time."

Cross stared hard at Reo. "I believe my client has information valuable to your investigation. In consideration of same—"

"You want to talk deal, we can talk deal. Depending on the information, the value thereof, and your client's full disclosure of his part and participation in the murder of Johara Murr and the viable fetus. We both know he's guilty. Again, it's late. Don't waste our time."

Eve handed what was left of her bag of chips to Mira. "Add this to the pile. If you're ready to get going again, counselor, we'll get going. Otherwise, your client goes back to his cell, and we bring up his mother. She may be more forthcoming."

She added a shrug. "First come, first dealt."

"We resume the interview."

Eve took the tube of Pepsi with her. "Record on. Resuming Interview with Singer, J. Bolton, and counsel. Dallas, Peabody, Reo entering Interview. Okay, J.B., spill it."

"Immunity—"

"Is off the table." Reo let out a sigh. "If your counsel is worth her fee, she explained to you we wouldn't make that deal."

"Five to ten," Cross said briskly, "in a low-security facility on-planet."

This time Reo just laughed. "You want us to give him a ride in a country club rehabilitation center? He murdered a woman and her thirty-two-week-old fetus."

"I didn't kill anyone! She did!"

"J.B." Cross gripped his arm. "You need to be quiet. My client has information regarding the death of Johara Murr. He is over eighty years old. Even a ten-year sentence is prohibitive and extreme. I believe any court would agree—"

"Then let's take it to court." Eyes glittering, Reo leaned forward. "You want to risk that, you'd risk that, knowing what he told you? What his wife told us?"

"You spoke with Marvinia! She can't say anything about it. We're married."

"Shut up, J.B. Fifteen years, on-planet, low security."

"Listen up. Twenty to twenty-five, on-planet, max security. And this is contingent on whether the information your client has is viable, valuable, and truthful. There will be no negotiation on those terms. If I take this to court, he will serve two life sentences, off-planet. Take the deal or don't, because he's just the type of defendant I like to prosecute."

"Indina. Twenty years!"

After a study of Reo's face, Cross turned to Singer. "I'm advising you to take this deal. On-planet, J.B. You'll have a chance to serve this time and get out, and live."

"But my God, my God." He held out his hands to Eve. "You have to understand, have some pity. I was coerced, I was in shock. I was afraid."

"Are you, on advice of counsel, taking the deal currently on the table?" Eve asked him.

"Yes, yes, I'll take it, if you promise you'll consider what I tell you, and my state of mind. If you promise to consider all of that and have some pity, perhaps renegotiate."

"We'll consider everything. Tell us about the murder of Johara Murr."

"It all goes back, you see. We were all worried about Bolt. He had this delusion he could make a living with his music. His mother went against us on this and indulged him. An obvious mistake, as he had a legacy, a duty here, and to the company his great-grandfather had started."

Duty, Eve thought. Legacy. Elinor Singer's words, no question.

"You kept tabs on him."

"My mother, thinking of his best interest, hired an agency to watch out for him."

"So she knew, you knew, when he became involved with Johara Murr."

"Yes, of course. Mother was upset, as you can imagine. She wasn't even an American, but I convinced Mother to let it go. Boys will be boys, after all. Even when it seemed to be more serious, we felt we should let it run its course. He was so stubborn, you see. If we forbade him from seeing her, living with her, it would only cement the connection. But then they were careless. She got pregnant."

"That must've been a blow," Peabody commented.

"It was impossible, of course. He was far too young and foolish. She was completely inappropriate. I expected her to terminate the pregnancy, then began to see, as Mother had, that she used it to trap him. That's why Mother went to London to speak to her parents."

Of course she had, Eve thought. "Elinor went to Johara's parents?"

"They were very unhappy to hear of the relationship and the pregnancy and, on Mother's advice, put on a bit of pressure to convince the girl to come home, to visit."

"Without telling her why."

"She was, as I understand, a very obedient young woman. When she went to them, they convinced her, as they should have, the relationship had to end, that she was far too young to raise a child, that she had disgraced the family. She agreed to go to her aunt, and to put the child up for adoption. A good home, of course. A stable home."

"But she changed her mind."

"We believe the aunt eventually told her about my mother's visit to her parents, and irresponsibly supported her change of mind, and her coming to New York. She was upset we'd interfered, and tried to convince my mother—whom she rightfully saw as the head of the family—that she and Bolton loved each other and the child."

He cleared his throat. "You have to understand, I had no idea what Mother planned when she insisted the girl meet us at the site. I believed it was to show her the scope of what the family stood for, what Bolton was part of. How misguided it was to push him off this path.

"And then we were there. It was a beautiful night, I remember, a beautiful night, the girl said how passionate Bolt was about his music. How he needed a chance to reach his potential. If we loved him, as she did, we'd support him. She—she said she was going to him, going to beg him to forgive her for leaving, and she would tell him everything we'd done.

"And Mother shot her."

He paused, covered his face with his hands. "I didn't know. I didn't. I was so shocked! She fell, and Mother said, 'Push her in. Push the tramp and her bastard in.'"

"And did you?" Eve asked.

"Yes. God forgive me. Yes. I didn't know what else to do. One of her shoes, and her purse, they didn't go in like she did. Mother picked them up. She said to go down and build the brick wall. She would mix the mortar."

"So you built the wall together."

"I didn't have a choice!" J.B. stretched his hands out, looked at Eve with a face full of fear and sorrow. "It was already done. It was too late, and we had to protect the family. She shouldn't have come back, she shouldn't have threatened us. Mother even offered her a hundred thousand dollars to go back, but she refused.

"I was sick, the whole time, just sick. Mother said for me to go to Marvinia and convince her to repair our marriage, and to agree to give Bolton another year or so. He'd come back, she'd see to it. So I did, and he did, and everything was fine again.

"Everything was fine again."

"Was it?" Eve shot back again. "Was everything fine for Johara and her child? For your son?"

"He has a very good life, the right kind of life. He would never have had a good life with this girl. She used him, she threatened us."

"Is that it?" Eve demanded.

"Yes, it's the truth. None of this would have happened if Bolt hadn't decided, without consulting us, to sell that property to Roarke. No one would have remembered her. Surely you must see I was given no choice. I didn't kill that unfortunate girl."

"At the very least, you were and are an accessory."

"And the deal stands—as long as it's proven out." Reo looked at Cross. "Are we done here?"

Cross merely lifted her hands.

"Then let's go to a conference room, make it official."

"But—but—I told you everything. You can see I was coerced. I didn't know. You have to have some pity."

Eve rose. "Sorry, all my pity's used up. It's all for Johara Murr. Interview end."

Eve took twenty minutes to recharge by sitting in her office, boots on her desk.

She turned her head into Roarke's hand when he came in, laid it on her hair.

"One wonders," he said, "the genetic miracle that makes a man like Bolton Singer with such a father, such a grandmother."

"We'd know about that."

"We would. You should take a blocker."

"Not yet. This last round won't take long. She's either going to spew or clam up and go to court. Either way, we've got her."

"You hope to make her spew."

"I'm going to give it a damn good shot." She sat up, rolled her shoulders when her communicator signaled.

"Tell me the good stuff."

"I've got good stuff," McNab told her. "I want to make out like it was hard, like I had to pull out super magic skills, but it's all on her office comp. Yeah, passcoded, but not much more. It goes back decades. But I've scanned through, and I can give you a whole bunch that ties her up in this."

"Gimme. Send it. I'm about to put her in the box."

"Really? It's almost midnight."

"She wants it."

"Okay then, I'm going to give you the cherry on top. True-heart found a passport in the name of Johara Murr in Elinor Singer's bedroom safe. Now, I did have to use some magic to open it. So credit there."

"Sick, sociopathic bitch. I need a copy of everything. Listen, if you want to break for the night after that, you're cleared for a hotel."

"I think we're into it, but we might want one after we're done."

"Good enough. Keep me informed. Good work, McNab. Good work all around."

"She kept the passport," Roarke said quietly. "So she could take it out, look at it, congratulate herself for seeing that the family line continues as she dictated."

"Yeah. Why don't you let Mira know about that? I need to— Busy around here," she said when her computer signaled an incoming. "What goes on top of the cherry on top?"

"Those sprinkles things?" he suggested. "Those colorful little candies?"

"We just got sprinkles."

Peabody stepped in. "She's up."

"So are we. Grab Reo. We need a few minutes before we take her."

Roarke read the screen over Eve's shoulder. "I'll update Mira and Jack. Take her down hard, Lieutenant."

"You bet your fine ass."

The jumpsuit didn't flatter Elinor any more than it did her son. She looked her age, at least around the eyes. Her very distinguished counsel sat in his very distinguished suit at her side as Eve started the record, read in the data.

"It's late, so why not make this quick? You're going to want to wait, Mr. Breathed," Eve added as he started to speak. "Just hold on to all the objections, the my client this and that. First, Mrs. Singer, your son just rolled all over you and back again."

"That's absurd."

"That's fact. I have his statement, and his confession and his play-by-play on record, and we'll get to that. Next, we have records accessed from your home office computer for a pallet of bricks to be delivered to the site and the building under construction where the remains of Johara Murr and her fetus were found. Your order, signed by you, for said bricks and for the mortar required to build the ten-by-eighteen-foot wall, dated September 8, 2024."

"Really, Lieutenant, Mrs. Singer, without a doubt, ordered material for that site and many others. This is hardly evidence of murder."

"She ordered the brick for a wall that was not on the blueprints, not in the plans, and was used to conceal the body of Johara Murr. Just wait, will you?" she snapped at Breathed. "Here, I have a copy of a passport found during the warranted search of your home. Found in your bedroom safe. A passport in the name of Johara Murr. Maybe you'd like to tell us how you came to be in possession of this item?"

"I know nothing about it."

"It just, what, popped in there by magic? It has a stamp on her entry to New York. It's dated September 8, 2024. The same day you ordered the brick—rush delivery, I'll add. Cost you extra." She pushed the copy across the table.

"I'll need a moment with my client."

"Fine, fine, but can you just wait until I'm finished piling on the evidence, so we can get the hell out of here sometime tonight? I have here the ballistic report—I can rush things, too—on the weapon you used to fire two shots at me, a police officer, this evening."

"My client was confused, and believed you were an intruder attacking her son."

"That's bullshit, as the record, which I'll play, clearly shows. You thought about trying that third shot, but you knew I'd stun you. I didn't stun you because you're really old and it could've killed you, even on low. But you really wanted to fire again, try for the head shot. Even better than the—on-record—attempted murder of a police officer, which will get you twenty-five to life, is the fact that the bullets fired from that gun tonight and the bullets fired thirty-seven years ago into Johara Murr match. Same weapon used. You should've gotten rid of it. Shouldn't have kept her passport, should've destroyed those invoices, but you didn't want to. They were like medals of honor for you."

"You won't put me in prison."

"Elinor, we need to talk."

She shoved Breathed's hand away. "She will not put me in prison. Do you know who I am?"

"Oh, yes, I do. You bet I do."

"You broke into my home, you planted all those things. I

will be believed over you. You're nothing. You're married to a competitor, a criminal. Everyone knows he's no more than a vicious Irish thug. You're trying to destroy what my family has built over generations for him, for some nouveau riche foreigner. People will believe me."

"Not a chance. Your own lawyer doesn't believe that line of bullshit. Science, you murdering bitch. Science, evidence, statements. A recording that shows you holding the weapon, firing it at me, just like you fired on the pregnant woman your grandson loved."

"Love means nothing. She was some tramp, some whore trying to worm her way into my family, our status, our money, our heritage with the bastard growing inside her."

"Your great-grandchild," Peabody mumbled.

"Nothing but a nit."

"Elinor, stop. My client has nothing more to say at this time."

"She thinks she can bully me." Elinor pushed his hand away again. "That whore thought the same. She found out differently, and so will you."

"So you shot her, killed her, had your son help you wall her in because you considered her a whore and the child inside her a nit that had to be killed so as not to infect your family."

"She was a threat. I eliminated the threat. That is my right as head of the family. You will not put me in prison for protecting my family from infestation."

"You'll never know another day of freedom," Eve promised.

"No, she won't," Reo agreed. "There will be no deal, Mr. Breathed, so let's not waste time on that. Your client has confessed. We have evidence on top of evidence. She will serve her two life sentences for murder and her twenty-five for attempted murder of a police officer, consecutively."

"Ms. Reo, consider my client's age and life expectancy."

"She'll live that expectancy out in prison. One concession I'll give, considering that age and the physical strain of transporting her off-planet, is she'll live what's left of her life in an on-planet maximum-security prison.

"Take me to court on it," Reo invited. "And that concession is deleted." She rose. "Speak with your client, but that's it, and that's all."

She sailed out.

"Reo exiting Interview." Eve rose, gathered the files. "We actually have more, but you get the gist. When you've finished with your client, she'll be taken back to her cell."

"I will not spend another minute in that hellhole."

"You're going to spend a lot more than a minute in hellholes. I only wish you had more years left to spend in them. Interview end."

Epilogue

Eve stepped out, rubbed her fingers on her gritty eyes, then over her face, then back into her hair.

She needed a shower, she thought, needed to wash off the sludge that excuse for a human had left behind.

"You sure called it, going for the son first." Peabody scrubbed at her own face. "Not only the way he rolled, but getting the time to get the ballistics, to have the search come around. Her lawyer barely got to play lawyer."

"He might try to push a little more, but I'm not budging." Reo bared her teeth at the closed door of Interview A. "Neither is the boss. I'll take a conference room if he wants to play with it awhile. She may overrule him. She may insist on going to trial."

"She may," Mira agreed as she walked to them. "She's a malignant narcissist, classic, and is certain she will never face consequences."

"She will, and there'll be more of them if she takes it to court. Either way." Reo rolled her shoulders. "Long day."

"He's going to push for bail, or house arrest."

Reo nodded at Eve. "He will, and he'll do so knowing he won't get either. The passport? That's gold. But the diamonds and rubies on the gold? She used the same gun she used to kill a twenty-two-year-old woman pregnant with her own great-grandchild to shoot a cop."

Nothing could have satisfied Eve more. "Now I'll take a blocker. Who has one?"

Peabody reached in her pocket, Reo in her briefcase, Mira in her purse. "Jesus, really? You all carry them?"

She plucked one from Peabody, knocked the tiny blue pill back.

"Ice those bruises," Mira told her.

"I appreciate you coming in for this. I know it all ran late."

"I wouldn't have missed it. Breathed will most certainly try to convince her to submit to a psychiatric evaluation, but she'll dismiss that. Nothing wrong with her. I'm going to re-watch those recordings, both of them, the first chance I have. Fascinating. I may do a paper on them. But for now, I'm going home. Dennis probably waited up, and, if so, we're going to have some midnight ice cream and talk this through."

"Midnight ice cream?"

"A family tradition. It's been a pleasure, in our way, to work with all of you on this. Get some rest."

"I'll wait this out," Reo said as Mira walked away. "No need for you to stay."

"I need to write it up."

"Write it up in the morning, which it already is. This was good work," Reo added. "Better than good work, but I'm getting a little punchy, and that's the best I can do."

"Don't let him string you out too long."

"Oh, believe me, Dallas, he knows she's cooked. See you next time."

"I'm just going to write up the broad strokes," Eve told Peabody as they headed back. "We can fill it in in the morning. Take an hour personal time there. Sleep in a little."

"Whole bed to myself."

"Right. We'll give you a lift home."

"I wouldn't mind it."

"Give me ten minutes."

Broad strokes, she told herself as she sat at her desk. And God, even she'd had enough coffee. She got water and laid down those broad strokes.

"Haven't you had enough for tonight?" Roarke walked in.

"Yeah, I have. I'm going to finish in the morning. I figured you were still playing with the commander, so I'd get started."

"He said to tell you very fine work, and he'd like to see you in his office tomorrow. Late morning. He was talking to Anna when he left. I believe she's very pleased."

"Well, that was the whole goal, pleasing the commander's wife."

She rose, looked at him, then moved into him.

"There now, my darling Eve."

She held on, and tight. "There are horrible people in the world. Ugly people, vicious people, but there aren't, under all that, so many genuinely evil people. Elinor Singer is one of them."

"She is, yes. She tried to take you from me. My heart stopped, just an instant. Even as I was moving, there was no breath in me."

"She tried, she failed. You gave me magic. You're not an Irish thug, but even if you were, I'd love you anyway."

Such was her fatigue she didn't hear Peabody clomping to her office until she heard her partner's: "Awww!"

"Shut up, Peabody."

But she kept holding on.

Read on for an excerpt from

ABANDONED IN DEATH

by J. D. Robb

Available 2022 in hardcover from
St. Martin's Press

1

BEFORE

The decision to kill herself brought her peace. Everything would be quiet, and warm and soft. She could sleep, just sleep forever. Never again would she hide in the dark when the landlord banged on the door for the rent she couldn't pay.

Or climb out a window again, to take off. Again.

She wouldn't have to give blow jobs to some sweaty john to buy food. Or the pills, the pills she needed more than food.

The pills that made everything quiet, even the pain.

Maybe she'd even go to heaven, like it looked in the books in Bible study where everything was fluffy white clouds and golden light and everyone smiled.

Maybe she'd go to hell, with all the fire and the screaming and eternal damnation. Taking a life, even your own, was a big sin according to the Reverend Horace Greenspan, the recipient of her first BJ—payment and penance when he'd caught her lip-locked with Wayne Kyle Ribbet, and Wayne Kyle's hand under her shirt.

The experience had taught her, at age twelve, it was better to receive than give payment for such tedious services.

Still, suicide ranked as a bigger sin than blowing some grunting asshole for traveling money or a handful of Oxy. So maybe she'd go to hell.

But wasn't she there already?

Sick, half the time sick, and her skin on fire. Sleeping in her car more often than in a bed. Driving from one crap town to the next.

Trading sex in steamy alleys for pills.

It wasn't going to get better, not ever. She'd finally accepted that.

So she'd take the pills, enough of the pills so the quiet went on and on and on.

But before she did, she had to decide whether to take her little boy with her. Wouldn't he be better off, too?

She shifted her gaze to the rearview mirror to watch him. He sat in his grubby Spider-Man pj's, half-asleep as he munched from a bag of Fritos she'd grabbed from a machine when she'd pumped all but the last few dollars of her money into the gas tank. They kept him quiet, and she needed the quiet.

She hadn't had time—or just hadn't thought—to grab anything when she'd scooped him out of bed. She had money—nearly gone now—and pills—far too few of them—stuffed in her purse.

They didn't have much anyway, and what they did she'd shoved into a trash bag weeks before. She had another couple of outfits for the kid—nothing clean. But she'd nearly gotten busted trying to lift a T-shirt and jeans for him from a Walmart in Birmingham.

If she got busted they'd take her kid, and he was the only thing completely hers. She'd wanted the best for him, hadn't she? She'd tried, hadn't she? Five years of trying after the asshole who got her pregnant told her to fuck off.

She'd done her best, but it wasn't enough. Never enough.

And the kid was no prize, she had to admit. Whiny and clingy, Christ knew, carrying on so she'd lost babysitters when she'd tried serving drinks or stripping it off in some hellhole.

But she loved the little son of a bitch, and he loved her.

"I'm thirsty, Mommy."

Thirsty, hungry, tired, not tired. Always something. She'd seen motherhood as something holy once. Until she'd learned it was nothing but constant drudgery, demands, disappointments.

And she wasn't good enough, just like everyone had told her all her damn life.

She slowed enough to pass the bottle of Cherry Coke between the seats. "Drink this."

"Don't like that! Don't like it! I want orange soda pop! I want it! You're a bad mommy!"

"Don't say that. Now, don't you say that. You know it hurts my feelings."

"Bad Mommy, Bad Mommy. I'm thirsty!"

"Okay, okay! I'll get you a drink when I find a place to stop."

"Thirsty." The whine cut through her brain like a buzz saw. "Thirsty *now*!"

"I know, baby darling. We'll stop soon. How about we sing a song?" God, her head felt like a soggy apple full of worms.

If she could be sure, absolutely sure, she'd die from it, she'd swerve into an oncoming car and be done.

Instead, she started singing "The Wheels on the Bus." And when he sang with her, she was, for a moment, almost happy.

She'd put one of her pills in his drink, that's what she'd do. He'd sleep—she'd given him a portion of a pill before when she'd needed him to sleep. But she'd give him a whole one, and wouldn't he just drift away to heaven?

He could have a puppy, and friends to play with, and all the toys he wanted. Orange soda pop by the gallon.

Little boys, even bratty ones, didn't go to hell.

She pulled off the highway and hunted up a twenty-four-hour mart. She parked well back from the lights where insects swarmed in clouds.

"You have to stay in the car. If you don't, I can't get you a drink. You stay in the car now, you hear? Be quiet, be good, and I'll get you some candy, too."

"I want Skittles!"

"Then Skittles it'll be."

The lights inside were so bright they burned her eyes, but she got him an orange Fanta and Skittles. She thought about sliding the candy into her purse, but she was too damn tired to bother.

It left her with less than a dollar in change, but she wouldn't need money where she was going anyway.

As she crossed back to the car, she dug out a pill from the zipped pocket in her purse. Thinking of puppies and toys and her baby darling giggling with the angels, she popped the tab and slipped it into the can.

This was best for both of them.

He smiled at her—sweet, sweet smile—and bounced on the seat when she came back.

"I love you, baby darling."

"I love you, Mommy. Did you get my Skittles? Did ya? Are we going on another 'venture?'"

"Yeah, I got 'em, and yeah, you bet. The biggest adventure yet. And when we get there, there'll be angels and flowers and puppy dogs."

"Can I have a puppy? Can I, can I, can I? I want a puppy now!"

"You can have all the puppies."

She looked back at him as he slurped some of the drink through the straw she'd stuck in the pop top. Her little towheaded man. He'd grown inside her, come out of her. She'd given up everything for him.

No one in her life had ever loved her as he did.

And she'd ruined it.

Windows open to the hot, thick air, she drove, not back to the highway, but aimlessly. Somewhere in Louisiana. Somewhere, but it didn't matter. She drove, just drove with the sweaty air blowing around her. Away from the strip malls, away from the lights.

He sang, but after a while his voice had that sleepy slur to it.

"Go to sleep now, baby darling. Just go to sleep now."

He'd be better off, better off, wouldn't he be better off?

Tears tracked down her cheeks as she took a pill for herself.

She'd find a place, a dark, quiet place. She'd down the rest of the pills, then climb in the back with her baby boy. They'd go to heaven together.

God wouldn't take her away from her baby darling or him from her. He'd go to heaven, so she would, too. The God in Bible study had a long white beard, kind eyes. Light poured right out of his fingertips.

That was the way to heaven.

And she saw a light instead of the dark. It seemed to shine above a small white church sitting by itself on a little hill. Flowers bloomed around it, and grass grew neat and smooth.

She could smell it all through the open window.

Dazed, half dreaming, she stopped the car. This was heaven, or close enough. Close enough for her baby darling.

She carried him to it like an offering to the kind-eyed God with his white beard, to the angels with their spread wings and soft smiles.

He stirred as she laid him down by the door, whined for her.

"You sleep now, my baby darling. Just sleep."

She stroked him awhile until he settled. He hadn't had enough of the drink, she thought, not enough to take him all the way to those angels and puppies. But maybe this was the best. Close to heaven, under the light, with flowers all around.

She walked back to the car that smelled of candy and sweat. He'd spilled the drink, she saw now, when he'd fallen asleep, and the Skittles were scattered over the back seat like colorful confetti.

He was in God's hands now.

She drove away, drove and drove with her mind floating on the drug. Happy now, no pain. So light, so light. She sang to him, forgetting he no longer sat in the back seat.

Her head didn't hurt now, and her hands didn't want to shake. Not with the night wind blowing over her face, through her hair. And the pill doing its magic.

Was she going to meet her friends? She couldn't quite remember.

What classes did she have in the morning?

It didn't matter, nothing mattered now.

When she saw the lake, and the moonlight on it, she sighed. There, of course. That's where she needed to go.

Like a baptism. A cleansing on the way to heaven.

Thrilled, she punched the gas and drove into the water. As the car started to sink, so slowly, she smiled, and closed her eyes.

NOW

Her name was Mary Kate Covino. She was twenty-five, an assistant marketing manager at Dowell and Associates. She'd started there straight out of college, and had climbed a couple of rungs since.

She liked her job.

She mostly liked her life, even though her jerk of a boyfriend had dumped her right before the romantic getaway she'd planned—meticulously—like a campaign.

Yesterday? The day before? She couldn't be sure. Everything blurred. It was June—June something—2061.

She had a younger sister, Tara, a grad student at Carnegie Mellon. Tara was the smart one. And an older brother, Carter, the clever one. He'd just gotten engaged to Rhonda.

She had a roommate, Cleo—like another sister—and they shared a two-bedroom apartment on the Lower West Side.

She'd grown up in Queens and, though her parents had divorced when she'd been eleven, they'd all been pretty civilized about it. Both her parents had remarried—no stepsibs—but their second round was okay. Everybody stayed chill.

Her maternal grandparents—Gran and Pop—had given her a puppy for her sixth birthday. Best present ever. Lulu lived a happy life until the age of fourteen when she'd just gone to sleep and hadn't woken up again.

She liked to dance, liked sappy, romantic vids, preferred sweet wines to dry, and had a weakness for her paternal grandmother's—Nonna's—sugar cookies.

She reminded herself of all this and more—her first date, how she'd broken her ankle skiing (first and last time)—every day. Multiple times a day.

It was essential she remember who she was, where she came from, and all the pieces of her life.

Because sometimes everything got twisted and blurred and out of sync, and she started to believe him.

She'd been afraid he'd rape her. But he never touched

her that way. Never touched her at all—not when she was awake.

She couldn't remember how she'd gotten here. The void opened up after Teeg ditched her, and all the shouting, and the bitching, her walking home from the bar, half-drunk, unhappy. Berating herself for haunting the damn stupid bar he owned, putting in hours helping out four, even five nights a damn stupid week.

For nothing but one of his killer smiles.

Then she'd woken up here, feeling sick, her head pounding. In the dark, chained up—like something in a horror vid—in a dark room with a cot.

Then he'd come, the man, looking like someone's pale and bookish uncle.

He turned on a single light so she saw it was a basement, windowless, with concrete floors and walls of pargeted stone. He had sparkling blue eyes and snow-white hair.

He set a tray holding a bowl of soup, a cup of tea on the cot and just beamed at her.

"You're awake. Are you feeling better, Mommy?"

An accent, a twangy southern one with a child's cadence. She needed to remember that, but in the moment, she'd known only panic.

She'd begged him to let her go, wept, pulled against the shackles on her right wrist, left ankle.

He ignored her, simply went to a cupboard and took out clothes. He set them, neatly folded, on the bed.

"I know you haven't been feeling good, but I'm going to take care of you. Then you'll take care of me. That's what mommies do. They take care of their little boys."

While she wept, screamed, demanded to know what he wanted, begged him to let her go, he just kept smiling with those sparkling eyes.

"I made you soup and tea, all by myself. You'll feel better

when you eat. I looked and looked for you. Now here you are, and we can be together again. You can be a good mommy."

Something came into those eyes that frightened her more than the dark, than the shackles.

"You're going to be a good mommy and take care of me the way you're supposed to this time. I made you soup, so you eat it! Or you'll be sorry."

Terrified, she eased down on the cot, picked up the spoon. It was lukewarm and bland, but it soothed her raw throat.

"You're supposed to say *thank you*! You have to tell me I'm a good boy!"

"Thank you. I—I don't know your name."

She thought he'd kill her then. His face turned red, his eyes wild. His fisted hands pounded together.

"I'm your baby darling. Say it! Say it!"

"Baby darling. I'm sorry, I don't feel well. I'm scared."

"I was scared when you locked me in a room so you could do ugly things with men. I was scared when you gave me things to make me sleep so you could do them. I was scared when I woke up sick and you weren't there, and it was dark and I cried and cried."

"That wasn't me. Please, that wasn't me. I—you're older than me, so I can't be your mother. I didn't—"

"You go to hell for lying! To hell with the devil and the fire. You eat your soup and drink your tea or maybe I'll leave you all alone here like you left me."

She spooned up soup. "It's really good. You did a good job."

Like a light switch, he beamed. "All by myself."

"Thanks. Ah, there's no one here to help you?"

"You're here now, Mommy. I waited a long, long time. People were mean to me, and I cried for you, but you didn't come."

"I'm sorry. I . . . I couldn't find you. How did you find me?"

"I found three. Three's lucky, and one will be right. I'm tired now. It's my bedtime. When you're all better, you'll tuck me into bed like you should have before. And read me a story. And we'll sing songs."

He started toward the door. "The wheels on the bus go round and round." He looked back at her, the face of a man easily sixty singing in the voice of a child. "Good night, Mommy." That fierceness came back into his eyes. "Say *good night, baby darling*!"

"Good night, baby darling."

He closed the door behind him. She heard locks snap into place.

She heard other things in the timeless void of that windowless room. Voices, screaming, crying. Sometimes she thought the voices were her own, the screams her own, and sometimes she knew they weren't.

But when she called out, no one came.

Once she thought she heard banging on the wall across the room, but she was so tired.

She knew he put drugs in the food, but when she didn't eat, he turned off all the lights and left her in the dark until she did.

Sometimes he didn't speak with the child's voice, the accent, but with a man's. So reasonable, so definite.

One night, he didn't come at all, not with food, not to demand she change her clothes. She had three outfits to rotate. He didn't come to sit and smile that terrifying smile and ask for a song or a story.

She'd die here, slowly starving to death, alone, chained, trapped, because he'd forgotten her, or gotten hit by a car.

But no, no, someone had to be looking for her. She had friends and family. Someone was looking for her.

Her name was Mary Kate Covino. She was twenty-five.

As she went through her daily litany, she heard shouting—

him. His voice high-pitched, like the bratty child he became when upset or angry. Then another voice . . . No, she realized, still his, but his man's voice. A coldly angry man's voice.

And the weeping, the begging. That was female.

She couldn't make out the words, just the sounds of anger and desperation.

She dragged herself over to the wall, pressed against it, hoping to hear. Or be heard.

"Please help me. Help me. Help me. I'm here. I'm Mary Kate, and I'm here."

Someone screamed. Something crashed. Then everything went quiet.

She beat her fists bloody on the wall, shouted for someone to help.

The door to her prison burst open. He stood there, eyes wild and mad, his face and clothes splattered with blood. And blood still dripping from the knife in his hand.

"Shut up!" He took a step toward her. "You shut the fuck up!" And another.

She didn't know where it came from, but she shouted out: "Baby darling!" And he stopped. "I heard terrible sounds, and I thought someone was hurting you. I couldn't get to you, baby darling. I couldn't protect you. Someone hurt my baby darling."

"She lied!"

"Who lied, baby darling?"

"She pretended to be Mommy, but she wasn't. She called me names and tried to hurt me. She slapped my face! But I hurt her. You go to hell when you lie, so she's gone to hell."

He'd killed someone, someone like her. Killed someone with the knife, and would kill her next.

Through the wild fear came a cold, hard will. One to survive.

"Oh, my poor baby darling. Can you take these . . . brace-lets off so I can take care of you?"

Some of the mad fury seemed to die out of his eyes. But a kind of shrewdness replaced it. "She lied, and she's in hell. Remember what happens when you lie. Now you have to be quiet. Number one's in hell, so number two can clean up the mess. Mommy cleans up messes. Maybe you'll be lucky number three. But if you're not quiet, if you make my head hurt, you'll be unlucky."

"I could clean up for you."

"It's not your turn!"

He stomped out, and for the first time didn't shut and lock the door. Mary Kate shuffled over as close as she could. She couldn't reach the door, but at last she could see out of it.

A kind of corridor—stone walls, concrete floor—harshly lit. And another door almost directly across from hers. Bolted from the outside.

Number two? Another woman, another prisoner. She started to call out, but heard him coming back.

Survive, she reminded herself, and went back to the cot, sat.

He didn't have the knife now, but a tall cup. Some sort of protein shake, she thought. He'd pushed one on her before. Drugged. More drugs.

"Baby darling—"

"I don't have time now. She ruined everything. You drink this because it has nutrition."

"Why don't I make you something to eat? You must be hungry."

He looked at her, and she thought he seemed almost sane again. And when he spoke, his voice sounded calm and easy. "You're not ready." When he stroked a hand over her hair, she fought not to shudder. "Not nearly. But I think you will be. I hope so."

She felt the quick pinch of the pressure syringe.

"I don't have time. You can drink this when you wake up. You have to be healthy. Lie down and go to sleep. I'm going to be very busy."

She started to fade when he walked to the door. And heard the bolt snap home when she melted down on the cot.

He had a plan. He always had a plan. And he had the tools.

With meticulous stitches—he was a meticulous man—he sewed the neck wound on the fraud. Over the wound he fastened a wide black velvet ribbon.

It looked, to his eye, rather fetching.

He'd already cut her hair before bringing her—with so much hope!—to this stage. Now he brushed it, used some of the product to style it properly.

He'd washed her, very carefully, so not a drop of blood remained, before he'd chosen the outfit.

While he worked, he had one of Mommy's songs playing.

"I'm coming up," he sang along with Pink, "so you better get this party started."

Once he had her dressed, he started on her makeup. He'd always loved watching her apply it. All the paints and powders and brushes.

He painted her nails—fingers and toes—a bright, happy blue. Her favorite color. He added the big hoop earrings, and he'd already added the other piercings, so fit studs into the second hole and the cartilage of her left ear.

And the little silver bar in her navel.

She'd liked shoes with high, high heels and pointy toes, even though she mostly wore tennis shoes. But he remembered how she'd looked at the high ones in store windows, and sometimes they went in so she could try them on.

Just pretending, baby darling, she'd told him. Just playing dress-up.

So he slipped her feet into ones she'd have wished for. A little tight, but it didn't matter.

And as a final tribute, spritzed her body with Party Girl, her favorite scent.

When he was done, when he'd done his very best, he took a picture of her. He'd frame it, keep it to remind him.

"You're not Mommy, but I wanted you to be. You shouldn't have lied, so you have to leave. If you hadn't, we could've been happy."

Number two and number three were sleeping. He hoped number two had learned a lesson—you had to learn your lessons—when he'd made her clean up the mess.

Tomorrow, he'd cut her hair the right way and give her the tattoo and the piercings. And she'd see all she had to do was be a good mommy, and stay with him always, take care of him always.

And they'd be happy forever.

But the Fake Mommy had to leave.

He rolled her out on the gurney—a man with a plan—out through the door and into the garage. After opening the cargo doors, he rolled her—with some effort—up the ramp into the van.

He secured the gurney—couldn't have it rolling around!—then got behind the wheel. Though it was disappointing, he'd known he would probably go through more than one before finding the *right* one, so he already knew where to take her.

He drove carefully out of the garage and waited until the doors rumbled down closed behind him.

It had to be far enough away from the home he and Mommy would make so the police didn't come knocking to ask questions. But not so far away he had to take too much time getting there.

Accidents happened.

It had to be quiet, with no one to see. Even at this time of night in New York, you had to know where to find quiet. So the little playground seemed perfect.

Children didn't play at three in the morning. No, they did not! Even if they had to sleep in the car because the mean landlord kicked them out, they didn't play so late.

He parked as close as he could, and worked quickly. He wore black, coveralls and booties over his shoes. A cap that covered his hair. He'd sealed his hands, but wore gloves, too. Nothing showed. Nothing at all.

He rolled the gurney right up to the bench where good mommies would watch their children play in the sunshine.

He laid her on it like she was sleeping, and put the sign he'd made with construction paper and black crayon over her folded hands.

It said what she was.

BAD MOMMY

He went back to the van and drove away. Drove back and into the garage, into the house.

He had the house because she'd left him. He had the house because she'd given him the deed and the keys and the codes and everything.

But he didn't want everything. He only wanted one thing. His mommy.

In the quiet house he changed into his pajamas. He washed his hands and face and brushed his teeth like a good boy.

In the glow of the night light, he climbed into bed.

He fell asleep with a smile on his face and dreamed the dreams of the young and innocent.

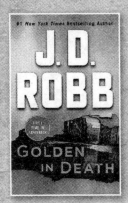  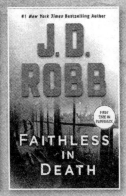
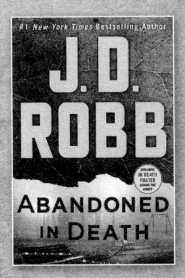